Volume One

# SIERRA JENSEN COLLECTION

*Only You, Sierra*

*In Your Dreams*

*Don't You Wish*

ROBIN JONES GUNN

MULTNOMAH
BOOKS

THE SIERRA JENSEN COLLECTION, VOLUME 1
published by Multnomah Books
*A division of Random House, Inc.*


International Standard Book Number: 978-1-59052-588-3

Cover photo by Steve Gardner, www.shootpw.com

Compilation of:
*Only You, Sierra*

*In Your Dreams*

*Don't You Wish*


Printed in the United States of America



For information:
MULTNOMAH BOOKS • 12265 Oracle Boulevard, Suite 200 • Colorado Springs, CO 80921

Library of Congress Cataloging-in-Publication Data
Gunn, Robin Jones, 1955-
The Sierra Jensen Collection Volume 1 / Robin Jones Gunn.
v. cm.
Previously published as separate works.
Contents: Only you, Sierra—In your dreams —Don't you wish.
ISBN 1-59052-588-4 [1. Interpersonal relations—Fiction. 2. Conduct of life—Fiction. 3. Christian life—Fiction.] I. Title.
PZ7.G972Sie 2006
[Fic]—dc22

2006008136

08 09 10—10 9 8 7 6 5

# TEEN NOVELS BY ROBIN JONES GUNN

## THE SIERRA JENSEN SERIES

<u>Volume 1</u>

Book 1: *Only You, Sierra*
Book 2: *In Your Dreams*
Book 3: *Don't You Wish*

<u>Volume 2</u>

Book 4: *Close Your Eyes*
Book 5: *Without a Doubt*
Book 6: *With This Ring*

<u>Volume 3</u>

Book 7: *Open Your Heart*
Book 8: *Time Will Tell*
Book 9: *Now Picture This*

<u>Volume 4</u>

Book 10: *Hold On Tight*
Book 11: *Closer Than Ever*
Book 12: *Take My Hand*

THE CHRISTY MILLER SERIES

Volume 1

Book 1: *Summer Promise*

Book 2: *A Whisper and a Wish*

Book 3: *Yours Forever*

Volume 2

Book 4: *Surprise Endings*

Book 5: *Island Dreamer*

Book 6: *A Heart Full of Hope*

Volume 3

Book 7: *True Friends*

Book 8: *Starry Night*

Book 9: *Seventeen Wishes*

Volume 4

Book 10: *A Time to Cherish*

Book 11: *Sweet Dreams*

Book 12: *A Promise Is Forever*

# Book One

# ONLY YOU, SIERRA

# one

SIERRA JENSEN GAZED out the train window at the cold, wet English countryside. In an hour she and her friends would be back at Carnforth Hall with the other ministry teams that had spent the past week in various European countries. She wedged her hands between her crossed legs, trying to warm them against her jeans. Endless pastures, frosted with winter's ice, flashed past her window. Sierra let out a sigh.

"What are you thinking?" Katie asked, uncurling from her comfy position on the train seat next to Sierra. Katie's red hair swished as she tilted her head to make eye contact with Sierra. Even though Katie was two years older than Sierra and they had met only two weeks ago, they had become close during the week they had just spent together in Belfast, Northern Ireland.

"About going back to the States," Sierra said. Her silver, dangling earrings chimed as she turned to Katie and smiled her wide, easy smile, but she was really looking past Katie. In the seat across the aisle from them, their team leader,

Doug, was sitting next to his girlfriend, Tracy.

"This whole trip went too fast." Katie folded her arms and settled back against the upholstered seat. "I'm not ready to go home yet."

"I know," Sierra agreed. "Me neither." She noticed that Doug was now slipping his arm across the back of the seat. Tracy slid closer to him.

"I'd like to come back," Katie said. "Maybe next summer."

"Me too," Sierra said, watching Tracy snuggle up to Doug.

"It would be great if out whole team could be together again for another trip."

"Me too," Sierra said. Tracy was tilting her heart-shaped faced toward Doug's, giving him a delicate smile that, by the look on his face, was melting him to the core.

"What do you mean, 'me too'? Of course you would be on the team." Katie looked over her shoulder to see what had distracted Sierra. Turning back to Sierra, Katie leaned forward and quietly said, "Don't they just make you sick?"

"Katie," Sierra said in a hushed voice, "I thought you guys were all best friends and had been for years—you, Doug, Tracy, and Christy. Why would it make you sick to see those two together?"

"We're all best friends. It's just...well, look at them! They're totally in love."

"I know," Sierra said, casting another quick glance at the couple who were now talking softly and looking deeply into each other's eyes. "I can't imagine ever being in Tracy's place and having a guy look at me like that."

"Are you kidding?" Katie pulled back and let her bright

green eyes do a quick head-to-toe scan of Sierra. "Have you ever looked in a mirror, girl? First, you have the hair going for you. You have great hair! Wild, blond, curly. Very exotic."

"Haven't you noticed?" Sierra said, tugging at a curly loop of her long hair. "Straight, sleek hair happens to be in right now."

"Oh sure, this week. Wait a few days. Everyone will be running out for perms so they can look just like you. And your smile happens to be award-winning, in case you didn't know. Blue-gray eyes that change with the weather are also quite popular. A few freckles. That's good. Fantastic clothes, all very original. And I don't ever want to hear you complain about your body."

"What body? I'm shaped like a tomboy."

"Better to be shaped like a tomboy than a fullback."

"You're not shaped like a fullback," Sierra protested.

"Okay, a halfback."

"You're both beautiful," Stephen, the German guy on their team, inserted into the conversation. He was sitting directly across from them and had appeared to be sleeping.

Sierra felt her cheeks blush, realizing Stephen had overheard their conversation. He was the oldest one of their group, and his beard added to his older appearance.

"Why do women find it a sport to criticize themselves to their friends?" Stephen asked, leaning forward and taking on the tone of a counselor. "You both are gorgeous young women on the outside and fantastically beautiful here," he patted his heart, "where it really counts."

"Then you tell us why all the guys aren't falling at our feet," Katie challenged.

"Is that what you want?" Stephen asked, and in an uncharacteristic move, tumbled to the floor and bowed at their feet.

Sierra burst out laughing.

"Get out of here!" Katie said. "You're making this a joke, and I'm serious."

Stephen returned to his seat, a satisfied little grin across his usually serious face.

"You're a guy; tell us what you're attracted to in a girl," Katie said.

Stephen took a quick look at Tracy and then back at Sierra and Katie. "Well," he began, but it was too late. His unspoken message seemed clear.

Katie threw her hands up in the air. "I knew it! You don't have to say anything. You men are all alike! You all *say* it's the personality and what's on the inside that counts. But the truth is your first choice every time is the Tracy-type, the sweet, helpful, cute ones. Admit it! There's little hope in this world for the few individualists like Sierra and me."

"On the contrary. You're both very attractive. To the right man, you will be a treasure. You just need to wait on God."

"I know, I know," Katie said. "And until then, we have our own little club, don't we, Sierra?"

Sierra remembered when she and Katie had formed the Pals Only Club at the beginning of their trip. She slapped Katie a high five and said, "P.O. forever!"

"That's right," Katie said. "We may have lost Tracy, but it's you, me, and Christy from here on out."

"You women do not need a little club," Stephen said. "Perhaps a caveman with a big club might be helpful..."

Instead of laughing at his joke, the girls gave Stephen a tandem groan and twisted their expressions into unappreciative scowls. He folded his arms against his chest, closed his eyes, and pretended to go back to sleep. But a crooked grin was on his lips.

"Come on," Katie said. "Let's get something to drink."

Sierra followed her down the rocking aisle that led to the back of the train car. They passed through the sliding doors and headed for the compact snack bar at the end of the next car. After buying Cokes, they stood to the side by the closed windows.

"Guys like Stephen really bug me," Katie said. "First they're all sweet and full of compliments, and then they make stupid jokes. You never know if they're serious about all the nice stuff or not."

"I think he meant it," Sierra said, shifting her weight from one foot to another. She was wearing her favorite old cowboy boots that she had worn for most of the trip. They were actually her dad's old leather boots. Very authentic. She had found them in the garage last summer when they were cleaning out stuff for a garage sale. Her mom had wanted to sell them and said, "I can't believe we still have these old boots! Howard wore them on our first date."

That's when Sierra knew they couldn't be cast off to some stranger at a garage sale. She tried them on, and to her amazement, they fit. She had worn them constantly ever since, much to her mother's dismay.

"Enough talk about guys," Katie said. "Let's talk about something else."

"It'll be great to see all the other teams tonight and hear about everything that happened to them."

"Yeah." Katie agreed. "I can't wait to hear about Christy's week in Spain."

"I still can't believe they pulled her off our team at the last minute and sent her all the way to Spain after the rest of the Spanish team had already left. I don't think I could have done what she did, traveling all by herself for two days and then joining up with a team of people she barely knew."

"It's like I kept saying," Katie said, making a muscleman pose. "She is Missionary Woman."

Sierra smiled. "I felt as if I was just getting closer to her, and then they shipped her off on a moment's notice. It must have been even harder for you to see her leave like that, since you guys have been best friends for so long."

"I'm sure it was a God-thing." Katie finished her drink and tossed her can into the bin marked "rubbish" as if she were shooting a basketball into a hoop. She made the shot and with two fingers gave herself a score of "two points" in the air.

Sierra finished her Coke and aimed her can at the rubbish bin. Her shot banked off the side. When she scooped it up, Katie said, "Try it again." Sierra did. This time she made it.

"All right!" Katie said, slapping a low five behind her back. "We're unstoppable."

Sierra thought about how much had happened during their week of ministry at the church in Belfast. Sierra and Katie had worked with the children, performed in a drama group, gone out street witnessing, prayed with teenagers when they said they wanted to give their lives to God, and had visited some elderly women of the church who treated them to tea and cakes. It had been a life-changing experience for

Sierra, and she was glad Katie had buddied up with her.

"You know," Katie said, as they headed back to their seats, "I'm sure God had a reason for taking Christy off our team. If nothing else, it let me get to know you, and I'm really glad for that."

"I am too," said Sierra. "I'm just starting to feel depressed now that it's almost over."

"Not so fast! We have two more days before we have to leave," Katie pointed out.

"Next stop is ours," Stephen said when they reached their seats. "Hey, Doug, we're almost there. Next stop."

Sierra watched as Tracy uncurled herself from Doug's shoulder and Doug resumed his role as team leader. He was a great guy. Sierra admired him, especially after all they had experienced together as a team this past week. She could easily see Doug and Tracy married and working together in ministry.

The group members gathered their belongings, as they had done dozens of times during their travels, and helped with each other's luggage. It was a familiar routine.

Sierra fought off the sadness that crept in when she realized the next time she boarded a train in England it would be to go home. Something caught in her throat every time she thought about returning to the States.

She hadn't been able to talk about it to Katie or anyone else. Maybe she should. Whenever she mentioned her situation, it had been with her usually cheerful, adventuresome spirit. No one knew that deep down she was nervous, knowing that everything in her life was going to be different when she returned home.

While Sierra was in England, her family had moved.

Instead of flying back to the small mountain community in northern California where she had spent her life, she was flying to Portland, Oregon, her new home.

The train came to a stop, and the group shuffled off and made its way through the station and then out to the small parking lot in front. A van was waiting for them in the late afternoon drizzle. They climbed in like a bunch of robots, all so accustomed to travel and so tired from their latest adventure.

Sierra sat in the back next to the window, curling and uncurling her cold toes inside the leather cowboy boots. She still had two more days in England, two more days to think through all the changes that were about to take place in her life. She wasn't ready for any of it. The nervousness about the move bothered her. Sierra had always been the bold, free-spirited type. But then, her whole foundation of home and family had never been rocked before.

Tracy slid into the van and plopped down next to Sierra. Doug sat in the front and patted the driver on the shoulder, thanking him for the ride.

Tracy said, "I can't wait to see Christy! I hope she had a good time in Spain."

Sierra smiled and nodded in agreement. She couldn't help but like Tracy. Everyone did. And of course Sierra was happy for Tracy that she and Doug had gotten together on the trip. Still, something made Sierra feel a little hurt and left out. Maybe it was jealousy that Tracy was getting one of the few truly wonderful guys left in the world.

The van wound around the narrow streets through the small town and then hit the country road leading to Carnforth Hall. The scenery looked exactly as it had a week ago when they left, with the exception of a few wild, purple crocuses popping up through patches of thawed earth. Sierra decided that if any more guys like Doug existed in this world, they certainly weren't in Pineville, Sierra's old hometown. And they certainly weren't on this trip.

"Tracy, by any chance does Doug have any brothers?"

"Does Doug have any brothers?" Tracy repeated with a skeptical look. "Why do you ask?"

"Oh, no reason. Never mind."

The van stopped in the gravel driveway at the front of an old castle, Carnforth Hall. Standing in front of the huge wooden doors was a tall brunette under an open umbrella. She waved wildly at their van.

"It's Christy!" Katie shouted, standing up in the back of the van and pounding on the closed window. "Hey, Missionary Woman!"

Sierra watched as Christy struck a muscle-bound pose with her right arm. Something on her wrist caught the glow of the amber porch light and sparkled brightly.

# two

KATIE LURCHED ACROSS the van seat and grabbed Tracy by the shoulder. "Tracy, look!" she yelled. "On her wrist! Is that…?"

"How could it be?" Tracy asked.

"Open the door, you guys!" Katie screamed.

Sierra couldn't figure out why Katie had gone berserk. Katie, who was the first one out of the van, grabbed Christy's wrist, looked at it, looked at Christy, and then screamed.

Tracy sprang from her seat and said, "Doug, it is!"

"It is what?" Sierra asked. "What's going on here?"

Doug was already out of the van's front door and joining Katie and Tracy in giving Christy a group hug. Then Doug asked Christy something and took off running in the rain without a jacket or umbrella to the administrative offices.

"Do you have any idea what's happening?" Sierra asked Stephen.

"They're Americans," he said. "This is normal behavior for them, isn't it?"

"Hey, I'm an American, and you don't see me freaking out here, do you?"

"Not yet."

"Come on," Sierra said. "Let's find out what it is." They climbed out of the van into the steady drizzle and tried to break into the wild chattering among Tracy, Katie, and Christy.

Katie kept saying, "I don't believe it. I don't believe it. This is like the ultimate God-thing of the universe! I don't believe it."

"Sierra," Christy called out over Tracy's head, "hi."

The two girls hugged, and Sierra said, "Well? So what is this 'God-thing of the universe'?"

Christy held out her right arm and showed Sierra her wrist. She wore a beautiful gold ID bracelet. Sierra touched it and saw that it had the word "forever" engraved across the top.

"It's nice," Sierra said. "Did you get it in Spain?"

"Sort of," Christy said. "I mean yes, but...well, it's a long story."

"I just don't believe this," Katie said. She looked as if she needed to sit down.

"I'm so happy for you!" Tracy said, grasping Christy's arm and squeezing it.

"Pardon us if it seems rude," Stephen said, pulling his coat collar up around his neck. "But it does happen to be raining. We're going inside."

"Come on," Christy said, holding her umbrella high enough to cover as many gathered around her as possible. "We probably should all go inside. I'll explain everything, Sierra."

The group members gathered their wet luggage and trudged through the gravel into the castle. The guys headed into their rooms, apparently not interested in Christy's secret. The four girls shook out their coats and hung them on the entryway pegs before heading for the great drawing room. A fire roared in the stone fireplace, but the couches around the fireplace were empty. Katie was the first to plop down.

"I still can't believe this," she said.

Sierra sat next to her while Christy and Tracy sat across from them. Sierra noticed that Christy looked different. Two weeks ago, when they had first met at Carnforth Hall, Christy had walked around every day with worry lines across her forehead and with a clenched jaw. Now she was radiant. Her eyes danced with the light from the fire, her cheeks looked warm and pink, and her smile was contagious.

"I'm dying to hear what's going on!" Sierra said. "You look like a different person, Christy. Please don't tell me it's because you're in love or anything."

"Sierra," Christy said, trying to make a straight face, "I am so totally in love it even makes me sick."

Tracy giggled joyfully. Katie slumped down in the couch and moaned. "I can't believe this is happening! Our club is dwindling, Sierra. It's just you and me now."

"I don't understand," Sierra said. "Can you really be this in love with someone from Spain? Someone you just met a week ago?"

"No, I mean yes. I mean, we didn't just meet," Christy fumbled. "Do you remember that night in our room when Katie told you about Todd?"

"Wasn't he the gorgeous blond surfer who went to be a missionary on some island?" Sierra asked.

Just then Doug's voice behind them said, "Well, you got three out of the four right. He didn't go to any island."

Katie sprang from the couch and gave the guy next to Doug a long hug while she cried, "I can't believe this!" Tracy was right behind her giving the guy an equally long hug and shedding just as many tears.

Sierra felt as if she didn't quite belong since she didn't understand what was happening. When Christy rose to give Doug a sideways hug, Sierra stood up, walked around the couch to where everyone was hugging, and stood there grinning and feeling like a dork. Why was this reunion such an emotional one for all her new friends? Who was this Todd guy anyhow? What was the big deal with his being there and Christy being in love with him?

Tracy let go of Todd, and he looked over at Sierra. She met his gaze and caught her breath. Sierra was looking into the most incredible blue eyes she had ever seen. It was more than his eyes, though. There was a look about Todd. She could tell he was different from other guys. God was going to do something special through this man.

"Sierra," Christy said, "I'd like you to meet Todd."

Todd stuck out his right hand and shook Sierra's. He gave her a broad smile, which showed off the dimple on his right cheek. "Christy's told me a lot about you," Todd said. "I'm really glad to meet you."

"And from what we overheard," Doug added, "Christy has told you all about Todd."

Sierra felt a little embarrassed that Todd and Doug had heard her call Todd gorgeous. She also had a fleeting thought that if Doug didn't have a brother, maybe Todd did.

"We all thought Todd had gone to Papua New Guinea," Tracy said. "None of us have seen him for almost a year."

"But he was in Spain!" Christy said triumphantly. "He met me at the train station." Tears beaded up in Christy's eyes. She looked up at Todd and smiled. "With a big bouquet and my bracelet."

"Don't tell me," Katie said. "White carnations. Am I right?"

"Yeah," Todd said. "And do you know how long it took me to find white carnations in January? I had to drive almost two hours down the coast and back. I almost missed her train."

"That's what he gave her when they first met," Katie explained to Sierra, "a dozen white carnations. She was only..." Katie turned to Christy. "How old were you? Fourteen?"

"No, it was right after my birthday. I was fifteen."

"Anyway," Katie continued, as if Sierra were the only one around, "Todd gave her white carnations when they met almost four years ago, and she has kept them all this time in a Folgers coffee can. They're all brown and withered, and they smell gross."

"They do not," Christy protested.

"You kept those?" Todd asked. He slipped his arm around Christy's shoulder and gave it a squeeze.

"I almost tossed them out a couple of times," Christy confessed. "But I still have them. And they *don't* smell." She made a face at Katie.

"Trust me," Katie said to Sierra, "they smell like moldy coffee. But that's not the point here. It's the bracelet. See, Todd gave her that forever bracelet for Christmas—"

"It was actually New Year's three years ago," Tracy corrected. "Right after the party at my house."

"Okay, so New Year's," Katie said.

Doug interrupted with, "All Todd gave me that year was the book *101 Things to Do with a Dead Hamster*. You remember that?"

"Yes!" Christy and Tracy said in unison. They didn't appear to have as many fond memories of the book as Doug and Todd seemed to.

Doug and Todd both had their arms around their girlfriends but managed to slap each other a high five in memory of the dead hamster book.

"Will you guys let me finish!" Katie said, stomping her foot. "So, you see, Sierra, they've been pretty much together for the past three years. But then Todd received this letter to go full time with some mission organization, but he didn't want to go because he and Christy were getting so close."

"It was really because I didn't want to have to sell Gus, my VW bus."

Katie continued, ignoring Todd's sarcastic comment. "But Christy broke up with him. She let him go, no strings attached, so he could serve God full time. It was the most noble act the world has ever seen. I'm not exaggerating. And when they broke up, she gave him back the bracelet. Todd said if they ever got back together again, it would be because God had done it. He said if he ever put that bracelet on her wrist again, it would be forever!"

"If I ever suffer a memory lapse, I'm coming to you, Katie," Todd teased. "You seem to know my life better than I do."

"I didn't know he was in Spain," Christy explained to Sierra. "I thought the mission had sent him to Papua New Guinea because that's where he always wanted to go."

"The need was greater in Spain," Todd explained. "Once I went through the training, it became clear that God wanted me to go to Castelldefels. It didn't hurt a bit that the surfing there is pretty decent." A grin crept onto Todd's face.

Christy went on. "Todd didn't know I was in England or coming to Spain until he received a fax the day before I arrived, explaining who he was supposed to meet at the train station. That's why this is such a shock to everybody. We couldn't have planned getting back together like this. God did it. And we had such a fantastic week of ministry!"

"I want to hear all about it," Tracy said. "Is that the dinner bell?"

They all paused to listen. It was indeed time for dinner.

"I need to wash up," Sierra said. She felt as if she needed to walk away from all of them. The sooner, the better. "I'm glad to meet you, Todd. And Christy, I'm really happy for you. For both of you. That's amazing how God worked it all out. I'll see you guys at dinner."

Sierra was about to slip out when Todd reached over and gently grasped her shoulder. "Sit by us at dinner, okay?"

"Okay," Sierra said, not sure why he was being so nice to her. She made her way into the nearest bathroom and, locking the door behind her, turned on the water and splashed her face two, three, four times. With each splash her tears mingled with the chilly water and washed down the drain.

"This is stupid," Sierra muttered to herself. "Why are you crying?" She looked at herself in the mirror above the sink. "I'm happy for Christy. I really am. And for Tracy and Doug too. Am I so self-centered that I can't share their happiness just because I didn't meet anybody on this trip? That is so immature, and I hate myself for even thinking it!"

Sierra washed her face again and commanded the tears to cease. She was surprised when they obeyed. Smiling at her reflection, Sierra felt her confidence returning. She had never felt so overwhelmed by her emotions.

*Maybe I wanted to cry like everyone else was because I was happy for Christy, but I didn't feel I could because I'm not part of their group. I mean, I am, but only for a week. They have been friends forever. Forever. Just like her bracelet. Will there ever be anyone who will promise to love me forever?*

Sierra took a deep breath and ran a finger through the wet, matted curls around her forehead. *They're all older than I am*, she reasoned. *Christy and Katie are two years older; Doug's five years older; and Todd must be at least four or five years older. So why am I comparing myself to them? They're all in college, and I still have a year and a half of high school. I knew it would be awkward on this trip being one of the youngest. I guess I thought I was mature enough to handle it.*

She smiled again and adjusted one of her earrings. If Todd was the kind of guy she thought he was, he would save a seat for her at dinner. She would sit with Christy and Todd and all their friends—make that, all *her* friends—and she would be just as mature as they were. And if all else failed, she would pull her chair next to Katie. She and Katie could always call an emergency meeting of the P.O. Club and go off together and sulk.

# three

SIERRA ACTUALLY HAD A GOOD TIME at dinner. The conversation switched from all the love stories and turned into equal-opportunity sharing time. Sierra felt like one of the group again. She sat next to Katie on one side and Doug on the other. Christy and Todd were across the table from them.

A couple of times Sierra caught Christy and Todd giving each other heart-stopping looks of admiration and mutual affection. It reminded Sierra of her brother. Cody had been enamored with his wife, Katrina, all through high school. They started going together when they were sophomores and were married right out of high school, with the blessing of both sets of parents. Cody and Katrina were meant for each other. It was obvious to everyone. They were still intensely in love. They had an adorable little boy, Tyler.

*Maybe I want it to be easy for me, like that. Maybe I feel behind since Cody was so in love when he was my age.*

"I can't believe I'm saying this," Katie said toward the

end of dinner, "but being around you guys like this is making me homesick."

"You miss your family?" Todd asked.

"Maybe a little bit. I'm mostly homesick for being young again. You know, going to the beach and everything we did together. Our high school years were the best. Don't you think so? I don't know how we got so old so fast."

"I know what you mean," Christy agreed. "My brother, David, is thirteen. I don't know when he grew up. He's somehow turned into this lanky teenager, and I hardly know who he is. He answered the phone when I called this afternoon, and I had no idea it was he. My baby brother! All grown up!"

"Well, almost grown up," Katie said. "David will always be a little dweeb in my book."

"What about you, Katie?" Sierra asked. "Do you have brothers or sisters?"

"Two older brothers. They're both big dweebs."

"And you, Todd?" This was the answer she was most interested in. What if Todd had a brother just a few years younger? Someone just like him, only closer to Sierra's age.

"None. I'm the only kid. What about you, Sierra?"

"Four brothers and one sister."

"You have six kids in your family?" Doug asked. "Do you guys wear name tags to keep everyone straight?"

"Of course not! Six isn't a lot. My dad came from a family of nine kids. I have two older brothers. The oldest one is in college, and the next one is married and works in construction. My sister is two years older than I, and then there's Dillon and Gavin. They're eight and six."

"Sounds like your mom kind of did kids in pairs," Katie said. "At least you each had someone your own gender to share a room with."

"I hate sharing a room. Tawni is super picky about everything. Whenever I have a really good dream, it always involves *not* having to share a room with Tawni."

"Do you guys really all have cowboy names?" Katie said.

"They're not cowboys names," Sierra said.

"Okay, then western names. What's your oldest brother's name?"

"Wes."

Everyone started to laugh.

"No, wait, you guys!" Sierra held up her hands, trying to get their attention. "That's just his nickname. His real name is Wesley. That's because Wesley was my mom's maiden name. She's related to Charles and John Wesley, who were famous Christians a long time ago."

"And your next brother?" Katie prodded, on a hunt for more cowboy names and not at all impressed with Sierra's family history.

"My married brother's name is Cody."

Again everyone laughed.

"See? They're all cowboy names. What does your dad do? Run a ranch or something?" Katie said.

"No," Sierra said, and now she started to giggle.

"What does he do?"

"You're going to laugh. My dad was a county sheriff."

They laughed with Sierra, and Christy asked, "Did he have a silver badge and everything?"

Sierra nodded and wiped the laughter tears from her eyes. "I guess we are a bit on the western side. I never thought of it before. I always thought of us as Danish, since my grandma is from Denmark."

"What's her name?" Christy asked.

"Mae. Mae Jensen. We call her Granna Mae. I do have her name as my middle name, if that counts for anything. Mae's not a western name, is it?"

Christy shrugged. "I don't think so."

"What's your middle name?" Sierra asked Christy.

Christy looked at Todd with a shy smile. "It's Juliet."

Now everyone was laughing, especially Doug.

"All right, Douglas!" Tracy said with a hand on her hip. "If you think that's so funny, tell everyone your middle name."

Doug turned sober. Tracy's eyebrows rose. "Would you like me to tell them?"

Doug quietly said, "Quinten."

Another round of laughter followed as Doug tried to explain that it was a family name, just like Mae and Wesley, and there was nothing funny about it all.

By the time the six of them left the dining room and headed for the chapel for the evening meeting, they had laughed themselves silly. All of them were weary from their travels, which made them all the sillier. Especially Katie.

Sierra couldn't believe how fast Katie's mind seemed to be working, providing a funny response to everything everyone said. It was going to be hard to come back down to earth in chapel.

The assistant director of Carnforth Hall stood at the chapel's back door and greeted each of the students. When Sierra arrived with her group, he grasped Todd by the arm and said, "Dr. Benson had to go to a funeral in Edinburgh so I'm heading this up. Have you guys got the music covered?"

"We're all set," Todd said. He let go of Christy's hand, and he and Doug headed toward the front of the chapel. Sierra sat next to Christy, Tracy, and Katie. It was back to just the girls, and it was kind of nice.

Four guys were up front with guitars, and Todd seemed to be in charge. Since Todd and Doug were so wired from dinner, they started off the music with three rowdy, hand-clapping songs. They got the whole room full of students singing and clapping. It seemed that all the returning groups were pretty keyed up.

Sierra loved it. Her little church in Pineville was pretty conservative. They would never have been so vigorous in their worship.

After the fourth song, the assistant director came to the microphone and asked everyone to sit down. "Before we move into the worship and praise portion of chapel, I wanted to make a few announcements. First, I'd like to introduce Todd Spencer here on the guitar."

Todd smiled and gave the casual chin-up gesture to the group of forty or so gathered in the chapel.

"Todd is our mission director in Spain. He's on a two-year commitment, working with the teen outreach at Castelldefels. Todd is also completing his college degree by correspondence. When his term is up with the mission a year from this June, he'll have a B.A. in intercultural studies. It you have any interest in finishing up your degree while in full-time ministry, see me, and I'll get you all the necessary information." He looked back at Doug and the other guys playing the guitar. "Was there anything else?

Doug? Were you the one who said you had an announcement?"

Doug shook his head.

Katie, who was sitting next to Sierra, suddenly blurted out, "Doug wanted to announce that his middle name is Quinten!" At first people around the room didn't laugh. They all looked at Doug, who took it good-naturedly. He gave Katie a thumbs-up gesture and then threw back his head and laughed. The rest of the room joined as the assistant director shook his head. "It's always the Americans," he said in the microphone.

Katie leaned over to Sierra and said, "I've been waiting for that one for a long time. Ever since Doug gave me a black eye right before the first day of my senior year in high school."

The crowd settled down as Todd began to strum a set of familiar chords on his guitar that led into a moderately lively song. Soon the group was singing as one, song after song. They went from fast tempo to slower. Then a hush settled over the room as they prayerfully sang the final chorus. Sierra closed her eyes and sang from her heart, listening to her voice blend perfectly with Christy's and Tracy's.

A time of prayer followed in which people spontaneously thanked God for what had happened with their teams in the cities they had just returned from. Many of them prayed by name for people they had met. Sierra prayed for an elderly woman in Belfast who said she believed she would get to heaven simply because she was a good person. She had refused to believe she needed to trust Christ for her salvation. Something in the woman's appearance or mannerisms had reminded Sierra of Granna Mae, only Granna Mae was one of the strongest Christians Sierra had ever met.

The group prayed and shared for more than an hour. Reports of all that God had done among them during the past week were amazing. After the meeting, Katie and Sierra went to the main hall where their luggage was still sitting in the entryway. They hauled it up to their room and settled in for the night.

"Doesn't it seem like a couple of years have passed since we were last in this room?" Katie asked.

"I know," Sierra agreed. "And it's only been a week."

"It's really going to seem weird when we go home. We've changed so much in just a few short weeks. Probably everything at home will be exactly the same," Katie said.

"For you, maybe," Sierra said with a laugh, crawling into her bed and rubbing her legs up and down against the sheets, trying to warm them. "Brrr! I forgot how cold this room is."

"What do you mean 'for me'? Don't you think everything will be the same in your family?" Katie pulled her bed closer to Sierra's before climbing in and pulling the thick covers up to her chin.

"Well, you see, Katie, when I left a few weeks ago, my family moved. I've heard of parents trying to drop hints to their children about leaving the nest, but my parents are a little extreme."

"You're kidding, right?"

"Not exactly. They really did move. That was one of the reasons they agreed to my coming on this trip in the middle of the school year. I'll start my new school at the beginning of the semester."

Katie fluffed up her pillow and said, "What did you do, ace all your finals early?"

"Sort of. The high school I went to in Pineville was really small. I would have been in a graduating class of fifty-seven. Only two hundred students are in the whole high school. All my teachers were real nice and let me take exams early."

Just then the door opened, and Christy and Tracy entered, giggling about something. Katie looked over at Sierra and raised her eyebrows. "The Juliets have returned from their Romeos."

"Did you girls have a good time?" Sierra said in her best motherly voice.

"I'm sorry," Tracy said. "Are we being totally obnoxious?"

"Only partially obnoxious," Sierra teased. "I guess that's what Katie and I have to look forward to when we fall in love someday."

"Yeah, someday," Katie quipped. "Like when I'm eighty-five and some old guy at the rest home starts to chase me around in his wheelchair."

"Oh, do you think it will happen that soon?" Sierra teased. "That's encouraging. I might still have some of my original teeth!"

"You guys shouldn't be so sarcastic," Christy warned, sitting on the edge of her bed and slipping off her shoes. "Love can hit you when you least expect it."

"Oh really?" Katie sat up in bed and nimbly pulled out her pillow. "Like this?" She whacked Christy on the side of the head. Christy let out a startled shriek and immediately retaliated by tossing her pillow at Katie. But she missed and hit Sierra in the face. Sierra sprang into action. Then Tracy grabbed her pillow, and it was a free-for-all.

The four friends squealed like little kids and whacked each other silly until Sierra's pillow burst open and tiny white feathers fluttered everywhere. They were laughing so hard they were crying and fanning the floating feathers away from their faces.

A brisk knock on the door turned into several solid thumps. The girls squelched their laughter.

"Yes?" Sierra called out in a controlled voice.

"Ladies?" The deep male voice called through the closed door. "What on earth is going on in there? We can hear you in the south wing of the castle!"

"Um, we're just laughing, sir, but we're going to bed now," Sierra answered, still maintaining her straight face.

"Good night then, ladies. Lights out."

"Yes, good night, sir." Sierra reached over and switched off the light. They listened as the footsteps echoed down the hallway and then turned the light back on.

"Very impressive," Katie said, brushing her red hair out of her eyes. "How did you do that?"

"I grew up in a big family, remember? I've had a lot of practice. What you really have to do is learn how to have silent pillow fights."

Christy plopped down on her bed and stared at the ceiling. "Truce, you guys. I can't take another round, silent or otherwise. I don't think I've ever laughed so hard or so much in my whole life as I have today. It's good to be back together!"

Tracy started to clean up the feathers.

"Let's leave them until tomorrow," Sierra said. "It'll be

easier to clean up in the morning. I think there's another pillow in the closet I can use."

"I'll get it for you," Tracy said, walking across the room. "I feel bad about the mess."

"Don't worry. It'll still be a mess in the morning," Sierra said. "That's what I always tell my sister, but she's so picky. Everything has to be in place before she can allow herself to go to bed."

Tracy stepped out of the closet and handed a pillow to Sierra. "Does anybody else need anything while I'm up?"

There was no answer.

"Christy, can you change in the dark if I turn off the light?"

Silence.

"I think she's asleep," Katie said, settling back under her covers.

Sierra peeked up over her blanket and sure enough, Christy was asleep on her back with a smile on her lips. "Tracy, we better try to get her under the blankets. She's going to freeze like that," Sierra said.

Tracy, ever the helpful type, spoke softly to Christy, coaxing her to roll over enough for Sierra to pull up the blankets and wrap them around her. Christy cooperated but seemed as if she were doing so in her sleep.

Within minutes they were tucked in bed. One lone feather fluttered through the air and landed on Sierra's cheek. She batted it away and slipped off into dreamland.

# four

SIERRA DIDN'T WAKE UP until almost ten o'clock. The other girls were still asleep when she opened her eyes, and the floor was still covered with a carpet of feathers. Sierra tiptoed to the hall closet and returned with a broom. Quietly she cleaned up with feathers without waking the others.

She could hear voices in the room next door. Some of the other girls were starting to wake up. Anticipating the exhaustion, the mission directors had forgone breakfast and were offering a buffet brunch from ten to noon. Sierra decided to quickly shower while some hot water remained.

By the time she finished and returned to the room, the other three girls were awake and trying to get themselves going.

"I can't believe how tired I am," Christy said. "I can't remember ever falling asleep with my clothes still on!"

"Do you mind waiting for us, Sierra?" Tracy asked. "We can all go to brunch together."

"I don't mind. Take your time." Sierra towel-dried her

wild, caramel-colored hair and pulled on her boots. She opened a zippered pouch on the inside of her suitcase and fished for a matching pair of earrings. Today she chose the ones with the moon and the stars suspended from thin silver chains. She searched for her silver hoop bracelets, eight of them all looped together, and pushed them up her left arm. Around her neck hung a string of tiny multicolored beads that looked like bits of confetti against her forest green knit shirt. She felt refreshed after her shower, hungry, and ready for that brunch.

She didn't mind waiting for the others, though. It gave her a chance to read her Bible, which she pulled from her brown leather backpack. The medium-sized book was covered with a handmade, tooled-leather cover that her dad made for her years ago. The design was of a tree that had "Psalm 1:3" embossed at the bottom of its trunk.

That had been Sierra's favorite verse as a kid, which she had memorized in second grade. This morning she turned to the book of Psalms and picked up where she had left off reading a few days ago, at Psalm 62.

Verse 8 really stood out to her: "Trust in Him at all times, you people; pour out your heart before Him; God is a refuge for us."

Sierra thought of how she had been holding in her discomfort about the move to Portland. She hadn't poured her heart out to anyone, not even God.

The door opened right then, and Sierra's roommates returned, all three wearing towels wrapped around their heads. They stood in the doorway with goofy looks on their faces. On Katie's signal they all held up their right hands out in front of them, wiggled their hips, and sang in their most soulful voices, "Stop! In the name of love!"

Sierra started to laugh, and pretty soon the three soul sisters were giggling so hard their "beehive" towel-dos came tumbling down.

"Hurry up, you goofs," Sierra said. "It's almost eleven-thirty. They're going to close down the buffet before we get there!"

About fifteen minutes later, they all descended on the dining room. Sierra filled her plate and ate every bite. Just as Mrs. Bates was clearing away all the food, Doug and Todd walked in.

"Those two are going to be sorry they slept in," Christy said.

It looked as if Todd was sweet-talking Mrs. Bates into letting them scrape the bottom of the serving bowls for whatever was left.

Tracy giggled as they watched the guys coax the pan of ham slices out from underneath Mrs. Bates' protective arm. Todd stuffed hard-boiled eggs into the front pouch of his navy blue hooded sweatshirt while Doug snatched a basket of rolls from the serving table and held it behind his back. "She doesn't realize those two will eat anything," Tracy said, "especially Doug. She could let them empty all the leftovers in her refrigerator, and they'd be just as happy."

The guys, with their arms full of loot and expressions of brave conquerors across their shaven faces, joined the girls.

"You guys get the bamboozle award for the day," Katie said. "I think you two could hoodwink even the Queen Mother if she were here today!"

Doug and Todd gave each other mischievous smiles.

"What?" Christy asked. "I know that look. What did you guys do?"

"Oh, nothing," Doug said.

Todd poured himself a glass of juice and tried to repress his chuckling.

"Tell us!" Tracy demanded.

The grin on Todd's face kept growing. He avoided eye contact with Christy and lifted the glass of apple juice to his lips.

Doug looked as if he were about to burst. He glanced at Todd and then at Tracy. Looking directly at Katie, he furrowed his eyebrows and said in an extra-deep voice, "Ladies, what on earth is going on in there? We can hear you in the south wing of the castle!"

Katie's mouth dropped open.

"Good night then, ladies," Doug continued. "Lights out!"

"It was you!?" Katie rose from her seat with both hands outstretched, ready to strangle Doug.

Todd started to laugh so hard that the apple juice squirted out of his nose. He grabbed a napkin, rose from the table and turned his back to the group until he could stop coughing.

"You guys are so immature!" Katie squawked, plopping back down in her seat and folding her arms across her chest. "It's as if your little brains froze at about the level of twelve-year-olds. I can't believe you guys!"

"Us!?" Todd said, regaining his voice sans any stray liquids. "And just what were you *mature* women doing last night? It sounded like an all-out, junior-high-style pillow fight to me!"

"It was, " Sierra said, laughing with the rest of them. "Too bad you guys weren't in on it. We would have creamed you!"

"Oh, yeah?" Doug said. "Would you like us to take you up on that challenge tonight? Huh?"

"I dare you!" Sierra rose to her feet and stuck her chin out at Doug the way she had done many times with her older brothers.

"Tonight," Doug said, pointing a finger at Katie and Sierra trying to look tough. "We'll be there."

"Yeah," said Todd, echoing Doug's macho voice, "tonight!"

Dr. Benson stepped into the dining room and announced that chapel would begin in fifteen minutes. He looked tired. Sierra remembered he had been at a funeral in Scotland. Perhaps he had just arrived.

In the chapel the guys played guitar again, and for the first half hour they sang, which Sierra loved. Then Dr. Benson gave a talk about adjusting to life when they returned home. He instructed each of the students to take his or her Bible and find a place to read, pray, and prepare for returning home.

Sierra chose a bench at the back of the chapel. Nearly everyone else had filed out, except three or four people who were scattered around the chapel having their own quiet time with the Lord. She read her chapter again from that morning and prayed.

"You say You want me to pour my heart out to You, God. Well, here goes. I'm scared. Yeah, me. Scared. Doesn't happen too often, but I am. I didn't want to move. I don't want to go to a new school. Not that I don't want to meet new people. It's just that I guess I like being sort of popular at Pineville High. Now I'm going to be a nobody. And that's okay, if that's who You want me to be. But I feel intimidated by it all, and You know it takes a lot to intimidate me. As long as I am pouring out my heart here, the other thing that's driving me crazy is the way everyone is getting a boyfriend, and I'm not. These guys are really solid, quality guys. I'm afraid there won't be any more like them left for me. I know I'm supposed to trust You..."

Sierra opened her eyes and peeked at verse 8 again: "Trust in Him at all times."

"Okay," she prayed, "so I'm supposed to trust in You at all times, even in boyfriend-less times, and I *am* trying. But I would like You to make note that I am sweet sixteen and never been kissed. I haven't even had my hand held. Can You see how that would make someone like me feel a little insecure about her looks and personality and everything? Just so You understand, which I know You do."

Feeling surrendered, Sierra left the chapel and took one last walk about the grounds. She kept talking silently with God as she walked.

Sierra talked with God like this often. She had given her heart to Jesus when she was five and had continued a close walk with Him ever since. It had been fairly easy in her strong Christian family and in the safe community of Pineville. She knew challenges lay ahead for her in Portland.

That evening after dinner, Sierra and her team gathered together one last time. Last night there had been unstoppable laughter. Tonight the tears began and didn't seem to stop. Even after the girls were in bed with the lights off, they kept talking and crying and making promises to stay in close contact with each other. With the flood of emotions, everyone forgot about the challenge of the pillow fight.

The next morning, even though Sierra thought she had emptied herself of all her good-bye tears the night before, she cried when she joined the group on the 5 a.m. shuttle van to the train station. It was still dark outside and very cold. Everyone in her group was up and dressed to see her off.

Sierra received endless hugs from her friends. Katie hugged her first and said, "Somehow it's not so hard saying good-bye to you because I know I'm going to see you again. We'll get together this summer, if not before."

Todd even hugged her good-bye, and when he did, he said, "I guess we'll have to reschedule that pillow fight."

"Okay," Sierra agreed. The tears welled up in her eyes. She knew she might never see Todd or Doug again, and the promised pillow fight was an empty threat.

Christy hugged her the last of everyone and said, "I hold you in my heart, Sierra. I always will." The two young women held each other at arm's length, and each wiped away the other's tears. Christy then placed her hand on Sierra's forehead and said, "Sierra, may the Lord bless you and keep you. The Lord make His face shine upon you and give you His peace. And may you always love Jesus first, above all else."

Sierra waved and stepped up into the van. The rest of them were going to London that afternoon and staying overnight at a boardinghouse. Their flights went out early the next morning with Doug, Tracy, and Christy flying to

Los Angeles and Todd flying to Barcelona. Sierra hated being the first one to leave. "Good-bye, you guys!" she called out and waved one last time.

Even with such a blessing and send-off, Sierra felt as if a dark cloud had settled over her head and hung there all the way to the Heathrow Airport. She stood in line at the ticket counter, checking her bag, and asked directions to her gate. Everything was going smoothly. Her plane was scheduled to leave in an hour.

She decided to call her mom and dad and let them know she was on schedule. Sierra had to fumble through her backpack to find her new phone number. If felt weird not knowing her own number by heart.

When she located the phones, they were all in use so Sierra stood patiently to the side and waited her turn. A guy on the second phone turned around and, noticing Sierra standing there, put his hand over the receiver and said, "Excuse me, but do you have any coins? I'm desperate!"

By his accent, she knew he was American. "I'm not sure." Sierra hurriedly opened her backpack and rummaged around the bottom of the bag for any loose coins. She walked over to the frantic-looking guy and handed him four coins. Then she searched for more.

"You're a lifesaver!" he whispered as he fed the coins into the phone. "Yes, this is Paul. Is Jalene there?" He motioned for more coins. Sierra struck pay dirt in the zippered pouch on the front of her backpack and pulled out nine of them. She wasn't sure what they were, how much they were worth, or how much she had just given away to this stranger. He eagerly received her gift and fed the money into the phone.

"Hi! I only have a minute on this phone," he said. "Let me give you my flight number. Are you ready? It's flight 931 to San Francisco and then flight 57 to Portland. Have you got that?"

Sierra took a few steps back and nonchalantly looked at her ticket. She was on the same flights.

"I arrive in Portland at 8:24 p.m. Got it? Great! Okay, I'll see you then. Thanks a lot. 'Bye!" He pulled the phone away from his ear and held it out to Sierra. "Just enough." She could hear the dial tone. "I owe you. How much did you give me?"

"I have no idea," Sierra admitted. As she spoke, she took a good look at "Paul" for the first time. He had thick, dark brown hair that had a natural wave at the top of his broad forehead. He wore a tan leather jacket and attached to his backpack was an Indiana-Jones style hat.

Sierra was surprised to find herself thinking, *Fight for this man*.

"I'll pay you back in dollars," he said, reaching into his pocket.

"Sorry," said a man next to Sierra with a British accent. "Are you waiting for that phone?"

"Yes, I am." Sierra stepped forward and took the phone from Paul and began to place a collect call to her parents. Paul stood next to her, still scrounging for the money to pay her back. He acted as if they were together. Sierra held the receiver in place with her shoulder. She could smell a strong, earthy cologne. She guessed it to be Paul's.

Sierra's dad answered the phone, and she spoke in low tones, leaning into the phone, fully aware this guy stood only feet away, waiting for her. She assured her dad that everything was fine and on schedule. He promised to be at the gate to meet her when she deplaned. "I love you, too," Sierra said softly and then hung up.

She turned around and met Paul's eyes. They were gray. No, they were blue. No, they looked gray. And very clear, like water. "I only have two dollars on me," he said. "Do you mind following me over to the money exchange booth? I can cash a traveler's check and pay you back. Is that okay? Are you in a hurry?"

"All right," Sierra said, shrugging her shoulders. "I'll follow you."

"My name's Paul," he said. "I apologize for presuming on you. You were very kind to help me out. Thanks."

"It's okay. Don't worry about it."

They stood in line at the money exchange booth. Sierra felt Paul staring at her. When she couldn't stand the sensation any longer, she turned and looked at him. He didn't turn away or act embarrassed.

"You don't wear any makeup, do you?" Paul noted.

Now Sierra felt really odd. This guy was blunt. That was her usual approach, and it had gotten her in trouble more than once. "No, do you?" she countered playfully.

Paul looked shocked at first and then a delighted smile inched onto his face. "Not that you need to or anything."

Sierra leaned a bit closer to him, as if scrutinizing his complexion right back. "And neither do you," she said flatly.

This time Paul laughed.

They were up to the window now, and Sierra stood to the side as he pulled out his passport and wrote out a traveler's check. The clerk counted the money back to him and slid it on the metal tray under the glass window.

"Here you go," Paul said, stepping away from the window and handing Sierra a twenty-dollar bill.

"I don't have change for a twenty."

"All I have is twenties," he said. "You'll have to take it."

"But then I'll owe you," Sierra said.

"Don't worry about it." He looked at his watch. "Hey, thanks again. I have a plane to catch."

"Me too," Sierra said as he dashed away, his backpack flung over his shoulder.

Sierra began to hike to her flight gate, a few yards behind Paul. She thought about calling out to him and walking with him since she knew they were on the same flight. But something held her back, which was not typical of her. Usually she could approach anyone at any time.

She watched him as she waited to check in at the ticket counter. Paul was ahead of her in line, with three rather large people in between them. Paul never turned around. He left the waiting area as soon as he checked in and returned only when they called the flight. Sierra was standing by the window and watched him get in line to board the plane.

*This is ridiculous! What am I doing watching this guy?*

Sierra entered the single-file line of passengers with her ticket in hand and backpack over her shoulder. She watched the well-worn hat looped over the top of Paul's leather backpack as he shuffled through the line. About eight people were between them this time.

A crazy thought danced through her imagination. *What if our seats are next to each other?*

Sierra smiled at the flight attendant and made her way

to the rear of the plane. She could still see Paul's bobbing hat down the aisle in front of her. It was a good sign; he hadn't reached his seat yet. Only a few more and he would be at her row. Suddenly Paul stopped. Sierra held her breath.

# five

SIERRA WATCHED AS PAUL slung his backpack off his shoulder and ducked his head beneath the overhead compartment. He hadn't seemed so tall at the phones in the terminal but now he seemed not only tall but also broad-shouldered. Of course, since Sierra was five foot five and a half most guys did seem tall to her. She checked her seat number again.

*Rats! I'm three rows behind him. Will he notice me when I walk by?*

Sierra slowly shuffled past him. Paul had his head down, stuffing his backpack under the seat in front of him. She lingered just a minute, wondering if she should say something. He straightened up but kept his eyes lowered as he adjusted his seat belt.

Aware of the line of people behind her, Sierra made her way to her row and slid next to the window. An older gentleman sat in the aisle seat.

*Why couldn't this have been Paul's place?* she thought, looking at the vacant middle seat between her and the older man. *Then again, he didn't have anyone next to him yet. Maybe I should think of an excuse to go up and casually sit by him, as if I think that spot is mine. No, too cheesy. Maybe I should slip out and search for a pillow or magazine or something to see if he notices me when I walk past. Let him make the first move. I'll stand there, chatting nonchalantly with him, then the stewardess will come by and tell me to take my seat. I'll have to sit down right then and there! What am I thinking? This is ridiculous.*

"Good day to you," said the man in the aisle seat. He was bald with little round glasses. His hands were contentedly folded across his round middle, and his short legs were stretched out and crossed at the ankles. He looked awfully comfortable, and Sierra couldn't bear to ask him if she could slide past him to parade down the aisle. She returned his greeting and then gazed out the window.

A luggage tram pulled up next to the plane, and two men began to toss bags onto a conveyor belt that inched its way up into the plane's belly. Sierra thought she would prefer to ride in the cargo with the luggage than spend the next fifteen hours peering over three rows of seats to spy on the back of Paul's head.

Reaching for a magazine in her seat pocket in front of her, Sierra forced herself to think about something else. She flipped through the pages, pretending to scan the articles. Her mind felt mushy. She had no idea what time it was or how much longer it would be before the plane took off.

The flight attendant made her way down the aisle, checking seat belts and offering pillows and blankets. Sierra accepted both. Suddenly she felt sleepy. A nap before dinner would do her good. She pulled the blanket up to her chin and balanced the pillow behind her neck.

Closing her eyes, she tried to sort out all the thoughts, feelings, and experiences of the past few weeks. This was the first time she had been "alone" for any significant time the entire trip. Maybe it was good she wasn't trying to carry on a conversation with Paul.

The plane taxied down the runway and took off. Sierra looked out her window. In less than a minute the nose of the plane pierced the thick blanket of fog that hung over Heathrow Airport, and all Sierra could see was a shroud of gray. She tried to catch a glimpse of Paul ahead of her. Was he looking out the window too? Was he reading? Sleeping? She reclined her seat, closed her eyes, and went back to categorizing and filing the events of her trip.

Sierra felt herself begin to doze off. Then, just for good measure, she moved her pillow over to the window and leaned against it with her face open to the aisle. Actually, she was more comfortable with the pillow behind her head and her chin down. But her hair fell across the side of her face in that position. This way, if Paul *did* happen to walk by, he would certainly notice her. She only hoped she wouldn't start drooling while she slept.

When Sierra next opened her eyes, the flight attendant was offering her a dinner tray. She lowered her tray table, adjusted herself in her seat, and tried to shake awake enough to eat. A movie followed that Sierra tried to watch, but she fell asleep again, dozing uncomfortably off and on for many hours.

At one point, she shifted in her seat and noticed the man in the aisle seat was gone. She decided to use the opportunity to go to the restroom at the rear of the plane. Several people stood back there in cramped quarters, waiting for one of the four restroom doors to open. Sierra stood with them, yawning and glancing around.

Paul was standing only six feet away by the small serving area, asking the stewardess for something to drink. Once again, Sierra was paralyzed. Paul wasn't looking at her. He seemed oblivious to her existence. Why should she be so interested in him? Thanking the stewardess, Paul accepted the beverage and started to return to his seat. Suddenly he turned and looked back over his shoulder in Sierra's direction.

This was the encounter she had been waiting for. And what did she do? She immediately turned her head away and studied the silver "occupied" sign on the bathroom door in front of her.

*What a dork I am! Did he notice me? Did he know I was here, and was he looking back to see if I had recognized him? I guess I'll never know, will I?*

Sierra chanced a peek over her shoulder through a wild mass of her unruly curls. He was gone. Now she had to make those silly cat-and-mouse decisions all over again. Should she return to her seat by walking the long way around the plane so she could saunter past his seat and they might make eye contact?

She entered the tiny restroom and took a look in the mirror. "Night of the Flying Zombies," she muttered to herself. Her eyes were puffy, and across her right cheek was a deep crease from the pillow. At least she didn't have to be concerned with mascara smears.

Sierra thought back on Stephen's comments to her and Katie a few days ago. He had said she was beautiful. Gorgeous. Her dad told her that all the time. But no *real* guy had ever said anything like that to her. Stephen didn't count because such a compliment would only matter if it came from an "eligible" guy, a guy whose opinion really mattered to her.

"So why do I think Paul is that kind of guy? Why am I obsessed with him? This is getting out of control."

Sierra finished in the bathroom and returned to her seat by the most direct route, avoiding Paul. She crawled back under her blanket and silently prayed about her bothersome obsession. She didn't know if her unbridled thoughts about Paul were wrong or if they were normal. In either case, she knew it would be good to pray and surrender the whole thing to Christ. She remembered the verse she had read in Psalms about trusting Him at all times and pouring out her heart to Him.

It worked. She felt more peace about Paul after praying. Only now all she could think about was arriving in Portland in a few hours and everything being brand new for her. She went right back to praying and pouring out her heart.

The plane landed on time in San Francisco. Sierra knew she had to walk from the international terminal over to another section where a much smaller plane would take her to Portland exactly forty-two minutes after this flight landed. It didn't leave much time for customs.

Fortunately, Sierra hadn't bought many souvenirs and had marked on her form that she had nothing to declare. She was directed to a fast-moving line. Paul, she noticed, wasn't in her line. She was tempted to turn around and scan the crowd behind her but resisted the urge. It was more important that she get her passport cleared and find her way to the other end of the terminal to catch her next flight.

She made it with a few minutes to spare. Breathing hard and feeling the perspiration beads form on her forehead, Sierra settled into her seat and gazed out the plane's window.

"Pardon me," a deep voice said. "I think you're in my seat."

She turned to look into the surprised blue-gray eyes of Paul. "It's you! How did you get here?" He said it sincerely enough that Sierra believed he really didn't know she had been on the flight from London.

"I swam," Sierra said with a smile, wiping away the perspiration off her forehead and flipping her hair back over her shoulders.

Paul slid into the middle seat next to her, holding his backpack and hat on his lap. "Were we just on the same fight?"

She felt like saying, "Duh!" but instead she said, "As a matter of fact, we were."

"I wish I'd known," Paul said. He rose to put his gear in the overhead compartment and asked, "Do you want me to put anything up here for you?"

"No thanks," Sierra answered. She couldn't believe this was happening. Nearly sixteen hours ago in England she had hoped to sit next to Paul, then she had given up, and now here she and Paul were, and it all seemed so natural. "I didn't realize I was in the wrong seat," she said as he ducked to sit down. "Do you want the window seat?"

"No, that's fine. You deserve it. I feel as if I still owe you."

"You don't," Sierra said. "If anything, I owe you." She bent over, unzipped the outside pocket on her backpack, and pulled out a small white sack.

Once again she felt Paul staring at her. She smelled his aftershave, and it made her think of Christmas back in Pineville. This time she didn't try to catch him staring.

Since this had developed into a most interesting turn of events, she decided to play it for all it was worth. Let him stare. What did he see? Was he deciding she was worth pursuing?

Even as she entertained these thoughts, Sierra felt guilty. What a flirting game! She knew nothing about this guy except his name was Paul, he was going to Portland, and he was gutsy enough to beg money from a stranger but honorable enough to pay it back with interest.

Now it was her turn to pay back with interest. "I still don't have any change," she said, holding out the sack and smiling at him. "But will you take this? It's chocolates from Finland."

Paul raised an eyebrow and peered at the crumpled bag. "Chocolate?"

"Here," Sierra offered. "Consider it change for your twenty."

Paul accepted the gift and reached into the sack. He took out one of the small cubes of chocolate and popped it in his mouth. "Oh yeah," he said, closing his eyes. "Now *this* is chocolate! Where did you say it was from?"

"Finland."

"Is that where you've been?"

"No, I was in England and then in Ireland. One of the other girls from our group was from Finland, and she gave some to everyone the last day of our missions outreach."

Paul stopped sucking on the chocolate and looked closer at Sierra. "You weren't at Carnforth Hall, were you?"

"Yes, I was!"

"I don't believe it!" He leaned back his head and closed his eyes as if the news distressed him. Sierra peered closer to him, searching for a clue as to why that bothered him.

"Have you been there?" she ventured.

Paul looked at her, a normal expression returning to his face. "More times than I can count. My grandfather bought Carnforth Hall right after World War II. He used to run summer Bible camps until about six years ago when he turned it over to the mission group that now operates it."

"You're kidding!"

Paul shook his head. "My grandfather just died. His funeral was in Edinburgh three days ago."

Sierra remembered that Dr. Benson had gone to Edinburgh for a funeral. "Was Dr. Benson there?"

"Charles? Yeah, he was there along with about eight hundred other people. My grandfather was a well-loved man." Paul looked contemplative and then switched to a less serious expression. "Did you meet a guy from San Diego named Doug at Carnforth?"

"Doug was my team leader! How do you know him?"

"He's friends with my older brother. My dad is the pastor at Mission Springs in El Cajon. Have you heard of it?"

Sierra shook her head. "Should I have?"

"It's a big church. Four thousand members. Doug goes there, and that's where he met my brother, Jeremy. They have this Sunday night group called God Lovers that meets at Doug's apartment. I used to go there when I was in high school. It was a big deal, hanging out with all the college kids."

Sierra knew exactly what Paul meant. She had felt that way this whole trip. "Did you ever meet a friend of Doug's named Todd?"

"Surfer type? Plays guitar?"

"Yeah. He's the mission director now in Spain."

"Figures."

"Small world, isn't it?" Sierra replied.

"The circles in life are very small." Paul said it as if he were quoting someone. "So, what brought you to Carnforth?"

Sierra shrugged her shoulders. "God, I guess. I heard about it from one of my cousins and decided to go."

Paul looked away. The plane was taking off. It was much smaller and noisier than the wide-body had been from England.

Once they were airborne Sierra pursued their conversation.

"Why are you going to Portland? Don't you live in San Diego?"

"I'm going to school at L. and C."

Sierra looked at him as if the initials meant nothing.

"Lewis and Clark College." Paul reached in the white bag and took out another chunk of chocolate. "Would you like some of your own candy?"

Sierra took a small piece and thanked him. The incredible chocolate melted in her mouth.

"You know what?" he said, lowering his voice and leaning a bit closer. "I don't even know your name."

"Ah, but you know the really important stuff about me," Sierra said, feeling flirty. "Like I loan money to strangers, I don't wear makeup, and I'm generous with my world-class gourmet chocolate."

"True, true. And those are good qualities in a person. But what's your name?"

It was fun, stringing him along like this, but she decided to give in. "Sierra."

He gave her a peculiar look, as if her name pleased him, as if this were a test, and she had given the right answer. One hundred percent correct.

# six

"SIERRA," PAUL REPEATED her name as if he were savoring it. "I like your boots."

She glanced down at her worn-out doggies and said, "They're my dad's."

"And this quick wit?" Paul asked. "Is that your dad's too?"

"As a matter of fact, it is," Sierra said.

"And you're going to Portland because..." Paul waited for her to fill in the blank.

"Because I have a free place to eat and sleep there."

"Your parents' house?"

"Actually, my grandmother's house. My family moved in with her while I was in England. It's a huge old Victorian, and Granna Mae refused to sell it. She can't keep it up or take care of herself anymore, so my dad made a career change, and we all moved in with my grandma."

"Sounds like something my dad would do. We grew up in a pretty small house and always drove junker cars. But every year my dad spent his saved up pennies on airline tickets so all five of us could spend the summer with our grandparents in Carnforth. Be glad that you can spend time with your grandmother now. It's a gift."

"I know," Sierra said. "She's my soul mate."

"Really?" Once again Paul looked at Sierra as if she had given him the correct answer. "Most people don't feel that way about their grandparents or elderly people in general. I was closer to my grandfather than any other person I've ever known. It was like we had the same heart."

"And now that he's gone, how do you feel?" Sierra saw the hurt in Paul's face and the glistening in his eyes. She wanted to reach over and take his hand and comfort him.

"No one will ever take his place in my life. I feel as if I have a big hole right through the middle of me. At night, I can almost hear the wind whistling through it."

Sierra felt so connected with this poet of a man. Their eyes met, and neither of them said anything for a moment. Paul seemed to be staring deep inside of her, drawing strength from her silence. She gazed back at him.

"Something to drink for you two?" the flight attendant asked, breaking their communion. They both turned to him, and at the same time said, "Orange juice with ice, please."

"Okay!" the uniformed man said with a laugh. "Two OJ's on the rocks. Are you two brother and sister?"

Sierra and Paul looked blankly at each other and then back at the flight attendant. "No, what made you think that?" Sierra asked.

"Your eyes. You have the same eyes." He moved on to the row behind them.

"Why did he say that?" Paul asked, turning back to look at Sierra.

"Beats me," she said, comically crossing her eyes and trying to stare at the freckles on her nose.

Paul laughed. "You don't suppose we really are twins, separated at birth, do you?"

"Not a chance. You're older," Sierra said.

"By how much? I was nineteen in December."

Sierra smiled and didn't answer.

"What? Are we about six months apart? Maybe nine?"

"Well my birthday is November fourteenth..."

"You're kidding," Paul said. "That's my mom's birthday! So what, you're eighteen then?"

"No."

"Seventeen?"

"No."

"Sixteen?" he said slowly as Sierra nodded. "You're only sixteen?"

Sierra watched him physically draw back, and as he did, something changed between them. All the closeness evaporated. She wanted to defend herself, to tell him nothing was wrong with being sixteen, and actually she was mature for her age. But he was gone, closed off emotionally from whatever connection they had experienced.

They silently sipped their orange juice. "Is your boyfriend picking you up at the airport?" Paul suddenly asked.

"My boyfriend?"

"I heard you tell some guy on the phone in London that you loved him."

"That 'guy' was my dad."

"Oh." Paul looked at his plastic tumbler and said, "My girlfriend is picking me up."

"It's too bad she wasn't able to go to the funeral with you. I'm sure it would have been nice for you to have her there." Inside she felt all chewed up. Why was he telling her about his girlfriend? She could be mature about this, she coached herself. Just ask lots of questions.

"Actually, it wouldn't have been a good idea for her to have been there."

"Why?"

Paul swished the ice cubes around in his nearly empty cup. "Jalene is...well, she's different."

"You mean she's not a Christian," Sierra said.

Paul looked at her, startled at her discernment. "I didn't say that."

"You didn't have to."

A tense silence hung between them. Sierra was bugged. Why would a guy like Paul, with such a godly background and all kinds of potential for ministry, fall for a girl who wasn't a Christian? She wanted to tell him exactly what she thought and realized she had nothing to lose. He obviously wasn't interested in her, not only because she was sixteen but also because he had a girlfriend. Sierra shifted into high gear.

"What are you doing with her? I mean, don't you see the potential for destruction in a relationship that's so lopsided? It's like a trap to get you to settle for less than God's best for your life."

Now Paul looked mad. "And where do you get off telling me what to do with my life? You think you're some prophetess or something? You don't know anything about me or my life or what God's best is for me!"

"And Jalene does?" Sierra asked. Tact had never been one of her strengths.

Paul looked really mad now. "What's it to you? Who do you think you are, anyway?" He looked away, as if the sight of her disgusted him.

Shaking his head, Paul fumbled for a magazine in the pouch in front of him and then reached up to turn on the light above his seat. Obviously he was shutting her out.

Sierra decided two could play this game. She swished her head away from him, pretending his behavior didn't bother her a bit. But one of her long, flying curls caught in the band of his wristwatch.

"Ouch!" Sierra tugged angrily to get free. It only tangled her hair more.

"Don't move," Paul snapped. "You're making it worse. Hold still."

Sierra couldn't see his face, but she could feel him pulling each thread of hair, releasing it from his watch.

"Man, you really torqued it in here." The angry edge seemed to subside from his voice. "I almost have it."

"Just pull it out," Sierra said stubbornly. "I don't care."

"Relax, will you? Now hold on. There. You're free. None the worse for wear."

Sierra smoothed down her ruffled mane but didn't turn to look at him.

"Thanks for the souvenir," Paul said.

She turned slightly to see what he meant. He was still pulling blond hairs from his watchband. "When you're caught like that it doesn't help to pull away." He sounded like Wesley when he was in one of his big brother moods.

"Oh, right!" Sierra said, giving him a scolding look. "And you're one to tell me about jerking away! You can't even have a conversation about your girlfriend without pulling away."

Paul's reaction startled her. He started to laugh. It was deep, from the heart, merry laughter.

"What's so funny?" Sierra asked defensively. "You know I'm right."

"What are you?" Paul asked, still smiling. "My guardian angel or something?"

"I'm no angel."

"Some mystic warrior, then? Sent to guide me back to the right path?"

Sierra recalled the thought that had occurred to her when she first met Paul. "*Fight for this man.*" Maybe a battle was going on in his life. Maybe the Holy Spirit was calling her to be a prayer warrior for him. She had heard stories of people feeling compelled to pray for someone without knowing why. Later they had found out that God had used their prayers to redirect the course of that person's life.

"Maybe," she answered calmly. The whole chance encounter with this guy was a little too weird for her. "Just remember, you're the one who asked me for phone money. I wasn't trailing you, as you seem to think."

Paul looked at her again, studying her intensely. It didn't bother her. She felt open, with nothing to hide. What was it he was searching for?

"Sierra, you are an exceptional young woman. I pity the man who falls in love with you."

"And I pity any young woman who falls in love with you, if you're running away from God. Jonah tried that, remember?

Unless you have an affection for whale barf, I'd encourage you to get your act together."

"Man!" Paul said, running his fingers through his dark, wavy hair. "You just don't quit, do you?"

Like an alarm going off in Sierra's head, she felt the call to retreat. She suddenly realized how brazen she was being.

"I'm sorry," Sierra said, looking down and feeling herself calm down. "I come on a little too strong sometimes. I apologize if I said anything out of line."

Paul raised an eyebrow. "From full-on in-your-face to innocent lamb. You do that very well. You must have some Scottish blood in you." A smile pulled up the corners of his mouth. "I imagine you'll grow into that zealous spirit. Right now I'd say it's a little too big for you."

It bothered Sierra that he was putting her down with such tender words. It bothered her that their intense conversation had gone nowhere. She had surrendered. What good had that done? She withdrew by tearing open her tiny bag of airline peanuts and chewing each one a dozen times so her mouth would stay busy.

Her mouth had gotten her into trouble so many times that she couldn't begin to count them all. When would she ever learn to keep quiet? Why couldn't she and Paul have talked about normal things like the weather? Why did she always have to speak her mind and be so intense, even with strangers?

That's what bothered her the most. Paul didn't seem like a stranger. Somehow they connected. Even Paul had to admit that. There was something between them, and it was powerful.

The plane landed on time in Portland. Paul and Sierra

had spent the last ten minutes talking about hiking. He recommended several of his favorite places in the area. It was a calm, friendly chat, like two strangers are supposed to have on an airplane. She expressed her condolences about his grandfather, and he thanked her politely.

When they deplaned, Paul walked down the hallway beside her as if they were together. He didn't say anything. He was just there.

As soon as they entered the terminal, Sierra scanned the greeters, trying to pick out Jalene before he went to her. She found her immediately. With jet black hair cut severely short, Jalene wore a long skirt and black boots. She looked normal enough. Kind of cute and fun-looking, except for a cat smile that curled up in her lips. Paul seemed to hesitate for an instant before walking up to her open arms.

Sierra kept moving with the crowd, walking toward the baggage claim where she had arranged to meet her parents. On impulse she turned and looked over her shoulder one last time. She expected to see Paul kissing Jalene. However, from the looks of it, Jalene was the one doing the kissing.

Sierra stepped on the escalator and tried to shake thoughts of Paul from her mind. She had enough to deal with, including adjusting to the new house and a new school next week.

*I don't even know his last name. I'm never going to see him again. It was nothing more than a strange encounter with an even stranger guy. I opened my mouth way too much, as usual. End of story.*

Sierra spotted her dad the minute she stepped off the escalator. His eyes were all crinkled up in the kind of smile he wore when he was trying not to cry. Her mom stood beside him, looking slimmer than Sierra remembered. She was a youthful-looking woman who jogged regularly. Her blond hair was a short bob, and she had on the black pants and red sweater Sierra had given her for Christmas.

Sierra hurried into their embrace. First Dad hugged her, with a big kiss on the cheek, and then Mom, whose tears smeared across Sierra's face.

"It's so good to have you home!" Dad said. He looked young too, except for his receding hairline. Where the brown wispy hairs had thinned on top, rows of faint worry lines ran all the way up his extended forehead.

"It's weird thinking of Portland as home," Sierra said. She and her mom looped arms and walked over to where the other passengers were forming a line around the long luggage conveyor belt.

"I think you'll like it here," Mom said. "Granna Mae has been doing better since we arrived."

"Are we all moved in?" Sierra asked.

"Pretty much. A bunch of boxes are in the basement full of my knickknacks and books and things. There's no room for them on the shelves yet. Granna Mae and I need to do some sorting and cleaning. She's been asking for four days straight when you're coming home. Time is still a problem for her. Days and years all sort of blend together, and she has a hard time remembering where she is. Don't be surprised if she is confused when she sees you and can't quite place who you are."

"She'll know me," Sierra said confidently. "I'm glad she's feeling better."

A loud buzzer sounded, and the luggage conveyor belt began its cycle. Sierra stepped deeper into the crowd of travelers and stretched to see if her suitcase was coming yet.

She spotted it and was about to reach for it when someone stepped in front of her and grabbed it.

"Hey, that's my bag!"

"No, it's mine," the guy said. He turned to face her. It was Paul.

# seven

"I DON'T BELIEVE THIS," Paul said. "Your bag must look like mine, but this is my bag."

"Sorry, it's mine. Check the luggage tag."

He did, and it was hers.

"My mistake," Paul said, putting the bag down in the midst of all the people crammed around the conveyor belt.

"Yeah, well, try not to make any more," Sierra said, deliberately looking beyond Paul to Jalene, who was waiting for him in the background.

A smile slipped onto Paul's face. "I hope I never see you again," he said. "You're making my life very complicated."

Sierra thought of about four sharp comments she could make back to him, but she held her tongue. She wasn't sure why. Perhaps because all the bold comments on the plane had seemed so futile. Or maybe because her parents were standing only a few yards away, not to mention Jalene, watching them.

Sierra said nothing but stood her ground and stared into his blue-gray eyes the way he had stared at her more than once. Paul stared right back. Their thirty-second stare-out felt as if it lasted an eternity. Sierra was the one who blinked first.

"Have a nice life," she said and walked away.

"Hey!" Paul called out after her. She ignored him and kept walking.

"You forgot your bag!"

Sierra turned around. Paul was about two feet away from her, emerging from the crowd with her luggage.

Paul handed her the heavy travel bag and, without making eye contact this time, said in a low voice, "Don't ever change, Sierra." Looking up at her for just an instant, he smiled, then turned and headed back to the mob of people.

To her, this was the final truce. To the average observer she was sure the exchange seemed to be nothing more than a stranger helping someone locate her luggage.

However, Sierra's dad didn't happen to be an average observer. After they arrived home and Sierra had been thoroughly hugged and welcomed by her two younger brothers, her dad invited her to sit out on the front porch with him. Granna Mae was already asleep, having apparently forgotten that Sierra was coming home tonight, and Tawni hadn't returned yet from her job at the Clackamas Town Center Mall.

Sierra made herself a cup of hot peppermint tea and grabbed a thick lap comforter from the front hall closet. The screen on the door squeaked as it had every summer that Sierra had come here since she was a baby.

Only now it was winter, and the wide, wraparound front porch was a chilly place to sit. Her dad was waiting for her on the swing. She sat next to him, balancing her tea and pulling the comforter over her legs.

"We all missed you, Sierra. It's a good thing you're home." She could see his breath as he spoke to her.

"Do you want some of my tea?" Sierra offered the steaming cup and he took a sip.

He made a face. "What is that?"

"Peppermint."

"I think I'll stick to coffee." He liked it dark and thick, a tradition in his Danish family but one Sierra was unable to bring herself to participate in. On the few occasions that she did have coffee, she tempered it with lots of cream and sugar. Artificially flavored creamers were even better. For the most part, Sierra was an herbal tea drinker.

"What was his name?" her father said.

"Who?"

"The young explorer with the hat who couldn't take his eyes off of you." Sierra's dad rested his arm across the back of the porch swing, inviting Sierra to draw closer to him and share her thoughts.

She knew better than to beat around any bushes with her dad. When it came to his six children, Howard Jensen knew each of them by heart. Sierra did her best to reconstruct the unusual encounter with Paul and even told her dad about the impression to fight for Paul.

He rubbed his chin after she finished. The worry lines on his forehead began to smooth away. "That is what you must do then," he concluded.

"I don't even know his last name," Sierra said.

"God does. All you must do is pray for him. I'll pray

with you. Every day. Now tell me about the rest of your trip."

"I don't know where to start. It was the most incredible experience of my life. I'm so glad I went." Sierra put down her empty mug and slipped her cold hands under the comforter. She began with a day-by-day rundown, then her mom joined them with two mugs of coffee. She handed one to Dad. Mom had on a long coat with her favorite mukluk slippers. She curled up in a white wicker chair across from the swing. Sierra's dad wore only a sweater and pants yet seemed warm enough. He loved the cold. Must be his Scandinavian blood.

"Oh, good," Sierra's mom said, sipping her rich coffee. "I don't want to miss anything. I tucked in the boys and told them to let you sleep tomorrow, even if you end up sleeping all day."

"Thanks," Sierra said. "I probably could sleep all day. I don't even know if it's daytime or nighttime, according to my body."

Just then a white sedan pulled up and parked in front of the house. Sierra's sister, Tawni, stepped out and pushed a button on her key chain, which made a melodic tune as it locked the car doors.

"Did Tawni get a new car?"

"Last week," Mom said. "Isn't it a beauty?"

Stately Tawni, with her model-like figure, sauntered up the five wide steps that led to the porch. A sweet fragrance preceded her, the aftereffect of her job at a perfume counter at Nordstrom's. "You're home!" she said when she noticed Sierra. "Did you have a good time?"

Sierra slid off the swing and went over to hug Tawni

since she didn't seem to be moving toward Sierra. "It was fantastic! You should go next time." Sierra couldn't quite imagine Tawni traveling unless she was guaranteed a hot shower every morning and a place to plug in her curling iron. "I like your new car," Sierra said.

"Thanks." Tawni warmly reciprocated the hug. That's how Tawni was. She wouldn't initiate any sign of affection, but she responded sincerely when Sierra did.

Tawni was a beautiful woman and looked older than eighteen. Her appearance was enhanced by her expert use of makeup, her highlighted blond hair, and her tinted blue contacts. She had worn braces for three years and had had singing lessons since she was ten. They were congenial because they were related. Under other circumstances, they probably wouldn't have sought each other's friendship.

"I'm so broke now you wouldn't believe it," Tawni said. "This job at Nordstrom's opened up just in time. I'm only scheduled for twenty-five hours a week to start, but it should turn into full time by the first of March."

"That's great," Sierra said. "You want to grab a blanket and join us out here?"

"If you don't mind, I'm really tired. I'll hear all about your trip tomorrow. Did you see our room yet? At least it's bigger than the one we had in Pineville."

"The boys showed it to me right away. I take it my bed is the one by the window?"

"You don't mind, do you?" Tawni said. Sierra knew that since Tawni was already settled, it wouldn't matter if she did mind.

"No, it's fine. It's a great room. It's just weird to come

home and have everything all turned around and you guys settled and living here without me."

"Well, welcome home," Tawni said, moving toward the front door. "I'm going to bed."

"Good night, honey," Dad said.

"Sweet dreams," said Mom.

Sierra called out, "I'll try to be quiet when I go to bed."

Tawni went inside, and Sierra thought again, as she had hundreds, if not thousands of times, that she wished she could find a way to change her sister. Tawni seemed to carry a big chip on her shoulder because she was the only one of the six Jensen children who was adopted. Obviously she was wanted. She was always treated equally by Mom and Dad, and Sierra thought of Tawni as her one and only sister. But Tawni had labeled herself years ago and moved about their family with slight alienation.

"I didn't even ask you guys how you like it here," Sierra said, snuggling back under her comforter.

"It's home," Dad said.

"Well, of course it is to you, Dad. You grew up here. How are you doing, Mom? And the boys?"

"Actually, thing are going better than I'd expected. Granna Mae has some good days when she's bright as a berry, but then other days her memory lapses, and she doesn't know who we are. This morning she asked Howard if he was here to fix the plumbing."

"Doesn't it kill you to know your own mother doesn't know who you are?" Sierra asked.

"It's not her fault. I told her yes, I was the best plumber in all of Portland, and where was the leaky pipe. She led me right to the washbasin in the basement and told me how it stopped up because a yo-yo was caught in it."

"That really happened," Mom told Sierra. "When your dad was about seven, he stuck his yo-yo in the sink, and they had to call a plumber to remove it so the rest of the drains wouldn't stop up. It was an expensive visit from the plumber, and Granna Mae talked about it for years."

"So now she's remembering things that happened in the past and sort of acting them out?" Sierra asked.

"Something like that," Dad answered.

"It's going to be hard for me to be around her when she's spacing out like that," Sierra said. "She was perfectly fine last summer. What happened? Can't they give her something? Medicine of some kind or treatment?"

Mom shook her head. "We just have to keep an eye on her. It seems best to play along whenever she's having one of her memory lapses. It upsets her when we try to tell her who we really are or force her back into the present."

Sierra and her parents talked for almost an hour before it became too cold and Sierra was yawning so much that she couldn't complete her sentences. She hugged her mom and dad and climbed the curved staircase up to her new room.

Tawni had left on a small light on the bed stand between their twin beds. It cast a soft yellow glow on the striped rose wallpaper and the white wooded shutters lining the bottom half of the bedroom window.

This room had belonged to Aunt Emma, Dad's baby sister. When Emma moved out years ago, it had become a catchall room since it was so large. For every summer that Sierra could remember, coming into this room was like exploring an old attic. With all the old clutter cleared out and the room now cleaned up and filled with Sierra's and

Tawni's familiar belongings, it had turned into a wonderful bedroom.

Sierra noticed it was especially cold by the window. She made sure the shutters that covered the old glass panes were completely shut, blocking out the night draft. Her feet were still cold from sitting on the porch. It would feel good to slide in between those flannel sheets.

But before Sierra climbed into bed, she felt she should do something to christen her new room. It had to be something quiet so she wouldn't wake Tawni.

Sierra decided to pray. She knelt beside her bed, with the chilly window to her back and with her hands folded and eyes closed. She prayed silently for Granna Mae, her family, herself, and her friends from Carnforth Hall. The she prayed for Paul.

When Sierra opened her eyes, a scream caught in her throat. Someone was sitting on her bed. The silent figure wore a white gown and a glow came from around its head. Sierra could feel her heart pounding as the figure rose and pulled back the covers for Sierra. It moved away from the light and spoke to her. "Did you remember to pray for Paul, Emma dear?"

"Granna Mae," Sierra whispered. The confused woman stood in her flannel nightgown, her white hair all fuzzy around her head, waiting for Sierra to climb into bed. Sierra remembered what her mom had said about playing along so she obediently crawled into bed.

*Why did she ask if I prayed for Paul? Does she know about the guy on the plane? Why does she think I'm Emma? Because I'm in Emma's room?*

Granna Mae had a peaceful smile on her face as she tucked the covers in all around Sierra and kissed her on both cheeks as if she were a little girl who had just said her prayers.

"Repeat after me, Emma dear: 'The Lord thy God in the midst of thee is mighty.'"

Sierra hesitated.

"Go ahead, Emma dear, 'The Lord thy God...'"

"'The Lord thy God in the midst of thee is mighty.'" Sierra repeated in a small voice. Her heart was still pounding.

"'He will save, He will rejoice over thee with joy; He will rest in His love,'" Granna Mae said tenderly.

Sierra repeated it.

"'He will joy over thee with singing.'"

Again Sierra repeated, "'He will joy over thee with singing.'"

"Amen," said Granna Mae.

"Amen," Sierra echoed.

Then, as silently as she had appeared in the bedroom, Granna Mae shuffled out in her bare feet, shutting the door behind her.

# eight

"MOTHER, YOU CAN'T TELL me that's normal," Sierra argued in a hushed voice the next morning in the kitchen.

"For her, for right now, it is normal. We all have to be understanding. That's what we agreed to when we came here, Sierra." Mom turned off the whistling teakettle, and the stove's black knob came off in her hand. She held it up in front of Sierra and said, "And this is the other reason! This old house is falling apart. It's not safe for her to be here alone."

"But is it safe for us to be here with her?"

"Of course it is! Her mind is playing tricks on her, that's all. You did the right thing last night by playing along and letting her think she was tucking Emma into bed. That was probably a very soothing and warm memory for her."

"But why did she ask if I prayed for Paul?"

"I'm sure she meant her son Paul. Did you remember that Dad had a brother who was killed in Vietnam?"

"I didn't even think of him," Sierra said, pouring the hot water into a bowl of instant oatmeal. "It's too spooky for me, Mom. I felt as if I should sleep with one eye open just in case she came back in the middle of the night."

"Try to imagine what it must be like for her," Mom said. "Treat her with dignity."

"I'll try." She poured some milk into her oatmeal, stirred it around, and lifted the spoon to her mouth. Just then, Granna Mae stepped into the kitchen.

"Well, look who's here!" she said. Sierra wasn't sure if Granna Mae thought she was looking at Sierra, Emma, or maybe even someone else, like the plumber.

"Good morning," Sierra said with a smile. She slowly pushed the stool away from the kitchen counter and stood before Granna Mae, waiting for her cue as to who Sierra should be for her grandmother this morning.

"Well? Don't you have a little hug for me, Lovey?"

Sierra knew her grandmother recognized her when she said "Lovey." She had pet names for all her grandkids, and that was Sierra's. With a sigh of relief, Sierra met her grandma's hug and even gave her a kiss on the cheek. Granna Mae smelled like soap, all clean and fresh.

"Don't let me interrupt your breakfast," she said. She stepped lightly to the cupboard, pulled out a china teacup, and poured herself some of the strong, black coffee warming in the Braun coffeemaker on the counter. She always drank from a china cup, even water with her daily pills. Perish the thought that she would ever lift anything plastic, or horrors, Styrofoam to her lips. It was a china cup or nothing. Sierra remembered going on family picnics as a child, and wrapped in a cloth napkin at the bottom of the picnic hamper would be Granna Mae's favorite china teacup.

"I'd love to hear all about your trip, Lovey. I was simply too tired last night to wait up for you. I hope you understand."

"Of course," Sierra said. "My trip was wonderful. I loved Ireland, and I made a lot of great friends." For the next twenty minutes or so Sierra chatted about her trip. Granna Mae sat on the cushioned bench along the back kitchen wall and listened with clear-eyed interest. Sierra found it hard to believe this was the same person who had done the angel imitation in Sierra's bedroom last night.

During the next three days, Granna Mae seemed normal, spunky, quick-witted, and hardworking. Sierra loved being around her. They talked lots and laughed about silly things. They worked together helping Mom clear off bookshelves in the downstairs library. Most of the photos and mementos were moved up to Granna Mae's room, where Sierra's dad had built new shelves along one entire wall. Granna Mae seemed pleased to have all her new things near her.

Sierra was impressed that her grandma was so willing to share her well-established home with Sierra's family. After living in the same house for forty-two of her sixty-eight years, she was gracious about letting Sierra's mom come in and rearrange everything. Mom had even ordered new furniture for the family room, including a couch that folded out into a queen sleeper. Granna Mae's little television was sent up to her room, where she'd have better reception than she had ever gotten downstairs.

The TV corner was now empty, which made the family room look lopsided with all the new furniture in place. Dad was building an entertainment center out in the cottage behind the house that he had turned into his workroom. It was actually an old playhouse with tacky gingerbread trim around the roof and windows. But nothing was childish about what went on inside it now that Dad had set up his workbench and lined the wall with Peg-Board and all his power tools. Dillon and Gavin loved going out there and with their own hammers and saws creating "masterpieces." Granna Mae referred to it as "the boys' clubhouse."

Then, the night before Sierra started school, Granna Mae had one of her relapses at dinner. They were sitting around the mahogany table in the formal dining room when all of a sudden Granna Mae turned to Gavin and said, "You cannot leave this table until you eat your peas, young man." She stood up and cleared her place, taking her still-full dinner plate into the kitchen.

Six-year-old, freckle-faced Gavin looked at his mom with distress. "We're not even having peas," he said.

"I know, honey. She's confused. It's okay."

Granna Mae returned a few moments later wearing a mitt pot holder on her hand and carrying in an apple pie. In the other hand she held a knife. She had a smile on her face. "Now I told Ted we would save him a piece of this pie. You children mind that you don't take too much for yourself." She set down the pie on the table. "I suppose I should cut it for you so it will be fair. This is the only pie we have, and it must go around." She pressed the knife into the center of the pie, but nothing happened. "Oh, me. I brought the wrong knife." Granna Mae drifted back into the kitchen.

"It's frozen," Sierra said.

"I know. I put it out on the counter to let it thaw," Mom said. "I planned on putting it in the oven after dinner."

"Mom," Dillon said, "is it safe for her to be walking around with knives like that?" Dillon was eight and looked like Sierra's dad only with more hair. Dillon was the serious, responsible child, who seemed to believe his mission in life was to make sure his fearless younger brother, Gavin, lived to be a teenager. Dillon had caught Gavin playing Ninja warrior with Mom's chef knife about three years ago. When he wrestled the knife away from Gavin, Dillon received a minor cut on the palm of his hand. His concern for Granna Mae was sincere.

"We'll keep a close eye on her," Mom said. She looked to Dad for support.

"I better go check on her," Dad said and strode into the kitchen. It was quiet as they all waited, eating and listening.

Dad finally returned with Granna Mae beside him. "It was a fine dinner," he was saying to her.

"Did the children save you enough pie?"

"Yes, yes they did. You go on up to bed now. I'll have the children do the dishes for you."

"If you're sure you don't mind," Granna Mae said, heading for the hallway that led to the stairs.

"Not at all. You get some sleep now."

Granna Mae shuffled off down the hallway, and Dad returned to the table. He seemed upset.

"Is she okay?" Dillon asked.

Dad nodded and silently stuck his fork into his now cold mashed potatoes. "She was doing so well the past few days. I didn't expect her to switch on us so quickly."

"What was she doing?" Gavin asked.

"She thought we were her children, and she was serving dinner like she always did. She's gone to bed now. She'll be fine."

Sierra watched her mom give Dad that look that said, "How can you be sure she'll be fine?"

The situation with Granna Mae tore at Sierra that night as she tried to sleep. Her body still had nights and days mixed up, and she was fighting off feelings of uncertainty about starting school the next morning. All this emotional energy focused on Granna Mae. Sixty-eight wasn't old for a grandmother. Her body was strong and healthy. It seemed cruel and unfair that her mind would fail her when her body had so many more healthy years left.

Sierra's Grandpa Ted had died when Sierra was little. She only had a vague memory of the funeral and wasn't sure what had caused his death. He had been a builder for thirty-some years, as his father had been for many years before him. Sierra's great-grandfather built this house in 1915, which was partly why Granna Mae couldn't bring herself to sell it. Sierra knew her father was too compassionate to ever send his mother to a rest home. So here they were, adjusting to a new life in a new city with a grandmother who was slowly going crazy.

Tawni entered the bedroom quietly while Sierra was deep in her disturbing thoughts. A distinct sweet fragrance entered with her. "You don't have to tiptoe, Tawni. I'm still awake."

"Do you mind if I turn on the light?" As she asked the question she turned it on.

Sierra pulled up the blanket to cover her eyes. "How was work?"

"Fine."

"Granna Mae flipped out a little at dinner. She thought we were all her children."

"You should have seen her the day we moved in," Tawni said. "She acted as if we were all workers who had come to repair her house. I wish they could do something for her."

"I know. Doesn't it kind of scare you to think about getting old and losing your mind like that?" Sierra asked.

"I don't know." Tawni slipped off her shoes and sat on the edge of her bed. "It's probably hereditary. You have her genes; I don't. At least you know. Who knows what hereditary diseases I'm carrying around."

Sierra had heard Tawni talk like this before. It was sort of a martyr thing. At the same time, what she said was true. She didn't know the medical history of her birth family. Sierra would probably feel the same way if she were in Tawni's position.

"But I intend to find out," Tawni said, scooping up her shoes and walking over to the closet. Tawni's side of the closet was perfect. Everything had a proper place, and that's how she kept it. All the time.

Sierra had a much more liberal system for keeping track of her things. If it was in the way, move it. If you can't find it, wear something else.

Tawni's comment sank in. Sierra raised herself on one elbow and squinted at the light. "What do you mean, 'find out'?"

"I'm going to find my birth mother," Tawni said, without turning around. "As soon as I save enough money."

"Why do you want to do that?"

Tawni spun around, looking surprised and almost hurt that Sierra would even have to ask.

"Never mind," Tawni said. "You wouldn't understand."

# nine

MONDAY MORNING MOM DROVE Sierra ten miles across town to Royal Christian Academy. It was raining, as usual, and Sierra shivered in the front seat of their old VW Rabbit, waiting for the heater to kick in. She looked at her blue knit shirt, her long patchwork skirt, and her cowboy boots. She touched her earrings again, trying to remember which ones she had put on.

For one of the first times in her life she felt self-conscious about her clothes. Being an individual in Pineville had been cool. Her high school was small, and she was popular, especially because all the teachers had liked her two brothers and sister who had gone before her.

Now she was starting her first day at a private Christian school, and she imagined all 279 of the other students were a bunch of clones, wearing navy blue outfits with white socks.

"Mom," Sierra said, as they sped down the freeway, "I'm beginning to think this Christian school idea isn't the way for me to go. I've always been in public school except when you home-schooled me. I don't think I'll like it. It's just not *me*."

Sierra's mom was generally a patient counselor. Sierra felt she could come to her anytime and talk to her about anything. This morning was different. Her mom seemed on edge.

"We've been through this," she said sharply. "When we made the decision to move here, we talked with you about it, and you decided you would like to go to the Christian high school since you never had that opportunity in Pineville."

"I know," Sierra said. "But that was before I went to Europe. I don't think I'm going to have anything in common with any of the people at this school. I'm just not like them."

"And how do you know all this without having even seen the school or met a single student, hmmm?" Mom turned the windshield wipers on full speed. "It's not like you, Sierra, to be afraid of the unknown like this. What happened to your adventuresome spirit?"

"I don't know."

"Give it a try." Mom pulled off the freeway and drove four blocks to the high school. "One week is all I ask. Then we'll have this conversation again. Okay?" She stopped the car in front of the two main doors.

Sierra hesitated. It looked like a normal school. She spotted a few students entering the building who had on normal-looking clothes, nothing uniform-like or old-fashioned.

"One week," Sierra said.

"Do you want me to come into the office with you?" Mom asked.

"No, I'm fine." Sierra pulled her backpack over her shoulder and opened the door.

"I'll pick you up at 3:15," Mom said, leaning across the seat. "Have a good day, honey!"

Sierra forced a smile.

The office was easy to find, and as soon as she walked in, a frizzy-haired woman with glasses said, "You must be Sierra Jensen. Welcome to Royal!" Sierra didn't smile back.

"Here's your class schedule and some other papers for you to look at, including our handbook."

*I knew it! Here come all the rules.*

The secretary began to run through a list of information such as where her locker was, what time they broke for lunch, how she could sign up for the girls' basketball team (if she were interested), and how chapel was on Fridays. Most of the information bounced off of Sierra.

"Randy should be here any minute," the lady said. "I asked him to show you around." She glanced at the large, round clock on the wall. "Well, where is he? You only have ten minutes before the bell rings."

"I'm sure I can find everything on my own. Thanks."

"Don't be ridiculous. This is a big school, and we don't want you getting lost on your first day."

Sierra felt like telling the woman that last week she had managed to get herself from the Lake District of England all the way to Heathrow Airport and then to Portland. Certainly she could find locker number 117 without a Seeing Eye dog.

Just then a tall guy with longish hair walked into the office. Sierra was surprised. She would have expected a rule about hair length in the handbook.

"Hey, new girl!" Randy said.

"Her name is Sierra," the secretary said. "Now show her around quickly before classes start."

Randy stuck out his arm as if he were supposed to escort her down the aisle at a wedding. Sierra motioned that both her hands were full of papers.

"Whatever," Randy said and walked out into the hallway, which was now beginning to thicken with students. "Cool boots," he said.

"I like your jacket," Sierra said.

"My dad bought it in Nepal. Now, your locker is right here. Did they give you the combination?"

Sierra was delighted that at least one person in this school was related to someone who had been outside the U.S. She found the paper with the combination on it and spun the numbers around. It opened right away, and a dozen purple and gold balloons tumbled out.

"That's our traditional welcome," Randy said. "Now you're official or whatever."

Sierra didn't know what to think. People were walking past them, looking but not stopping. She still had her arms full, and yet she had to try to collect all the balloons and figure out what to do with them. Randy just stood there watching. Still, it was a nice surprise, something she would have never experienced at Pineville High.

"We can pop 'em." Randy pinched the latex on one balloon and bit into it so that the air came hissing out. He popped a few more while Sierra tried to cram the rest back into her locker. She didn't have any books so nothing else needed to fit in her locker yet.

Once she shut the locker door, Randy said, "Come on. I'll show you where the classrooms are. What do you have first period?"

Sierra followed him down the hall and scanned the papers in her hand. "If this is it, then I have English first."

"Cool," Randy said. "So do I. It's right here." He pointed to a door on the left but kept walking. "Down the hall is the gym. For P.E. you go into the door on the right at the very end." He kept walking. "Now that hall," he said, motioning to the left, "is the low-life ward. It leads to the junior high wing. You don't ever want to get lost and wander off down there!"

A bell rang above their heads. Randy turned around and started to walk back the way they had come. "I'll look for you at lunch," he said. "Did I show you where the cafeteria is?"

"No. But don't worry. I'm sure I can find it."

They were back at the door to their English class. Randy stopped by the door and let Sierra enter first. He followed her in and said in a loud voice, "This is Sierra, everybody." Then to her, in a lower voice he said, "You can sit wherever you want."

Sierra slid into the closest desk, aware that everyone was looking at her. Somehow all the friendly-welcome stuff bugged her. She was sure the administration meant well, sending Randy to show her around and filling her locker with balloons, but it made her feel uncomfortable. She felt too welcomed. She had expected a school of stuck-up students all ignoring her. That would have made it easier for her to slip in and out unnoticed. It would have also made it easier for her to leave after a week and never be missed.

"Look!" said a dark-haired girl. "We match."

Sierra had not expected that. Her clothes *never* matched anyone else's. Ever.

"Did you get your skirt at A Wrinkle in Time?" the girl asked. She had dark, expressive eyes and olive-toned skin. "That's my favorite vintage store in Hawthorne."

"I've never been there," Sierra said. And then, because it came out so abruptly, she added, "My skirt came from a thrift store in Sacramento."

"Is that where you're from?" the girl asked.

"No." Sierra didn't offer any further explanation because the teacher was starting the class and everyone was seated except the girl in the matching patchwork dress.

The teacher briefly welcomed Sierra, who felt relieved a big deal wasn't being made over her. The class time was mostly lecture and not discussion, which was good. She could melt into the background a little more easily.

Melting in turned out to be Sierra's goal for the day. She remained quiet and reserved in each class. At lunch she sat with Randy and some of his friends because he made such a fuss about it when she walked into the cafeteria. But when she answered their initial questions with only a simple "yes" or "no," they all turned their attention to other topics and closed her out. And that's what she wanted.

"Lovey?" Granna Mae called from the kitchen when Sierra and her mom walked in after school. "I'm all ready to go. Will you drive me to Eaton's?"

Sierra looked to her mom for an explanation. Mom only shrugged her shoulders. Sierra thought her grandmother was dealing in the present since she had used the term "Lovey." But what was this plan of hers to go to Eaton's Drug Store?

"Do you need to pick up a prescription, Granna Mae?" Sierra asked.

"No." She buttoned the big black buttons on her red coat and pulled the black fur collar up around her neck. Then, adjusting a black mohair tam on her head, she moved toward the door. Granna Mae looked cute, like a little girl on her way to a Christmas party.

"I guess we'll be back in a little while." Sierra dropped her backpack by the front hall coatrack and scooped up the keys to the Rabbit from off the entry table. With Granna Mae's arm looped through hers, they took the wet steps down the front porch slowly.

Sierra drove the six blocks to the pharmacy carefully. The roads were slick, plus this was the first time she had driven a car in more than a month. It felt funny to be behind the wheel, especially in an area she had never driven before.

During her summer visits to Granna Mae's, she and her brothers and sister had walked to Eaton's many times on the warm afternoons. Inside an original fountain and grill with a long Formica counter and red vinyl stools waited for them. Sierra had consumed many ice cream cones and root beer floats at that counter. It was one of the few businesses in the area that had remained operative since the day it opened more than fifty years ago. Some of the other older businesses along the same street had been torn down or renovated and turned into gift shops or espresso stands.

Granna Mae hummed contentedly as they pulled into

the small parking lot and maneuvered through the puddles to the back door. A bell rang as they entered, and Sierra was flooded with memories of the place.

"What do you need today, Granna Mae?" asked Sierra, automatically heading for the pharmaceutical counter.

Granna Mae headed in the other direction, toward the fountain. Sierra followed her and sat down on a stool next to her grandmother, still a little confused as to what was going on.

"Mae, how are you doing today?" the woman behind the counter in the white apron asked. Sierra recognized her. She had been working there ever since Sierra had first come in.

"Very well. Did you notice Howard's daughter here with me, Angie?" Granna Mae asked, removing her coat and hat and draping them over the vacant stool next to her.

"Why, is that little Sierra? My, how you've grown, honey! I heard you had a rather exciting trip to the Emerald Isle. Did you find it to your liking?"

"Yes, thank you. It was a great trip. I'd love to go back again one day."

"I imagine you will," the sweet woman said. "Mae always said you had the spark for the lark. Now, what can I get you ladies today?"

"We need the usual first-day-of-school treat with two glasses. And I'd like a cup of coffee too. Anything else for you, Lovey?"

Since Sierra wasn't exactly sure what the "usual" was, she ordered a glass of water.

Granna Mae's soft face turned up in a smile as she

transferred her attention from Angie to Sierra. "Did your father ever tell you how I used to do this with all the children? On the first day of school we walked over here to Eaton's and ordered chocolate malts. It used to be the little ones couldn't wait for their first day of school just so they could have their chance to come. I haven't done this since Emma was in grade school."

Angie set the glass of water and cup of coffee in front of them. Granna Mae went to work, preparing her coffee. First, just the right amount of cream was poured in from the silver-colored creamer Angie slid across the counter to them. Then precisely half of a packet of sugar, torn open only at the corner, was added.

Sierra enjoyed Granna Mae's hands. They were dancing hands. Each movement of her fingers seemed liquid and smoothly connected to the next movement. She lifted her spoon as if it were a feather and created a whirlpool within the white ceramic mug. Apparently Eaton's coffee mugs were an acceptable substitute for a china cup.

"One year," Granna Mae said, picking up her thought, "we had seven Jensen children and myself lined up on the first day of school. We nearly took up the whole counter!"

Sierra knew that Granna Mae had always been careful with her money. She was surprised that her grandma would spend money on seven chocolate malts simply to celebrate the first day of school.

"Now tell me about your first day, Lovey."

Sierra shrugged. "There's not much to tell."

"That's not an answer. Tell me about everything. I want to hear it all."

"Well, it's different from Pineville in a lot of ways, especially when my English teacher started the class with a Bible verse and prayer. That was a nice change from public school."

"Indeed it was! And that's how things should be in school."

Angie placed two fluted glasses in front of them, filled with the rich chocolate malt. She also gave them the metal canister she had used to blend the ice cream.

Granna Mae chuckled. "And to think I used to be able to finish off one of these by myself!"

Sierra stuck her straw into the glass and savored the treat. "Thanks, Granna Mae. This is really nice of you. I appreciate it."

"It's my delight, Lovey. Now tell me more about your school."

Sierra tried to think of things to say. Inwardly she was still planning to finish out the week and then tell her parents she wanted to enroll in the public high school. She told Granna Mae about the balloons in her locker and how she popped them and threw them away at the end of the day so she could stick her books inside.

"Oh, and then, if you can believe this," Sierra said, "a girl in three of my classes had a dress on that was made out of the same material as my skirt. The chances of that happening are pretty slim, don't you think?"

"You should go shopping with her then. She has your taste."

The comment felt abrasive to Sierra. Nobody had her taste. Her clothes were her trademark. That wasn't something shared.

"As a matter of fact, why don't you invite her over sometime? What's her name?"

"I don't know."

Granna Mae looked at Sierra with a hint of disappointment pulling down her sometimes droopy right eye. She didn't say anything, but her hands danced to her coffee mug. She lifted it and sipped slowly.

Sierra felt the need to redirect the conversation. "Do you remember that one girl I told you about from Carnforth? Katie? I invited her to visit me sometime. She might come up this summer. You'll like her; she's a lot of fun."

"Did you learn the names of any of the other students today?" Granna Mae didn't fall for diversion.

"Yes."

"And what are their names?"

"Well, I met a guy named Randy. He had a really nice coat. He said it was from Nepal."

"And?" Granna Mae prodded.

"And his father bought it for him." Sierra knew that wasn't the trail of conversation Granna Mae had been trying to direct her down. She couldn't help it. All this questioning made her feel guilty, even though Granna Mae hadn't said anything that should make her feel scolded.

Angie stepped back over to fill Granna Mae's coffee mug. She made friendly conversation with Granna Mae, which Sierra was glad for. It meant she didn't have to give any more answers about school. It had been hard enough finding satisfactory answers for her mom on the way home from school.

Granna Mae took her time on her malt and coffee. An elderly man came in and sat a few seats down. He and

Granna Mae greeted each other and asked the customary questions. The man seemed to know who Sierra was, even though she couldn't remember if he was a neighbor or what. His presence added a further opportunity for sidetracking Granna Mae from her mission to probe into Sierra's first day of school.

When they left, Granna Mae paid the check and left a quarter for a tip. Sierra thought that was awful chintzy. She wished she had some money on her so that she could leave more.

As they stepped outside, they found the sun had broken through the clouds, making rainbows in the oily puddles in the asphalt.

"Thanks again for the treat," Sierra said as they drove through a maze of old houses in the Mt. Tabor district of Portland. She could see why Granna Mae had put down her foot about moving out of this area. Besides being a beautiful neighborhood, she also had lifelong friends and neighbors. She was connected. And in a real way, Sierra envied her.

# ten

THE SECOND DAY of school Sierra continued her role as the uninterested observer. Nothing anybody said or did received much of a response from her until she was at her locker after school. She had just closed the metal locker door and turned around, when right in front of her was a brown leather backpack on the back of a guy. She had seen that backpack before. It was like Paul's.

Sierra hurried down the hall so she could pass the guy and then nonchalantly turn around and look at him. She knew it wasn't Paul. No way. What would he be doing there? Still, she had to look.

When she was about five feet in front of him, Sierra turned her head and looked at the backpack's wearer. She recognized him as the guy who sat in front of her in biology. He caught her glance and gave her a shy smile.

*Oh great! Now he thinks I am trying to get his attention.*

He wasn't an ugly guy or anything, sort of average in every way—average height, average brown hair, average facial features. He looked like the kind of guy whose favorite ice cream flavor was vanilla. Not at all the sort of person she was drawn to. He was probably nothing like Paul.

For a moment Sierra was bothered that she had used Paul as a standard by which to judge other guys. How could she compare them? She didn't even know Paul. She would never see him again. Why should he even be in her thoughts?

Sierra kept walking down the hall and out the double doors until she spotted her mom in the line of cars.

"So?" Mom asked as she maneuvered the little car out of the school parking lot. "Was today any better?"

"It was fine," Sierra said.

"I don't need the car tomorrow," Mom said. "You can drive if you want to. If you need to stay after school for anything, that would be fine too."

Sierra knew what her mom was hinting at. She had brought up the topic of joining a school club at the dinner table the night before. Sierra had quickly used the excuse that all the clubs met after school. Now Mom was eliminating the obstacle.

"Sure," Sierra said, careful to avoid any suspicion, "I'll take the car tomorrow." The rest of the way home she paid careful attention so she could find her way back tomorrow.

She had no trouble finding her way *to* school on Wednesday. However, she met with difficulty getting back home. She left right after school was out and entered the freeway with no problem. Then she missed the off-ramp and ended up driving into thick traffic that led to downtown Portland. She didn't want to exit off the next off-ramp unless she was sure an on-ramp existed that would take her back the direction she had come. That way she would be sure to find her way home.

Sierra passed up the next two off-ramps. The first one didn't have a freeway return. The second one did, but she couldn't tell until she had already driven by. Before she realized it, she was approaching one of the huge bridges that crossed the Columbia River and led to downtown Portland.

"Oh, man! What am I going to do?"

She felt dwarfed in her little car by all the vehicles passing her on either side. She drove slowly, trying to think through her next move. Just knowing water was underneath her gave her the heebie-jeebies. Nothing like this bridge existed in Pineville. And she had never driven in so much traffic.

Sierra curled up her toes inside her boots and quickly tried to think through her choices. She could find a phone, call her dad, and ask him to come rescue her. No. She could stop and ask someone how to get back to Granna Mae's house. At least she knew what district she lived in. That was a possibility. But the best scenario would be to find her own way back. If she could turn around and retrace her trail, she should be fine.

With renewed determination, Sierra clutched the steering wheel and exited the bridge into the business district and a maze of one-way streets. As soon as she found a place to turn, Sierra made a right and followed the one-way street until she could make another right. She was headed for a freeway on-ramp.

"Okay, okay!" she hollered at the driver behind her who honked because she was going too slowly. She gave the car a little more gas and wished her parents had acquired Oregon license plates. She could imagine the guy behind her yelling, "Californian, go home!" She refused to look at him in her rearview mirror. Besides, she had way too much ahead to concentrate on.

For example, which off-ramp to take. She drove for a while before any exits appeared. The first one didn't sound familiar at all so she tried to switch lanes to avoid the off-ramp. But it was too late. The car behind her was on her trail, and a steady stream of cars was passing her on the left. She had no choice but to exit.

Sierra drove off to who knows where. But at times like these her adventuresome spirit kicked in, and she refused to be overcome. She drove a few blocks until she came to a gas station, parked to the side, and walked into the mini-mart connected to the gas station. Then, acting as if this were all planned, Sierra bought herself a Mars candy bar and Portland map.

Just as Sierra was exiting the mini-mart, a sports car pulled in. The driver was Jalene, who appeared to be alone. Wondering if she would recognize her, Sierra considered talking to her.

As Sierra thought through her options, a black Jeep Wrangler bounced into the gas station, with its radio loudly playing music. Two college-age guys were in the Jeep. Sierra remembered seeing several older students in the mini-mart, and she realized she must be near Lewis and Clark. Now her options increased.

Sierra found herself smiling for the first time that day as she climbed back into her car and unfolded the Portland map.

*Katie would probably call this a God-thing, my getting lost and ending up so close to Lewis and Clark. What if I drove around campus and had a look? Maybe God has directed me here so I could bump into Paul.*

She felt her heart beating faster as she located her position on the map and realized she was less than two blocks from the campus. Her parents wouldn't worry about her being late since Mom had encouraged her to stay after school. Still, she felt sneaky.

Should she call? That would be a good idea. Sierra fumbled in her backpack for some phone change and the slip of paper that had her new phone number on it. She couldn't believe she hadn't memorized it yet. Numbers just weren't her thing.

Locating the paper with the phone number, Sierra unfolded it and let out a groan. The paper must have gotten wet, because all the numbers were now smeared. She could dial several combinations of numbers until she came up with the right one. No good. She had to use the pay phone and had less than a dollar in change after buying the map and candy bar.

*Of course, I wouldn't be stuck using a pay phone if I had a cell phone. Like* that's *going to happen anytime soon.*

Trying not to get sidetracked on her cell phone dilemma, Sierra spun the options, looking for an immediate solution. She could call information and ask. That would be good. Actually, that would be wise.

Sierra tore open the candy wrapper and took a nibble on her Mars bar. She remembered Cody once saying it was easier to say "I'm sorry" than "May I please." His philosophy certainly applied to this situation. If she did call home and say she was going to drive around the campus, her Mom would probably tell her to come home and they would go another time, together.

However, getting lost and ending up here wasn't something she had planned. It was really quite innocent. She could have a quick peer around campus and then, with the help of the map, find her way home. Her story would be as true as could be.

Chomping into the candy bar and chewing a big chunk now, Sierra decided to take the "I'm sorry" route. It wasn't as if she were disobeying or anything. This was one of those gray areas her dad had talked to her about, one of the many decisions a teen needs to make for herself and then be willing to live with the consequences of that choice. No problem. What kind of consequences could there be to a simple spin around some college campus?

A light rain began to fall as Sierra swallowed the last bite of her candy bar and backed her VW Rabbit out of the parking place at the gas station. She waited for an opening in the traffic before pulling onto the street. Glancing in her rearview mirror, she noticed Jalene's car was right behind her. She doubted Jalene had even seen her, let alone recognized her as one of many passengers at the airport baggage claim a week ago.

When the first clearing appeared in the flow of traffic, Sierra pulled out and puttered the two blocks toward the university with Jalene right behind her. Sierra wished it were the other way around—that she was the one trailing Jalene. Who knows? Jalene might even lead her to Paul. Now that would be interesting.

Something inside Sierra didn't feel quite right. A subtle voice kept telling her that she had stepped a little too far outside the safety zone. At the same time, an urge within pushed her forward, insisting she be daring. The rugged pioneer spirit of hers rose to the surface, and she forged ahead, entering the campus with Jalene right behind her.

Sierra kept an eye on Jalene's sports car as it turned into a parking lot beside a large building, which was about six stories high. One side of the building was glass windows. Sierra wondered what the impressive building was. She watched Jalene get out of her car and jog in the drizzle toward the building with some books under her arm. The library, maybe?

Sierra could venture into the library, couldn't she? She parked and swiftly darted into the building. It was the library. And it was full of college students. Sierra wondered what the chances were that Paul would be in the library right now. She didn't see Jalene anywhere.

Sierra walked past the front desk and past the card files on the left and stopped. All along the windows were sequestered nooks, each filled with students. What if Jalene had come to the library to meet Paul? What if they were sitting in one of those study areas right now, and Sierra happened to bump into them? What would she say, "Your girlfriend followed me over here, and now I'm following her"?

She glanced around one more time, impetuous enough to stay simply because she liked it there. She liked being around college students. This was where she felt she fit in, much more than at high school. These students and the campus had a maturity about them, and it suited her just fine. She saw herself as one of them.

"Excuse me," a male voice said softly.

Sierra spun around, expecting to see Paul and, at the same time, dreading it.

A bespectacled student who was shorter than Sierra stood next to her. He shifted the load of books under his arm and said, "You have a candy wrapper on your...well...back." His eyes moved to Sierra's behind.

She tried to turn to see what he meant. Somehow her Mars bar wrapper had gotten stuck on the seat of her jeans, and she had walked around the whole library that way.

"Oh, thank you," she said, peeling off the wrapper and appearing unruffled. A glob of chocolate and even caramel remained on her jeans. Sierra took even, steady steps through the library, out the door, and straight to her car.

# eleven

WHAT SIERRA HAD NOT counted on was the heavy after-work traffic. She had studied the map carefully and had found the freeway with no problem. The freeway, though, was more like a parking lot. Everyone in Portland seemed to want to go the direction she was going. The best she could do was inch along and flip through the radio stations, trying to find company for the commute home.

She located a Christian radio station, which was playing a song by one of her favorite performers. Sierra sang along with her and sneaked another peek at the map.

She arrived home at ten after five. The minute she walked in the door, she knew she was in trouble.

"I got lost," she quickly pleaded before her mother had a chance to explode. "I ended up at Lewis and Clark somehow. I bought a map and found out how to get home, but the traffic was really heavy."

"Why didn't you call?" Mom said. Her arms were still folded across her chest, and her face was still red. It did seem she was a little relieved to hear Sierra's explanation.

"I thought about it, but I didn't have the number."

"Sierra," Mom said, shaking her head. "I'm not going to buy that one."

"Look." Sierra reached into her backpack and pulled out the smeared phone number.

"You learned how to dial information long ago. The wet paper is no excuse."

"If I had a cell phone..."

"Sierra, don't try to change the subject. You could have found a way to call us. Now go wash up. Dinner is on the table."

This was the worst, going to dinner with an unresolved problem. It meant Sierra's situation would be discussed among the family members at the dinner table. She would have rather been yelled at by her mom and dad and gotten it over with.

The truth was, neither of them yelled very often. Almost all their family problems were handled with discussions. Everyone was free to express his or her feelings and opinions at any time.

After her father prayed over the meal, he asked Sierra to explain again what had happened, which she did. This time she included the part about going into the library.

"Did you see him?" her father asked.

"No," Sierra said. *Does my dad know me, or what?*

"See who?" Gavin asked, his six-year-old curiosity piqued.

"A young man named Paul," Dad said.

"Paul?" Granna Mae asked. She sat motionless, and Sierra feared her grandmother's mind would do another one of its time warps. Then Granna Mae looked down at her plate and began to quietly eat her peas.

"I met him on the plane coming back from England," Sierra said, hoping the current reference would help Granna Mae to know they weren't talking about her son.

"I see," she said. "You had an uncle named Paul. Did you know that, Lovey? He had a paper route in Laurel Hurst. One morning he had a flat tire right in the middle of deliveries, and do know what he did?"

Everyone was listening to her story, relieved that she was talking about the past in a normal way. Sierra was glad for the diversion, which took the attention off of her.

"Instead of calling home, he pushed that bike the rest of the way, delivered each paper. Then he pushed his bike all the way home in the rain. He was an hour and a half late. I thought he had been kidnapped or worse. Then he walked in that door, and just imagine, I yelled at him." Granna Mae cut her chicken into an extra small piece and lifted the bite to her lips.

A reverent silence followed.

"You could have called," Mom said, calmed but still determined to make her point. "This is not Pineville. You can't drive around a city this size and think it's completely safe."

"Tawni drives down to Clackamas every day," Sierra said.

"Yes, but we know where she's going, where she'll be, and when she'll be home. If she's late, we know where to start looking. It's completely different from what you did today. You mustn't do that again."

"You can drive back and forth to school, of course," Dad said. "But anywhere else you'll have to clear with us first. Fair enough?"

Since Sierra knew she had the freedom to speak her mind, she charged ahead, letting her feelings out. "Only a week ago I was on the other side of the world, remember? I managed to get myself here from England without any problems. Don't you think I can find my way around Portland?"

"That's not the issue," Dad said. "We all know you're capable of taking care of yourself. Your independence and maturity are beyond your years. Yet the fact remains that you're sixteen years old. God had entrusted us with your life. Until you're an adult, your mother and I are responsible for giving you boundaries. Whether or not you honor us and our guidelines is, of course, your choice. We try to base our guidelines on what we think is best for you."

"I know," Sierra said with a sigh.

"So, do you agree that you need to check in with your father or myself if you want to drive anywhere other than to school and back?" Mom looked calm now. Sierra wondered if her mom had experienced the same kinds of fears Granna Mae had about Paul. Sierra felt instant remorse that she might have caused that kind of concern.

"Yes, I agree. I realize I should have called. I apologize."

"Good!" Gavin said, pushing away his plate. "Can we have dessert now?"

"In a minute, Gavin," Mom said.

Sierra had only eaten a few bites of her dinner. As she and the rest of the family finished eating, Gavin asked, "What did you do in the library anyway?"

"I looked around. It's a huge building. I'd like to go back there sometime—with permission, of course."

Mom smiled. "Did you talk with anyone there?"

Sierra started to chuckle. "Only some guy who told me I had a candy wrapper stuck to my rear end."

"And you were walking around like that?" Dad asked.

"Yes!"

Everyone laughed with her.

"Only you, Sierra. Only you," her dad said. "Your mother has visions of you maimed for life in a car accident, but instead you're traipsing about a university library wearing a candy wrapper for a tail. And the guy who told you was probably more embarrassed about it than you were. Am I right?"

"I think so," Sierra said.

Mom went into the kitchen and returned with a plate of cookies and a pitcher of milk. Rather than join the others in eating dessert, Sierra excused herself and went upstairs to her room, promising to return in a few minutes to help with the dishes. She stretched out on her bed and tried to decide what it was that still made her feel unsettled inside.

Things with her parents were smoothed out. Her grandmother seemed to be doing well. She was even getting along with Tawni. Something wasn't right, though.

Was it school? Probably. She flat out didn't want to be in high school anymore. That was it. She wanted to be in college and be around college students like she was in England. That's where she belonged.

Then a vague thought fluttered through her mind. It was something Katie had said one of their nights at Carnforth. Something about how she was homesick for being in high school. At the same time Sierra had thought it was a strange thing to say, but it seemed even stranger now since Sierra couldn't wait to grow up.

*Will I be sorry for pushing ahead so fast? Will I wish I took my time and enjoyed high school more?*

Sierra still wanted to transfer to the public high school. That way she could slip right into the crowd. She didn't need to be popular like she was in Pineville. She just wanted this next year and a half to slip by as fast as possible. It would go much faster if she were lost in a school of several thousand students.

Her determination to leave Royal Academy kept her in a monotone sort of mood all the next day. She spoke only when spoken to and then responded as simply as possible. In her mind, all she had to do was finish out the week, as she had agreed to, and then she could discuss with her parents why she should go to public school. They had always been fair about hearing her side of things. Certainly they would agree with her that public school was the best route for her to go.

To make sure there were no wrinkles in her relationship with her parents, Sierra came right home from school on Thursday and even helped her mom give Brutus his bath, all without being asked.

Brutus was a fun-loving Saint Bernard they had owned for the past three years. Even though Sierra wasn't crazy about animals in general, she did love Brutus.

In Pineville, Brutus was king of the neighborhood. He roamed around freely but always showed up on time for dinner. Everyone in the neighborhood loved Brutus.

Since they had moved to Portland, Brutus had been acting strange. He moped around all day and begged to go inside the boys' clubhouse whenever anyone was in it. Brutus seemed uninterested in checking out the neighborhood or marking his territory.

Mom thought a bath might help. Sierra didn't understand the logic but agreed to assist in the sudsy mess. As soon as they plunged Brutus into the downstairs tub, he turned into a two-hundred-pound jellyfish.

"Come on, boy," Mom coaxed. "You have to help us out here. Stand up so we can scrub you all nice and clean."

The downstairs tub was the original cast-iron claw-foot and was difficult to maneuver around. Brutus filled the entire tub and seemed only interested in licking the faucet with his great pink tongue. Sierra and her mom scrubbed and rubbed and sweet-talked the big guy until the smell of wet dog was almost overpowering in the small bathroom.

"Are we going to dry him off in here?" Sierra asked.

"We could haul him to the kitchen, but I think he would only make more of a mess in there. Let's try it in here." Mom turned off the water after the final rinse.

Getting the big lug over the high sides of the tub was a real challenge. He didn't want to get out. That wasn't like Brutus either. He used to fight his baths in Pineville, and the minute he was freed, he was out of there, shaking like crazy.

"Look at him," Sierra said. "He's turned into a big baby. Come on, Brutus. Lift your paws. That's it. Over the side. Now the back paws. Okay, good. Now you stand right there and let us towel you off."

For the first time in history, Brutus complied.

"It's as if he's depressed," Sierra said, wiping the mellow dog dry.

"Do you think he misses home?" Mom asked.

"How can you make a dog understand that this is his new home?"

"I think he knows," Mom said. "That's why he's bummed. He's mourning the loss. You know what they say about how the bigger they are, the harder they fall. He'll come around. Wes is coming home this weekend, and I'm sure that will perk Brutus up. At least Wes will make sure he exercises."

Sierra's oldest brother was the one who had brought Brutus home three years ago. The dog was only an armful of brown and white fur, with an endearing little pouty face. There was no way anyone could say no to keeping him, especially Sierra's mom, who was a devoted animal lover. Wes had said the dog was for Mom. Since he was going away to college in a month, he wanted Mom to have somebody to fuss over.

"Okay, you big brute." Mom grabbed the dog by his collar and led him out of the house. "It's to the backyard for you. At least you smell better. Maybe you'll start perking up a little too."

Brutus plodded across the cold grass and stopped in front of the workshop's door. No one was inside. He could go through his doggie door if he wanted. But Brutus curled up on the doormat and laid his jowls down on his clean white paws.

Sierra and her mom stood at the kitchen window watching. Sierra thought she could almost hear him sigh.

"Did you know the green ones aren't good to eat?"

Sierra turned around and saw Granna Mae looking at a basket of fruit on the baker's rack by the refrigerator.

"They're okay, Granna Mae," Sierra said, walking over to see what might be in the basket. There were two oranges, three red apples, and one brown-spotted banana. "There aren't any green ones in here," she said. "Do you want a red apple?"

"I don't want an apple," Granna Mae said, looking at Sierra as if she were the one who was confused. She started to hum to herself and walked away.

Sierra and her mom exchanged looks of concern.

"It's so hard to stand by and watch a life thin out like that," Mom said. "I want to stop the clock and turn it back."

Sierra considered commenting on how she wished she could turn the clock forward in her life. She decided to keep that thought to herself. It wouldn't sound right if she said it aloud.

All these thoughts pushed Sierra to do something she had been thinking about for a week. She wrote a letter to Katie, who would speak her mind and explain to Sierra why she was struggling with growing up. Sierra also wanted to tell Katie about Paul. She decided to write out the letter instead of going downstairs and trying to get in line to use the computer. Besides, she wanted to take her time with her thoughts, and this was the best way to do that.

Lying on her stomach across her unmade bed, Sierra wrote on a piece of notebook paper, "Dear Katie, Okay, tell me if you think this is a God-thing or not. When I arrived at Heathrow, I was waiting to use the phone when this guy turned around..."

# twelve

ON FRIDAY AFTERNOON Sierra cleaned out her locker and took all her books home. She thought it would be easier for her mom to withdraw her from the school on Monday if she had all her books to turn in at one time. Sierra felt unemotional about her choice to leave Royal Academy. All week she had distanced herself from everything and everybody, which made it easier to walk away.

Sierra guessed it would help to take home her gym clothes as well. She walked to the girls' dressing room and worked the combination to her locker. Some girls who were on the other side of the row of tall metal lockers seemed to be so involved in their conversation they hadn't noticed anyone else come in.

"I think she's stuck-up," one of the girls said.

"That's not a fair judgment, Marissa," the other girl said.

"Well, look at how she has treated us all week. It's like she's too good for us. We're all little peons."

"I think we should give her a chance. Maybe invite her

over with a bunch of girls and see if she opens up."

"She's not going to open up," Marissa said. "I'm telling you, Sierra is totally stuck-up."

It had not begun to register with Sierra that they might be talking about her until Marissa used her name. Then she froze. Who were these girls? What right did they have to form such an incorrect opinion of her? Being a confronter by nature, Sierra stormed around the lockers and stated, "I am *not* stuck-up!"

Both of the girls looked stunned. Their mouths dropped, their eyes popped, and neither of them had anything to say. Sierra recognized them from some of her classes. With nothing else to add to her declaration, she turned and marched away, snatching up her gym clothes and storming out the door.

*That's it! That is it! I'm out of here. Who do these little prissies think they are, calling me stuck-up? I've never been called stuck-up in my life! I'm always the one who makes friends the fastest. I'm the one who goes out of my way to make each person feel she belongs to the group. I'm not stuck-up. They are! And that's why I'm leaving!*

Sierra unlocked the door of the Rabbit and threw her books and gym clothes onto the backseat. She wished this car had more oomph. If it did, she would peel out of that parking lot so fast that those girls in the gym would hear her tires squeal. Unfortunately, the car wasn't made for dramatic displays of emotion. It had difficulty just cranking over when she turned the key. Sierra drove away as fast as she could, telling herself to calm down, shake it off, block the incident from her memory.

By the time she arrived home, she was even more heated

up. Stomping into the house, she went right to her room. Tawni was changing clothes for work, which only infuriated Sierra more. She had no place she could go to be alone, no place that was completely hers. She scooped her clothes out of the rocking chair in the corner and heaved them over onto her bed.

"Why are you all bent out of shape?" Tawni asked, cinching a wide black belt around her slim waist.

"I hate it here," Sierra blurted out. "I wish we didn't have to move here. I wish we were back at home!"

"Have you even tried to make this place a home for yourself?" Tawni asked.

"Of course I have! You can't tell me you like it here better than Pineville." The rocker was empty and ready to soothe her, but Sierra refused to sit down.

"I love it here," Tawni said. "You will too, if you give it a chance. Portland has so much more to offer than Pineville ever did. What set you off?"

"Nothing."

"Oh, and I'm supposed to believe that? Come on. What happened?"

"All right, you want to know? I'll tell you. Those girls at this nice Christian school said I was stuck-up!"

"So have you been?"

"Of course not!"

"Were they friends of yours?"

"I don't have any friends here," Sierra said, surrendering to the rocking chair and folding her arms across her chest.

Tawni flipped her shoulder-length hair back and looked at Sierra. "You know, sometimes you amaze me. You can be so smart and so dumb at the same time, so mature and such a baby. You're really blind to this whole thing, aren't you? If you want to make a friend, you have to be a friend first."

"Duh!" Sierra said, making a face at Tawni. "Maybe I don't want to make friends here."

"Oh, well, that's intelligent!" Tawni grabbed her purse and headed for the door.

"You going to work?" Sierra asked. She couldn't wait to have the room to herself. Yet at the same time, she didn't want her sister to leave. Not yet. Not until she spilled her guts a little more.

"Yes, I'm going to work, and afterwards I'm going out for coffee with two of my *new* friends from the store. Watch and learn, oh stubborn one. This is how it's done." She opened the door and was about to leave when she turned around to deliver one final jab. "And I've already told Mom and Dad where I'm going and when I expect to be back, even though I don't have to because I'm eighteen."

Sierra picked up a slipper from the floor and heaved it at the door just as Tawni closed it. "I'm eighteen," Sierra mimicked. She hated being sixteen. Hated, hated, hated! What a horrible age. Nothing was "sweet sixteen" about it. She could drive, but only to school and back. She had no friends, no social life, nothing to do on a Friday night but feel sorry for herself.

At least back in Pineville she had dozens of friends to hang out with, friends she earned by working hard to keep the relationship going even when it would have been easier to walk away. Tawni didn't have to give her advice on friendships. Sierra knew all about them and could even teach a seminar on making friends, if anyone ever asked her to. But of course, no one ever asks a sixteen-year-old to do anything.

"Sierra?" Mom called out, gently tapping on her closed door. "Is it all right if I come in?"

"I guess."

Mom opened the door and came in, with Granna Mae right behind her. *Oh great, now I have double counsel. Just what I need!* Sierra didn't mind talking to her mom. And she loved talking things over with Granna Mae sometimes, too. But both of them, at the same time, when she was at about the lowest point in her life, felt suffocating.

Granna Mae sat on Tawni's neatly made bed and cast a skeptical glance around Sierra's mess. Mom pulled out the straight-back chair from the desk and sat facing Sierra about five feet away. They formed a tight little triangle.

"I know, my side of the room is a mess," Sierra said, throwing up a smoke screen to sidetrack both of them. "I'll clean it up this weekend."

"Good," said Mom. "I love it when you clean your room. I did want to talk with you, though, about something else."

Sierra shrugged.

"I've been noticing it's a little tough for you to make the adjustment of moving here. I wanted to know if I could do something to help out."

"You can let me go to the public high school. I don't want to go to Royal. I gave it a week, like you asked. It's not my kind of school."

"And what is your kind of school?" Granna Mae asked.

Sierra felt like saying, "A huge one where I can blend in with the crowd, make it through my next year and a half as soon as possible, and get out of there!" Instead she said, "I'm not sure. But it's not Royal."

"We'll need to talk to Dad about it," Mom said calmly. "I'm sure we'll have some time to do that this weekend. Is there anything else besides school that's bothering you?"

"No."

Mom paused and then said, "Wes should be here in about an hour. I thought we would all go out for pizza tonight. You and Wesley might want to catch a movie afterwards."

As Mom talked, Granna Mae stood up and ambled over to the antique dresser that had been in this room for several decades. She tilted her head and examined her reflection in the beveled mirror about the dresser. Sierra couldn't help but wonder if she were slipping into one of her time warps.

Granna Mae touched the wrinkled corners of her eyes and looked closer. "Isn't that odd," she said. "Why, just yesterday I was twelve. I'm quite sure of it."

Sierra and Mom exchanged quick looks.

"Or maybe we'll order a couple of pizzas and have them delivered," Mom said quietly. Sierra thought her mother must have been concerned about trying to take Granna Mae out to a pizza parlor when she was in a confused state of mind.

"You know," Granna Mae said, turning to face them, "it goes just like that." She snapped her wrinkled fingers and looked at Sierra. "It will come soon enough, Lovey." She headed for the door and said, "I'm going downstairs for a cup of coffee. Would either of you care to join me?"

Now Sierra and her mom were even more surprised. Granna Mae had called her Lovey, an indicator of which time zone she was functioning in. So what was the look in the mirror for and the speech about being twelve only yesterday? Sierra couldn't help but wonder if Granna Mae understood Sierra's passion to be all grown up and was, in her quirky way, trying to tell Sierra to slow down.

"Sure," Mom said, "I'll go with you."

"And I'll clean my room," Sierra said, "which I'm sure will make both of you happy."

"Tawni will be the most delighted," Mom said as she followed Granna Mae out of the room.

Sierra sat in the chair for a while, rocking back and forth. Then she went over to the antique mirror and looked into it closely, the way Granna Mae had. She almost expected it to be an enchanted mirror that would reflect back her image at sixty-eight years old. All she saw was her freckled nose, her wild hair, and blue-gray eyes that were not yet wrinkled. She smiled and tried to wrinkle them up the way her dad's did when he was laughing hard or trying not to cry. She thought it made her look kind of old. She uncrinkled them and looked again.

*They are the same color as Paul's,* she realized. *That flight attendant was right. We do have the same eyes. If only we saw things from the same perspective.*

Then, as Sierra had done dozens of times that week, she prayed for Paul.

# thirteen

"WHAT DO YOU GUYS WANT? Pepperoni and what else?" Wes stood next to his father at the order window of the Flying Pie Pizzeria and called to the rest of them.

Wes took after Mom's side of the family. He was tall, with lots of wavy brown hair, and a long straight nose. His eyes were like Dad's, brown and crinkly in the corners.

"I want pineapple," Gavin said.

"Olives," said Dillon.

"Why don't we try to find a table?" Mom suggested. "How many are we tonight?"

"Seven," Sierra said, taking a quick count. The room was full, which was probably a sign this was a good place to eat. The women and boys threaded their way to the back of the darkened eating area and managed to find a large booth in the corner. If they could locate an extra chair for the end, they would all fit. This is how it always was when their large family went anywhere. It was frustrating, though, since most places were designed with a family of four in mind.

The pizza parlor was cozy, with red vinyl seats, checkered

plastic tablecloths, metal pizza stands on each table, and red patio candles underneath the stands to keep the pizza warm. On the ceiling above Sierra was a table and two chairs hung upside down, complete with tablecloth, plastic food, and even a flower in a vase. It was all securely suspended, yet Sierra wondered if an illusion like that might throw Granna Mae into confusion. She seemed to be doing fine.

Gavin and Dillon came racing to their table, begging for quarters so they could play the video games in the adjoining room.

"I don't have any," Sierra told them after they had hit up Granna Mae and Mom and came up empty. She had no pockets, no backpack, and she never carried a purse. She didn't even own one. "Go ask Wes. He'll probably join you in the arcade."

The boys scrambled off to harass their oldest brother, who sometimes acted more like an indulgent uncle to them than a brother. As Sierra predicted, Wes joined the guys and pumped quarters into their machines until the pizzas arrived.

About forty minutes later, after nearly all two of the extra-large pizzas had been devoured, the Jensen troupe left in two cars. Mom, Dad, Granna Mae and the boys went home while Wes and Sierra headed across town to a movie Wes said he wanted to see.

She didn't say anything all the way to the theater. Wes didn't seem to notice. He had plenty to talk about, such as his truck, his classes at school, and his job stocking grocery shelves on the swing shift. This was his third year at Oregon State University in Corvallis. What Sierra liked most about Wes was that he treated her as an equal.

Wes seemed to know his way about Portland a lot better than Sierra did. She finally opened up and told him how she had gotten lost a few days earlier and ended up at Lewis and Clark.

"So do you think you want to go there next year, or are you going to come down to OSU?" Wes asked.

"I'm only a junior, remember? I have a few months before I have to really get serious about making that decision."

"Oh yeah, I keep forgetting. Ever since you got your driver's license, I've been thinking of you as about to graduate."

"Nope. Not yet. Although it can't be too soon for me."

"How do you like Portland?"

"It's okay. Tawni likes it here."

They pulled into the parking lot at the movie theater. Sierra hopped out of Wes's truck, and he made sure the doors were locked. Wes's stereo had been stolen from his old car once when it was parked at a friend's apartment complex. Now he was extra careful, especially since he was the one paying for his insurance and truck now.

They stood in line to buy tickets, and Sierra shivered in the damp night air. She wished she had a jacket with her. Theaters seemed cold to her. Or maybe it was just that she had the talent of sitting right under the air-conditioning vent. As they walked in, Sierra involuntarily shivered again. Her brother put his arm around her and rubbed her arm to warm her up. They had to wait a minute while a herd of moviegoers exited the show that had just concluded in the theater next to theirs.

As they stood waiting, Wes squeezed her a little closer

and said in her ear, "It's sure good to see you, Sierra. I'm glad you had a good time in England and that you got home safely."

Sierra smiled up at her brother with sincere admiration. "Thanks," she said.

Then the image of a brown felt hat caught the corner of her eye. Sierra snapped her head away from Wes and scanned the trail of people moving past them. There, only ten feet away, was Paul. He kept on walking with the stream of people, but his head was turned, and he was staring at Sierra. She stared right back.

"Did you see somebody you know?" Wes asked, removing his arm from her shoulder.

"Yeah."

"Did you want to go say hi? We have a few minutes before the movie starts."

Sierra didn't know what to do. Should she run after him? He was already out the door. What if someone were with him—like Jalene? Sierra hadn't noticed anyone.

*If he wanted to talk to me,* she reasoned, *he certainly could have stopped and said hi.*

Then she remembered that Wes had had his arm around her and was talking softly in her ear while Paul walked by. It must have looked as if Wes were her boyfriend.

"Do you want me to go with you, wait here, get us some seats, or what?" Wes asked.

"Let's go in," Sierra said. "I don't think I could catch him."

They started down the carpeted hallway. "Do you want some popcorn?" Sierra asked.

"Are you kidding? After all that pizza? How could you possibly have room for anything else?"

"Actually, my stomach feels kind of empty right now. Can I have some money?"

Wes, playing the role of the benevolent uncle, pulled a five-dollar bill from his pocket and said, "Get a large drink, too, and I'll split it with you. I'll save you a seat."

Sierra stood in line at the snack bar but kept looking out the windows that lined the front of the theater, wondering if by any remote chance Paul were still out there. Maybe if he saw her alone he would come back inside and say something to her. She knew it was a crazy thing to think.

The more she thought about it, it was crazy that she had even seen him. What are the chances of the two of them connecting in this huge city? To have seen Jalene at the gas station and now Paul at the movies was unsettling.

Katie might call it a God-thing, and it was insofar as it made Sierra think about Paul and then, consequentially, pray for him. However, Sierra thought the chance encounters were more like a "weird thing" or a "crazy-making thing." Why should she be so connected with this guy?

"May I help you?" the girl behind the counter asked.

"A medium buttered popcorn and a large Coke."

"We don't have Coke. Is Pepsi okay?"

"Sure. Fine." Sierra felt as if people shouldn't be allowed to ask such stupid questions, especially when she was so deep in thought about Paul and all the bizarre encounters they had had. Coke, Pepsi, what difference did it make?

"That will be $6.50," the girl said.

"Six dollars and fifty cents? For a Coke and a popcorn?"

"Pepsi and popcorn," the girl corrected her.

"Forget it. I'll just have the Co...Pepsi. I don't want the popcorn." Sierra held out the five-dollar bill. In exchange she received a huge drink, loaded with ice, and two crumpled one-dollar bills. "It's a racket!" Sierra spouted as she turned to go. "I mean, I know you just work here and everything and it's not your fault, but the snack prices are ridiculous."

She marched off, shaking her head. She didn't care that the people in line behind her had heard everything. All she wanted to do was find Wes, sit down, and get caught up in the movie. She needed to relax.

Then it occurred to her that she wasn't on the edge because of the popcorn prices. She had paid that much before and never flinched. Seeing Paul was what had rattled her. She had transferred all those emotions to the price of popcorn.

"Where's the popcorn?" Wes asked when she slid across him to take her seat. He always wanted to sit on the end of the row.

"I changed my mind. Here's your change. And I got Pepsi. Is that okay?"

"They didn't have Coke, I take it."

"What does it matter?" Sierra barked.

"Whoa!" Wes said, leaning back and taking a hard look at her. "What's up with you?"

"Nothing. Sorry." Sierra settled back in her seat. The movie began, and she was ready to relax.

Only one problem. The movie was centered around spies and skydiving and a high-speed motorcycle race. It was so suspenseful that Sierra was on the edge of her seat the entire two hours. She walked out of the theater with cramped toes from having curled them up inside her boots for most of the movie.

"Great show, don't you think?" Wes asked as they left.

"Sure was full of action. I didn't know I could hold my breath for so long."

"How long?" Wes asked, opening the truck door for her.

"Oh, about two hours."

Wes laughed. "Weren't the special effects amazing when the guy landed in the water, got himself out of the handcuffs, and then released the parachute?"

Sierra nodded. "It was a good movie. Thanks for taking me, Wes."

"Do you want to go anywhere for coffee?"

"No, I'm ready to go home. Are you?"

"Sure. I brought a ton of reading home with me. It would be good if I could chip away at some of it tonight."

Sierra went right to bed when they reached home. Her room was nice and clean after the hour she had spent on it that afternoon.

Putting away her clothes had been more of an anchor than she realized it would be. As long as her things were scattered around and her luggage from England hadn't been unpacked yet, she had felt her time in this room was only temporary. But once she had put things away and hung her clothes alongside all the others, which the moving fairies had brought to this closet while she was sleeping on the other side of the world, then her stay in this room became permanent. She wasn't sure if that was good or bad.

Tawni would be glad the room was clean, and that was a good thing. She wasn't home yet after going out with her friends from work.

*Of course she likes it here. She got to move her belongings into our room and put everything right where she wanted it. She's been here a month, and I've only been here a week. I feel as if everyone is settled, but here I am, walking into the middle of this new life and running to catch up.*

Sierra read her Bible until her eyelids became too heavy to stay open. She turned off the light and lay in bed flossing her teeth with an extra-long strand of peppermint-flavored dental floss she had found while unpacking her things.

In the dark, in the silence, the confusing thoughts came tumbling down around her all at once. Like a mental kaleidoscope, the thoughts twirled from hearing the girls in the locker room call her stuck-up, to the image of Granna Mae looking for her youth in the bedroom mirror, to that locked-in stare of Paul's. First in London at the money exchange booth, then on the plane, then at baggage claim, then again tonight, he stared at her. Why?

Sierra wondered if somehow her matching eyes were like a mirror to him. He was searching for something. What was it?

All she could do was pray for him. And she did. Like a determined warrior with sword drawn, Sierra prayed that God would protect Paul. She prayed that the enemy would release the hold on Paul's life. She prayed that Paul would break up with Jalene or that Jalene would become a Christian. And Sierra prayed that Paul would be miserable until he got back into a really tight relationship with God. Sierra prayed and prayed until she finally felt her shoulders start to relax. Time to retreat. Enough battle for one day.

Tawni entered the room, and Sierra pretended to be asleep.

# fourteen

SIERRA HAD ALWAYS liked her parents' openness and the way she could discuss things with them, even difficult or embarrassing things. So she was caught off guard when she talked to them about leaving Royal Academy, and they asked her to try it for one more week.

"But, Mom, you said I should try it for one week. I did, and I don't like it."

"We aren't convinced you gave it a fair try. It was your first week in Portland, right after your big trip. You didn't even have time to settle into your room." Dad spoke in such a direct yet gentle voice. "We need you to be fair, Sierra. Fair to yourself, fair to other students, fair to us. If we were sure you had actually done that, we would send you over to Madison in a minute. One more week. And be fair all the way around this time, okay?"

Wes walked into the kitchen just then, zipping up his jacket. "I'm going to take Brutus for a walk. Anyone want to go with me?"

"I do," Sierra said, hopping off the "hot seat" counter

stool and hurrying to duck out of this conversation. She was close to saying something she might regret later, and since she had done that so many times, she was beginning to learn it was better to walk away and think things over.

"Get your jacket. It's cold this afternoon. Did anyone hear the weather? Are we expecting snow?"

"I haven't heard," Dad said.

Sierra left the room and returned with a jacket and gloves a few minutes later.

"I hope you can coax Brutus out of his slump," Mom said. "He just hasn't been himself since we moved here."

"Looks to me like he's not the only one," Wes said.

"And what's that supposed to mean?" Sierra said, not sure if he meant her or not.

"Moving is high stress," Wes replied, looking over his shoulder at her. "It's right up there with death in a family or a job loss on the scale of how much a person's emotions can handle. We saw this chart in my human development class. It's really interesting to see the things that cause stress. Even term papers are on the list. And since that's my biggest source of stress now, I thought I'd try to downshift a little and relieve some of the stress by walking the dog. You ready, Sierra?"

"I'm ready. I have my own areas of stress to walk off. Let's go."

"Think about what we've been discussing," Dad said as they left. "We'll talk about it some more this weekend, Sierra."

"Okay. And will you guys think about my side of it, too?"

"Of course," Dad said. "By the way, I want my shirt back."

"You never wear this old flannel shirt," Sierra said. The ends of the red plaid shirt stuck out from underneath her jeans jacket, and she tugged on them to make her point. "I found it in a mound of clothes in the basement. I thought you were giving it away."

"It was in the mending pile. It's missing a button." Dad shot a teasing glance at Mom, who shrugged her shoulders.

Sierra didn't notice the missing button since she had on a thermal undershirt and wore the shirt like a jacket over it. But she knew what Dad's look meant. Mom had many fine abilities, but mending was not one of them. As long as Sierra could remember, Dad had been the one to go to with a missing button or a broken zipper. Mom tried, of course, to do her share of the clothes repair, but sometimes it took months before she got around to the pile of maimed clothing.

"Then may I have your blue work shirt?" Sierra asked.

Dad looked at Mom and said, "I never dreamed I'd be fighting with one of my daughters over *my* own clothes."

"Why don't you try some of the thrift stores down on Hawthorne?" Mom asked Sierra.

Sierra remembered that one girl the first day of school saying she bought her outfit at some vintage store on Hawthorne. What was the name of it? "Maybe I will after we take Brutus out. Do you want to go with me, Mom?"

"Ask when you're about ready to go, okay?"

Sierra joined Wes in the backyard where he was roughing up Brutus' fur and growling back at his old pal. "Come on, Brute Boy. Let's take Sierra for a walk." He hooked the leash onto Brutus' collar, and the big dog "ruffed" in agreement. They took off down the street with Brutus stopping every two seconds to sniff and scope out the neighborhood.

"I can see this is going to take all afternoon," Sierra said. It was so cold she could see her breath. Her jean jacket was too thin, and she could feel the damp chill right through her flannel shirt and thermals.

"This is good for him. I think he's been such a slug because he didn't know the neighborhood. I'm taking him on a round of social calls."

Brutus did seem to enjoy the romp. He growled through the fence at the bulldog three houses down, and the two exchanged their greetings in doggie language. Sierra could hear another dog across the street yipping.

"Looks as if a little one over there is trying to get in the act," she said. Wes tugged on the leash, and Brutus gladly galloped across the street to sniff and bark at the little black and white fur ball behind the chain-link fence.

For almost an hour, Wes and Sierra trailed after Brutus as he terrorized the neighborhood dogs. He seemed to be rebounding back to his old self.

Sierra was shivering, and her teeth were chattering as they rounded the corner that led to Granna Mae's grand white house. It was one of the largest houses on the block and certainly the one with the most personality. Two elms stood like silent guards between the front porch and the street. For more than eighty years they had stood their post, shading the elegant white lady in the summer and showering her with amber jewels in the autumn.

Sierra had to admit that she did love this old house. As a child it had seemed like a castle. She and her brothers and sister used to call it "Granna Mae's mansion."

When they came for their visit each summer, Sierra pretended this was really her house, and she would play that she lived there in the horse-and-buggy days. Iron rings were still fixed in the cement curb where nearly a century ago the residents would tie up their horses. Sierra and Tawni once tied their bikes to the rings with their jump ropes. Granna Mae helped right along, coming out to the curb with several lumps of sugar in her apron pocket, which she pretended to feed to the horses.

Now Sierra was experiencing her childhood dream of living in this wonderful mansion, and yet she didn't want to be here.

"Come on, Brutus. You've had enough for one day. And if you haven't, I certainly have!" Wes led the dog into the backyard and took off the leash. Brutus acted as if he weren't through exploring the neighborhood. He bounded over to the gate and barked a few times. Then he thundered to the other side of the yard and barked at some squirrels that were chittering at the top of the neighbor's tree.

"What did you do to him?" Mom asked, opening the back door and welcoming them into the warm house. It smelled like cinnamon, and Sierra was instantly hungry.

"What are you making?"

"Apple cobbler. How did you manage to revive Brutus?"

"We just took him around to meet his new neighbors," Wes said, opening up the oven to peek inside at the cobbler. What Mom lacked in sewing abilities, she made up for in baking. Apple cobbler was Wes's favorite. "You're the world's best mother! When will it be ready?"

"In about fifteen minutes. Why don't you two have some lunch first? Some turkey is in the fridge for sandwiches."

"I think I'll make some soup," Sierra said. Her throat was feeling raw, and she was still cold from the walk.

"After your soup do you want to explore a couple of thrift stores?" Mom asked. "Granna Mae just went upstairs for a nap so I think this would be a good time."

"Sure!" Sierra was always up for exploring, especially a secondhand clothing store. "Let's just go now. I can eat something when we come back."

"Okay. Wes, I know I can count on you to take the cobbler out on time, right? I'll grab my purse. If you have any money, you might want to bring it."

Sierra took the stairs two at a time and breathlessly opened her bedroom door.

"Where are you going?" Tawni asked. She was sitting at the desk, doing her fingernails.

"To some thrift stores. Mom is going with me. Do you want to come?" Sierra knew it was pointless to ask Tawni such a question. She only wore clothes from the finest department stores. Her idea of a bargain was a sale in a Spiegel catalog.

Tawni answered politely for once. "No thanks. Have fun!"

Sierra grabbed her cash and dashed down the stairs. Mom was waiting for her, wearing a full-length coat, gloves, and her favorite paisley scarf. Sierra considered changing into a warmer jacket but didn't. She reasoned it would be warmer in the car once the heater got going.

It wasn't. They drove the van, and its heater took forever

to produce any warmth. It was barely puffing out a few breaths of heat when they arrived at the first thrift store. Now Sierra was really chilled.

The shop was full of great items, but it was cold inside the building. Sierra felt her enthusiasm for shopping begin to drain away. But, stubborn as she was, she didn't bend away from her goal. She stuck it out through three stores and found more than she expected.

The best stuff they had was in the last shop, called A Wrinkle in Time. She remembered this was the store that girl had mentioned the first day of school. And that girl, whatever her name was, had been right. The store had a fantastic collection of low-priced, unique clothes that were Sierra's style. She wished she had a bundle of money so she could buy everything she liked.

In the end, Sierra came home with a black velvet hat, a cream-colored crocheted vest, two men's flannel shirts, and a long skirt from Bangladesh that had two tiny bells on the drawstring at the waist. She thought she would show the girl at school the hat she had found, but then she remembered she wasn't going back to Royal on Monday, if she got her way. Sierra carried her treasures up to her room and laid them out on her bed.

"Let's see what you bought," Tawni said from her curled-up position on the padded window seat. She was reading a fat paperback novel and had on her silly glasses that made Sierra want to laugh. Tawni was the sort of person who would die if anyone important to her ever knew she wore glasses to read.

Sierra popped the hat on first and tilted it to the side.

"That's actually cute," Tawni said. "And those are in style now. You bought it at a thrift store?"

"It was a recycled clothing place. It could be new. I don't know."

"Don't you want to spray it with Lysol or something before you put it on your head?" Tawni looked slightly disgusted.

Sierra ignored her and held up the rest of her finds. When she showed off the skirt, she said, "This is one of those you wash by hand and then dry by wringing it out to keep the crinkles in it. No ironing necessary. My kind of skirt, don't you think?"

"It smells funny," Tawni said. "Make sure you wash all that stuff before you wear it. It could be full of fleas or lice or worse."

"Don't worry," Sierra said. "I'll wash it all right now. I always do, don't I?"

"I guess. By the way, I wanted to say thanks for cleaning up the room yesterday. I appreciate it."

"I thought you might." Sierra took off the hat, pulled her hair back, and fastened it in a ponytail. "You must hate having to live with me," Sierra said. "No two people in the world are more opposite than you and I."

Tawni shrugged and went back to reading her book.

"May I ask you something?"

"Hmm?" Tawni didn't look up.

"What are you going to do when you find your birth mother?"

Tawni looked up slowly and peered at Sierra from over the top of her glasses. It seemed as if she were trying to decide how much of an answer she could trust her little sister with. "I don't know. Talk to her. Find out a few things, such as my medical history, who my father is, and why she gave me up for adoption."

"You're not going to move in with her or anything, are you?"

"Of course not! What a ridiculous question. She obviously didn't want me eighteen years ago. Why would she want me now?"

"Maybe she *did* want you but couldn't keep you," Sierra suggested. "I think if I were you, I'd do the same thing. I'd try to find my biological mother. I just don't know what I'd do with the relationship after I reestablished it."

"I don't either."

"What do you think she's like?"

"I have no idea. Hopefully I'll find out soon. I've got to save up some money first. My new car wiped me out financially. You're lucky you don't have to worry about all that stuff, Sierra. You just wait. These next two years are the cruise years."

"I know," Sierra said. "But I'll bet being older isn't as bad as you make it sound."

"Just wait until you see what kind of responsibility comes with being an adult. Right now you have it easy. You don't have to pay for your own car or car insurance, you don't have to worry about getting a job, and you don't have to start thinking about whether or not to rent your own apartment. Enjoy it while you can, little girl. It goes fast."

# fifteen

EARLY SUNDAY EVENING Sierra brought up the topic of school again with her dad. He was paying bills at the big rolltop desk in the library and had on his favorite CD of classical Bach. She hadn't planned on talking to him yet, but Tawni had brought up the cordless phone into their bedroom and asked Sierra if she would mind letting her have some privacy for about an hour.

Sierra had been sitting on the bedroom floor, shuffling through a box of her possessions that hadn't been unpacked yet. She was making two piles, one of things to keep and one of others to throw away.

She left her mess and ambled down the hall to Granna Mae's room. The only TV in the house was in her grandma's room since the family was waiting for Dad to finish the entertainment center before they bought a new one for the downstairs den. Dillon and Gavin were sitting on Granna Mae's bed watching a cartoon special, and Granna Mae was dozing off, stretched out on the love seat in the rounded window alcove.

This was the most charming room in the house. A fire danced in the hearth to the right of the alcove.

Grabbing a quilt from the end of the bed, Sierra slipped over to the love seat and covered up Granna Mae. As she gently tucked the blanket around her grandmother, a little smile crept up Granna Mae's face.

"The Lord thy God," Granna Mae muttered without opening her eyes, "in the midst of thee is mighty. He will rest in His love."

Sierra planted a tiny kiss on Granna Mae's forehead and finished off the verse, whispering, "He will joy over thee with singing."

Then, heading out the door, she told her brothers, "You guys should wake up Granna Mae when your show is off so she can get in her own bed."

"She said she didn't mind if we sat on it," Gavin said.

"I know. She doesn't mind a bit. I'm sure she's glad for the company. It's just not good for her to sleep all night on the couch curled up like that."

"We'll wake her," Dillon promised.

Sierra left them and wandered downstairs. That's how she ended up in the library with her dad. She plopped down in the overstuffed chair by the French doors that led to the back deck. This chair was fast becoming her favorite spot in the house. Usually no one was in the library. It smelled old and musty from all the books that were stacked on the floor-to-ceiling shelves. To the left of the chair was a broad-hearthed fireplace with a thick mantel. On the mantel was an antique clock that ticktocked steadily in the silent room. It sounded every hour with a dainty chime that reminded Sierra of an ice cream truck.

"How are you doing, honey?" Dad asked without looking up from his paperwork.

"Okay. I wanted to talk to you some more when you want to take a break. You don't have to stop what you're doing."

Dad put down his pen, turned down the CD player, and turned to face her. Leaning back in the swivel captain's chair, Dad said, "This is a good time. The bills can wait. What do you want to talk about?"

"School."

He titled his head to the side and folded his arms across his chest. If Sierra were reading his body language correctly, he was indicating to her that he was a rock in his decision.

"I feel strongly about not going back to Royal. If I go one more week, it will only prolong the inevitable and make it harder for me to make the switch."

"And what will make the switch harder?" Dad asked.

The truth was she didn't feel nearly as convinced of her decision as she had on Friday. She had found herself thinking about some of the students this weekend, and she wondered about their lives. Like Randy. What was his dad doing in Nepal when he bought that coat? And those girls in the locker room. Surely they must think she was a jerk for the way she acted on Friday. She was beginning to wish she could apologize to them. Sierra hated unresolved relationships.

Another reason she became mellowed about going to Royal was Brutus. She found that she and Brutus had a lot in common. In Pineville, Brutus was the most popular dog in the neighborhood. In Portland, he was nobody. Then Wes took him around the neighborhood and helped him break the ice, so to speak, with all the other dogs on the block. Sierra had thought during their walk that she had withdrawn and felt sorry for herself, just as Brutus had. She had convinced herself the solution was to withdraw more and hide in a huge school. Now she wondered if maybe she needed to "make the rounds" and get acquainted at Royal. It would be a lot harder now, since she had proved to those two girls that she was stuck-up by yelling at them that she wasn't stuck-up.

"I don't know," she finally said to her dad. "I'm mixed up about the whole thing. I don't know what I want."

Dad unfolded his arms and leaned forward. "Do you know what, honey? None of us really gave a thought to how hard this transition would be for you. You went from a life-changing experience in Europe to an instant new home and new school all within a few days. You've held up remarkably well."

"I don't know about that," Sierra said.

"Wes got me thinking about it when he mentioned that stress list yesterday. You've had double, no triple the changes. The rest of us had a three-week head start on you. Somehow we expected you to fall right in line with where we were in this transition. I can understand why it seems confusing. And that's why I believe we should stick with our original choice, which you made almost two months ago. I think you should give Royal another try."

Sierra let out a sigh. She knew her dad was right. But she found it hard to concede. "Okay," she said at last.

Then it hit Sierra that she had homework. When she was sure she wasn't going back, she had mentally written off the assignment.

"Thanks for talking to me about it," Sierra said.

"Any time," Dad replied, twirling the chair back to the desk.

"Good night." She hurried back upstairs. Tawni was still on the phone and made a face when Sierra entered.

Sierra snatched her backpack and headed for the kitchen, hoping she could remember what chapters she was supposed to read. She was fortunate to snag the last piece of Mom's apple cobbler. Then, pouring herself a glass of milk and warming the cobbler in the microwave, Sierra planted herself on a kitchen stool and spread her books across the counter. That's when she remembered she needed book covers for all of them as well.

*It was a lot easier when I thought I wasn't going back. I can't believe I changed my mind so easily. Maybe Dad is right. Maybe I've been under more stress than I realized, and that's what made me act stuck-up to those girls.*

Sierra decided the first thing she would do tomorrow at school would be to find those girls and apologize. But, when Sierra woke up the next morning, her throat was so swollen she could barely swallow.

"I'm not faking it," she told her mom after dragging herself downstairs and turning on the teakettle. "My head is pounding, my ears are stopped up, and it hurts to swallow."

"You're past the age where I decided whether or not you can make it to school. You decide for yourself."

"I can't go. I feel awful."

"Probably jet lag," Dillon said, as if he knew all about it.

"It's not jet lag, Dillon. You don't get jet lag a week and a half after you've been somewhere. I'm coming down with the flu or a cold or something." The teakettle began to whistle, and Sierra poured herself a cup of lemon herbal tea and dipped in a spoonful of honey. Then, carrying it upstairs with shaky hands, she went back to bed.

Tawni was already gone. She had a seven o'clock class on Monday at the community college.

With the room to herself, Sierra closed the door and headed for her snug bed. On the floor sat her unfinished project from the evening before—packing box, paper, and two piles of her things. Tawni would be ticked off, but she would have to walk around it for another day. All Sierra could do was crawl back into bed.

Something happens to a person's imagination when she's sick. For Sierra, the morning turned into a strange limbo between fast-paced, no-time-to-think-it-through reality and wild, worst-case-scenario dreams. One of her bizarre episodes included Paul. Jalene was standing next to him at the library, kissing him the way she had at the airport. Paul turned into a robot and followed her up and down the aisles, carrying her books. Jalene kept piling on the books until Paul couldn't carry any more.

Then, in her dazed imagination, Sierra arrived on the scene, driving her super mobile shaped like a huge Mars bar. She was steering it up and down the library rows, chasing Jalene.

When Sierra forced her eyes open and scanned the bedroom for familiar things, she could feel the perspiration forming on her forehead. All she wanted was a nice hot bath. That triggered another round of crazy imaginations in which she was trying to bathe Brutus. But he ended up putting her in the tub, and with his great, furry paw, he was lathering her hair. Then Brutus was walking her to school and coaxing her to make friends with students who were behind chain-link fences, yipping at her.

A cool hand on her forehead drew her back to reality. She opened her eyes.

"How are you feeling, Lovey? I brought you something for your throat." Granna Mae nudged Sierra to sit up and receive the glass of dark green liquid held out to her. One of her grandmother's herbal concoctions, no doubt. Sierra knew it was harmless. Still, it could be nasty-tasting, and she wished she could somehow turn it down without hurting her grandmother's feelings.

Knowing it would be rude to plug her nose, Sierra did her best to hold her breath and chug the liquid down her swollen throat. The aftertaste made her shiver. "Is there any water in here?" She knew her tea was gone but wondered if she had brought up a glass of water and forgotten it.

"I'll get you one, Lovey." Off Granna Mae padded to fetch a drink of water.

Sierra waited and waited. The remedy began to taste fermented. Finally she couldn't stand it any longer and forced herself to venture down the hall to the bathroom and get her own drink. Walking only made her head spin more. She barely made it back to her bed before her headache overpowered her.

A few minutes later her mom walked in with a glass of orange juice and a thermometer.

"Thanks," Sierra said, eagerly sipping the orange juice. "Did Granna Mae tell you I asked for a cup of water?"

"No. Was she up here?"

"About ten minutes ago."

"That's odd. She's been rather mixed up this morning. Did she know it was you?" Mom asked.

Sierra thought hard. "I'm pretty sure she called me Lovey. She gave me a glass of some green stuff to drink."

"You didn't drink it, did you?" Mom looked stunned.

"Yes." Suddenly Sierra realized she couldn't assume anything with her grandmother anymore. For all she knew, Granna Mae fed her plant food or the soaking solution for her dentures. "Wasn't too smart, was it? I thought it was one of her vitamin or herbal drinks."

"It very well may have been, but we can't be sure about anything with her. Did you say she gave it to you about ten minutes ago?"

"About that."

"Well, if it were poison you would know it by now."

"Great," Sierra said, placing the orange juice on her nightstand. Then, because she wasn't too sick to play a joke on her mom, Sierra suddenly bulged out her eyes and clutched her throat. With a gasp and a wheeze, she closed her eyes and flopped lifeless on her pillow.

"Very funny," Mom said. "I take it you're feeling better."

"Actually, I kind of am."

"Must be the orange juice."

"Or Granna Mae's green gunk. Can we at least try to find out what it was? I can't believe I drank it. I didn't want to hurt her feelings."

"Here," Mom said, leaving the thermometer. "I'll check on Granna Mae. Take your temperature and let me know what it is."

It was only 99 degrees, a slight fever but not one that warranted a trip to the doctor. Sierra fell back asleep. This time it was deep, restorative, dreamless sleep.

Tuesday she had a hard time deciding if she should

attend school or not. Mom had left the choice up to her. Sierra missed the days of grade school when her mom would stick the thermometer in Sierra's mouth and then look at her watch, waiting for it to reveal its secret. She would pull it out and read a secret message inside the glass tube that only moms could read. If it bent to Sierra's favor, Mom would say, "Stay in bed today." If not, Mom would say, "I think you can make it." The thermometer was as much of a mystery to Sierra in her childhood as the groundhog's seeing his shadow. In her mind, the thermometer made the decision about school or no school. Not Sierra. Not her mom.

Now it was all up to Sierra. She was beginning to feel the realities of Tawni's comments about having more responsibilities the older she became. She decided to go to school.

Sierra settled on jeans and a flannel shirt with her thick hunter's jacket and new velvet hat. She drove herself to school so she could leave if she felt too sick.

As soon as she made a trip to her locker, Sierra waited in the hallway until she spotted the girls from the gym last Friday. She saw one of them and made eye contact. The girl immediately looked away and kept walking to her locker.

Sierra marched up to her and said, "Excuse me." The girl looked timid. "I just want to apologize for the way I acted on Friday. I was a jerk, and you were right. I did act stuck-up last week. I'm really sorry. I hope we can start over."

The girl looked surprised but relieved. She had silky brown hair parted down the middle and tucked behind each ear. She wore tiny pearl earrings and had thin eyebrows above green eyes. "Sure," she said. "My name's Vicki. Don't worry about Friday. Marissa and I were out of line to talk about you behind your back. I'm sorry."

"That's okay," Sierra said. "It was actually a God-thing because it made me realize what I was doing."

"A God-thing," Vicki repeated with a smile. "That's good. Did you make that up?"

"No. I heard it from a friend I met in England."

"You've been to England?" Vicki asked. Before Sierra could answer, Vicki was motioning to someone over Sierra's shoulder. Marissa joined them, chewing on her lower lip as if she were in trouble.

"I want to apologize," Sierra said again. "I was out of line Friday and I'm sorry I acted the way I did."

"It's okay," Marissa said. "We were wrong for gossiping about you. I'm sorry, too."

"I was hoping we could all start over."

"Good idea," said Marissa. She smiled but didn't show her teeth. Marissa was shorter than Sierra. She had on a denim jacket and wore her medium-length, cinnamon-colored hair in a loose ponytail.

"Sierra was saying she's been to England," Vicki said.

Just then another girl walked up to them and said loudly, "I don't believe it! This time you have to say you bought it at A Wrinkle in Time."

Sierra turned to see the girl who had commented on Sierra's outfit her first day. Today she had on the same black velvet hat as Sierra's. Sierra laughed. "I did," she said. "On Saturday. When did you buy yours?"

"Last Thursday," the girl said. "By the way, if you want the notes from English yesterday, I have them with me. I noticed you weren't there."

"Thanks. I'm sorry; I don't remember your name."

"Amy," the girl answered. She looked Italian, with thick black hair and dark, expressive eyes. The hat looked really cute on her. Sierra wondered if it looked that good on her.

"Amy, I want to apologize to you too, about acting so stuck-up last week. I'm trying to make a fresh start."

"Then you're at the right school because the people here are very good at forgiving." She shot a sideways glance at Marissa and still smiling, said, "Most of the time."

# sixteen

"YOU WERE RIGHT," Sierra said when she arrived home that afternoon. "I was wrong. I stand corrected. There, do you feel better?"

Mom was standing at the kitchen sink, scrubbing potatoes. "Let's see, could it be you enjoyed school?"

Sierra poured herself some cranberry juice and sat on a stool by the kitchen counter. "I apologized to everyone I thought I'd been a brat to, and they treated me as if I were a totally different person."

"Probably because you treated them like different people," Mom suggested.

"My throat even feels better," Sierra said.

"Sounds like a wonderful day for you all around."

"How was your day?"

"Good. Granna Mae had a doctor's appointment. I talked with him some after she left the room. He seems to think a lot of the disorientation last week was due to the move and changing things around in her house and in her bedroom. She might be doing a little better now that we're all together in one place without any more major changes for a while."

"That's encouraging."

"Oh, and a letter came for you today." Mom motioned with her hand. "It's on the front entry table."

"Thanks. Do you want some help with dinner?"

"No, I'm fine, thanks. I might take you up on the offer after dinner."

Sierra placed her emptied glass on the counter and went in search of her letter. She guessed it might be from one of her friends from Pineville. She was pleasantly surprised to see it was from Katie. Carrying the thick envelope into the library, Sierra curled up in her favorite chair and began to read.

*Hey, Sierra!*

*How are you doing as you readjust to real life? My first week was hard. I don't think I was much fun to be around. I've mellowed out now that I'm back in the routine of school.*

*I went down to San Diego this weekend to see Doug and go to the God Lover's Bible Study that meets at his apartment. Boy, the stories I could tell you about that place! I'll save those for another time, like this summer when we get together.*

*Anyway, Doug gave me this letter to send on to you. A guy named Jeremy at the Bible study gave it to him and asked him to get it to you.*

Sierra pulled the folded-up envelope out of Katie's envelope and looked at the handwriting. All that was written across the front was "Sierra" in bold black letters. She wanted to rip it open, but read the rest of Katie's letter for a clue.

*I'm dying of curiosity, Sierra. You'll have to write me immediately and tell me who wrote this mystery letter to you. I can't help but think it's from that Paul guy you wrote and told me about.*

*Well, stop wasting your time reading this nothing letter from me and read the mystery letter! Then write me and tell me all about it.*

*Oh and one more thing. You asked about what I meant about being homesick for being a teen again. I'd give anything to be sixteen again. I was a dork so much of my time because I kept trying to be more independent. My parents kept putting a halt to that. They wouldn't even let me be a counselor at summer camp for one measly week! I used to think their decisions to hold me back from doing all these wild, independent things were because they aren't Christians and most of the things I wanted to do were with my Christian friends or with the church youth group. Now I think I understand that they just wanted me to take it slow and stay home as much as possible. I'm the youngest of three kids, and so I guess they wanted me to stay anchored a little longer.*

*I don't know if that answers your question, but if you want some free advice, take each day as slowly as you can and enjoy it when you can find simple solutions to your day-to-day problems. Believe me, it only gets more complicated from here on out!*

*Hey, are you still reading this? Why? Open that letter!*

*I hold you in my heart,*

*Katie (Phil. 1:7)*

Sierra carefully tore open the sealed back of the envelope. She had to admire Katie. If she had been the designated courier for a mystery letter, she couldn't guarantee her curiosity wouldn't keep her from trying to see who the letter was from.

Sierra pulled out one sheet of nice-quality paper. The writing was in bold, black ink and was a mixture of printing and cursive. It was signed "Paul."

Feeling as if her heart were pounding fiercely in her already-tight throat, Sierra swiftly read the letter. Then she read it again, letting each word sink in.

*Sierra,*

*You've ruined my entire life. Are you happy now? I couldn't sleep for two days after I got back. Jet lag, I'm sure. Or was it the angels of torture you sent to harass me? Well, they did their job. I broke up with Jalene and walked away with my honor. Then I even went to church last Sunday for the first time in ten months. I imagine you're smiling right now. Feeling quite proud of yourself, are you? Well, don't give yourself any medals yet. I'm still on the fence. Only now my back is probably turned in the right direction. My mother thinks you're an angel. I told her you're only a little girl with a smart mouth. You don't fly, do you?*

*Paul*

At the very bottom, in small letters, was a post office box number. Sierra interpreted that as an invitation to respond, especially since he ended his letter with a question.

Sierra folded the letter in her lap and tried to slow down her rapid breathing.

*He must have written this letter last week if he sent it to his brother in San Diego, and I received it before Sunday. So why didn't he say anything about seeing me at the movies?*

Then Sierra remembered that when Paul saw her, Wes

had his arm around her. Paul obviously thought Wes was her boyfriend. She liked the idea of Paul thinking she was going out with a guy who was obviously older than she. She sat for a long time, lost in her thoughts.

When Mom called her to come for dinner, Sierra folded the letter, which she had now read at least fifteen times, and ran it up to her room. Tawni wasn't there. Sierra tucked it under her pillow, and as she did, she remembered how one of the girls in England talked about writing letters to her future husband and keeping them in a shoe box under her bed. Maybe Sierra would do that too one of these days.

On her way to the door, she tripped over her piles of stuff on the floor and told herself she had to pick it up right after dinner.

All through the meal, Sierra's imagination was floating somewhere above the table, weaving in and out of the antique chandelier from Denmark. She decided she would write Paul tonight, before she had time to change her mind. She would be witty and brief. Just enough of a note to let him know she could return the volley with ease.

There was a slight problem, though, she suddenly realized. She didn't know his last name. He didn't write it, and Katie didn't mention what Jeremy's last name was. Would the letter be delivered to a post office box without a last name? It was worth a try. His letter had reached her through Jeremy, Doug, and Katie. That was very resourceful of them.

"Can you help me with the dishes?" Mom asked Sierra just as she was about to flee to the sanctuary of her room.

"Okay," she answered halfheartedly. As she loaded the

dishwasher, she considered saying something to Mom about the letter. She almost expected Mom to ask about it. But she didn't, and Sierra decided to keep the secret to herself for a while. Of course she would tell her mom and dad eventually. But not yet. The secret was too good to share with anyone just now. She thought she might even wait a day or two before writing back to Katie.

With an energetic snap of the dial, Sierra turned on the dishwasher and dried her hands.

"You seem to be feeling better," Mom said.

"I guess I am," Sierra said before hurrying up the stairs. She shut her bedroom door and pulled out the letter. She read it one more time. Then two more times. Now she was ready to write back.

But on what? She didn't own any nice paper. Maybe Tawni did. Sierra looked through the desk and didn't find anything she wanted to use.

Then, slipping the letter back under her pillow, Sierra went down the hall to Granna Mae's room and knocked softly on the door.

"Come in." Granna Mae was watching a rerun of *The Waltons* her favorite TV show.

"I wondered if you had a piece of stationery I could borrow."

Fortunately, the commercial came on just then. Granna Mae slowly slid off her bed and shuffled to the old desk in the corner of her room.

"I didn't mean for you to get up," Sierra said. "I could have gotten it."

"No, no, Lovey! I have different stationery for different letters. Is this to a boy or girl?"

"A guy," Sierra said, feeling a little funny admitting it for the first time.

"I have just the thing." Granna Mae pawed through a whole drawer of random single sheets that must have taken her a lifetime to collect. Letterhead stationery from hotels that weren't even in business any longer came out of the desk, as did pink sheets and aqua-colored sheets. Then she pulled out one piece that was the color of wheat. In the bottom right corner in faint calligraphy letters was written "Zephaniah 3:17."

"This is the very last stationery I used to write to my Paul every day." She handed it to Sierra. "Will this work for you, Lovey?"

The coincidence rattled Sierra a bit. Did Granna Mae somehow know she was writing to a Paul, too? "Sure. Yes, thank you. It's perfect. Good night."

She scooted down the hall to her room and closed the door. Sierra stood for a moment with her back against the door, feeling her heart pound.

"You are so real," she breathed into the empty room. "Sometimes, God, You boggle my imagination! Is this a sacred piece of stationery or what?"

Sierra didn't have to look up the verse at the bottom. She knew it was the one Granna Mae had made her repeat the night she tucked her in, thinking Sierra was Emma. For a flicker of a moment Sierra wondered if maybe Granna Mae wasn't smarter than all of them put together. What if she were only faking this memory lapse thing to make them all move in with her and to give her opportunities to get all her points across without being held responsible? No, that couldn't be.

Stretching out on the bed, Sierra held her pen poised over the paper and carefully began to write. She couldn't make any mistakes. This guy had no idea how highly she valued handwritten letters over e-mails. She wanted to make sure her response to Paul came out clear and neat at the same time.

*Paul,*

*Aren't you the clever one, sending messages through your big brother! Big brothers can come in handy sometimes. Like last Friday when my big brother took me to the movies. The funny thing was, I thought I saw someone that looked just like you. I probably should have said something. One always expects little girls with big mouths to say something, doesn't one?*

*Oh, and about your life. It doesn't sound demolished to me. Of course, it's hard to tell yet. You must get a great view up there on that fence. Maybe a few splinters?*

*Please tell your mother she's a saint for putting up with your garbage these past—what was it? Ten months? And yes, I do fly. We* did *meet at an airport, didn't we?*

*Sierra*

She carefully addressed the envelope, folded the letter, and placed it inside. Before she sealed it, Sierra had one last thought. Across from the verse she printed her street address in tiny letters the same way Paul had left his box number.

She thought of how much had changed in her life in the past few weeks. She had been to Great Britain and back all by herself; she had her faith stretched during the outreach in Northern Ireland; made some wonderful friends; met

Paul; settled in a new, old house with a grandmother who was changing right before her eyes; started a new school; and, after letting God break down her stubborn resistance, decided she liked Royal and the people there. Sierra felt as if her emotions and her life were beginning to even out.

Glancing down at the letter one more time, she noticed an open space after her name. She decided to add one final thought that summed up her life right now.

*P.S. By the way, yes, I am happy now. Thanks for asking.*

# Book Two

# IN YOUR DREAMS

# one

"HOW CAN YOU STAND to live like this?" Sierra Jensen's sister, Tawni, snatched a pair of ragged jeans off the floor from her side of the room and hurled them onto Sierra's unmade bed. The jeans landed on a mound of clean clothes Sierra had removed from the dryer on Monday. It was now Thursday afternoon, but she never quite found the time to put her clothes away.

"I'm not bothering your stuff!" Sierra said, grabbing the jeans and depositing them on the top of her dirty clothes pile on the floor. "Just because you're Miss Tide Queen doesn't mean everyone else has to be like you."

"You don't have to be like me, Sierra. Just try to be normal."

"Normal! Normal? I am normal! You're the neat freak, Tawni. Never a blond curl out of place, never seen in public without makeup, never a chipped fingernail. Don't you ever get tired of living the life of a mannequin?"

"You are so rude."

"Oh, and you're not?"

"How am I rude?" Tawni challenged.

"You're throwing my stuff around. I'd call that slightly rude."

"I wouldn't have to throw your things around if you would clean them up once in a while. Like this weekend, for example. Do you think you could manage to keep my side of the room the way it is right now and try to clean up your side by Sunday night when I come back?"

Sierra bit her lower lip to keep her angry words inside. Letting them out never seemed to help. And the times she had, she regretted it later. But having to share her room with an older sister who was a clean nut had to be listed somewhere as one of the world's cruelest tortures. If she could find that list and show it to her parents, they would understand how much Sierra had suffered during her sixteen years of life with the perpetually perfect Tawni Sage Jensen.

"I mean it, Sierra," Tawni said, zipping closed her luggage. "You're going to have to give up your sloppy ways one of these days. I vote you start this weekend." Tawni turned with a swish and marched out of the room.

Sierra plopped onto the floor next to her pile of dirty clothes and took inventory of the surroundings. The two sides of the room couldn't be more opposite. Tawni's bed was made without a wrinkle, and her embroidered pillows were positioned on it just so. Her dresser was covered with a lacy white cloth and set like a stage. Front and center was a slender vase with three red tulips picked from the front yard that morning. To the side were two porcelain frames, one containing Tawni's high school graduation picture and the other her baby picture. Each of her four bottles of perfume lined up in a row with their labels facing the audience. Perfume, or as Tawni called it, "fragrance," was her thing. She worked at a "fragrance bar" at Nordstrom's. There she had accumulated a bunch of new friends, and this weekend they were going skiing at Mount Bachelor.

Sierra had plans for this weekend too. Not with friends, though. Since their family had moved to Portland a few months ago, Tawni was the one who'd made all the new friends.

For Sierra, the problem of not having friends wasn't as pressing at the moment as her prolem of not having money. Hopefully that would be taken care of soon. She had a job interview Saturday afternoon at a flower shop on Hawthorn, about seven blocks from the old Victorian house where they lived. Sierra liked flowers, but she wasn't sure she would catch on to how to arrange them. She had what she thought of as a different artistic eye than most people. This was evident by the way she dressed. Casual. Simple. Not on "display," the way Tawni was with her appearance and her room.

That's how Sierra felt about herself too. Natural. Approachable. Her wild, curly blond hair flowered unhindered to her shoulders. Her blue-gray eyes, the shade of a winter morning sky, lit up her honest face. And the sprinkling of freckles across her nose had yet to be covered with makeup.

Sometime last summer, when Sierra was examining her freckles in the mirror, she had decided her best feature was probably her lips. They were equally proportioned on top and bottom. Round and full. Just right for kissing. But then, she wouldn't know. The only male that had kissed her smack on the lips lately was her three-year-old nephew, Tyler.

"Sierra?" A tap on the door followed Mom's voice.

*Oh great! Tawni told Mom to bug me about my room.*

"Come in," Sierra said. "I already know what you're going to say."

Mom appeared in the doorway. Her normally calm demeanor was replaced with a frenzied look. She had on a straight denim skirt, a white shirt with the sleeves rolled up, and she carried a slip of paper in her hand.

"What's wrong?" Sierra asked. "Are you okay?"

"Uncle Darren just called. Gayle's in the hospital. She and the twins were in a car accident. The boys are okay, but Gayle broke both arms. I told Darren I'd try to catch the first flight out. There's one that leaves at seven tonight."

Sierra stood up, instinctively feeling she should do something. "Is Aunt Gayle okay?"

Mom nodded. "Yes. She'll be in the hospital at least until tomorrow. But with both arms fractured, she'll be in casts for weeks. She obviously can't take care of Evan and Nathan. They were both asleep in the car seats when the other car hit them at an intersection. Darren says they're doing fine."

Sierra knew how close her mom was to her youngest sister, Gayle, and how Mom felt responsible to help Aunt Gayle in her time of need. Mom had gone to Phoenix eighteen months ago when the twins were born. She had taken the role of mother to Gayle when their mom had passed away twenty years ago, and now she had become a substitute grandma for the twins.

"Are you going tonight then? At seven?" Sierra asked.

"I need to talk it over with your dad when he comes home, which—" Mom glanced at her wristwatch—"should be any minute now. With Tawni off on her ski trip and Dad planning to take the boys camping this weekend, that would leave you home with Granna Mae."

"It's okay."

"I know you can handle everything," Mom said. "It's just that it can be a bit tricky sometimes when Granna Mae has one of her memory lapses."

"I can handle it, Mom. She's almost always clearheaded with me."

Mom tucked her short, dark-blond hair behind her ear and gave a close-lipped smile. Sierra noticed her mom had nice round lips too.

"Are you worried about Granna Mae being home all alone tomorrow during the day? I could stay home from school, if it would help."

"No, you don't need to miss any school. I guess she'll be okay. After all, she managed for all those years by herself before we moved in."

"Mom," Sierra said, folding her arms across her chest. "I'm telling you it will be fine. Give me a chance to prove myself."

"You don't need to prove anything," Mom said.

Just then, Dad's footsteps pounded up the stairs. A moment later he appeared in Sierra's room. He was an energetic man whose receding hairline was the only hint that he was well into his fourth decade. "I heard," he said, giving Mom a quick kiss.

Sierra had wondered if her dad ever noticed that his wife had lips shaped just right for the kiss he had given her.

Do men even notice things like that? Especially after nearly twenty-five years of kissing the same lips every day?

"I can take a flight at seven," Mom explained, showing Dad the slip of paper. "Or there's one with a stopover in Los Angeles that leaves at 10:20 tonight."

"Take the seven o'clock. The boys and I will cancel our trip."

"You don't have to," Sierra said. "I'm staying with Granna Mae. We'll be fine."

Mom and Dad exchanged hesitant glances.

"What?" Sierra said, stepping over a mound of her clothes and preparing to plead her case. "You guys are looking at me as if you think I can't handle this. Less than a month ago I managed to travel to England and back all by myself, remember? I think I can handle being alone with my grandmother for a few days."

"You're not the one we're concerned about," Dad said.

"Granna Mae has been fine lately," Sierra said. "Her memory lapse hasn't been a problem for the last week or so. Didn't she visit the doctor a few days ago?"

"Yes." Mom quietly closed Sierra's bedroom door behind her and spoke softly so only Dad and Sierra could hear. "He ordered some tests, and I took her in for them this morning."

"And?" Dad asked.

"I suppose the results will come sometime next week. Besides, what can the tests tell us that we don't already know? Her mind is slipping. Aside from that, she's in fine health."

"You guys can trust me," Sierra said. "She and I will be

fine. Really." *And it isn't as if I have to cancel my social life this weekend or anything, since I don't have one.*

Mom let out a deep sigh. "The boys have been looking forward to the camping trip..."

"Okay. We'll go," Dad said in a quick decision. "Sierra, you're in charge. Honey, I'll take you to the airport in an hour, and then the boys and I will leave on schedule at four-thirty in the morning. Any problems, Sierra, you call Cody or Wes, okay?"

Sierra didn't think it was too practical to call either of her older brothers. Cody, his wife, Katrina, and their son, Tyler, lived in Washington, more than an hour away. And Wesley was going to school in Corvallis, almost two hours away. What good would they be in an emergency? She knew she could handle whatever problems arose.

"You're incredible, Sierra. Did you know that? I never cease to be amazed by you and proud of you." Mom kissed her on the temple. "Oh, and by the way, if you find some spare time this weekend, you might want to straighten up your room."

# two

"SIERRA," A DEEP VOICE WHISPERED in her ear. "Honey? The boys and I are leaving now."

Sierra pried open her sleepy eyelids. "Dad?"

"Don't wake up all the way. I wanted to let you know we're leaving now. You have an alarm set, don't you?"

"Yes."

He planted a quick kiss on her cheek. "Thanks for holding down the fort. Remember, if you have any problems, call Mom at Aunt Gayle's, or call Wes or Cody."

"I'm sure everything will be fine," Sierra mumbled, snuggling deeper under the covers. "Have a great time. Catch a bunch of fish."

"We will. 'Bye, honey."

Sierra lounged a long time in the buoyant corridor between wake and sleep. Her fleeting dreams consisted of her sweet Granna Mae absentmindedly looking for a feather in the downstairs closet and her six-year-old brother, Gavin, teetering on the edge of a creek as a huge fish on the end of his line tried to pull him into the water.

Then all of a sudden the missing feather fluttered onto an open page of Sierra's biology book. She reached over to pick it up and out of the corner of her eye spotted a figure wearing an Indiana Jones-style hat and a leather backpack.

She immediately opened her eyes. Only the dark shadows of her room greeted her. *Paul.* Letting out a deep breath, Sierra closed her eyes and tried to go back to sleep. She wanted to fall into a deep sleep, where fragmented dreams have room to dance like crazy and then disappear with the morning light. That's where Paul belonged. In her dreams.

The next two hours she wrestled with the covers, trying without success to fall back into sleep. At seven she finally rolled out of bed in a bad mood and stumbled into the bathroom for a shower. She wasn't sure if she should wake Granna Mae or simply leave a note saying she had gone to school and would be back around four.

After deciding on a pair of baggy jeans (which Tawni thought looked ridiculous) and an embroidered peasant blouse (which Tawni thought was pathetic), Sierra took a long look in the full-length mirror at the end of the upstairs hall. She was glad Tawni couldn't force her fashion advice on Sierra today.

She heard Granna Mae stirring in her room. Sierra gently tapped on the door.

"Come in, Lovey!" This was a good sign. Granna Mae's nickname for Sierra was "Lovey." It had also become a clue as to whether Granna Mae was operating in this time zone or not. If she didn't refer to Sierra as "Lovey," she might be thinking Sierra was someone else from another era in Granna Mae's life. This morning Sierra harbored fears that

Granna Mae's mind might slip into its precarious time machine and transport her mind and soul into another time frame.

"Good morning," Sierra said cheerfully as she stepped into the large bedroom.

Granna Mae was making her bed, pulling up the thick down comforter and covering it with her favorite old handmade blanket. It was a patchwork collection made from squares of fabric she had kept over the years from clothes she had made for her children. The bedroom was cheery and charming, with a window seat in the rounded window alcove and a fireplace that was used often.

"I'm almost ready to leave for school. What are you going to do all day?" Sierra asked.

"Oh, I thought I'd do the usual: Go roller skating this morning and bowl this afternoon. There might be time to take tea with the mayor before you come home." The mischievous twinkle in Granna Mae's eye let Sierra know she was spry this morning and her usual self.

"Sounds fun," Sierra teased back. "Be sure you wear your elbow pads."

The phone rang, and Sierra reached for it on the nightstand before Granna Mae could make it around to that side of the bed. The large green letters on the digital clock read "7:58." Sierra needed to leave for school in two minutes.

"Is this Mrs. Jensen?" the male voice on the other end asked.

"This is Sierra Jensen, Sharon's daughter."

"I'm trying to reach Mrs. Mae Jensen."

"Oh, she's right here." Sierra covered the mouthpiece with her hand and said, "It's one of your boyfriends.

Probably wants to add bungee jumping to your list of today's activities."

Granna Mae took the phone while Sierra finished making the bed. She heard her grandmother say, "Oh, yes. Good morning...Oh...Oh...No...Okay...Yes...Well, no...Okay. Good-bye." She hung up the phone just as Sierra was scooting out the door.

"So?" Sierra called out over her shoulder. "What are you doing today? Bungee jumping or skydiving?"

"I'm having my gallbladder taken out," Granna Mae replied.

Sierra laughed at her grandmother's quick wit. "Well, have fun!" She bounded down the stairs and reached for her backpack off the coat tree by the front door. "Have a great day!"

"Oh, Sierra," Granna Mae's high-pitched voice called from the top of the stairs, "could you give me a ride?"

Sierra stopped in her tracks, irritated that she would be late for school now. She often drove her grandmother to the pharmacy or the grocery store, but why couldn't her grandma's errand wait till Sierra came home? "I'll give you a ride wherever you want to go as soon as I get home."

She was about to close the door behind her when she heard, "But I need to be there before nine."

"Before nine this morning or nine tonight?"

"Nine this morning," the twittering voice replied.

Sierra stepped back into the house and tried not to sound irritated. "Where do you need to go?"

"The hospital."

Now Sierra knew something was off in Granna Mae's thinking. "Not today, Granna Mae."

"Yes, today," she said. "This morning. Dr. Utley said I shouldn't drink or eat anything and to be there by nine o'clock. I can call a cab." With that she turned at the top of the stairs and padded back to her room.

"Okay," Sierra called after her. "I'll see you around four this afternoon."

"I won't be here. I'll be at St. Mary's Hospital. You can come directly there to see me."

How could her grandmother's mind slip so suddenly? Sierra didn't know what to do. She couldn't leave Granna Mae like this. She might actually go call a cab and have herself carted somewhere. Then what would Sierra do if she came home and Granna Mae wasn't there? With a frustrated huff, Sierra dropped her backpack on the floor and took the stairs two at a time. She found Granna Mae in her room, neatly folding some of her underclothes and tucking them into an overnight suitcase.

"He said nothing to eat or drink, not even water. And now I'm hungry, just because I know that. It's such a good thing Dr. Utley checked the test results this morning. He's leaving today at three and won't be back for a week. I can't wait that long." Granna Mae reached for a bottle of lotion and kept chattering as she packed her hospital bag. "So that's why I don't mind going on such short notice. I want Dr. Utley to do the operation, of course. He's the one that took out Paul's appendix."

Paul was one of Granna Mae's sons. He had been killed in Vietnam, and his death had left a heavy mark on Granna Mae. Whenever she started to talk about Paul, she had almost certainly dipped into la-la land.

"Well, I tell you what," Sierra said, sitting down on the edge of the bed. She reached over to touch her grandmother's hand and thus coax her to stop packing. "You wait right here at home today. Right here in your room. You'll be just fine here. You can watch some TV or read a book. And when I come home, we'll go see Dr. Utley together. How would that be? Would you like that?"

Granna Mae gave Sierra an irritated look and calmly withdrew her hand. "I don't know why you are speaking to me that way, Sierra Mae Jensen. But let me tell you right now that I am completely serious. That was Dr. Utley on the phone. The test results show that I must have my gallbladder removed right away. If I want him to do the operation, I must go in this morning. Now don't you worry about a thing. You go on to school. I don't need a ride. I'll call a cab."

Sierra didn't know what to believe. And she didn't know what to do.

"I...I can stay a bit longer." Sierra decided she would wait out this waking hallucination with her grandma and go to school as soon as she knew Granna Mae was thinking clearly again.

"Oh, dear!" Granna Mae said, looking at the clock. It's 8:25. I've made you late for school, haven't I, Lovey?"

Sierra froze. *She called me Lovey. She's never called me that unless she's thinking in the present. What if she's telling the truth?*

With her mind scrambling at a furious pace, Sierra popped up and said, "That's okay. Why don't you finish up here? I'm going downstairs for a few minutes." She closed the door behind her and raced down the stairs to the study.

In the top drawer of the old rolltop oak desk was the phone book. Sierra pulled it out and frantically flipped the pages until she found Dr. Utley's number. She dialed, and the minute the receptionist answered, she said, "Yes, I need to talk with Dr. Utley right away. It's very important. My name is Sierra Jensen."

"One moment, please."

The moment felt like an hour as Sierra waited. She could hear her grandmother's footsteps upstairs in the bedroom right above her. "Come on, come on!" she breathed into the phone.

"Dr. Utley speaking."

"Yes, hello. My name is Sierra Jensen, and my grandmother is Mae Jensen. I'm sorry to bother you, but she thinks that you called her this morning, and that she's supposed to have an operation. But, you see, I don't know exactly what to believe because her mind sometimes plays tricks on her and—"

"I see," the doctor said, interrupting her. "Is your mother there?"

"No," Sierra said. "I just wondered if you'd mind talking with her and setting her straight."

"Actually," the doctor said. "I think you're the one I need to set straight. Your grandmother had some tests yesterday, and her regular doctor sent me the results. She has several gallstones. One has escaped from her gallbladder and is clogging her bile duct. I've scheduled her for surgery this morning at eleven. She needs to be at the hospital by nine."

Sierra felt as if someone had sucked all the air out of the room. "Okay," she finally managed to say. "I'll take her right away." She hung up the phone and took a deep breath. Her heart pounded.

"Lovey," came the calm, birdlike voice from the stairs, "I'm ready to go."

# three

ST. MARY'S HOSPITAL was only a few miles from Granna Mae's house. Sierra found a parking place near the entrance, and they checked in at the front desk at ten minutes before nine. Granna Mae had to sign papers, and then they were sent up the elevator to a room where Granna Mae was instructed to change into a hospital gown and wait on the bed.

"I'll be right back," Sierra said, thinking this would be a good time to call her mom.

"Not yet, Lovey. You need to watch the door for me. I don't want one of those male nurses barging in on me while I'm changing."

Sierra drew the curtain around the bed and stood watch by the door. She had to stop a lab technician. "She's changing," Sierra explained. "It'll just be a minute."

"Is that Ted?" Granna Mae called out.

Sierra bit her lip and felt her heart pounding at top speed again. Ted was Sierra's grandfather. He had died when she was a toddler. This time Granna Mae *had* to be confused.

"My name's Larry, ma'am. I need to take a sample of your blood. You let me know when you're ready for me."

"I'm ready," the calm voice replied.

Sierra drew back the curtain. Granna Mae was in the bed with the white sheet pulled up to her chin. She had an innocent, passive look on her face. The sparkle she had exhibited earlier this morning was gone.

"Make a fist for me," Larry said as he reached for her creamy white arm. "A little poke here...Hold on, I'm almost finished...There. Bend your arm and hold this right here."

Granna Mae didn't even flinch. She glanced at Sierra and smiled. *Oh, my dear Granna Mae! Who do you think I am when you look at me? One of your daughters? A nurse? Do you even know I'm here? I wish I knew what you do!*

For the next hour Sierra didn't leave Granna Mae's bedside. They didn't talk much. At least Sierra didn't talk much. Granna Mae asked for things like a blue scarf she said she had left in the car and a cup of coffee. She wanted to know what time they were leaving. None of it made sense. Sierra agreed to everything but didn't move.

Granna Mae didn't seem to notice. She willingly signed a form listing all the items she had brought to the hospital. She went to the bathroom when the nurse told her to, surrendered her arm for the IV, and only winced slightly when the needle was inserted. In a way, Sierra was thankful for the cushion of illogical thought that padded her grandmother's preparation for surgery.

When it came time to wheel her off, Sierra asked if she could speak briefly with the doctor.

"Come with us," the nurse advised. Sierra followed her, walking alongside of Granna Mae's rolling bed. Impulsively Sierra reached over and grasped her grandma's hand, squeezing it as they moved down the corridor. Granna Mae's hands were elegant, silky white, and softly wrinkled.

"Do you mind waiting here?" the nurse asked.

The hospital bed was wheeled forward, and Sierra reluctantly let go of Granna Mae's hand. "'Bye," she whispered.

A moment later, an older man dressed in mint green hospital garb approached Sierra. "Are you Mae's daughter?"

"Granddaughter," Sierra corrected him. "Yes, I'm Sierra. I wanted you to know that she's a little confused. She was fine this morning, after you called, but now she seems mixed up. I don't know if that makes any difference with the surgery, but I wanted you to know."

"I appreciate it," he said, patting Sierra's hand. "Don't worry. She'll be fine. Will you be able to sit with her in the recovery? I think it would help her to see a familiar face when she wakes up."

"Yes, I'll be here."

Sierra felt a huge knot tightening in the pit of her stomach. She knew she had to call her mom and let her know what was happening. But dozens of obstacles were in her way. First, she didn't know Aunt Gayle's phone number, and she didn't know if she should go home to find it or stay nearby while Granna Mae was in surgery. She decided she shouldn't leave the hospital.

Maybe the best thing would be to call her brother and

his wife. They would have the number, and they could call Mom.

Sierra scrounged through the bottom of her backpack and found she didn't have enough money to make a long-distance phone call. She would have to phone collect. Katrina would understand. *Oh, how I hate not having my own cell phone!*

The only problem was Katrina wasn't home, and the operator wouldn't let her leave a message on the answering machine. So there she was, with no money and no further along in her quest. Her only choice was to go home.

Once inside the big, empty house, Sierra went about placing her phone calls. First, she phoned Aunt Gayle's, where she left a message on the machine. She didn't want to freak out Mom by telling her Granna Mae was in the hospital. All she said was, "Hi, it's Sierra. Mom, when you have a chance, could you call home today...right away. I need to talk to you." She hung up and wondered if the message should have been more urgent.

Jotting down the number, Sierra tucked it in her backpack and decided to try to call it later from the hospital. Then she punched in Cody's number again and left a message on his machine for him to call her at home. Again, she didn't mention Granna Mae or the operation.

Sierra grabbed a carton of orange juice, a couple of granola bars, and all the spare change she could find in the kitchen drawer where Mom kept her stash. It was mostly coins recovered from the dryer, which Mom claimed were her "tips."

Then Sierra hurried back to the hospital, where she waited for nearly two hours. Twice she tried Aunt Gayle's, but each time she hung up right before the answering machine picked up on the call so she could retrieve her change. She didn't know what else she could do but sit and wait for Granna Mae to be released from surgery. It seemed like the slowest couple of hours in her life.

At about one-thirty a nurse came into the waiting room and told Sierra she could be with her grandmother in the recovery room. There, in a straight-back chair, Sierra waited for a few hours, half dozing, half flipping through a few magazines. She thought she should try to call Mom again but didn't. What if Granna Mae woke up while she was gone?

Sierra pulled out the last granola bar and took a chomp. Just then she heard a low groan.

"I'm right here," Sierra said, hopping up and standing beside the bed. Something inside her welled up and made her want to burst into tears. Her sweet grandma looked so helpless, lying there hooked up to all those tubes. She gently reached for Granna Mae's hand. "It's okay," Sierra said, as much to comfort herself as Granna Mae. "You're going to be fine."

A nurse came in and went about her duties as Sierra stepped to the side. "I'll be right back," Sierra said. "If she says anything, tell her Sierra will be right back."

She scooted down the hall to the pay phone and tried Aunt Gayle's number. It was busy. She waited a few minutes and tried again. Still busy. It made her nervous, as if she were going to get in trouble for bringing Granna Mae in for surgery without asking anyone's permission.

She tried the number again. This time it rang. She assumed someone was there and let it ring four times, but the answering machine picked it up after the fourth ring.

"Hi, it's Sierra again. Mom, I really need to talk to you. Ummm..." She didn't know how much she should say. "I, uh...," she stammered. Then fearing that she might run out of time to leave her message, she blurted out, "I'm at the hospital with Granna Mae—" Before she could finish her sentence, the machine beeped loudly in her ear and cut off her sentence.

"Oh great," she muttered, fumbling to find some more change, then realizing she didn't have enough. Not enough to call Phoenix. Feeling exasperated, Sierra hurried back to the recovery room to check on Granna Mae. But when she got there, Granna Mae was gone.

# four

"EXCUSE ME. I'm looking for Mae Jensen. Do you know where they moved her?" Sierra asked.

A uniformed nurse with a clipboard scanned her list and said, "Room 417. The elevator is at the end of the hall."

Sierra breathed a sigh of relief. For a moment she had feared something had gone wrong, and they had taken her grandmother back into surgery.

Sierra stepped calmly into the elevator and decided she had been watching too many hospital shows on TV lately. Room 417 was in the middle of the hall near the nurses' station, and Granna Mae appeared to be sleeping soundly when Sierra entered.

Granna Mae had a distinctive snore. It was faint and steady, a sort of ruffling of the air.

Sierra stood beside her and spoke softly. "It's me, Sierra. Are you feeling okay? I prayed for you. I'm sure everything went just fine."

Just then Dr. Utley stepped into the room and asked, "Has she awakened yet?"

"Not really. Not all the way."

"She'll probably sleep for the next few hours. The anesthesia has most likely worn off by now, but she's on some pretty strong painkillers, and those tend to cause drowsiness." Dr. Utley looked closely at Granna Mae's face and did a quick scan of the IV tubes. "She looks good. I'm sure she'll be fine. We were fortunate we spotted the problem when we did. She only had two gallstones, but they were both large. I had to make an incision about six inches long right here." He traced his fingers across his abdomen, under his right rib cage.

Sierra resisted the urge to clutch her stomach. She felt queasy just hearing about the surgery and decided she didn't want to see the incision.

"I'll need to keep her here about a week. She'll be groggy the first few days, but it will help her to know you're here." Dr. Utley smiled at Sierra. "You do know, don't you, that your grandmother is a remarkable woman?"

Sierra smiled back. "I've always thought so."

"It wouldn't surprise me a bit if she bounced back from this in half the time of most patients her age."

Sierra lowered her voice, just in case Granna Mae could hear her. "It makes it even more difficult to see her body still strong but her mind..." She trailed off, not sure how to complete that sentence.

"I know," Dr. Utley said, nodding his understanding. "A little patience and a lot of love go a long way." He glanced at his watch, and then with a renewed spring in his voice, said, "Well, I have a plane to catch and a very long-overdue vacation waiting for me. I've assigned my associate,

Dr. Adams, to take over for me. He will probably stop by sometime this evening."

"Thank you," Sierra said. "And have a great vacation!"

"I plan to," he answered on his way out the door.

Sierra moved closer to the bed and tried to talk to Granna Mae again. "Did you hear that? Dr. Adams will be checking in on you. I'll stay as long as you want me to. If you need anything, just tell me, okay?"

When Granna Mae responded with a slightly deeper snore, Sierra settled into the upholstered corner chair. She tucked her legs up underneath her and looked out the window. The room faced another row of hospital rooms. Four floors down, in the center of the complex, was a lush garden. It was raining, and in the sky above, streaks of dark gray clouds seemed to be dropping lower while another layer of lighter gray clouds appeared fixed in place, blocking out the blue sky. A typical spring afternoon in Portland.

Sierra thought about all that had happened to her during the past few months. In January she had gone to England on a missions trip. She had become close friends with three of her roommates, Christy, Katie, and Tracy. Even though they were older, Sierra felt she could fit in with them just fine, better than she fit in with most people her own age. While she was in England, her family had moved to Portland from a small mountain community in northern California. In Pineville, Sierra had known everyone, and everyone knew her. She was one of the most popular girls in her high school. Here, she was nobody.

Going to a Christian school in Portland had seemed like a good idea because it was so much smaller than the public schools and therefore more like the high school she had attended in Pineville. But after returning from England, Sierra found it hard to settle back into her junior year. She started off poorly, and although things had leveled out, she still hadn't connected with any of the other students. Of course, a lot of it was her fault. She hadn't worked very hard to make friends. But still, it was a Christian school, and she would have thought the students would be friendlier to her than the mobs at the public school. It didn't seem to be turning out that way.

Granna Mae stirred, and Sierra peeked over at her. She settled back into a rhythmic snore, and Sierra went back to daydreaming out the window.

Sierra knew she had to keep her appointment for the job interview at the flower shop tomorrow, even though she felt as if she shouldn't leave Granna Mae. Without the job, she had no spending money. Without the spending money, she would never break into the circles of students at Royal Academy.

One time, some of the girls had invited her to go out for pizza on a Friday night. Sierra had agreed to go, but when Amy came by to pick her up that evening, her parents weren't home to ask for money, and Sierra didn't have even a dollar in change.

Amy seemed to understand when Sierra used the excuse of not being able to clear going out with her parents. But that was two weeks ago, and Amy hadn't invited her to do anything again. Sierra felt certain the job would be the key to her social life.

For hours she sat listening to Granna Mae's breathing, greeting each nurse who slipped in to check on the patient. Sierra's stomach began to grumble, and she thought she should go home to find something to eat and to try to call Mom again. But she didn't want to leave until Granna Mae had awakened enough to know Sierra was there.

Finally, when it was growing dark, she gave in. Sierra stopped at the nurses' station and explained that she would be gone only an hour or maybe even less. They smiled but seemed absorbed in their routine and not nearly as concerned about Granna Mae as she was.

It felt strange walking up the dark steps of the old house and unlocking the front door. She had never been there by herself. In a family of six children, she rarely had been home by herself. It gave her the creeps to step into a silent entryway and grope for the light switch on the wall.

The smell comforted her. It was a subtle mixture of cinnamon and mothballs. The scent hinted at childhood memories of her favorite hiding place during a game of hide-and-seek, the great, deep downstairs hall closet with the fuzzy red and yellow wallpaper. She would scrunch up in the back corner behind the winter coats and draw in that mothball, cinnamon fragrance.

One summer her dad had read a story to them about four children stepping through a closet full of old coats and entering a magical place called Narnia. Sierra believed it really could happen. As a matter of fact, she was convinced that Granna Mae's closet was equally enchanted, and if she entered it at just the right time, she too would be transported to Narnia. She had tried many times, up until about the age of eleven. Even though she stopped trying, in her heart, she still believed.

It was a wonderful dream, and one she wished she could surrender to right now. How comforting to curl up in that closet. But she was sixteen and responsible for her grandmother's welfare.

The first thing Sierra did was try to call her mom again. This time her uncle answered. "Hi, it's Sierra."

Before she had a chance to say another word, her uncle started to shout into the phone. "Where are you? What is going on? What was the phone message all about? Sharon, come here! It's your daughter."

Uncle Darren had never been Sierra's favorite.

Sierra's mom spoke into the phone. Her voice sounded calm in a forced way that told Sierra her mother was stressed. If Mom were home now, she would put on her jogging clothes and run until she was good and sweaty. "Are you okay, Sierra?"

"I'm fine. It's Granna Mae. This morning Dr. Utley called and said the test results showed she needed to have her gallbladder out immediately. He did the operation at eleven this morning."

Mom listened calmly as Sierra gave the details. Sierra could hear Uncle Darren breathing heavily, listening in on the extension. That bugged her. As soon as she finished, Uncle Darren said, "We've been trying to reach you all afternoon. Do you know what you've put your mother through?"

"It's okay," Mom said quickly. "How is she?"

"She was still sleeping when I left. I'm going back as soon as I eat something. Mom, do you know if there's any money around here? I had to raid your dryer tips to find enough change to call you."

Mom directed Sierra to an envelope taped to the inside of one of her desk drawers in the study and told her to take as much as she needed. Sierra pulled out twenty dollars.

"I'll see what I can do about coming home tomorrow," Mom said.

"Oh, great," Darren muttered and hung up his extension.

Mom was quiet for a minute before saying, "Things are a little rough here. Do you think you'll be okay by yourself for the night?"

"I'm going back to the hospital. I want to stay with Granna Mae all night."

There was another pause before Mom said, "You're a mother's dream, Sierra. Do you know that? Call me if anything at all goes wrong, okay? Even if it's the middle of the night. If I don't hear from you, I'll call the hospital early tomorrow morning."

"Okay. That'll be fine. I'm sure she's going to be all right," Sierra said.

"That's what I'll be praying," Mom said.

# five

SIERRA SPENT THE NIGHT curled up in the corner chair of Granna Mae's hospital room. Sometime around three-thirty in the morning, Granna Mae woke up. She moaned terribly and sounded as if she might be crying.

Tumbling out of her chair, Sierra went to her grandmother's bedside and quickly pressed the call button for the nurse. "It's okay, Granna Mae. The nurse is coming. Do you want a drink of water?" Sierra reached for a cup at the bedside and offered Granna Mae the straw. But she didn't drink. She didn't open her eyes. She only groaned and tried to move.

"Where is that nurse?" Sierra muttered. "Are you uncomfortable? Can I help you move or something?"

The nurse entered the room. "Yes?"

"She's groaning." Sierra said, trying not to sound as frantic as she felt. "I don't know what to do."

"How are you doing there?" the nurse said, gently lifting Granna Mae's hand and taking her pulse. "Are you having some pain?"

Granna Mae only moaned louder.

"We can give you something for that." She checked the IV bag and said, more to herself than to Sierra or Granna Mae, "And we'll hang another bag of fluid for you."

"Does she know I'm here?" Sierra asked the nurse.

The nurse nodded. "She's just groggy. It's good that you're here. Keep talking to her. I'll be right back."

Sierra reached for Granna Mae's hand and held it gently. It felt cold and clammy. "How's my favorite lady?" Sierra asked brightly. Cheering up the elderly and the sick wasn't Sierra's thing. But Granna Mae was her favorite lady, and she would do anything for her—even act brave when she felt queasy.

Granna Mae settled back to sleep after the nurse took care of her, and Sierra returned to her blanket and her curled-up position in the chair. Sleep didn't return to Sierra's mind or body. During the chilled, hazy hours of the early morning, she thought and prayed and thought some more.

The phone jarred her from limbo-land sometime after seven o'clock. Sierra jumped to answer it.

"Hi, it's Mom. How are you doing?"

"I'm fine. Granna Mae had a pretty good night. She's still sleeping," Sierra whispered into the phone.

"No, I'm not, Lovey. Who is it?"

Sierra looked over at Granna Mae. Her eyes were puffy, but she was obviously awake. "It's Mom. Do you want to talk to her?"

"I suppose. Not much to say." Her voice sounded low and raspy.

Sierra held the phone next to her grandmother's ear.

"No, I'm fine," Granna Mae said, apparently in answer to Mom's question. "I don't think I can move, though. They have me all wired up here."

As Sierra watched, a cloud seemed to move over Granna Mae's face like the clouds Sierra had observed out the window yesterday afternoon. Dark gray streaks of confusion began to gather in Granna Mae's eyes. She looked up at Sierra and then at the phone.

"Tell them I don't want any!" Granna Mae snapped. She turned her head away from the phone and tried to inch her shoulder away.

"Mom?" Sierra quickly pulled the phone to her ear. "I think she's a little confused."

"I just don't want any," Granna Mae muttered. "If I wanted another dish towel, I would have told them."

"Mom?"

"It's okay, Sierra. You just stay calm and steady. It'll be all right. Listen, I'm at—"

Sierra dropped the phone and reached for Granna Mae's hand. She had started to tug at the IV tubes, trying to pull them out. "You need to leave that there," Sierra said firmly. "You can't take this one out yet." She wrapped one hand around Granna Mae's wrist so she couldn't pull out the tube and hunted with the other hand until she found the call button for the nurse. From the dangling phone, she could hear her mom calling to her. "There you go." Sierra patted Granna Mae's hand and gently pushed it away from the IV. "You're okay."

"But I don't want it!" Granna Mae squawked. "They should have asked me!" Then she started to cry like a little girl with all the fight drained out of her.

The nurse stepped in. It was a nurse Sierra hadn't met yet. "Hi," Sierra greeted her nervously. "She's trying to take out the IV."

"Naughty, naughty," the nurse said, half teasing and half sounding as if she were scolding a toddler.

It made Sierra mad. "Hey," she said defensively. "She doesn't completely understand what's going on, okay?"

The nurse gave Sierra a startled look and reached for Granna Mae's free hand to take her pulse. Sierra cautiously let go of the hand with the IV and retrieved the phone. "Mom?"

"I'm right here, honey. Is everything all right?"

"I don't know. I think so. She just sort of clouded over and..."

"You did the right thing. Listen, I was trying to tell you that I'm calling from the airport."

"In Phoenix?"

"No, I'm in Portland. I took the first flight out this morning. Do you want me to grab a cab to the hospital?"

Sierra hesitated. She knew it would only take half an hour to drive to the airport and back to the hospital. "No, I think she'll be okay. I'll come pick you up." Sierra kept a keen eye fixed on Granna Mae and on the nurse. "I'll meet you out in front of baggage claim."

She hung up and watched the nurse as she entered some data on the wall computer where all notes and medications were logged. Granna Mae appeared to have slipped back into a restless sleep.

"I'll be right back," Sierra said to the nurse. "Please keep an eye on her."

"That's what I get paid big bucks for," the nurse said in a snippy tone.

Sierra dashed out of the room and wished she had told Mom to take a cab after all.

Easing the little Volkswagen Rabbit out of the hospital parking lot and scooting down the freeway toward the airport went smoothly. But the tricky part was making sure she took the right exit. Sierra had gotten lost more than once on the freeways around Portland, and this morning she didn't have any time to spare. She felt so responsible for Granna Mae.

The sign for the Portland airport loomed ahead of her, and she pulled into the turn lane with no problem. She found Mom in front of the baggage claim and hopped out to give her a hug.

Sierra felt like crying the moment Mom's arms encompassed her. But she refused to give in. She had been too strong this long, so she should be strong for Mom too.

Mom chucked her luggage into the back of the car, and Sierra slipped into the passenger seat. She let out a sigh of relief as they exited the busy terminal area. In more than one way, Mom was now in the driver's seat.

"How are you doing?" Mom asked, shooting a sideways glance a Sierra. Before she could answer, Mom added, "I wish we could contact your father. Did the doctor say how long she would be in the hospital? Has she eaten anything yet?"

"Fine, I don't think so, and no," Sierra said, using her brother Wesley's approach of answering Mom's string of questions. Sierra hoped the technique would lighten the situation.

Mom smiled. "I don't even remember my questions. I've been so concerned for you both. Let me start over. Are you okay?"

"Sure. I'm fine."

"I'm proud of you, Sierra."

"I didn't do anything. Actually, Mom, I almost blew it." Sierra told her about not believing Granna Mae at first when the doctor called.

Mom shook her head. "I'm glad you had the sense to stay home. I don't know if I would have. Do you want me to take you home so you can sleep?"

"No, I'd like to go back to the hospital with you." Sierra glanced out the window as they entered the freeway. That's when she remembered her job interview at ZuZu's Petals that morning at nine. "Actually, maybe I better go home so I can shower before my interview. I'm feeling a little bit crumpled."

"You'll have to walk to your interview then," Mom said.

"That's fine. It's only a few blocks."

At five minutes to nine, Sierra felt like her "few blocks" had turned into a few miles. She hoofed it a little bit faster, grabbed a handful of her wild, curly blond hair, and flipped it up and down. It was still wet underneath. She had on a gauze skirt that hung a few inches below her knees and her favorite footwear, her dad's old cowboy boots. As unique and beat-up as they were, those boots were Sierra's good ol' buddies and her trademark. She wore a long-sleeved T-shirt covered by an embroidered vest.

A light drizzle followed her down Hawthorne as she trekked the final block to the flower shop. She passed a bakery, buzzing with locals waiting in line for hot, fresh

Saturday morning cinnamon rolls. The door opened, and a wonderful blast of cinnamon assaulted Sierra, beckoning her to join the others in line. She knew she didn't have the time if she was going to keep her nine o'clock appointment at ZuZu's Petals, three doors down.

In twelve long strides, she was there. Sierra breathed a quick prayer and turned the knob on the large wooden door. It was locked.

# six

SIERRA PEERED THROUGH the side window of the flower shop and gently tapped on the glass. The lights were off inside, and she didn't see anyone stirring in the back room.

*This is bizarre. I know the interview was for this morning. It's after nine. Why isn't anyone here?*

She looked around, thinking maybe the owner had gone out for a cup of coffee or one of those hot cinnamon rolls. Sierra reviewed the phone conversation she had had with the owner a week ago. She was sure the time had been set for this morning at nine.

Granna Mae was the one who initially had arranged for the interview. She loved flowers, and for years ZuZu's Petals had been "her" florist. More than once Sierra heard Granna Mae say, "If I had two dollars, I'd use one to buy bread and one to buy flowers. Bread may feed the body, but flowers feed the heart."

Granna Mae had called ZuZu's Petals last week to order flowers for one of Sierra's aunts back East who had just had a baby. Before her grandmother had hung up, she had handed Sierra the phone and said, "They'd like to hire you, Lovey." The appointment was set up in a few sentences, and now Sierra stood in front of the vacant shop wondering if the whole thing had been in her dreams.

An older man and woman walked by in the steady morning drizzle with cups of coffee in their hands and a white bag that probably held cinnamon rolls. "Good morning," they said in unison to Sierra.

She smiled and returned the greeting. Two women strode past her, caught up in lively conversation. A short man leading a huge black dog on a leash trotted right after them. Sierra felt like a hotel doorman, standing her post under the green canopy of the shop's front door. Her taste buds were shouting, "Get a cinnamon roll!" Her logic was droning out all the reasons she should stay put and wait for someone to show up. Her stomach was constricting with the thought she should have gone back to the hospital with Mom and rescheduled this interview. For a full twenty minutes she stood in place.

At last a white minivan pulled up in front of the shop and parallel-parked. The words "ZuZu's Petals" were painted in fancy pink script on the sliding side door.

"Are you Sierra?" The driver hopped out and sprinted to join Sierra under the protection of the awning. "I'm Charlotte. Sorry to keep you waiting." She unlocked the door and flipped over the closed sign. "We had two huge weddings to deliver this morning. Come on in. Would you like some coffee?

"No thanks."

"So, you're Mae's granddaughter. She's a favorite of mine. How is she?" The energetic owner had very short black hair and snappy dark eyes to match. In her right ear she had at least six silver earrings. Sierra hadn't decided yet if she liked her or not.

"Well, actually, she's in the hospital. She had her gall-bladder removed yesterday."

Charlotte stopped in her tracks and looked at Sierra, horrified. "She's okay, isn't she? I had no idea! Is she at St. Mary's?"

"Yes. She seems to be doing all right."

"Are you going to see her today? I'll send some flowers with you. I got some gorgeous daffodils in yesterday. I'm so sorry to hear she's in the hospital!" While Charlotte rapidly gave her condolences, she poured herself a cup of coffee behind the counter and opened a small refrigerator with her foot. In one motion she grabbed a carton of French vanilla-flavored coffee creamer, poured it into her cup, returned the carton to the refrigerator, and closed the door again with her foot. "Sure you don't want some coffee?"

"No thanks."

"I live on this stuff!" Charlotte whirled around and flipped a switch that turned on all the lights in the charming shop. Sierra wondered how much of Charlotte's vivaciousness came naturally and how much was caffeine-induced.

"Okay," Charlotte said, boosting herself onto a stool behind the cash register and taking a sip from her ceramic mug. "The pay is minimum wage, the hours are Saturday and Sunday, eight to five, and you need to use your own car, but we'll reimburse you for gas and mileage. Do you want the job?"

Sierra stood there, stunned. *That was my interview?* "I'll work Saturday all day, but I can't work Sunday, and I can't guarantee I'll always have a car. I thought you were looking for someone to work here at the shop, not run deliveries for you."

"Nope. I need a gofer. That's why I was out this morning; my two associates are still out. The three of us need to run the shop. We're looking for someone to do the deliveries. And Sunday is part of the package deal. I'm not interested in hiring you if you can't work both Saturday and Sunday."

"Then I guess this won't work out," Sierra said just as directly as Charlotte was being with her. "Thanks anyway. I hope you find someone."

She turned to go, and Charlotte called out, "Wait!" She hopped off her stool and hurried into the back of the shop. A moment later she returned with a huge bunch of bright yellow daffodils mixed with long-stemmed blue irises all wrapped in green paper with a pink bow. "For Mae. Tell her we all send our best."

Sierra received the bundle of flowers. The only way to carry them was like a beauty queen, cradled in her arms. "Thanks. She'll really appreciate these."

"I know," Charlotte said, reaching for her coffee mug. "See you around, Sierra."

Stepping out onto the wet sidewalk, Sierra wished she had an umbrella. The light rain was steady now, and although she didn't mind getting a little wet, she felt the flowers should be protected. It was an unusually large bouquet, beautiful, but a little overpowering. The awkwardness of toting such a bundle made Sierra change her mind about waiting in line at the bakery for a cinnamon roll. It was all she could do to carry the flowers. Anything else in her arms would surely meet with disaster, especially in the rain. She passed the bakery, promising her taste buds she would be back one day soon.

The rain was coming down hard now. Sierra wished she had worn a jacket. Her T-shirt clung to her arms, and her skirt stuck to the back of her legs. She could feel her hair drooping down her back and adhering to the sides of her face. A chill swept through her as she walked even faster, trying to protect the innocent bouquet from being soaked. She felt miserable.

All her emotions seemed to have collected into one big bundle, and Sierra felt fifty pounds heavier carrying them home with her in the rain. She hadn't gotten the job. She still had no money, no social life, no hint at things getting better in the near future, and her dear Granna Mae was in the hospital and slowly loosing her mind. The calm, steady days of her family's predictable life in Pineville were over. Community picnics, horses, and fields of wildflowers were exchanged for crowded neighborhoods with barking dogs, pollution-belching busses, and flower shops run by quirky people amped on caffeine. Sierra felt terribly alone.

Then, because she thought it would help her feel better, Sierra let herself cry. Big, fat tears rolled down her cheeks, feeling hot in contrast to the chilling raindrops that joined them. She tilted her face to the sky and let the cool rain wash over her. Sierra felt little sieges of sobs tremble inside her chest. She didn't care who saw her or what the people who passed her on the sidewalk thought. A few whimpers escaped her lips. She didn't try to stop them. Nothing in her life seemed to be going the way she thought it should.

The rain poured over her. She felt as if she had been

doused with a bucket of water. Only five more blocks to go, and she would be home where she could crawl into bed. Or a hot bath.

Sierra came to a stoplight and had to wait before she could cross the street. Out of the corner of her eye, she noticed a black Jeep that had come to a stop at the red light only a few feet from her. Even though the windows were rolled up, she could hear the beat of the music blasting from the Jeep radio. She also heard laughter. Male laughter. Deep and rowdy laughter. She couldn't help but wonder if they were laughing at her. And she couldn't blame them if they were. She probably would be laughing at the sight of her if she were the one in the Jeep. Sierra knew she must look ridiculous, like a runner-up in the Miss Drowned Rat Beauty Contest.

The sound of their laughter only added to the hurt already coursing through her. It made her mad. Sierra blinked away her tears and, with a jerk of her head, glared at the insensitive males inside the Jeep. The guy in the passenger seat was looking right at her. Their eyes met. Sierra stopped breathing. The grimace on her face vanished. And the guy in the passenger seat stopped laughing.

It was Paul.

The light changed, and the Jeep jerked forward as Paul turned his head to get one last look at Sierra. Then he was gone.

She put one foot in front of the other, sloshing into a puddle as she crossed the street. Everything inside and outside had gone numb.

*It was Paul. He saw me. He was laughing at me.*

Sierra barely remembered the final blocks home. Her

mind had been transported back to the phone booth at Heathrow Airport in London where she had met Paul. He had asked to borrow some change for his phone call, and somehow, something inside of Sierra and Paul had connected. They spoke later on the plane and found they had mutual friends. It was all very promising. Then he found out how old she was. He was a big college student, and she was only a junior in high school. His interest in her seemed to evaporate. But then he wrote her a letter, and she answered it. That was several weeks ago, and he hadn't written back. Now, after this morning's curbside encounter, she was sure he never would. It was one more thing to cry about. And cry she did.

# seven

SIERRA STRETCHED OUT her legs in the warm water of the antique cast-iron tub. She hadn't soaked in the claw-foot tub since she was a little girl visiting Granna Mae during summer vacation. After her family had moved to the old Victorian house, she had taken showers in the upstairs remodeled bathroom. Now she sank deeper into the soothing water.

The minute she had reached home, she had called the hospital. Mom said Granna Mae was resting and doing fine. Then Mom suggested Sierra get some sleep to make up for the restless night she had spent in the hospital room chair. After lunch, they would go back to the hospital together.

The leisure time was just what Sierra needed. A nice hot bath, a change into old sweats, and a cup of jasmine tea lifted her emotions out of the bog that had entrapped them just an hour earlier.

Just as Sierra was pouring her second cup of tea, the phone rang. "Hello," she said. A far-off part of her heart hoped it would be Paul.

"Hey Sierra! Whatcha' doin?" the female voice asked.

"Not much. Who's this?" It drove Sierra crazy when people started to talk before she knew who they were.

"You mean you've forgotten us already?" the voice teased.

"Hi, Sierra," another female voiced chimed in. "It's Christy. I'm sure you can guess the other mystery caller."

"Katie? Christy! Hi! How are you guys?"

"We're peachy," Katie said. "How about you?"

"That's her new word," Christy interjected. "I guarantee you'll get sick of it real fast."

Sierra pulled the tea bag out of the mug and headed to the office with the phone balanced on her shoulder. She curled up in her favorite chair and placed the hot tea on a coaster on the end table. "I'm so glad you guys called! It seems like years since we were in England."

"I know," Katie agreed.

"But it's only been a few weeks," Christy pointed out. "What's happening with you?"

"Don't ask!" Sierra warned, sipping her tea. "It's been a not-so-happy couple of weeks topped off by a couple of disastrous days. You guys tell me about you first. Maybe it will cheer me up."

"Well, we're baking cookies right now," Christy said. "At least we're trying to—if Katie will stay out of the chocolate chips.

"I only had a handful," Katie responded. "Besides, if we add raisins, no one will know the difference."

"Todd will," Christy said.

"Is Todd there too?" Sierra asked.

"No, he's at his dad's in Newport. We're going there

this afternoon because Tracy is having a party at her house tonight. We really wish you were going to be at the party, Sierra."

"Don't taunt me like that. You know I would love to be. I would give anything to see you guys again!"

"So come on down," Katie said in her best game show voice.

"Oh, right. There is this little matter of a thousand or so miles that separate us."

"Ever hear of airplanes?" Katie asked. "Marvel of the modern world. You could be here in a few hours."

"Ever hear of money?" Sierra said. "As in, I don't have any?"

"Then get some," Katie said.

"I tried." Sierra tucked her feet underneath her to keep them warm. "I had the world's fastest job interview this morning, and I didn't get the job. It was for a flower shop. They wanted me to work all day on Sundays and use my own car for flower deliveries."

"Did you tell them you couldn't work Sundays because you go to church?" Christy asked.

"No. She didn't even ask why. I just told her I couldn't work on Sundays."

"I used to work at a pet store," Christy said. "My boss understood when I told him I couldn't work Sundays because I went to church. Maybe you could try explaining it to her."

"It doesn't matter," Sierra said. "I don't have a car. My mom and I share an old beater that's not so dependable. I know I couldn't take it for the whole day even if they just hired me for Saturdays. It wouldn't work out."

"That's too bad," Christy said. "Are you going to apply anywhere else?"

"There are plenty of shops and fast-food restaurants around where we live. I'm sure I'll find something."

"When you do," Katie advised, "be sure to tell them you can't work during Easter vacation because you're coming down here to spend the week with us."

"If I get some money."

"You have to. It's mandatory," Katie said.

Sierra heard a low munching sound on the phone.

"Katie, are you eating those chocolate chips again?"

"Just a few."

"Katie," Christy said, "we're going to have to buy some more. I never thought I'd say this, but maybe that health food kick you were on wasn't so bad. At least every bit of chocolate didn't disappear when you were around."

Sierra laughed. "I'm so jealous of the two of you."

"Jealousy is not a good thing," Katie said.

"You know what I mean. You've been best friends for all these years. Since we moved here, I haven't found anybody I could even ask to come over and make cookies."

"You'll find someone soon," Christy said.

"Oh yeah? How?"

"Advertise," Katie said with a crunch.

"What?"

"Put a classified ad in the school newspaper."

Sierra laughed. "What would I write? 'Wanted: Kindred Spirit'?"

"That would work," Katie said with another obvious munch. "What could it hurt?"

"Where do you come up with these ideas, Katie?" Christy asked. "And stop eating those chocolate chips!"

"Didn't you know that chocolate is the best brain food on planet earth? It heightens one's awareness of the obvious. And it's obvious Sierra needs a soul mate, and I still think advertising is the way to go."

"I'll be praying God brings a wonderful, peculiar treasure right to your door," Christy said.

"She's not ordering a pizza," Katie pointed out. "Take my advice, Sierra. Advertise. It's the best way. Very peachy. But speaking of peculiar treasures, and peachy peculiar treasures, what happened with Paul?"

"Funny you should mention him," Sierra said.

"Who's Paul?" Christy asked.

Katie explained in one long breath. "Remember that guy I told you about that Sierra met at the airport in London on the way home? Last month when I visited Doug at his God-Lover's Bible Study, it just so happened that Paul's brother was there and gave me a letter from Paul to give to Sierra."

"You never told me any of this," Christy said.

"Of course I did!"

"No, you didn't. I would have remembered."

"I'm sure I told you, Christy. You seem to have a selective memory lately."

"And what's that supposed to mean?"

Sierra sipped her tea and listened to her friends rant with each other on their long-distance call to her.

"If it has to do with Todd, your memory is perfect. Anything else is up for grabs lately."

"Oh, that's real nice, Katie. Thank you very much. The point is, you never told me about Sierra meeting this guy...what's his name?"

"Paul," Sierra and Katie said in unison.

"And I saw him today," Sierra inserted quickly, before Christy and Katie had a chance to continue their friendly spat.

"How peachy! Tell us everything," Katie said.

Sierra recounted the drowned-rat-with-extra-large-bouquet scenario. There was complete silence on the other end except for the rustling sound of a bag of chocolate chips.

"Hello? Did I bore you to death with my story?"

"Of course not," Christy said. "It's just weird, your seeing him like that. What are you going to do?"

"Nothing. What can I do?"

"Maybe he'll call you to see if you're okay," Katie said. "That's what happens in the movies."

"No," Christy said, "in the movies he would have told his friend to stop the car, and he would have run back to you with an umbrella and walked you the rest of the way home, and you would have made him a pot of tea."

Sierra laughed. "I am drinking tea right now," she said. "Maybe my life is a low budget 'B' movie, and all I get is the tea. No hero. No umbrella."

"Yeah, well then my life is a class 'Z' movie," Katie said. "No hero. No umbrella. No tea. No plot—"

"Yours is more of a mystery," Christy interrupted cheerfully. "The ending will surprise all of us."

"And your life," Katie said to Christy, "is turning into a

rather predictable romance. Girl meets boy. Boy is a dork for four years. Girl blossoms into a gorgeous woman. Boy finds his brain. Girl turns into starry-eyed mush head."

Sierra laughed. "I take it things are still going great with you and Todd."

"Slightly," Katie answered for Christy. "You have to hurry down here, Sierra. I'm calling an emergency meeting of the Pals Only Club. Since you and I are the only remaining members, you are obligated to come. You do remember our club, don't you?"

"How could I forget?" Sierra said. "I do have to say I still qualify for membership. No guys are in my life—not even as pals." Then, because she was feeling rather perky, Sierra added, "Unless Paul was actually so taken with my ravishing appearance this morning that he's on his way over here as we speak, so he can sweep me off my feet."

"In your dreams!" Katie said. "I'd say you can check that loser off your list. Maybe your ad should be for a new member of Pals Only; we could even add some guys to our tiny band."

"Don't advertise," Christy advised. "Just start praying. I am going to pray that you'll meet some fun people up there."

"Then start to pray that I find a job. Easter vacation is only three weeks away."

"I will," Christy promised.

Just then the front door opened, and Sierra jumped. She wasn't expecting Mom until this afternoon. The antique clock on top of the oak desk read 10:57. Sierra listened to the footsteps on the wood floor in the entryway.

She wished she had locked the front door. Cupping her hand over the phone, she said, "You guys, somebody is in the house."

"Are you the only one home?" Christy asked.

"Yes," Sierra whispered back, feeling her heart pound faster as the footsteps headed toward the kitchen. They sounded heavy, like a man's. "Don't hang up. Stay on the line. If you hear me scream, call the Portland police immediately."

# eight

SIERRA HELD HER BREATH. In the phone receiver she could hear Katie slowly smacking her lips, and Christy whispering, "Katie, shhh!" With her other ear, Sierra listened as the footsteps clomped through the kitchen and seemed to come closer.

"He's coming into the study!" Sierra whispered.

"What's happening?" Katie whispered. "Who is it?"

A figure suddenly appeared in the doorway. "What are you doing here?" Sierra demanded.

Tawni marched in, her heavy snow boots thumping across the polished wood floor. "What are you doing here?" she asked. "Where's the car? I didn't think anyone was home, and I couldn't figure out why the front door was unlocked."

"Who is it?" Katie shouted into the phone.

"It's my sister," Sierra said. Then turning to Tawni she said, "Mom has the car. She's at St. Mary's with Granna Mae. She had her gallbladder out yesterday."

"Who?" Tawni squawked. "Who had her gallbladder out? Mom or Granna Mae?"

"Yeah," Katie chimed in, "you didn't tell us this!"

"Granna Mae. Mom came home this morning to be with her. She's doing okay."

"Who?" Katie asked. "Your mom or grandma?"

"Both," Sierra said. "Can I call you guys later?"

"We'll be down at Tracy's tonight. You can call there," Christy suggested. "Or we'll try you again in a week or so to see how things are working out for you to come down at Easter."

"Okay, great. 'Bye, you guys. Say hi to Doug and Tracy and Todd for me!"

"We will. 'Bye, Sierra."

She hung up and faced Tawni, who had her hands on her hips. "What is going on?" Tawni demanded. Sierra repeated the information, and Tawni said, "I'm going to the hospital."

"I'll go with you," Sierra said, hopping up. "Let me put on some shoes."

"I'm going to change, and then we'll go," Tawni said, leading the way up the stairs in her ski apparel.

"What happened with your ski trip?" Sierra asked. "I thought you were staying until Sunday."

Tawni opened their bedroom door and shouted, "Sierra!"

"What? I'm standing right here!"

"The room looks as if it hasn't been touched since I left on Thursday!"

"It hasn't, Tawni. I was slightly busy. What happened with your ski trip?"

"Nothing!" Tawni snapped. "I decided to come home early, that's all. It looks like a good thing I did. How did you manage to get Granna Mae to the hospital?"

"I drove her."

"You ditched school?"

"I *missed* school." Sierra pulled on some warm socks and slipped her feet into a pair of tennis shoes. "It was an emergency."

Tawni didn't have a real cheerful personality, and she often got mad at Sierra, but today she seemed more irritable than usual. Sierra chose not to push her sister for an explanation as to why she had come home early.

Tawni changed her clothes in silence, neatly hanging up her ski jacket and arranging her boots in the corner of her closet. They walked downstairs with Tawni in the lead. Sierra grabbed her backpack, which was still wet from her walk this morning, and was about to lock the front door behind her when she remembered the flowers in the kitchen sink.

"Wait. I need to grab some flowers." She hurried into the kitchen, searching for a vase large enough for the huge bunch and ending up grabbing a plastic water pitcher. In her hunt through the cupboard, something familiar caught Sierra's eye. She reached for it carefully, wrapped it in a dish towel, and stuffed it in her backpack.

Tawni had her car running and was checking her makeup in the pull-down mirror on the visor. Sierra had to brush a white paper bag off the front seat so she could sit down. A slight scent of cinnamon sugar hovered in the car. As soon as she had her seat belt on and the flowers balanced on her lap, she poked at the white bag. It was empty.

"What was in there?"

"In where?"

"The white bag. Was it a cinnamon roll from Mama Bear's?"

"Yes. What about it?" Tawni's voice still had that irritable edge to it.

"Nothing. I've been craving one of those rolls, that's all." Sierra swallowed the saliva that had filled her mouth. If she had been with anyone else, she probably would have had no qualms about slashing open the bag and licking up the crumbs. Sierra thought, *You hang on, tummy. I promise you a cinnamon roll from Mama Bear's will visit you very soon.*

Sierra led Tawni to the hospital room, where they found Granna Mae asleep in the bed and Mom dozing in the chair.

"I'll fix these," Sierra whispered, motioning with the pitcher and flowers as she stepped into the small bathroom. Mom stirred and greeted Tawni with surprise. They whispered as Sierra filled the pitcher with water. She wished she could hear what they were saying. Tawni would tell Mom what the problem was with the ski trip before she would tell Sierra.

"Lovey?" Granna Mae called out, her voice cracked.

"I'm right here," Sierra said, going to her bedside with the pitcher of flowers. "Charlotte at the flower shop sent these for you. Aren't they beautiful?"

"Daffies," Granna Mae said with a hint of delight. "My favorite."

"I'll put them right over here," Sierra said. "Mom and Tawni are here too."

The two women came over to her bedside, and Granna Mae lifted her free arm to grasp Tawni's hand. "Nee-Nee," Granna Mae said, receiving Tawni's kiss on her cheek.

Granna Mae had nicknames for all her grandchildren. Sierra just happened to be the one who was endowed with the most "normal" sounding one. Tawni had actually acquired hers compliments of Sierra. When Sierra couldn't pronounce "Tawni" as a toddler, she called her big sister "Nee-Nee," and it had stuck for Granna Mae. Sierra's two younger brothers had both called Sierra "Sissy," but that didn't stick. Granna Mae had christened Sierra her "little lovey" from day one.

"How are you feeling?" Tawni asked.

"Okay, but not quite wonderful." Granna Mae tried to prop herself up. Tawni adjusted the pillows for her.

"You've been through a lot, Granna Mae. You don't have to feel wonderful for a least another two days." Tawni smiled and smoothed back Granna Mae's fluffy white hair. "I brought some lotion. Would you like me to rub your feet?"

"Oh, would you, Nee-Nee? They feel so cold. And could you see about possibly getting me a warm washcloth for my face?"

"I'll get it," Sierra volunteered, slipping back into the bathroom.

"Think you can eat a bit more of your lunch here?" Mom asked.

The three women went to work, tending their favorite patient. And Granna Mae ate it up. Sierra felt grateful for this window of time when Granna Mae was coherent. She wondered how long it would last.

"What day is this?" Granna Mae asked.

"Saturday," Mom said.

"Aren't you supposed to be at Mount Bachelor, Nee-Nee?"

"I came home early," Tawni said. "It didn't turn out to be the way I thought it would."

"Did you ski at all?" Mom asked.

"Yesterday I skied all day. The snow was a little icy and it was too foggy for me at the top. But it was a good day."

"So the night was a problem," Granna Mae surmised, her eyes clear and her mind obviously sharp.

Tawni looked at Mom and back at Granna Mae. She held the bottle of lotion in her hand. Before she poured any, she said, "I guess you could say that. I need to find some friends who have the same idea I do of what constitutes a fun time."

Sierra wondered if she should bring up the subject of where they went to church. She and Tawni had talked about it with their parents before, but Mom and Dad were reluctant to approach the topic with Granna Mae. The church they all attended was Granna Mae's. It was a good church, small, traditional, and full of wonderful, sweet, elderly people with a few young families thrown in. No teenagers attended, and no youth programs or even Sunday school existed for them.

The family discussions had always come to the same conclusion: "We go to church as a family to worship, not fulfill our personal social needs." Yet here they were, with Sierra and Tawni both facing the same dilemma of unmet social needs. They had tried to convince their parents that when you're sixteen and eighteen years old, spiritual needs and social needs are closely related.

"We need to find a church that has a strong youth group and college group," Sierra said as she smoothed the warm washcloth across Granna Mae's forehead. The minute she said it, she saw Mom give her a facial signal that Sierra shouldn't have spoken.

"Don't let me stop you," Granna Mae said with her eyes closed, awaiting another swipe from the washcloth.

Sierra held the cloth over Granna Mae's eyes just a moment longer than needed so she could catch Mom's expression. Tawni was looking at Mom expectantly too. Mom looked surprised. She gave her shoulders a slight shrug and nodded.

"We'll still come with you to your church sometimes, Granna Mae," Sierra said, boldly plunging forward. "You don't mind though, do you, if our family finds another church that sort of meets all our needs? And maybe you can visit our new church with us sometimes."

"That would be fine with me, Lovey."

Sierra ran one more wipe of the cloth over the eyes and flashed a wry smile, expecting looks of admiration from her mom and sister. She had just accomplished something her dad wouldn't even try—extracting Grandma's blessing to try another church.

Mom and Tawni beamed their appreciation.

Patting Granna Mae's soft face dry with a second washcloth, Sierra said, "I brought something else for you." She reached in her backpack for the wadded-up dish towel and carefully unwrapped a china cup and saucer and held them for Granna Mae to see. She always drank from a china cup at home. Juice, coffee, or water, whatever the liquid, a cup was always her choice. But coffee was her favorite beverage. "Shall I ring the maid to bring you some hot coffee?"

# nine

"I THINK WE SHOULD try the one in Vancouver," Tawni said. She was stretched out comfortably on her bed that night while Sierra was making an honest attempt to pick up her clothes. Mom sat on the corner of Sierra's unmade bed.

"It's so far away," Mom said. "That's been the benefit of Granna Mae's church. It's only three blocks from here. Besides, it seems odd to go to a church in another state."

"But Washington is only across the river. It would take no more than fifteen minutes to drive there. And I've heard that this church in Vancouver has the best college group around," Tawni said.

"I've heard something at school about a church out in Gresham that's pretty good," Sierra added.

"Gresham is at least a twenty-minute drive in the opposite direction," Mom protested.

"See? We're better off going to Vancouver. I already called. The service is at ten tomorrow morning." Tawni put on her ridiculous-looking glasses she wore only to read and opened up her paperback book.

"I wish your father was home so we could all discuss this. Maybe we should go to Granna Mae's church one last time tomorrow morning, and then next week we can start to visit other churches."

"Why?" Sierra asked.

"What would be the point of that?" Tawni chimed in. "Granna Mae won't be there. This is the best time to make the change."

Mom let out a sigh and held up her hands in surrender. "I'm too tired to argue. You two make the decision. I'll go wherever you choose. Right now I'm going to bed. Has anyone checked the answering machine?"

"Nope."

"I'm concerned about Gayle. She wasn't doing too well when I left, and I'm afraid Darren isn't much help."

"Why is he so uptight all the time?" Sierra asked. "I thought he was going to bite my head off on the phone yesterday."

Mom sighed again. She hesitated before saying, "Their marriage is in a difficult place right now. He was laid off last month, and the insurance might not cover Gayle's hospitalization. You know what a handful the twins are. It's rough for them."

"Do you wish you would have stayed with them?" Sierra asked. "We could have taken care of Granna Mae."

Mom shook her head. "Darren's sister was coming in this evening. She'll do a better job than I did with Darren and the twins. If you two have never thought about thanking God for the father He gave you..."

"You mean instead of someone like Darren?" Sierra asked.

"I'm just saying, be thankful for the daddy you got. I sometimes forget what a wonderful husband and father Howard is." Mom rose to leave and then stopped. "You know what? Let's pray together before I go to bed. Just like when you two were little."

Sierra followed Mom over to Tawni's bed, where the three women sat cross-legged in a circle and joined hands. They prayed for Granna Mae, for Dad and the boys, and for Aunt Gayle and Uncle Darren. Mom choked up as she was praying for Gayle and Darren, and Sierra felt a knot tighten in the pit of her stomach as Mom asked God to rescue their marriage and protect the twins.

Then Mom did something very tender. She prayed for Tawni's and Sierra's future husbands. She prayed that they surrender their lives to the Lord, if they hadn't already, and that they would be set apart as godly men who would one day love Tawni and Sierra and their children. As Mom prayed, she wept.

Sierra felt the tears well up in her own eyes as she silently agreed with her mother's prayer. She knew her mother had prayed this for her many times, just as Granna Mae had once prayed for the spouses of her children. Sierra's mom had been the answer to Granna Mae's long years of prayers for Howard. All her life Sierra's parents and Granna Mae had prayed for Sierra and for her future husband. She had become used to it.

Until tonight. Tonight her mother's prayers sounded fresh and powerful in Sierra's ears. In her heart, she realized she was holding hands with a mighty warrior. Supernatural events were being released on her behalf because of her mother's prayers to almighty God.

Mom closed her prayer with "In the name of Jesus, may it be so."

Sierra looked up through her teary eyes. "May it be so," she repeated.

"Amen," Tawni echoed.

"I love you two." Mom gave them each a hug and kiss on the cheek.

"I love you too, Mom." Sierra brushed a kiss across Mom's cheek. "And I even love you," she said to Tawni with a smile and a lightening of her serious tone. Tawni accepted Sierra's peck on the cheek but didn't respond in kind.

"Sleep well," Mom said with a yawn. "Wake me if I'm not up by nine."

"We're going to Vancouver then?" Tawni asked.

"Fine with me," Sierra said.

"Sure." Mom yawned again and stumbled out the door.

Sierra shoved her stuff off the bed and crawled under her covers. She could feel Tawni's critical glare. "What?" she asked without looking at her sister.

"Aren't you going to finish picking up your junk?"

"Tomorrow. I'll do it tomorrow," Sierra said in her best Scarlett O'Hara voice.

"Tomorrow" turned into several tomorrows. Finally, on Tuesday Sierra attacked the mound of clothes again. This time she was determined to clean up everything. Or at least Tawni was determined that Sierra change the landscape of their room.

Granna Mae was improving nicely, and the doctor said she could go home Saturday if all went well the rest of the week. She slept most of the time, but her memory had been good when she was awake.

Sierra sorted out the dirty clothes from the clean. Then she scooped up the dirty clothes and headed for the washing machine in the basement. She had just put her first load in when she heard her dad's voice upstairs. Dad had spent most of his free time at the hospital since he had returned from camping. Gavin and Dillon had quickly filled the house with lots of noise again. Everything seemed back to normal.

But not quite. While the crisis had passed for Granna Mae, Sierra's problems remained unsolved. She still didn't have a job. She still didn't have a social life. And she desperately wanted to go to Southern California during Easter vacation. And now that Dad had settled back into a routine, it was time to ask.

Sierra took the basement steps two at a time. She found her father in the kitchen, washing off an apple before taking a big chomp out of it.

"Oh, Daddy, my wonderful Daddy-o!" Sierra began, looping her arm around his shoulders.

"How much is it going to cost me?" Dad asked without blinking.

Sierra drew back her arm. "What makes you think I'm going to ask for money?"

"You are, aren't you?"

"Well, not exactly."

"But whatever it is you're going to ask, it's going to cost money, right?"

Sierra circled her arm around him again and playfully rested her head on his shoulder. "How did you ever get to be so wise and wonderful, oh, Daddy, my wonderful Daddy-o?"

He looked down at her, and she batted her eyelashes for emphasis. Howard Jensen broke out laughing and nearly choked on his bite of apple. "Looks like this is serious," he said, still laughing. "Better step into my office."

"Dad!" Gavin called from the backyard in his high-pitched, six-year-old voice. "Can you come out and help us?"

"What do you need, son?"

"The pulley on the tree house rope broke."

"I'll be out in about..." Dad looked at Sierra. "What do you think?" he asked her. "Twenty minutes? Half an hour? Three hours?"

"Twenty minutes," Sierra said. "It's a simple request, really,"

"I'll be out in twenty minutes," Dad called back. "Don't try to fix it without me, okay, guys?"

"We won't," Dillon, the ever-clever eight-year-old, called back.

"Yeah, right," Dad muttered under his breath. He took another bite of his apple. "Right this way," he said, leading Sierra into the office.

This was Dad's favorite room in the house, and it was becoming Sierra's favorite hideaway too. One whole wall was a floor-to-ceiling bookshelf. Several rows were stacked with old books from Granna Mae's lifelong collection. Many were Danish, her original language. The books had an intriguing, musty smell that made the room feel important and familiar at the same time. It was a room full of silent friends who stood ready to give, yet who demanded nothing in return except perhaps an occasional dusting.

Sierra's favorite chair was nestled in the corner next to

the French doors that opened to the back patio. When the sun shone in, it hit that chair just right. Any cat would love to claim the seat as its own private tanning booth. No sun was beaming through the windows today, but that didn't stop Sierra from settling into the chair and stretching out her legs so her feet rested on the matching stuffed footstool.

Dad took a seat in the revolving oak captain's chair by the rolltop desk and leaned back. "Okay, shoot," he said, chomping into his afternoon snack.

"I want to go see the friends I met in England. They've invited me for Easter vacation. I'd fly down to San Diego or Orange County airport, and I'll pay for the whole thing myself. It's just that I don't have any money. Zilch."

"Oh," Dad said calmly, "is that all?"

"I tried to get a job at the flower shop, but they wanted me to work Sundays and use my own car. I haven't tried anywhere else, but I want to get a job around here so I can walk and not have to depend on the car."

"Sounds wise," Dad said.

"So, may I go?"

"I'll talk with your mother about it. I'm sure it'll be fine for you to go for the week, but you're right. You'll need to pay for the airfare. The recent quick trip to Phoenix for your mom wasn't exactly in the budget. I'll tell you what. Why don't you work on finding a job, and I'll work on finding the lowest airfare. Does it matter which airport? Your friends are going to pick you up, aren't they?"

"Of course. I don't think it matters. They live kind of in between both airports."

"Okay," Dad said. "I'll check out the airfares."

Sierra flashed a big smile. "Thank you, my wonderful Daddy-o."

"Don't get too confident now, Sierra. It's still contingent on your coming up with airfare."

"I know. But thanks for just being my dad."

"Any time." Dad opened the French doors and headed toward the tree house. "By the way," he called over his shoulder, "did you see the mail on the desk? There's a letter for you."

# ten

SIERRA SPRANG from her cozy chair and grabbed the stack of letters on top of the desk. Bills, bills, advertisement. Her hand stopped on a white envelope addressed to Sierra Jensen in bold black letters. She immediately recognized the handwriting. She had only received one other letter with that script, but she had read it at least fifty times. Maybe more. Right this minute, that letter with the matching handwriting was under her pillow. And today, its twin had come.

Cradling the letter in her hands, Sierra hurried upstairs to her room where she turned the envelope over and over before she opened it. *Did Paul write it before he saw me on Sunday or after? What if he's writing just to make fun of me?*

Unable to stand it another second, Sierra carefully opened the envelope and lifted out the one sheet of white writing paper. Only a few lines in Paul's distinctive handwriting, which was a combination of cursive and printing in bold, black letters, appeared on the page. It said:

*Dear Daffodil Queen,*

*I was wondering, and of course it's none of my business, but just out of curiosity, do you have pneumonia yet? And if you do, should I send flowers? Or will your lovely bouquet last you the duration of your convalescence?*

*Sincerely,*

*A Casual Observer*

Sierra read the letter four times, deciphering it differently each time. At first it was funny. Then it was sort of sweet. The third time it seemed pretty rude to her. By the fourth time reading, she was mad.

Marching over to her desk, Sierra found a piece of lined notebook paper and started to write before she had a chance to change her mind:

*For your information, Mr. Hotshot, my grandmother is in the hospital. I was the only one home with her Friday morning when we received the call that she needed emergency surgery. I stayed up with her all night in the hospital room. When you saw me, I was walking home from a job interview with daffodils that had been given to me to take my Granna Mae because those happen to be her favorite flower.*

*To answer your questions:*

*Yes, it's none of your business.*

*No, I don't have pneumonia.*

*No, I don't want any stupid flowers from you. I already told you the flowers were for my grandmother, who, by the way, is still in the hospital.*

*And, in case you're wondering, no, I didn't get the job.*

*Oh and don't go around signing things "sincerely" unless you really are.*

*Very Irritated,*

*Sierra*

Then, before she had a chance to change her mind, Sierra folded the paper, tucked it in an envelope, and fished around in the top drawer for a stamp. She looked back at the letter just long enough to obtain the necessary post office box number and then wadded it up and tossed it at the wicker trash can. She missed. The letter landed near a stack of school papers.

Sierra galloped down the stairs and called out to her dad in the backyard. "I'm going to mail a letter, Dad."

"Hang on, Sierra," he called back from his workshop. It was an old playhouse he had turned into a shop. Inside it were all his power tools, but the outside looked as if Hansel and Gretel might stop by at any moment. Dad opened the Dutch door, wiping his hand on a towel. He reached in his pocket and pulled out some money. "Can you swing by Mama Bear's and pick up a box of cinnamon rolls? I told Granna Mae I'd bring her breakfast tomorrow morning."

"You don't know how much I'd love to do that for you, Dad." Sierra said. "And I don't need any money."

"I thought you were broke. Zilch."

"Mom told me to take some out of the desk when she was gone. I've been using it for lunch money and gas money. I have enough left for a box of cinnamon rolls."

Dad grinned and said, "I guess I'll have to find another hiding place for my loot."

"Come on, Dad," Gavin called from the tree house.

"Do you want to take my car?" Dad asked.

"No, I need the exercise. I'll be right back." Sierra took off with long strides, clutching the letter in her hand the four blocks to the mailbox. It was a good thing the box wasn't further away or the sweat on her palms might have soaked through the envelope. With a yank of the handle, she shoved the letter into the dark abyss.

Instantly she regretted it. Sierra stood there, glancing around to see if anyone was watching her. She wondered if she could retrieve the letter. It soon became obvious that she couldn't. What was done was done.

She realized she needed the consolation of a cinnamon roll from Mama Bear's. She covered the next three or so blocks at near-jogging pace. The moment she entered the shop, she felt relieved, as if she had run a race against her hurt and anger and had beat them.

The store was empty except for three people who were huddling over fragrant coffee in the middle of some sort of meeting at one of the side tables. The scent of cinnamon wasn't as strong as it had been on Saturday morning, but it was still there, permeating the room.

"Are you still open?" Sierra asked the round woman in the white ruffly apron who was wiping down the counter.

"Another five minutes," the rosy-cheeked woman said, glancing at the clock that broadcast the time as "5:55." It was a wooden clock in the shape of a brown bear. Its big round tummy was the clock's face.

"Good! I'm glad I made it," Sierra said. "I need a box of rolls."

The woman reached over to the rack behind her and grabbed a box. "Can I get you anything else?"

Whenever a waitress would ask that question, Sierra's brother Cody would answer, "Yeah, a couple of tickets to Maui. To go, please." Sierra smiled and answered, "A ticket to San Diego."

The woman looked a little confused for just a moment, but then she smiled. "Getting a little tired of the rain, are you? Anxious to see some sunshine?"

Sierra nodded. "Actually, I'm hoping to visit some friends down there during Easter vacation. All I need is the money to buy my airplane ticket. But first I need a job to earn the money to buy the ticket." Sierra realized she was pouring out her heart to a stranger and quickly said, "But for today, all I need is a box of your world-famous cinnamon rolls. I've been craving them for days."

The woman took the money Sierra held out to her and rang up the purchase on the cash register. "You're not going to eat this whole box by yourself, are you?"

"I'll try not to." Sierra smiled as the white-aproned Mama Bear tucked the box into a large, white paper bag. "I need to save at least one of these for my Granna Mae, who's waiting for it in the hospital."

"You don't mean Mae Jensen, do you?"

"Yes, she's my grandmother."

"Well, I'll be! And which one are you?"

"Sierra."

"And your parents are..."

"Howard and Sharon."

"No!" the sweet woman said, clasping her hands around her middle like an opera singer. "My brother went to school with Howard. I used to have such a crush on him! Tell him you saw Amelia. Amelia Kraus now, but I was Amelia

Jackson. And tell him to come in sometime."

"I know he's been here before," Sierra said.

"I don't usually work at the counter. My husband and I own this shop. But it's been so busy lately that I've had to put the apron back on. And your grandmother? Is she okay?"

"She had her gallbladder out. She's doing fine."

"Goodness gracious! You be sure and tell Howard hello for us and get him in here sometime."

"I will," Sierra said, tucking the bag in the crook of her arm. "Thanks again! It was very nice meeting you."

"You too, Sierra," Mrs. Kraus said, following her to the door, where she turned over the "open" sign. "'Bye now."

Sierra stepped out into the chilly street, where the smell of wet sidewalks and car exhaust instantly assaulted her. They were a rude contrast to the warm cinnamon and coffee smells of Mama Bear's. She took about four steps when she was overpowered by the obvious. Turning around, she walked two steps before the door of Mama Bear's opened again, and Mrs. Kraus popped out her head. Both of them spoke at the same time, and then they both laughed.

"You first," Sierra said.

"It just occurred to me, you said you were looking for a job, and—"

"I had the same thought," Sierra said.

"Well, then, come back in, my dear," she said, opening the door wide. "I believe Providence has designed this moment."

# eleven

"I'M HOME!" Sierra called out, as the front door slammed behind her.

"We're in here," Mom called out from the dining room.

Sierra shelved the cinnamon rolls in the pantry and found her family seated around the antique dining room table eating Mom's favorite "speedy dinner"—baked potatoes with steamed broccoli and cheese.

"Guess what?" Sierra said breathlessly.

Everyone looked at her expectantly.

"You ran into an Elvis impersonator from Mars who eats human brains," Dillon said.

"Yeah," Gavin added, "and he tried to suck your brain, but he starved."

"Boys," Dad said firmly. "What's the news, Sierra?"

Not even her brothers' dumb jokes could dampen her enthusiasm. "I got a job! At Mama Bear's. I start Thursday. My hours are four to six on Tuesdays and Thursdays, and eight to four on Saturdays. It's perfect! And Mrs. Kraus knows you, Dad. Her name was Amelia Jackson before she got married, and she said you should come in sometime. And she gave us an extra box of cinnamon rolls free. But the best part is, she already said I could have the time off during Easter vacation!" Sierra paused just long enough to catch her breath. "And she's a Christian. Can you believe that? Did you know they don't open their shop on Sundays? Is that incredible or what?"

"It's incredible," Mom agreed.

"Mrs. Kraus called it 'Providence.' Something about God leading in ways we can't see or understand." Sierra speared a potato from the serving bowl and poked it open with her fork, allowing the steam to escape.

"Our God is an awesome God," Dad said. It was his favorite saying, and he often sang a chorus with the same words. "I guess I better start to check on those airline tickets."

"Where's she going?" Dillon asked.

"Please don't talk with your mouth full, Dillon. Sierra wants to go down to Southern California during Easter to visit her friends," Mom explained.

"So it's okay with you, Mom?" Sierra found it impossible to suppress her excitement.

"With the conditions as Dad explained them, sure."

Tawni, who hadn't said anything yet, dropped her fork onto her plate and said, "Does anyone else have a problem with her getting to fly off to England and California while the rest of us stay home?"

"We went camping," Gavin said.

"Yeah, and you went skiing," Dillon said. "And Sierra was the only one home that time."

Tawni rolled her eyes. "That ski trip was a disaster!"

"You can come to San Diego with me if you want," Sierra blurted out.

"Oh, right! And what would I do there? Hang out with you and your little friends?"

"They're not 'little friends,'" Sierra said. "I'm the youngest of all of them. Katie and Christy are your age; Tracy, Doug, and Todd are all in their twenties."

Tawni gave Sierra a strange look as if this was new information to her. "And what are they doing inviting you down there?"

"They're my friends. They treat me as an equal." Sierra exuberance began to dwindle as she defended herself to her sister. She *did* see herself on the same level with Katie, Christy, and the others. With Tawni, she always felt inferior.

"Congratulations on the job," Mom said, redirecting the conversation. "I'm sure it will be a fun place to work."

"I couldn't do it." Tawni excused herself from the table and cleared her plate. "I'd gain twenty pounds a day just smelling those rolls. Too bad the flower shop didn't work out. Much less fattening."

Sierra had never been seriously concerned about her weight. She had her mom's quick metabolism and had always been active enough to burn off excess sweets. Tawni was the relentless calorie counter in the family. She was adopted and more than once expressed her fear that her biological mother might be a blimp.

"Do we get to have cinnamon rolls for dessert?" Dillon asked. He was an eight-year-old version of their dad and had inherited his sweet tooth.

"Let's wait till breakfast," Mom said. "Is anyone planning to see Granna Mae tonight?"

"I can go over," Dad said. "Do you boys want to go with me?"

"Whose turn is it to help with the dishes?" Mom asked.

"Sierra's," Gavin said.

"Naturally," Sierra muttered, rising to clear the dishes. The first handful of plates clattered as they came to rest in the stainless steel sink.

"Take it easy in there," Mom called out.

"I am," Sierra said. She didn't know why she hated doing the dishes so much. Rinsing them off and loading them into the dishwasher certainly wasn't hard. Mom always worked alongside her, and they usually had good talks. But something happened inside Sierra every time she was told that it was her turn to do the dishes. It was like a mean button was pushed inside her. And if she opened the dishwasher and found it full of clean dishes that hadn't been put away yet, the "mean-o-meter" automatically turned up about three notches. She knew it was dumb. Still, there it was. Tonight her fully operative mean-o-meter quickly rose as she opened the dishwasher and found it full of clean dishes.

The chore only took fifteen minutes or so, and as always, Mom thanked her for helping. Sierra mumbled, "You're welcome," and excused herself to do her homework.

When she reached her room, Tawni was already at the desk working on her homework from one of the courses she was taking at the community college. Without a word, Sierra cleared a spot on her bed and started to read her very boring government textbook.

The two sisters worked in silence for more than an hour before Tawni said, "Were you serious about my going to San Diego with you?"

Sierra hesitated. She had extended the invitation in a jovial moment. In truth, the last person she wanted to spend Easter with was Tawni. And never, in her right mind, would she have thought to let Tawni loose on her circle of sacred friends. One look at the perfect Tawni and Sierra would be an instant castoff. "Why do you ask?" Sierra asked cautiously.

Tawni turned to Sierra. Tears were in her eyes. "I just wanted to know if you really meant it."

"Sure," Sierra said, instantly motivated by the uncommon display of emotion. She knew Tawni was trying to make friends too. That need was about the only thing they shared right now.

Tawni didn't respond. She turned back around and bent over her books.

"So?" Sierra prodded. "What are you saying? Do you want to come with me or what?"

"I'm not sure," Tawni said in a low voice. "I'll let you know."

Sierra felt like throwing a pillow at her sister. It was bad enough that Sierra had made the crazy invitation. Tawni could at least say yes or no so Sierra would know whether or not her life was about to be ruined. This limbo game was not to Sierra's liking. But it was typical of Tawni to keep others waiting on her.

Whenever Sierra felt this frustrated or angry, she knew the best thing, the only thing, that helped was to get her face into her Bible and leave it there until she had an answer.

She reached for the leather-covered treasure on her nightstand and opened to where a crinkled candy bar wrapper marked her place. She began to read where she had left off a few days ago.

Sierra's method of devotion was to read through a whole book at a time. Some days she would read only a few verses, but other days it would be several chapters. Whenever she missed a day, instead of feeling guilty, Sierra would just pick up where she had left off. She also kept a notebook in which she logged thoughts that came to her as she read.

The marker was in the twenty-sixth chapter of Isaiah. She had been reading in Isaiah for more than a week and admittedly skimmed some of the earlier chapters. The last few had been more interesting to her, and she had underlined some passages.

Tonight she read slowly and stopped at verse 3. "You will keep him in perfect peace, whose mind is stayed on You, because he trusts in You."

Sierra turned her back to her sister and read the verse again. She wondered how much she trusted God and how much she depended on herself to make things happen in her life. She read on. The next phrase that stopped her was in verse 9: "With my soul I have desired You in the night."

*I don't know if I desire You like that, God. I want to. I want to trust You every day for everything. I also want to...*she read the phrase again...*I want my soul to desire You, Father God. I want You in my whole life. Not just in my crazy days. I want You in my restless nights. I want You in my dreams.*

Instead of feeling stronger and peaceful and more spiritual, Sierra felt bummed out. Not so much about Tawni. Tawni was her ongoing unsettled relationship. What Sierra felt yucky about tonight was the letter she had sent to Paul. Her words had been an impulsive reaction that showed her sassy side and would surely sever any potential relationship that might have been developed with Paul. And it was too late to do anything about it.

# twelve

SIERRA REACHED into the bag and pulled out another Sun Chip. French onion. Her favorite. In the other hand she held a copy of the school newspaper. She was scanning the back page, reading the classifieds and contemplating the notice in the lower right-hand corner. "All personals and ads must be submitted by Friday at noon. Please bring them to the journalism office along with exact payment at two cents a word."

Filtering out the lunchroom noise around her, Sierra pulled out the piece of paper and fiddled with a few words. She had thought Katie's idea of advertising for a friend was silly at the time, but today, as she sat alone again at the indoor lunch table, the idea seemed to have some merit.

"Wanted," she scribbled. "Someone to each lunch with." She crossed it out and tried again. "Looking for a pal? I've been looking for you." She skipped down a few lines and tried, "New girl in school seeking a way to break into one of your extremely tight cliques. Please advise."

"That's easy," a male voice behind her said. Sierra

snatched up her scratch paper and spun around to give whoever it was a dirty look.

"Whoa!" he said. "My advice is to lighten up." It was Randy, the first student she had met at Royal Academy. He had shown her around the first day and more than once had tried to start up conversations with her. Sierra had usually answered with one-syllable responses, shrugged her shoulders, and pulled away. Even though she had made a few tries here and there to talk to people in her classes, more often she had drawn back and kept to herself.

Sierra suddenly realized how she must look to the other students. It was as if her mean-o-meter, which clicked on every time she had to do the dishes, had also become fully activated at school. She had not made much effort to break into any of the circles of friends.

Randy sat down next to Sierra even though he hadn't been invited. He gave his head a shake and a tilt, flipping back his straight blond hair. "You know what, Sierra Jensen? It's time we had a talk."

"Oh, really?" she said, her tone teasing.

"Really," Randy said. "It's time for you to get a life."

She felt a twinge of anger surfacing.

Randy must have read it on her face because he leaned closer and broke into his crooked grin. Sierra noticed the stubble of a faint beard shading his jawline. "May I start over?" Randy asked.

Sierra nodded.

"Will you be my friend?" His eyes reflected his sincerity.

"Why? You already have plenty of friends."

"See?" Randy slapped his hand on the table for emphasis. "That is the problem! Why won't you let anyone in?

Why are you so guarded all the time?"

"I don't know," Sierra said honestly. She felt unwanted tears building up in her eyes and quickly blinked and swallowed so they wouldn't break free.

Randy kept looking at her; his open expression didn't change. The bell rang right over their heads, and the lunchroom began to clear out, but Randy didn't move. He sat there, looking at Sierra, waiting. She glanced away, feeling uncomfortable. Part of her wanted to open up to him and tell him that she didn't feel accepted here, that she felt like an outsider. But deep down she knew that 90 percent of that was her fault. Maybe even more. She had withdrawn big-time.

The odd part was that such behavior was the opposite of her personality. Up until this point in her life she had always been the initiator. She had been the "Randy" at school and church, trying to make everyone else feel welcome. Now she was the new girl, and she didn't know how to play the role.

"Well, when you decide you're ready to conduct interviews for a buddy, I'd like to apply for the job."

Sierra let her smile surface. She felt foolish and immature for being unwilling to talk to him.

"Randy," she began, "it's hard—"

"No, it isn't," he said. "You haven't tried yet."

Sierra wished she had some magic words to make everything better. Words that she could use like a ticket to allow her to try this ride again.

Then she remembered something one of the speakers had said on her missions trip to England. She had written it in her notebook and had noticed it a few nights ago. He had said, "When all is said and done, there will only be two phrases to sum up every relationship. The first is 'Forgive me.' The second is 'Thank you.' Say the first one often in your youth, and you will need only the second one on your deathbed."

"Randy," Sierra said quickly, "forgive me."

"Okay. But what am I forgiving you for?"

"For being a brat. I would rather be your buddy."

Randy tossed her one of his crooked smiles. "You mean I got the job?"

"Yup." She stood up and held out her hand to shake on it. "You're hired."

Instead of a handshake, Randy looped his arm around her shoulders and gave Sierra a sideways hug.

"Pals?" Randy asked.

Sierra remembered the Pals Only Club she and Katie had joked about. "Pals," she echoed.

"Come on," he said. "We're going to be late."

Sierra grabbed her backpack and tossed her crumpled-up ad for a new friend into the trash can on their way out the door. For the first time, she had someone to walk with her to class.

After school, Randy and two other girls, Amy and Vicki, stopped her before she reached her car in the parking lot. Sierra had talked with some of the girls before, and they had both tried to pursue a friendship with Sierra, but she hadn't done much to reciprocate.

Amy looked Italian with thick black hair and dark, expressive eyes. More than once she had come to school wearing an outfit similar to one of Sierra's.

Vicki was very popular. Her stunning looks had something to do with that. She wore her silky brown hair parted down the middle, and it billowed at her shoulders with a slight wave. Her almond-shaped green eyes were arched by thin eyebrows, and she had a rather "womanly" figure. Because Vicki was so attractive, Sierra had assumed she was stuck-up and hadn't thought much about talking with her before.

The three friends gathered around Sierra and said, "We're going to McDonald's. You want to come?"

"I have to work," Sierra said. "Today's my first day. I have to be there by four."

"Where do you work?" Vicki asked.

"It's a little shop on Hawthorne that makes cinnamon rolls."

"Mama Bear's?" Amy said. "I love that place. You know where it is, Vicki. On the same side of the street as my favorite dress shop, A Wrinkle in Time."

"Oh yeah," Vicki said. "Maybe we should go there instead of McDonald's."

Sierra swallowed hard. This making new friends thing was pretty awkward for her. Starting a brand-new job would probably be uncomfortable too, but combining both activities sounded like a disaster. She felt relieved when Randy said, "They don't have burgers there, do they? I'm in search of some real food."

"Aw, come on, Randy," Amy said. "They have lattes."

Apparently the lure of fancy coffee drinks wasn't enough to coerce Randy to change his mind. "How about another time?" he suggested.

"Sounds good to me." Sierra let out her breath, which she realized she was holding.

"We'll see you tomorrow," Vicki said.

They turned to go. Sierra unlocked the car door and then stopped and called out, "Hey!" They turned around. "Thank you," she said.

"Sure," Randy answered for the three of them. He didn't seem quite clear on what she was thanking them for.

Sierra felt good as she drove to Mama Bear's. She was making progress. This wasn't a result of chance. When peace came blowing in like this, riding on the wind of the Holy Spirit, God was at work.

She rolled down her window, stuck out her elbow into the cool afternoon air, and peeked through the windshield into the cloudy sky. "Thank You," she whispered.

# thirteen

"SIERRA, IS THAT YOU?" Mom called from the kitchen.

"Yes, it's your very own walking disaster." Sierra dragged herself into the kitchen, dropped into a chair, pulled her hair back, and held it on top of her head in a ponytail. "You will not believe what happened."

Mom turned down the flame on the big pot of soup and said, "Oh, I might. Give me a try."

Sierra let down her hair and started her story. "I got to Mama Bear's on time. A little early, actually. They had this nice blue apron waiting for me, and Mrs. Kraus started to show me how to make cappuccinos. Should be simple, right?" Sierra shook her head. "I go to make my first one for this guy who's standing right there watching me, but I didn't tighten the little filter thing enough. You know, the thing with the handle that you use to put the coffee grounds in and clamp it onto the part where the super-hot water comes out."

"Don't tell me," Mom said.

"I did. I turned on the machine, and it spit scalding

water all over my pretty new apron, all over the floor, and all over the counter. When I tried to stop it, it spewed soggy coffee grounds all over. And I do mean all over. It was a disaster."

"That's awful, honey!"

"Wait. There's more. Mrs. Kraus is nice, calm, and sweet, and she tells me to start over and not to worry about it. So I clean up everything, and I try again, very carefully. Everything is perfect. The steamed milk frothed up just right. Wonderful. Only one problem. I forgot to put any coffee grounds in the machine. All he got was hot water and steamed milk. I can't believe it! I was so worried about the machine that I wasn't paying attention to the cup. Then I hand the guy his cappuccino after he's been waiting for ten minutes. He takes one sip and practically sprays it out of his mouth and all over the counter."

"Oh, Sierra," Mom sympathized.

"He gets really mad, and in front of about ten customers, he demands his money back and says he's never coming back. I thought he was going to throw the cup at me. I thought Mrs. Kraus was going to fire me right then and there."

"Did she?"

"No. She was totally calm and said, 'These things happen. Try again.'"

"What a marvelous attitude."

"I know. She's a very sweet woman."

"And did you try again?"

"Yes. I got it right the next time. I made another cappuccino for the very next customer. He was smiling at me the whole time, which made me slightly nervous. Then when I handed the cup to him, he handed me a dollar tip and said, 'I think all champions should be rewarded.'"

Mom smiled and shook her head. "Only you, Sierra. And all this on your first day!"

"That's not all," Sierra said.

"You're kidding!"

Dad had entered the kitchen with Brutus's dog leash in his hand. As he hung it on the hook of the back door, he asked, "Is this the recap of day one at the bakery? What have I missed so far?"

"I'll fill you in later," Mom said. "Just listen. She's on a roll."

Sierra started to laugh. She laughed until little tear crystals shimmered in her eyes. "Actually," she said, "the roll was on me."

"This ought to be good," Dad said, resting his arm on Mom's shoulder and giving Sierra his full attention.

"I reached for a box of a half-dozen cinnamon rolls that was on this rack behind the cash register. I didn't know, of course, that the box was open. I wasn't paying attention, and the whole thing tumbled onto me." She held up the ends of her hair. "Frosting everywhere."

"I wondered what happened to your hair," Mom said. "But frankly, I wasn't sure I wanted to know."

"Well, now you know. I tried to wash some of it out in the sink at work, but it was impossible. I can't believe they didn't throw me out and threaten my life if I ever darkened their doorway again. Oh, and then the grand finale. Right before it was time for me to leave, I caught my apron on the edge of this big mixer they have in the back, and I tore the apron."

"A lot?" Mom asked.

Sierra held up her two index fingers in the air to indicate a rip of about seven inches.

Mom covered her mouth. Sierra knew her mother was trying hard to suppress her laughter.

"And they still want you to come back on Saturday?" Dad asked.

"Yes. Absolutely amazing, isn't it?"

"By any chance did the job description call for someone to provide comic relief?" Dad teased. "You know, perk up the business a little by putting on a sideshow. Customers will be lining up on the days you work just to see what's going to happen next."

Sierra grabbed a pot holder off the counter next to her and threw it at her dad. "You meanie!"

"Meanie?" Dad said, catching the pot holder before it hit Mom. "What happened to 'wonderful Daddy-o' who was checking on airline tickets for you?"

"What did you find out?" Sierra asked, ducking as the pot holder came flying back at her.

"What's for dinner, honey?"

"Chicken soup. It's ready."

"Dad!" Sierra pleaded.

"Chicken soup?" he said, lifting the lid and giving it a stir. "Who's sick?"

"You're going to be if you don't tell me about the airplane tickets!" Sierra jumped up and grabbed his arm before he could reach for another pot holder.

"Oh, getting tricky in your old age, are you?" Dad leaned over and took a whiff of Sierra's hair. "I like your new perfume. It has that fresh-from-the-oven fragrance. Subtle, yet tasty."

"You're going to be fresh from the oven if you don't tell me about the tickets!"

"Okay, okay," Dad said, raising both hands in surrender. Some numbers were written in blue ink on the palm of his right hand.

"What's this?" Sierra said, grabbing his hand and taking a closer look.

"I didn't have a piece of paper handy. I was on hold for so long that when they finally came back on the line..."

Mom shook her head at her husband's antics.

"That one in the middle," he said, pointing, "is the fare into John Wayne. It's the best price."

"John Wayne?"

"That's what they call the Orange County airport. Do you think you can come up with the money in less than three weeks?"

"I think so," Sierra said, twisting her head to read the last two numbers. "Is that a two or a five?"

"Five. I think. Let me see. Yeah, that's a five."

"When do I leave, and when do I come back?"

"You would leave on Friday evening and return the following Thursday. No seats were left for a return on the weekend, and they only had a few seats left on Thursday at the reduced price."

"You asked them to hold it for me, didn't you?"

Just then the phone rang and Mom reached for the extension on the wall.

"I most certainly did. What kind of secretary would I be if I didn't make reservations for my boss?"

"Oh, dear," Mom said.

Sierra and Dad stopped their teasing and turned their attention to Mom.

"Yes...I see...Thank you for calling right away. Good-bye."

She hung up. Her face was creased with worry lines. "We need to go right now," she said.

"Was it the hospital? Were they calling about Granna Mae?" Sierra asked.

Mom nodded. "Sierra, can you serve dinner to the boys? They both need baths, and they need to be in bed by eight. Tawni should be home from work around nine-thirty. Call us at the hospital if you need anything."

"Is she okay?" Sierra asked.

"I'm not sure. Howard, are you ready to go?"

"Right with you, sweetheart. Let's take the van. I have the keys."

With a whoosh, they were out the door. The kitchen, which had rung with laughter only moments before, had turned painfully still. Sierra forced herself to take a deep breath. "Gavin! Dillon!" She called out the back door. "Time to eat."

# fourteen

SIERRA STEPPED OUT of the bathroom with a towel wrapped around her head. She fought the urge, which had been nagging her for the last two and half hours, to call the hospital. The boys were fed, bathed, and in bed. She had solemnly loaded the dishwasher and cleaned up the kitchen. Tawni should be home soon. And Sierra really needed to start on her paper for English. It was due tomorrow, and procrastinator that she was, she hadn't begun the five-page report.

Fortunately for Sierra, she managed to come out of such situations unscathed. Her teachers wrote on her report card in the comment column, "Sierra is bright and intelligent. She has not yet pushed herself to her full potential." It was true. She had never been motivated to try harder. Why should she, when, with a minimum effort, she could meet the class requirements and come home with a sterling report card?

She slipped into her favorite T-shirt pajamas and searched under her bed for her fuzzy slipper. Not there.

She tried the closet. Nope. Sierra glanced around the room, looking for the missing slipper. Then, as if she truly noticed her side of the room for the first time, she said aloud. "What a slob! No wonder you can't find anything, girl."

That did it. She couldn't stand the mess another minute. In a frenzy of motion, Sierra kicked into high gear and started to clean her room. It didn't matter that it was after nine and she still had a paper to do. She could not stand to live in this messy room another second. She was actually feeling sympathetic for Tawni, who had to look at her disastrous mess every day.

Panting hard, her wet hair dripping down her back and wearing only one slipper, Sierra worked with lightning speed to hang up clothes, throw away papers, stuff necessary junk into drawers, and clean off the top of her dresser. She even stripped her bedsheets and jogged to the hall closet for clean, neatly folded sheets that smelled like lemon fabric softener. With a few quick folds and a snap of her comforter, Sierra's bed was made—probably for the first time since they had moved here.

Then, scooping up an armful of dirty clothes, she trucked down to the washer in the basement and started up a load. Her clothes from a few days earlier were all folded and waiting for her in a plastic laundry bucket. On top of clothes was the missing slipper—a clean, fresh contrast to the one of her foot. In the slipper was a little note in Mom's handwriting. "Some bunny wuvs you!"

*I wonder if I'll be such a terrific mom someday,* Sierra thought, lugging the clean clothes upstairs. Just as she reached the entryway, a key turned in the front door. Tawni stepped in.

"Mom and Dad were called to the hospital," Sierra said. "I don't know what's going on."

"Why didn't you call the hospital?" Tawni said, hanging her purse on the same peg she always used on the hall coat tree.

"I thought they would call or just come home if everything was okay."

"What time did they leave?" Tawni asked, heading for the kitchen phone in a huff.

"Around six-thirty."

Tawni dialed the number for St. Mary's written in chalk on the wall blackboard. She asked for Granna Mae's room. They waited while it rang. "No one's answering," Tawni said. "What do you think is happening? Wouldn't a nurse answer it at the station?"

"I guess. I don't know." Now Sierra was feeling panicked. "Do you think we should go to the hospital?"

"Are the boys asleep?"

Sierra nodded.

Tawni held out the phone for Sierra to hear it ring. "That's the seventh ring. Nobody is there." Hanging up the phone, Tawni headed for the door. "I'm going. You stay here with the boys."

"Call me as soon as you get there," Sierra said.

"I'll try." Tawni swished out the door, closing it hard behind her.

Sierra stood in the entryway next to the full laundry basket. She didn't know what to do. Finally, she reached for her backpack, took it back to the office. With supreme concentration, she turned on the computer and began to punch out her report.

Her mind was only half in gear as she waited for the phone to ring. Then, to make sure the phone was working, she reached over, picked it up, and checked for a dial tone. It was working. Sierra went back to her paper. She wrote nonstop for twenty minutes.

*Come on, Tawni! Call me! What is keeping you?*

Sierra pushed herself to finish the report. It was like walking uphill against the wind. She checked the wall clock every few minutes and picked up the phone twice to call but decided to wait for Tawni.

Her paper was almost finished. Sierra glanced out the French doors at the inky black backyard. It reminded her of the verse she read in Isaiah. Something about "my soul I have desired You in the night." Sierra sat in the silent room, staring at the phone, praying for Granna Mae.

She forced herself to finish her paper, ran a spell-check, and then pressed "print." As soon as she heard the printer kick in, Sierra went into the kitchen and dialed the hospital. It was 10:40, more than an hour since Tawni left. The phone rang in Granna Mae's room. Mom answered it on the second ring.

"Mom, is everything okay? What's going on? Tawni was supposed to call me."

"I know," Mom said calmly. "I'm sorry we didn't call. Why don't you go to bed? We'll be home shortly."

"Can't you tell me what's going on?" Sierra asked.

Mom paused. "We'll be home soon." Then she hung up.

Now Sierra was really stumped. Why couldn't Mom say anything on the phone? Sierra retrieved her paper out of the printer and checked her e-mail, which was depressing when she saw it was almost all spam. She shut down the computer and cleared her things out of the office. Then she lugged the laundry basket upstairs to her room and started to sort clothes on her smoothly made bed. All her T-shirts were in one pile and all the clothes that needed hangers in another pile, while the third stack consisted of her underwear. One of her socks was missing its mate. For some reason, she thought she had seen it in her backpack.

Sierra went downstairs, retrieved her backpack, and brought it up to her room. Then, because she was in a cleaning mood, she dumped its contents out in the middle of the floor and started to sort through all the junk.

The sock was there, but it was dirty. She decided to run down to the basement and toss in another load so her laundry would be all caught up. On her way back up through the kitchen, Sierra decided a little midnight snack would be nice. She popped a piece of bread in the toaster oven and poured herself a glass of milk. The only way to eat toast late at night, according to Dad, was with butter and honey. That had become Sierra's favorite way too.

Balancing the plate in one hand and carefully sipping the milk as she walked, Sierra returned to her room. She sat cross-legged on the floor, sorting through the backpack mess and munching on her toast, trying not to panic over Granna Mae.

In the thick of her sorting frenzy, she heard the front door open. She jumped up and ran downstairs. "Well? Is she okay?"

Tawni hung up her purse. "What a mess! That has to be the most unorganized hospital in the world."

"What happened?"

"Granna Mae was confused. She got out of her bed and walked down the hall."

"With the IV in?" Sierra asked.

"She pulled it out. Then she took the elevator to the lobby and went into the gift shop. She slipped and fell. Mom and Dad have been sitting with her this whole time in X-ray. That's why they didn't call. They were worried about leaving her."

"I thought you were going to call," Sierra said.

"Don't you want to know how she is?"

"Of course I do."

"She broke her foot," Tawni said. "They just started to put the cast on when I left. I think Mom and Dad will be with her another hour or at least until she settles down for the night."

"Is she still confused?" Sierra asked.

"Very. I think the doctor is going to put her on some stronger medication to sedate her."

"When will she come home? Don't you think she would do better here where she would be in familiar surroundings?"

"I don't know what the doctor is going to say. I wasn't convinced the guy even knew what he was doing."

"He isn't her regular doctor," Sierra said, turning to go back to her room. Tawni followed her upstairs.

"Well, I didn't think much of him," Tawni said.

The minute Tawni stepped into their room, she barked, "Aren't you ever going to clean up this disaster?"

"I did!" Sierra protested. Then she glanced around and realized that, even though her side of the room had been cleaned up for about ten minutes, now it was a disheveled mess with clothes on the bed, backpack innards strewn across the floor, and the remains of her midnight snack on her previously tidy dresser.

"You could have fooled me," Tawni said, kicking off her shoes and placing them in her closet.

Sierra jammed most of her loose stuff into her backpack. Then, because Tawni had irritated her, she purposely shoved all her clean, folded clothes off her bed and onto the floor. She climbed into bed, unable to enjoy the fresh, clean sheets, and snapped off her light.

# fifteen

THE ROLLER COASTER on which Sierra's emotions had been riding came to a halt Saturday afternoon for a few precious moments. Then, without warning, the ride began all over again.

She was at work and had successfully made it through the first five hours without a mishap. She felt kind of eerie, as if she was just waiting for something to go wrong.

It had been a wildly busy morning. The time flew by. At noon, Mrs. Kraus told her to take a break and get something to eat. A tray of slightly burnt cinnamon rolls were up for grabs in the kitchen, so Sierra picked at one of them. But she had lost her appetite for cinnamon rolls after being around them all morning.

As she sat there, her hands sticky and her clothes smelling like coffee, Sierra felt content. Her job was going well, her dad had made the airline reservations, yesterday she had eaten lunch at school with Vicki and Amy, and this afternoon the sun had come out.

Sierra adjusted the dangling silver earring in her right

earlobe and smiled to herself. She thought of another verse she had read in her speedy journey through Isaiah that morning. "In quietness and confidence shall be your strength." Right now she felt a little bit of that quietness and confidence in the Lord. It was very sweet.

Then the roller coaster ride started up again. Mrs. Kraus called into the back room, "Sierra, you have a visitor."

She walked out into the busy shop and glanced around, looking for who it might be. Randy was standing by the cash register.

"Hi," he said. "Do you want to go out tonight?"

Sierra felt her cheeks instantly flush. Several people were staring at her. "Ahh, tonight?"

"Around seven." Randy said. "I thought maybe we could see a movie or something. When do you get off?"

"At four." Sierra realized that Mrs. Kraus was beside her, trying to ring up a purchase at the register. "Oh, excuse me." She stepped to the side.

"Randy—" Sierra began.

"Just say yes," he said, lowering his voice. "Don't make everything so hard, Sierra. We're just friends, right? Friends can go to the movies without it being a big deal, can't they?"

"Is anyone else going?"

"No. Do you want someone else to go?"

"Well…" Sierra didn't know how to tell him that she had never been on a date before. She had never been asked, so she had never gotten an okay from Mom and Dad. Her parents had said that when she turned sixteen she could date, but her sixteenth birthday had come and gone without any dating prospects. "Could you do me a favor, Randy?"

"Sure," he said, his crooked smile lighting up.

"Could you give me a call at home sometime after five? I need to check with my parents." Then, because she thought it sounded kind of babyish, she added, "My grandmother is in the hospital, and I'm not sure if it would work out for me tonight."

"Sure. I understand. Now can I ask you a favor?"

"Sure."

"Can you give me your phone number?"

Sierra reached for a napkin and wrote it down.

"Thanks," he said. "Now may I buy a cinnamon roll from you, or do I have to go back and stand in line?"

"I'll get it for you," Sierra said. "With or without frosting?"

"With. Definitely with."

Sierra made sure she was paying attention as she pulled out a tray of hot, frosted rolls and used the wide spatula to scoop one into a container to go. She even plopped a little extra frosting on top before she closed the container's lid. Randy took the roll from her and handed her the exact amount of cash. "I'll call you," he said. With a wave, he was gone.

Sierra let out a tight-chested breath and glanced at the clock. Her break was over, so she moved on to helping the next customer. None of her coworkers made any comments about Randy. She was thankful for that.

At the same time, she was dying to talk to someone about this major event in her life. She had been asked out on a real date.

As the afternoon continued at a sporadic pace, Sierra had more time to think about this date. She had dreamed about what it would be like when she was asked out for the first time and who the guy would be. But she never had dreamed it would be like this, rather unromantic and so direct. And she never had dreamed it would be with a guy like Randy.

Nothing was wrong with Randy—or so she tried to convince herself. He was valuable "buddy" material. But she had never thought about going out with him. It made her wonder how long he had contemplated asking her out. Did he like her the first day he had met her at school? Or did something spark for him the other day in the cafeteria when she offered her hand in friendship? And if it did for him, why hadn't anything sparked inside of her?

In the midst of wiping off tables and filling the little ceramic baskets with packs of sugar, it hit Sierra that maybe he was doing this out of pity. Maybe he felt sorry for her since she opened up a little about not having any friends. Sierra jammed a blue packet of artificial sweetener into the white basket and thought, *He can forget it if that's what this is all about. I don't need his sympathy. I would much rather have no dates—ever—than to accept a charity date, especially from someone I thought was my friend!*

She held to that course of logic the rest of the afternoon. That is, until she started to walk home and passed the mailbox into which she had dumped her flaming letter to Paul earlier that week. She still regretted sending it. If only she had waited and thought it through a little more clearly. Paul was teasing her, not attacking her.

She had had such strong feelings for Paul when she first

met him. For weeks she had prayed fervently for him. And now she had ruined even the little bit of friendship they had had. Maybe it wasn't friendship, but it was something. And it was still there, inside her head.

"Mom," Sierra called out when she entered the house. "Are you home?"

"She's at the hospital," Tawni shouted back from the family room.

Sierra went into the family room, which was being remodeled. Dad had made an entertainment center and had christened it fully operational the night before. The boys were sprawled on the floor playing a video game, and Tawni was labeling some videotapes and filing them in a new tape drawer.

"Make sure you put them in alphabetical order," Sierra said.

"What's that supposed to mean?" Tawni shot her a glance over her shoulder.

"I'm just sure that you'll be happier once everything is in its proper place." Sierra dropped onto the floor next to the boys and asked, "Who's winning?"

"Nothing is wrong with being organized, Sierra," Tawni snapped. "But then you wouldn't know anything about that, would you?" She went back to her task, and the two sisters ignored each other.

"Do you want to play the winner?" Dillon asked Sierra.

"Sure," she said. Then she remembered. Randy was calling at five. "Do you guys know when Mom and Dad will get home?"

"Dad's here," Gavin said. "He's out in the workshop."

"I'll be back." Sierra bounded to her feet and hurried

out to the backyard. She found Dad in the dollhouse-looking workshop with goggles on and an electric saw revved at full speed in his hand. She covered her ears and waited for him to notice her.

He reached the end of the board he was cutting and saw her. Dad turned off the saw, flipped up the safety glasses, and said, "You're home! So how did today go? Any adventures to add to Thursday's account? By the way, I've called the people from *Guinness Book of World Records*, and they're considering your experience for the 'worst first day' page."

"Tell them to find some other klutz to write about. My dork days are over. Today was relatively uneventful."

"Relatively?"

"I was asked out," Sierra said.

Dad put down his saw and stepped closer to look into Sierra's eyes. He had done that with all his children when they were little to see if they were telling the truth. As they grew older, he continued the gesture. Sierra thought it was his way of reading pains and joys they had learned to bury deeper inside the older they became. Dad always said that eyes were the heart's mirror. "Tell me about it," he said.

"It was a guy from school, not someone I just met at work, if that's what you're thinking. He kind of ate lunch with me one day at school this week. His name is Randy. He came into work and asked if I wanted to go out tonight at seven o'clock. I told him I'd need to talk to you. He's calling at five. What should I do?"

A slow smile spread across Dad's face. Sierra wasn't sure what it meant. "Five o'clock, huh?" He checked his watch. "Leave it to me." He revved up his radial saw one more time before turning it off and placing it on the workbench. Like a man on a mission, Dad whipped off his safety glasses and, with long strides, made his way out of the workshop toward the kitchen phone. "Yep," he called over his shoulder, "you just leave this one to me, Sierra."

# sixteen

"DAD," SIERRA PLEADED, glancing at the kitchen clock. It was quarter to five, and Dad stood next to the kitchen wall phone looking ready to "draw" the instant it rang. "You're not going to do anything weird, are you?"

*"Moi?"* he teased.

"I don't want you to do to Randy what you did to Tawni's old boyfriend, Martin," Sierra said.

"Who, Martin the Martian?" Dad asked.

"Are you guys talking about me?" Tawni said, stepping into the kitchen at just the right moment.

"Did Sierra tell you?" Dad asked. "She's been asked out on a real, live date."

"You're kidding!" Tawni said.

"Nope. It's true. Some poor, unsuspecting fellow named Randy asked her out at work today."

"Where did you meet him?" Tawni asked.

"At school. He's just a friend, you guys. I never would have thought he would ask me out."

"It's time you realized what a beauty you are, Sierra. I'm

sure Randy will only be the first in a long line," Dad said.

"Yeah, well, I just don't want him to be the last after you get ahold of him," Sierra said, crossing her arms and giving Dad a stern look.

"Oh, you're not going to do to him what you did to Martin, are you?" Tawni asked. It was the first time she had taken Sierra's side on anything in a long time.

"Listen to her, Dad," Sierra said.

"That interview stuff you did with Martin was too much, Dad. Don't do that with this guy. What's his name?"

"Randy."

"Don't do that to Randy. You scared off Martin, and I gained a reputation for being the least accessible girl in Pineville! Don't you remember how everyone made fun of me and said that whoever wanted to go out with Tawni Jensen had to first go out with her father?"

"It didn't hurt you any, and I got a free game of golf and two dinners out of the deal," Dad said. "Besides, that's the kind of reputation I want my girls to have."

"It doesn't have to be extreme, Daddy," Tawni said, slipping into her mushy side and pleading on Sierra's behalf. "Maybe you could invite him over for dinner or something casual with the whole family. That one-on-one male bonding approach is too severe. Okay?"

Dad thought a minute and said, "I have an idea."

Just then the phone rang.

Sierra looked at the clock: five o'clock on the button. She looked at her dad and then shot a skeptical glance at Tawni.

"I'll answer it," Dad said. He waved a hand at Sierra and Tawni as if to say, *Don't worry about a thing.*

Sierra bit her lower lip and listened.

"Hello...Yes, Sierra's right here. By any chance is this Randy?"

A short pause followed.

"Nice to meet you Randy. Hey, before I hand the phone to Sierra, I was wondering...ah, Sierra said you two were trying to make plans to do something tonight around seven."

Another short pause.

"Well, if you're interested, we're having pizza here at six o'clock. You're welcome to join us if you would like."

Another pause.

"Okay. Did you want to talk with Sierra?... Oh, okay. 'Bye." Dad hung up. His expression didn't give any clues to what Randy's answer had been.

"He said no, didn't he?" Sierra said. "He canceled the whole thing and said he would never bother me again, right?"

Dad's sly grin crept up his face, and the corners of his eyes crinkled the way they did when he was trying not to cry.

"What did he say?" Tawni asked, grabbing one of Dad's arms.

Sierra grabbed the other arm and gave it a yank. "Tell us or we'll pull you apart at the seams."

"What kind of pizza do you ladies want?"

"He's coming, then?"

"At six o'clock."

Just then the phone rang. Sierra grabbed it before Dad had a chance to. "Hello?"

"Sierra?"

"Yes."

"Oh, hi. It's me again. I can't believe this, but I forgot to ask where you live."

Sierra let out a nervous laugh. While Dad and Tawni listened in, she gave Randy directions and then asked, "So you don't mind having pizza with my family?"

"Are you kidding? I never turn down free food!" Randy laughed when he said it, and Sierra felt more at ease.

"I'll see you in about an hour then. 'Bye."

"See you!" he said.

Sierra hung up and turned to face Dad and Tawni with a hint of a smile on her face.

"I told you to leave it to me. I know the way to a man's heart. It's through his stomach. Always has been, always will be. Trust me on this one, girls."

"So what's going to happen when the poor guinea pig arrives?" Tawni asked. "Are you going to lock him in the office and make him sign release papers before they can go out?"

"Noooo." Dad gave Tawni a quick kiss on the forehead and then repeated the gesture on Sierra's temple.

"What are you going to do to him?" Sierra asked.

"You'll see." He headed for the front door and called into the family room, "You guys want to go with me to pick up a pizza?"

"You're going to change, aren't you?" Tawni asked.

Sierra looked down at her worn-out jeans and white, short-sleeved T-shirt. "What's wrong with this?"

"You've been wearing it all day, not to mention that you wore it to work."

"So? It's comfortable."

"Sierra, you could at least make a little effort to act like this is your first date. You know, brush your hair or something. You can borrow some of my makeup if you want."

Sierra forced herself to swallow the immediate laugh that came to her. She never had worn a pinch of makeup. Why would she start now? And for Randy of all people. It was a ridiculous thought. But she refrained from laughing because it was one of the most generous and un-Tawni-like things her sister had ever said to her. Tawni rarely shared anything, but especially nothing personal like her thoughts, her clothes, her jewelry, or her makeup. Sierra didn't want to ruin the moment.

"Thanks, but I don't think so. Not for sitting around eating pizza and going out to the movies."

Tawni scrutinized Sierra's face and kept pushing. "A tiny bit of mascara. That's all I suggest. It's your choice."

"Well, okay. I guess so. Just a tiny bit, if it means so much to you."

"I'm only trying to help!" Tawni snapped.

"I know, and I appreciate it. I really do. But just a little bit of mascara, okay?"

Tawni coached Sierra all the way to their room. "You should change into something other than jeans."

"What's wrong with these jeans? They're my favorite."

"They make you look fat."

"They do not."

"Yes they do. And they look sloppy, like you bought them in the boys department at Sears."

"I did not!" Sierra protested.

They stopped in front of their bedroom door, and

Tawni turned to give Sierra one of her I'm-right-and-you're-wrong looks.

Sierra stared right back at her. "I did not get them at the boys department at Sears." Then, lowering her voice and adding a mischievous grin, she stated, "For your information, I bought them in the boys department at T.J. Maxx. They were three dollars cheaper."

# seventeen

AT TEN MINUTES TO SIX, Sierra studied her reflection in the antique beveled mirror above the dresser in her room. Tawni stood behind her, admiring her own handiwork. Sierra's hair was pulled back in a loose braid fastened at the end with a large wooden clip. She wore no earrings, which made Sierra feel naked. Tawni said they were too cumbersome. The simple, fresh-faced look was what Tawni was after tonight.

"Innocence with a punch of attitude," she said while twirling the mascara wand over Sierra's upper lashes. "That's you to the core, Sierra. You should look the same on the outside as you are on the inside. Now hold still. You're not making this easy."

"You're going to poke me in the eye."

"No, I'm not. Relax. I know what I'm doing."

"You're trying to make me look like you, Tawni. I'm not you!"

"I'm *not* trying to make you look like me."

"So why are you doing this?"

Tawni pulled back and in a curt voice said, "Why do you make it so hard for anyone to treat you nicely?"

Sierra's comeback was, "Maybe it's because I'm used to certain people criticizing me rather than complimenting me."

Tawni let the challenge fall to the floor. She went back to running the mascara wand over Sierra's row of eyelashes. "There." Tawni stood back, and they studied the results together. "You look really good," Tawni said. "See what a difference a tiny bit of personal care can make in your appearance?"

*Oh brother!* Sierra still wasn't sure how she felt about being "all dolled up," as her dad called it. She looked at her face without making a comment. Her eyes did look larger. They even looked a little bluer than usual. But the freckles sprinkled across her nose made her look more girlish than sophisticated like Tawni. No amount of makeup could counterbalance that.

Still, she looked older than sixteen. At least, she thought she did. And Paul had thought so too, when he had first met her in London. He hadn't believed her when she told him her age.

*I wish I were going out with Paul tonight instead of Randy,* Sierra thought. *If I were, I'd let you give me the full treatment, Tawni! I'd want to look as fabulous as I possibly could. But I'm not going out with Paul. I will probably never see him again. I should be happy a guy like Randy is interested in me.*

"Well?" Tawni asked. "What do you think?"

Sierra remembered when Granna Mae had stood before this same mirror a number of weeks ago. She had looked closely at her reflection and had touched the wrinkles in the corners of her eyes and said something about being twelve just yesterday.

Somehow Sierra felt she was at a milestone too. It was odd thinking that her grandmother had seen her own reflection in this mirror when she was twelve and when she was sixteen and many more times during the five decades that followed. It was strange to think about Granna Mae being sixteen.

"Aren't you going to say anything?" Tawni prodded.

"It's weird."

"Oh, thanks a lot."

"I'm not talking about the makeup. I'm saying it's weird to think we have only one chance to cross the bridge from childhood into adulthood. And then we can never go back. This feels like one more step across that bridge."

Tawni looked startled at Sierra's comment. "Since when did you turn into a philosopher?"

"Don't you ever think about stuff like that?"

"Yes, of course I do. I never thought you did."

"I do sometimes. Like now."

Tawni put away her makeup bag and selected a bottle of fragrance from the collection on her dresser top. She squirted a tiny bit into the air above Sierra's head. "I think you're a light, sweet fragrance kind of person. Do you like this?"

Sierra took a whiff of the air. It didn't smell like Tawni. It was more like a fresh shower scent. "Yes, I like that."

"Then close your eyes, and I'll scent your hair."

"You'll what?"

"Close your eyes." Sierra did, and Tawni gave her hair several squirts. "There. Now you're ready. Except for your outfit, that is."

"Let's make a deal," Sierra said. "You got to do all the stuff above the neck, so I get to pick what goes on below the neck."

Tawni shrugged. "Suit yourself." She put the perfume bottle back where it belonged and picked the hairs from her brush.

Sierra sorted through the heap of clean clothes on the floor and pulled out a blue shirt and another pair of jeans. Ignoring her sister's small sounds of disapproval, Sierra carried the clothes down the hall to the bathroom, where she could change in peace.

Dad returned with the pizza before Randy arrived. Sierra could hear Dad and her brothers in the kitchen. As she headed downstairs, the door opened, and Mom came in, looking tired.

"How's Granna Mae?" Sierra asked, meeting her in the entryway.

Mom took a second look at Sierra. "You look wonderful! Did you do your hair?"

"No, I was Tawni's project for the afternoon. I kind of have a date tonight."

Mom's tired lines vanished as her face brightened. "You didn't tell me! Does Dad know?"

"Of course. He invited Randy over for pizza with the family. He should be here any second. Do I look silly?"

"Sierra Mae Jensen," Mom said, taking Sierra's hand in hers. "You look adorable. You have no idea how attractive you are."

Just then they heard heavy footsteps on the front porch and the sound of a male clearing his throat. Then the doorbell chimed. Sierra and Mom squeezed hands and exchanged silent giggles with their facial expressions.

"I think it's for you," Mom whispered, slipping into the kitchen.

Before Sierra could answer the door, Gavin and Dillon charged in from the kitchen, fighting over who was going to open the door. They both jerked the old doorknob at the same time, and the knob fell off in Dillon's hand.

"You broke it!" Dillon yelled. "Dad, Gavin broke the doorknob."

"I did not! You did!" Gavin shouted back, pushing his brother.

"Hey, you guys!" Sierra yelled above their shouting. "Cut it out!"

Dad came around the corner from the kitchen with Mom right behind them, both loudly asking what the problem was. At the same time, Tawni appeared at the top of the stairs and hurried down to find out what was going on.

"I'll need a screwdriver," Dad said. "Dillon, run out to the workshop and find a Phillips head and a flat head."

"But I didn't do it!" Dillon protested.

"I didn't say you did. Just get them for me, will you? Hang on there, Randy," Dad called through the closed door. "We'll open the door in just a minute here."

Sierra felt herself wilting in the midst of all the frenzy. Randy certainly could hear all the commotion. She wouldn't blame him if he turned around and ran all the way home. Everyone was talking at once, trying to solve the problem. Dillon returned with three different-sized screwdrivers, and Mom was saying a missing piece probably had fallen on the floor. She got down on all fours and started her safari in between everyone's legs. Gavin joined her and immediately found a dead bug he wanted to save.

"Try opening it with just the screwdriver," Tawni suggested. "You don't need to put the handle on to open it. The same thing happened before with the bathroom doorknob, remember? Granna Mae just uses a coat hanger and sticks it in there."

"I know how to do this," Dad said, sounding irritated. "I did grow up in this ancient house, you know." He pressed something inside the doorknob hole with the flathead screwdriver. It clicked and Mom popped up her head, colliding with Dad's elbow.

"Ouch!"

"You okay?"

"Open the door!"

"Stand back, you guys!"

"Wait a second. Let me stand up."

"Look out for my bug."

The door opened, and six eager faces smiled to greet Sierra's date. No one was there.

Sierra thought she was going to cry.

"Hi, guys," a voice behind them said. They all spun around and saw Wes, Sierra's oldest brother. Randy was standing next to him. "I found this poor guy out on the porch. Does anyone claim him?"

"I do," Sierra said, feeling her cheeks turn flaming red.

Mom rushed over to hug Wesley and give him a big kiss. "You didn't tell us you were coming home from college this weekend."

"What? Do I need to make reservations now or something? Maybe that was your problem," Wes said to Randy. "You didn't call ahead. They only open the door if you call ahead. But now you know my secret: Sneak in through the back door."

Everyone laughed, and Sierra said, "Everybody, this is Randy. Randy, this is my family. I forgot to warn you about them."

More laughter.

Randy just stood there with a dazed look on his face.

"Let's attack this pizza while it's still hot," Dad suggested, motioning with his arm that they should all follow him into the kitchen. As he passed Randy, he said, "So, do you like anchovies, Randy?"

"Uh...well, not too much, sir."

"Oh, too bad," Dad said.

Sierra stepped over beside Randy and said, "Don't worry. He didn't get anchovies. He hates them. He's just teasing you. He probably got pepperoni or something. Don't worry."

"Oh, I'm not worried," Randy said, his half grin barely inching up the side of his jaw.

Sierra smiled her best smile at him. But Randy looked worried. Very worried.

# eighteen

ONCE THE TROOPS were seated at the dining room table, eating pepperoni pizza off of paper plates and sipping Pepsi from the cans, Randy appeared to relax more.

"You look like that guy in that rap group," Gavin said to Randy. "Are you that guy?"

Randy shot a glance at Sierra and said, "I don't think so."

"Are you in a band?" Gavin wanted to know.

"No."

Gavin looked disappointed.

"My dad used to be, though," Randy said. "He played the drums."

"That's pretty cool," Dillon said. "Do you play the drums?"

"A little. I play piano some too."

"Oh." Apparently piano wasn't nearly as cool as drums when it came to Dillon's choice of instruments.

"What does your dad do now?" Mom asked.

"He's a scientist."

"Da' mad Mr. Science-Head," Gavin said in a deep voice with his arms raised over his head and his hands hanging down like a gorilla.

"It's a cartoon," Dillon explained on behalf of his little brother.

"We could have guessed," Wes said.

"What kind of scientist?" Mom asked.

"He's sort of a geologist."

"Sort of?" Tawni challenged.

Randy looked at Sierra, and then with a hopeful expression he said, "He's actually with a team of men and women who are searching for Noah's ark." Randy scanned everyone's face looking for feedback.

"Fascinating," Dad said. "Wouldn't it be something if they found it?"

Randy looked relieved. "Some people think that's weird. He also works with a team of scientists who study Mount Saint Helens, but he's really into the Mount Ararat project."

"Is that where you got that really great coat you wear to school?" Sierra asked. "You told me your dad bought it in Nepal."

"He brought it back for me last year when he was over there."

"Does your mom work outside the home?" Mom asked.

"She teaches third grade at the Christian school."

Sierra glanced around and felt relieved that things were going much more smoothly than they had at first. The conversation continued until all the pizza was gone. Dillon challenged Randy to a game of "Agitated Alligator," his new video game, and Wes said he would play the winner.

"Do you mind?" Randy asked Sierra. She could tell he was dying to play the game.

"What time do we need to leave for the movies?" Sierra asked.

"It depends on what you want to see," Randy said. He handed his empty plate to Sierra's mom as she moved about the table collecting them. "Thanks," he told her with a smile. "Great dinner."

"Yes, I slaved all day over a hot pizza oven. Glad you liked it."

"What do you want to see?" Sierra asked, trying to regain Randy's attention.

"It doesn't matter to me. As long as it's good and clean."

"Randy," Dillon called from the family room, "it's all ready."

Randy looked at Sierra. She was trying to decide if she should be upset. Everyone else had stepped out of the dining room, and she knew she could say whatever she wanted. "Oh, go ahead. We don't have to see a movie. We can just hang around here."

Randy smiled. "You don't mind?"

She shook her head. "Not this time."

"Randy!" Dillon called again.

"I owe you a movie," Randy said.

"I know," Sierra said. "And I won't let you forget it, either."

Sierra showed Randy into the family room, where Wes was already at his place at the controls. "I'll show you how to work this thing," Wes said.

"Oh, I think I can manage it," Randy said.

Wes handed him the controls and said to Dillon, "Look out, little buddy! When they act cool like that, they're really master video game champions trying to cover up their expertise."

"What's 'expertise'?" Dillon said.

"Watch and learn." Randy made himself comfortable on the floor and pushed the start button. Sierra had a feeling she wouldn't see him again the rest of the night. She went into the kitchen for a drink of water. Pepperoni always made her thirsty.

Tawni was at the sink, helping Mom with the few dishes that had accumulated during the day. She turned to Sierra and said, "I can't believe you're letting him do that!"

"Let who do what?"

"You turned your date over to your brothers. Those guys will play video games all night long. Don't you care that he jilted you like that?"

"Actually, no. I think I feel more comfortable with my first date being like this."

"This isn't a first date. Not when he dumps you for a runt!"

"Tawni," Mom said gently.

"This is a first date," Sierra said firmly. "This is how *I* do first dates. And I happen to like it this way."

"Well, I sure wouldn't," Tawni said.

"It's not your first date," Mom said to her older daughter. "Although I remember yours being a bit of a disaster. Didn't he take you to a restaurant that was out of business?"

"His dad told him it was a good place. They just hadn't been there for a year."

"I remember that," Sierra said. "You ended up at a Dairy Queen or something, and you were all dressed up with your hair fancy and everything."

"We still had fun," Tawni said with a slight pout.

"And I intend to still have fun tonight," Sierra said. "Anyone for a round of Trivial Pursuit?"

"Great idea," Mom said. "I'll tell Dad to set it up."

"I get Wes on my team," Tawni said.

Within twenty minutes, four teams were steeped in battle over the Trivial Pursuit board. Sierra and Randy were the team in the lead, followed by Mom and Dad. Gavin and Dillon were last, and they pooped out after half an hour and went back into the den to watch a video.

The game went on. At nearly ten o'clock, Sierra reached her hand into the popcorn bowl and drew another fistful to her mouth. Randy rolled the dice, and she said, "Okay, this is it. Game point!"

Randy moved their marker to a hot-pink square, and Wes pulled the question card from the box. "Oh, perfect!" he said, reading the question to himself. "You'll never get this, Sierra."

"Let me see," Tawni said, looking over Wesley's shoulder. "I have no idea what the answer is. You'll never get it, Sierra."

"Just read it," Mom said.

"Okay. For the game, the question is, what was Elvis Presley's middle name?"

Sierra let out a groan, but Randy immediately answered, "Aaron."

Tawni and Wes exchanged poker-face glances. "Is that your answer? It must be a team decision."

Sierra looked at Randy. "Aaron? Are you sure?"

Randy nodded.

She couldn't tell if he was right or not. He had come up with really bizarre and very wrong answers earlier in the game. She didn't know him well enough to know if he was faking it or not. Sierra drew in a deep breath. "Okay," she said. "I'll go with Aaron."

"I don't believe it!" Wes said, slapping the card onto the table. "It's right."

Randy slapped Sierra a high five. "We're the victors!"

"All right! How did you ever know that?

"I told you my dad used to be in a band. I didn't say it was a Christian band."

They all pitched in to clear the table and carry the empty popcorn bowls and glasses to the kitchen. Everyone sat around talking for another half hour or so before Randy stood to leave.

"I better get going," Randy said. "Thanks for a really great evening. 'Bye, everyone. Nice meeting you all."

Sierra's family had said good-bye to Randy, and she walked him to the front door. Dad had fixed the doorknob. Still, Sierra opened it carefully. "Thanks for coming over and everything," she said. "It really was a fun night."

"This was the best first date with someone I've ever been on," Randy said. Then looking over Sierra's shoulder to make sure no one was listening, he added, "Can I tell you something?"

"Of course."

"This was my first date of any kind."

"You're kidding! Mine too." She started to laugh and Randy joined in.

"It'll make the second date a whole lot easier," Randy said. "I still want to take you to the movies. Maybe next weekend."

"Sure. That would be fun."

"Well, good night," Randy said, giving her a crooked smile.

She held up her hand in a casual wave and said, "See you at school Monday." He left, and she carefully closed the door behind him before returning to the kitchen.

"Well, did he kiss you?" Wes wanted to know.

"Of course not! We're just friends. And you want to know something? He said it was his first date too."

"It seemed as if he had a good time," Mom said. "Once he got over the initial shock of our crazy introduction."

"Thanks, you guys, for 'double-dating' with me," Sierra said.

"Any time," Dad said. Then, turning to Tawni, he asked, "Well, was that better than the Martin the Martian disaster?"

"It depends," Tawni said.

"On what?"

"On whether or not he asks her out again. That will be the test."

# nineteen

SIERRA HAD A HARD TIME falling asleep that night. She felt as if she should think about Randy, what a fun guy he was, and how great the evening had gone. But she was thinking about Paul, wondering what it would be like to have him come over for pizza with her family. How well would Paul do at Trivial Pursuit? Would Paul have known Elvis's middle name?

She kicked at the covers and turned on her side. *What does it matter? Why am I thinking about him? My letter to him was enough to frighten anyone away. I can't believe I wrote all those things.* She thought back on how she had ended the letter, first by accusing him of using the word *sincerely* when she knew he wasn't. *And then by signing the letter so stupidly. What was it I wrote? "Irritatingly yours"? No, "very irritatedly." Why did I do that?*

With a groan she flipped over onto her back and stared at the dark ceiling. She remembered the notes in her journal about saying "forgive me" and "thank you," and the wisdom of using them often in her youth. She wanted to say "forgive me" to Paul. Even if he still thought she was an immature nerd, she didn't care. It was better than living with the memory of the unbridled words she had put into writing and mailed without thinking.

Sierra thought of how Granna Mae had told her last summer that whenever she had a big decision to make or if something was bothering her, she would bury it for three days and not think about it at all. Then, if on the morning of the third day, she found the choice or concern was alive, it would be evident God had resurrected it.

At the time, Sierra didn't understand what Granna Mae meant and had thought her grandmother was rambling. Now Sierra understood. If she had buried that letter right after she wrote it, then when she went back and looked at it three days later, her emotions would have calmed down, and she would have been thinking more clearly. That's what she would do next time. But for now, she needed to apologize.

In the stillness of the room, Sierra began to make her plan. Sunday afternoon she would write a letter of apology to Paul, and then she would call Katie and Christy to tell them that her dad had made the airline reservations.

As she began to doze off, feeling much more settled, Sierra remembered one of her recent verses from Isaiah. *With my soul I have desired You in the night.*

Sierra thought that was about the most romantic thing anyone could ever say to someone else. She whispered it aloud to the Lord. "With my soul I have desired You in the night, Jesus. Do You become tired watching me bumble things? Sometimes I get stuff right. Like tonight. That was a wonderful first date. Thanks for making it that way. Thanks for my family."

Sierra thought again about the thank-you, forgive-me quote. It seemed that with the Lord, as with all her important relationships, the words she said most frequently were "forgive me" and "thank you." She thought of how much better she would feel once she said "forgive me" to Paul.

But her eyes popped open when she remembered she had crumpled up his first letter and tossed it away. She wished she hadn't. Once again the three-day resurrection principle would have been helpful.

The next morning, as Sierra dressed for church, Mom tapped on the bathroom door. "Sierra, may I come in?"

"Sure."

"I just called the hospital to check on Granna Mae and guess what? The doctor was in her room, and he said we can bring her home this morning. Would you like to help me pick her up? He wants us to be there right away so he can go over instructions."

"Of course I'll go with you. Hang on. I'll be ready in a minute."

Dad took the rest of the family to visit the church Tawni liked in Vancouver while Mom and Sierra drove to the hospital.

"I'm relieved to have her come home," Mom said. "I know it will be a lot of work at first, but I'm glad I can count on you and Tawni to help out. She has her left foot in a cast, and I think they're going to give her a cane. She should be able to walk upstairs if we help her. I think she'll be glad to get back in her room."

The doctor was waiting for them and had a list of printed instructions. One page was on caring for a patient with a broken bone, and the other was for a patient recovering from a gallbladder surgery. Sierra wished they had one for dealing with an elderly person who was losing her mind.

"How are you feeling?" Sierra said, leaning over and giving Granna Mae a kiss on the cheek. "Did the doctor tell you that you get to go home today? This is earlier than we thought. You're doing so well!"

Granna Mae smiled and said, "Only a few like him are left in the world. Don't let him slip away."

Sierra assumed Granna Mae meant the doctor, who was standing right there. Granna Mae's favorite doctor, Dr. Utley, who had performed the operation, was still on vacation. Tawni hadn't thought much of this other doctor, but apparently Granna Mae did. Either that or she was rambling again.

"We'll send up a wheelchair," the doctor said as Mom signed some papers.

A nurse who had been standing nearby suggested, "You might want to make a trip to the car first to find a place for all these flowers."

"I'll take them," Sierra said. "I can probably do it in a couple of trips." She reached for the first gorgeous bouquet and read the card tucked in the plastic holder. It was some of Granna Mae's neighbors. The next one was from her friends at Eaton's Drug Store. There was a live plant from her friends at church. Sierra tried to balance the two bouquets and hold a vase in her hand. She got a good grip on them and was able to carry them all the way to the car only to discover it was locked.

On her second trip, she brought the keys and unlocked the car. All the flowers fit in the backseat just right, with enough room for Sierra to perch next to them on the way home.

She jogged back into the hospital, thinking about how great it was going to be to have Granna Mae home. She was glad Granna Mae had come through her surgery okay. Even with her broken foot and her memory problems, she was still alive.

When Sierra had met Paul, he was returning from his grandfather's funeral in Scotland. They had talked about how close they each were to their grandparents. Sierra had always considered Granna Mae a good friend as well as her grandma. Paul had seemed to understand that.

*Why am I thinking about Paul? I have to move on. I have other friends to think about—Randy, Amy, and Vicki, and maybe even Tawni in a unique way.*

Sierra remembered she had invited Tawni to go to California with her over Easter. She still wasn't sure why she had done that. The subject hadn't appeared again on Tawni's lips, so Sierra had determined not to bring it up either. Tawni had probably forgotten about the invitation. In two weeks, Sierra would be on her way to visit her good friends.

Until then, she had friends to eat lunch with at school, a possible date to the movies next weekend, more cinnamon rolls to serve, a dear Granna Mae to care for, and an apology letter to write.

When Sierra stepped back into the room, Granna Mae was already in the wheelchair, and her face was looking much brighter. "One more flower, Lovey!" she said. "I want to take all my daffies home with me. He was such a dear young man. Kept me company most of the evening after you left last night, Sharon."

"That's nice," Mom said, gathering Granna Mae's personal belonging from the restroom.

On the tray table was a small white vase with a single yellow daffodil. Sierra hadn't noticed it before. It almost seemed like a small decorative touch that had been served with breakfast. She wondered if someone from the hospital had brought it from his garden. Maybe the young man Granna Mae was rattling on about was a volunteer who had taken a shine to her and kept her company last night while Sierra and her family were all at home, busy playing Trivial Pursuit.

"Are we ready?" Mom asked, preparing to push the wheelchair out the door.

Granna Mae turned to the doctor and held out her hand. He grasped it, and she held his. From her lips came a gracious "Thank you." She thanked each of the nurses who came to say good-bye too. Sierra grabbed the final daffodil and followed the procession down the hall.

"Looks like you were pretty popular around here," Sierra said as two more nurses looked up from the central nurses' station and waved their good-byes. "I don't know about you, Granna Mae," Sierra teased. "Making friends everywhere you go, strange men bringing you flowers in the night..."

The small gift card attached to the daffodil vase rubbed against Sierra's thumb as she marched in Granna Mae's exit parade. Sierra glanced at it. The sight of the bold, black letters made her stop in her tracks. In a mixture of cursive and printing, the card held only two words: *"Sincerely, Paul."*

# Book Three

# DON'T YOU WISH

# one

"COME ON, BRUTUS, help me out here, buddy. I know you can't wait to get to the park, but you have to hold still." Sierra pushed away her St. Bernard's attempt to deliver a slobbery kiss and cinched the leash around his massive, furry neck. "Now remember what I said about being on your best behavior around Amy and her dog. She'll be here any minute, and I don't want you drooling all over her car's backseat."

Brutus returned Sierra's gaze with droopy brown eyes as he panted expectantly.

"Don't give me that innocent look." Sierra sat down on the floor of the front hallway and tugged on her old cowboy boots. "I'm serious. The only way to make a friend is to be a friend, and that's your job today. Be nice, okay?"

*Am I talking to Brutus or to myself?* Sierra wondered. Ever since Amy had asked Sierra if she wanted to go to the waterfront park on Saturday morning, she had been a little nervous. Making new friends in Portland had not come easily to her. Amy Degrassi was the closest thing Sierra had to a friend here, and she didn't want to blow it.

"That's the doorbell. Let's go, Brutus." That's all it took to persuade the big fur ball to take off.

Sierra grabbed his collar and opened the front door. Dark-eyed Amy met her with a laugh. "You weren't kidding! He is a monster."

"We don't have to take him if you don't want to," Sierra said, pulling hard on the leash to keep Brutus from knocking Amy over in his excitement to get outside.

"I think he would be fiercely disappointed," Amy said.

Sierra followed Amy to her car, a 1986 Volvo with a badly peeling paint job. On the backseat, with twig-like paws pressed against the window, was Peanut, Amy's itty-bitty Chihuahua.

"He's no bigger than a rat!" Sierra said. "I don't think this is such a good idea, Amy. I'm afraid Brutus is going to squash him. Or eat him."

"They'll be fine. Look, Peanut, I brought you a new friend."

Sierra expected the miniature dog to turn tail and look for a place to hide. Instead, he yipped merrily, clawing at the closed window. Brutus pressed both his paws on the glass and studied his new companion. He turned to give Sierra a look, which she imagined meant, "Is this a joke? You expect me to hang out with this little leftover?" But Brutus barked without malice, and when Amy opened the door, he even waited for Peanut to hop off the seat before he bounded inside.

"See?" Amy said. "They're going to be great friends."

Sierra's amazement didn't cease as they drove off and headed for Burnside Bridge. She peeked over her shoulder and saw the two unlikely companions sniffing each other and making all the right kinds of amiable dog motions.

"I never would have guessed," Sierra said, turning back around. As she did, a tangle of her long, curly blond hair caught in the headrest. "Ouch!"

"Ouch?"

"My hair got caught."

"I hate when that happens," Amy said, tossing her wavy, dark hair over her shoulder. "I'm ready to chop mine off. I wish I had Vicki's hair—straight and sleek."

Most of the girls at school wished they had hair like Vicki's. Not to mention a face, body, and personality like hers. She was the kind of person that made people, especially guys, stop to look twice.

"Don't you hate having naturally curly hair?" Amy asked.

"Yes." Sierra tugged the locks from the metal bar and left several strands behind. The truth was Sierra had given up wishing her hair were different. Cutting it only made it curlier. Living in the moist climate of Portland, Oregon, only made it curlier. Every kind of curl-taming shampoo she had ever used only made it curlier. She had decided long ago to let it just go wild.

"I think Vicki is interested in Randy," Amy said. "Did he say anything to you about her?"

"No, why would he? Randy has barely spoken to me this week."

"Why isn't he talking to you?" Amy asked as she eased into a parking place along a side street. She pulled out her ashtray and sorted through the coins. "I thought you guys were buddies."

"I don't know. I'd like to think so. Here, I have some money."

Sierra opened her backpack and pulled out three quarters for Amy.

In the backseat, both dogs were eagerly barking and yipping.

"Okay, okay," Sierra said. "You boys get out the side door. And mind your manners, Brutus." She opened the back door slowly, tangling with Brutus's leash until she had a firm grip. Amy put the coins into the meter as Peanut ran around her feet in circles.

"Are you excited about your trip next week?" Amy asked.

"Yes, I'm really looking forward to it." Sierra kept her answer nice and tame. Actually, she was so excited that the last two nights she had had a hard time falling asleep. She had been thinking about her friends Christy, Katie, Tracy, Todd, and Doug. She hadn't seen them since they were together in England three months ago. With Easter vacation around the corner, Sierra had big plans to spend the week with them. But she toned down her answer because she didn't want Amy to think she was so wrapped up in those friends that she wasn't in the market for a few new ones.

"I wish I were going somewhere fun." Amy said, dropping the last coin in the meter. "It's going to be pretty uneventful around here."

"Brutus!" Sierra cried. He had run out of patience during their small talk and taken off across the grass at a gallop, with Sierra sailing behind him at the end of his leash. Not to be outdone, Peanut yipped wildly, tippy-tap-toeing his way after them.

Brutus flew across the long stretch of grass and came to a screeching halt in front of the water fountain. This downtown Portland landmark was designed with several circles of holes bored into the concrete sidewalk. The holes shot arcs of water ten or more feet into the air before they all convened in the center. It wasn't a particularly warm April morning, yet a few kids were dodging in and out of the watery spires, trying to weave their way through the open spaces before the water pattern changed and the kids got soaked.

"Don't even think of it, Brutus," Sierra said, pulling him back toward the walkway. They waited for Amy and Peanut to catch up, and then Sierra and Amy tried to walk along the waterfront like normal people out for a Saturday stroll on a fine spring morning. Such an activity proved impossible.

Brutus galloped ahead despite Sierra's trying to slow him down. Peanut, not willing to be outdone, sprinted. He looked as if he would have a heart attack before they had gone more than a hundred yards. Joggers and bikers passed them, turning their heads for a second look at the giant bumbler and tiny toe-tapper. Some of them laughed at the strange sight.

"I don't think this is working," Sierra said, yanking Brutus to a halt, catching her breath. "Maybe we should try to carry Peanut."

"I wish we had brought Rollerblades," Amy said. "Brutus could have pulled both of us with no effort. Come here, Peanut. I'll carry you."

"Why don't we put him in my backpack?" Sierra suggested. "Here, hold this." She handed Amy Brutus's leash and took off her backpack, opening the top to make room for Peanut. Scooping up the little guy, she could feel his heart pounding.

"No, come back!" Amy screamed. The leash had slipped from her hand, and Brutus had bolted toward the fountain.

"Get him!" Sierra called, quickly stuffing Peanut into her backpack and looping the straps over her shoulders. She took off running and caught up with Amy at the fountain. Brutus had dashed into the center and was lapping at the water, standing on dry ground. The fountain, for some reason, was off.

"Well, that's a good thing," Sierra said, catching her breath. "Do they turn it off like that all the time?"

"Come here, Brutus," Amy said, patting her legs and whistling. "Come, boy." She turned to Sierra for only an instant to say, "The fountain turns off like this before it changes to the next water pattern. It's going to blast any second now."

"Brutus, get over here!" Sierra yelled.

Not willing to risk getting soaked when the fountain turned back on, both girls called, whistled, and clapped their hands. No use. Brutus found the refreshing drink, as well as all the attention, to his liking. There he stood, in the center of the fountain, as all the holes in the ground began to gurgle.

KETUSH! A dozen sprays of water shot like rockets directly under Brutus, nearly lifting him on impact.

"Look at that St. Bernard. What a chump!" Sierra heard a guy behind her say. Before she could see who was insulting her dog, the same voice said, "Sierra? Amy?"

Sierra turned to see Randy, his head tilted to the side, his straight blond hair hanging with a crooked part down the middle. He had a skateboard under his arm and was flanked by a shorter guy Sierra didn't know. "What are you two doing here?"

"Trying to get my dog out of the water. Come here, Brutus!"

Randy and the other guy joined the chorus, all calling Brutus out of the wet. Brutus had found a happy position, away from any direct shot of water but under an umbrella of mist.

Sierra shook her head. "It's hopeless," she said to no one in particular.

Peanut began to yip from the pack on Sierra's back. "Oh, and now I suppose you want to join him."

"What are you hiding in there?" Randy asked, stepping over and lifting the flap of Sierra's backpack. "Whoa!" he said in surprise as Peanut popped his head up and yipped in Randy's face. "Check it out, Dan. A big mouse."

"That's my dog," Amy said.

"That's a dog?" Dan asked.

"Come here, Peanut," Amy said in a cooing voice, lifting the quivering little animal from his nest. "Don't pay any attention to these mean ol' boys."

The four of them were standing with their backs to the fountain when Brutus decided to leave his invigorating shower and join them. Before Sierra could warn the others, he let loose with a might shake, dousing them all.

"Brutus!" Sierra reached for his collar and tried to pull the wet blob away from them. "Sorry, you guys."

"Hey, no problem. I needed a shower," Randy said. Then, catching Sierra's eye, he asked, "When do you work this week?"

"Today, next Tuesday, and next Thursday." She looked at Dan and then at Randy. "Why?"

"Just wondering."

Brutus gave one last good shake before Sierra firmly gripped his leash. "You're not making this very easy on me, Brutus. You think you could try to mellow out for a few minutes?"

For an answer, Brutus let out a mighty "ruff" and bolted for the fountain, taking Sierra along with him. She didn't even have time to yell at her wayward dog. Slipping on the wet cement, she was pulled involuntarily on her backside into the fountain, where she was thoroughly soaked in two seconds.

She expected to hear a burst of laughter from the others. Instead, Randy gave a war whoop. "Water war!" he yelled, leading the way into the fountain. Dan, Amy, and Peanut all followed, hooting and hollering—and barking, in Peanut's case. For a full five minutes, Sierra and Brutus were the focus of the frenzied splash attack. Everyone was laughing and getting soaked to the skin as Brutus barked and barked.

Then the water stopped, preparing to launch a new pattern into the air. The group took advantage of the break and stepped away from the gurgling holes. They laughed and tossed meaningless threats at each other, trying to shake themselves off. A breeze swept off the Willamette River, and Sierra began to shiver.

"I'm freezing," Amy said. Her dark hair hung in her face, and she held the quivering Peanut in her arms. "We're going to the car. 'Bye, you guys. See you later." Amy took off at a fast trot.

"I'll be right there," Sierra said and then turned to Randy. "Why did you ask about when I worked?" She was dripping wet, but her curiosity overruled her desire to run to the warm car. She had had one casual date with Randy several weeks ago. He had promised then to take her to the movies sometime. Sierra was stubborn enough to hold him to that promise, but something in her wanted him to be the one to bring up the subject.

"I'll probably stop by to see you," Randy said. Then, lowering his voice, he added, "I want to ask you something."

"So ask me now," Sierra challenged. Her teeth were chattering.

"No, you're freezing," he said. "I'll catch you at work, okay?"

Sierra gave him a look of pretend annoyance before surrendering to the chill and the persistent yank of Brutus's leash. Then, using one of Randy's favorite words back on him, she said, "Whatever," and jogged to the car with Brutus.

She hoped she hadn't appeared too disinterested. She liked Randy, but she wasn't dazzled by him. He was a buddy—that was all.

Amy had the heater on, waiting for her. "Well? Did he ask you out?"

"No, but he said he would see me at work. And that could mean anything."

"We both know what we hope it means," Amy said, popping the gearshift into reverse. "And don't worry, I won't say anything to Vicki."

"There's nothing to say," Sierra said, rolling down her

window halfway. "Phew! Does it smell like stinky, slobby dog in here or what? Brutus, you need a bath."

He let out a happy "ruff," as if he fancied the thought of more water.

# two

WHEN SIERRA REACHED HOME, she grabbed an old towel from the garage and dried Brutus off before leading him to his doghouse. She entered the kitchen by the back door and found her mom standing over the stove, scrambling eggs in a large frying pan.

A slim, energetic woman, Sharon Jensen managed to keep up with her six children, and nothing usually surprised her. However, when she turned to look at Sierra, her mouth dropped slightly and she said, "What happened to you? Or do I want to know?"

"Amy and I learned that the next time we go for a morning walk, we leave the dogs at home. Brutus dragged me into the fountain." Sierra grabbed her soggy hair and held it up in a ponytail as she leaned over the warm stove. "Those eggs smell good. Can you throw in a couple more for me? I'm going to take a quick shower to get warmed up."

"They'll be ready when you are," Mom said.

A fast ten minutes later, Sierra returned wearing her favorite ragged overalls. Her hair was wrapped in a bath towel, twisted on top of her head. She found a plate of eggs and toast waiting for her on the kitchen counter.

Her older sister, Tawni, was sitting on a stool, sipping grapefruit juice and showing Mom her little finger on her left hand. "It got caught on the edge of the cash drawer and ripped the nail right off." Tawni worked at Nordstrom's, selling perfume. At eighteen and a half, she seemed to have her life neatly in order, the same way she kept her side of the bedroom she shared with Sierra. Tawni was tall, slim, and poised, and she would never spend her Saturday morning running in a fountain the way Sierra just had with her new friends.

Mom made a sympathetic face over the broken nail.

"Do we have any honey?" Sierra asked. Mom reached into the cupboard above the dishwasher and lifted down a ceramic honey pot in the shape of a beehive.

"Did Dad tell you?" Tawni asked, turning her attention to Sierra. Tawni was dressed for work, with every hair in place. The two sisters could not look more opposite than they did at this moment.

"Tell me what?"

"About next week."

"What about next week?" Sierra said, taking a bite of eggs.

"I'm going to California with you."

"What?!" Sierra nearly choked. "Whose idea was that?"

Tawni looked surprised and then hurt. "It was your idea, Sierra. You asked if I wanted to come with you, and I said I'd let you know."

"But that was weeks ago," Sierra said, remembering her moment of weakness when she had felt compassion for

Tawni. The two of them had been in the midst of a rare civil conversation. They had agreed it had been hard for both of them to make new friends since the move to Portland.

Tawni's posture and facial expression turned to mush. "I thought you meant it," she said. "I asked Dad to look into airline tickets, and he has me booked on the flight with you. I suppose he could cancel it if you don't want me to go."

"It's just that..." Sierra didn't know how to say what she really felt—that she was going to visit her special friends and they were a part of her life that had nothing to do with Tawni. Sierra didn't want to compete with her sister over her Southern California friends as she'd had to compete her entire life with perfect Tawni. "I guess I thought you didn't want to come."

"I didn't know if I wanted to or not. Then I started to think about it, and it seemed like a fun idea. It was easy to get the time off work." Tawni stood and carried her empty glass to the sink. "But I won't come if you don't want me to."

Sierra felt her jaw clenching. She knew her mom was patiently observing, letting the two of them work things out, the way Mom always did.

"Tawni—" Sierra sucked in a nerve-replenishing breath. "I don't mind if you come. I was surprised, that's all."

A smile returned to Tawni's face, lighting up her blue eyes. "You really don't mind?"

"No." Sierra felt fairly sure she was telling the truth.

"Great! I haven't been anywhere in so long. Tell me what we're going to do so I know what to pack."

Sierra had a sickening feeling in the pit of her stomach. "Well, we're staying at the beach with Christy's aunt and uncle. Maybe I should call and make sure they don't mind another guest."

"I thought you said it was okay for me to come."

"I didn't exactly ask Christy before I asked you."

"Oh, great! Maybe you should call her before we make any more plans."

The phrase "before we make any more plans" hit Sierra like a renegade volleyball in gym class. *We? They used to be just my plans.* "Fine. I'll call her as soon as I finish eating." At least she could keep control over eating her meal, even though her appetite disappeared.

"Perfect," Tawni said. "I really appreciate this, Sierra. Well, I'm off. See you after five."

Sierra caught her mom's smile and nod of approval. She knew Mom thought she had handled the situation well. Too bad she didn't feel the same way. Now she had to call Christy and explain that her sister was coming. The odd part was that Christy, Katie, and Tracy were all Tawni's age—or older. Yet when Sierra roomed with these girls in England, she had felt more on their level than she did with any of her friends at home or with Tawni, who had never treated Sierra as an equal the way Christy and the others had.

Sierra put off the dreaded phone call all weekend. Her excuse to Tawni was she had to work from ten to four at Mama Bear's, and then there was church and homework and—poof—the weekend was over.

By Tuesday evening, Sierra was still stalling. She walked in the front door as Mom stepped out of the kitchen carrying a tray with a plate of steaming vegetables, turkey, and applesauce. "Oh, good, you're home. How was work?"

Sierra knew this wasn't the time to launch into a big story about how Randy had said on Saturday morning that he would stop by work, yet he hadn't come in on Saturday, he didn't talk to her at school the last two days, and he didn't come into the bakery this afternoon. Thursday was the last day she worked before her big trip to Southern California. Just when was Randy planning on stopping by?

It wasn't that Mom wouldn't understand Sierra's boy problems. But at the moment, she was standing there holding a tray of hot food in her hands. So Sierra answered with a simple "Fine."

"Good. Dinner's ready if you want to go sit down."

"Why don't I take that up to Granna Mae?" Sierra asked.

Mom looked as if she relaxed a bit. "Sure. And could you tell Tawni to come down?"

"Okay." Sierra took the dinner tray and headed up the stairs. She stopped by her bedroom first and called through the closed door, "Tawni, dinner's ready. Tell them to go ahead. I'm going to sit with Granna Mae while she eats."

Tawni opened the bedroom door and said, "Did you call your friend yet?"

"I didn't exactly have time," Sierra snapped. "I just walked in the door."

"You had better call her tonight. You're not being fair to me. I need to know, Sierra!"

"You're right, you're right. I'll call her after dinner."

Tawni swished past Sierra and headed down the stairs, an invisible trail of gardenia scent wafting in her wake, the remains of her day at work.

Sierra carefully balanced the tray and tapped on the

bedroom door at the end of the hall. "It's me, Granna Mae. I brought your dinner."

"Do come in, Lovey," a high, twittery voice called.

Twisting the old doorknob, Sierra entered the large bedroom of her grandmother, who was recovering from surgery. Granna Mae was wearing her favorite white cotton nightgown with a stand-up lace collar. And to Sierra's amazement, the collar wasn't the only thing standing up.

"Granna Mae!" Sierra quickly set down the tray and rushed over to where the tottering woman with a cast on her foot stood on the soft cushion of her built-in window seat. Her arm was extended over her head.

"What are you doing?"

"I decided I had watched that spider in her web long enough!" She showed Sierra the wad of silky thread stuck to one of her lacy handkerchiefs.

"I was about to name her Charlotte. Wasn't that the spider's name in that sweet children's book?"

Sierra took the hanky and placed it on the dresser. She reached for her grandmother's elbow and helped her down. "You shouldn't be doing things like that. Tell me or Mom or Dad, and we'll come kill spiders for you. You shouldn't be climbing on furniture. Come back to bed."

"Oh, really now!" Granna Mae swatted the air with her hand. Taking Sierra's outstretched arm, she limped back to her bed. "I've become quite tired of all this bed rest. Do you know what I'd really like? A walk to Eaton's Drug Store for chocolate malts. Yes, that's what I fancy for my dinner this evening. A look at the last tulips of spring around the neighborhood and a visit with my friends at Eaton's. You can take me there, can't you, Lovey?"

Granna Mae had broken her foot when she was in the hospital for emergency gallbladder surgery. She had decided to go for a little walk one evening, pulled out her IV, and then fell in the hospital gift shop. In recent years, Granna Mae's mind had begun to play tricks on her, so Sierra's family had moved here from a small town near Lake Tahoe, California, to live with her in her old Victorian home. Whenever she was thinking clearly, Granna Mae called Sierra "Lovey."

"I'll ask Dad," Sierra said. "First you need to eat your dinner before it gets cold." She held back the covers so Granna Mae could slip into bed.

"What did you bring me?" Granna Mae asked, slowly hoisting her legs under the covers. She leaned forward while Sierra adjusted the pillows behind her grandmother's back and tucked the blanket around her. With her hands folded on top of the handmade patchwork quilt, she looked at Sierra expectantly, innocently.

"Turkey, Granna Mae. Are you hungry?"

"Yes, I am, and turkey suits me fine. Are you going to eat with me?"

"No, but I'll stay with you."

Granna Mae reached over and slipped her cool hand into Sierra's. It felt like wrinkled silk, soft and familiar. "And you'll pray with me, won't you?"

"Of course." Sierra bowed her head and closed her eyes, allowing her ruffled emotions to settle down. She loved being with her dear grandmother alone like this and praying with her. With four brothers and one sister, Sierra had little time alone with her grandmother when Sierra was growing up. But every time her family visited through the years, Granna Mae had always found a way, found the time, to sit down with each of her grandchildren and pray with him or her. It always made Sierra feel special and singled out from the bunch. Sierra grew up believing that's how God thought of her too—as one-of-a-kind and worthy of His love and attention.

"Amen," Granna Mae said when Sierra finished praying. She squeezed Sierra's hand. "Now, tell me all about your day. How did you do on your science test?"

"That was yesterday. I did fine."

"Another A, I suspect," Granna Mae said, cutting her turkey with slightly quivering hands.

"I think so."

"Don't ever take those brains of yours for granted, Lovey. Do you hear me?"

Sierra nodded and smiled. Learning came easily to her. She still had to study to get A's, but it was never hard. The hardest part was feeling motivated enough to care about whether she was getting straight A's or not. Grades didn't matter that much to Sierra.

"And when do you leave for your great adventure in England?"

"I already went to England. That was last January, remember? I'm going down to Southern California on Friday to see the friends I met in England."

"Oh, yes." Granna Mae slipped a dainty spoonful of vegetables into her mouth and nodded at Sierra. She swallowed and asked, "And will Paul be there?"

Sierra quietly bit the inside of her lower lip. She had an uncle named Paul who had been killed in Vietnam. Often when Granna Mae's memory turned fuzzy, she would ask about Paul.

"Ah, no. My friends down there are Christy, Katie, Tracy, Doug, and Todd."

Granna Mae reached for the china teacup that held her strong black coffee, and she took a sip. "Pity that you won't see that nice Paul. You know he brought me daffies at the hospital and kept me company for hours my last night there. He is such a dear young man."

Now Sierra knew her grandmother hadn't slipped into another time zone. She was talking about a different Paul. This Paul was the one Sierra had met at the airport in England. Their relationship, if one could call it that, was a strange blending of chance meetings and a few pithy letters. That was all.

"No, Granna Mae, Paul won't be there."

"Pity," she repeated, stirring the applesauce.

Sierra settled in the overstuffed chair by the fireplace, slipped off her shoes, and curled up her legs underneath to keep her feet warm. She hadn't allowed herself the luxury of thinking about Paul for quite a few days, maybe even weeks. They had experienced such an intense connection when they had first met. Her grandmother almost sounded as if she had a strong affection for him, too. Why was that?

"You must pray for that young man," Granna Mae said. "Do you?"

"I did for a while, but..."

There was a quick tap on the door. Tawni opened it and said, "Sierra, you have a phone call. I think it's Christy."

# three

"ARE YOU SURE your aunt and uncle won't mind?" Sierra asked Christy on the phone down in her dad's study. She had retreated there to have some privacy. It was her favorite room in the house, and she was sitting in her favorite chair.

"No, I'm sure they won't," Christy said. "My uncle likes having us around, and my aunt likes to..." She seemed to search for the right word. "She likes planning things. I'm sure she'll like you and your sister. Tell me your flight number again so I can write it down."

Sierra repeated the information, and Christy said, "One of us will pick you up at the airport and drive you to Newport Beach. If Katie and I can't get up there soon enough, Todd said he would pick you up. Then we'll meet at my aunt and uncle's house. I'm sure they're planning on having dinner with us that night. The next day is open. We can hang out at the beach or go shopping or whatever you want."

"You guys don't have to entertain us," Sierra said. "We don't have to go anywhere. The beach is enough for me."

"Todd and Doug are bringing a bunch of their friends from the San Diego God Lovers' group."

"Sounds fun."

"I'm sure it will be. I'm really glad you're coming. Our time together in England went so fast. Makes me wish you lived down here."

"I know. Me, too. Thanks for inviting me, and I appreciate your letting Tawni come, too."

"Sure. You and Tawni must be pretty close."

Sierra tilted her head toward the phone receiver. The door to her dad's study was open, and she didn't know who might be able to hear her. "Not really. This was her idea, not mine."

"I'm sure it'll be fine," Christy said reassuringly. "The guest room is plenty big for the four of us—you, me, Katie, and Tawni. And there'll be so many people around all week. I'm sure Tawni will have a good time, and you will, too. It'll be like a big reunion. I can't wait!"

"I'm looking forward to it," Sierra said. "I hope I didn't sound negative about my sister. It's just that I guess it would have been easier or different or something if I were coming by myself." Then, changing the subject, she said, "How's Todd doing?"

"Great as always."

Sierra thought she heard a smile in Christy's voice. "Did he decide about going back to Spain?"

"Not yet. Lots of factors need to be considered. He's taking classes at the University of California, Irvine, this semester. I think I told you that before. And he's been in communication with the missions director at Carnforth

Hall. They'll gladly take him on staff in Spain or anywhere in Europe when he wants to make the commitment."

"And where does that leave you?"

"I want to get my AA degree in early childhood development as soon as possible. That's about all I have time for. After that, it's up to God."

"You and Todd haven't made any plans?"

"No. If one theme runs through our relationship, it's s-l-o-w. Everything has gone slowly for us, and just because we're both on the same side of the globe now, that hasn't changed. I don't mind, though. For now it feels just right. How about you? Whatever happened with the guy you met at the airport?"

"Paul? Nothing."

"Then what about the guy from your school who came over. Was it Randy? Did he ever take you out again?"

"No," Sierra sighed. "Until this weekend, he had been ignoring me. Then he said he would come see me at work, but he hasn't, and today he practically ignored me again."

"Sounds like an average guy to me," Christy said. "Don't get discouraged. Who knows? You might meet someone here next week. One of Doug's friends, maybe. Newport Beach is a wonderful place to meet someone special."

"I take it that's where you met Todd."

"Yep. Almost five years ago. Can you believe it?"

"Five years! You and Todd should be the poster couple for the 'Love Waits' campaign."

Christy laughed. "It doesn't seem that long. A lot has happened during those five years. But I do agree that true love is worth the wait. I'd wait another five years for Todd if I had to. He's the only man for me. Ever."

An hour after hanging up from her call with Christy, Sierra still felt a warm glow. There was something encouraging and beautiful about two people who were in love the way Christy and Todd were. It made Sierra wonder if she would be willing to wait ten years to marry a guy if she were so intensely in love with him. Maybe it was good that she had never had a boyfriend. Being in love at sixteen could create all kinds of problems.

The next evening the thought surfaced again in Sierra's mind while she was doing her homework. She asked Tawni if she felt ready to marry. Tawni stood over her open luggage, meticulously folding the pile of T-shirts she had laid on her bed alongside a pile of jeans, shorts, and enough accessories to open a jewelry stand at a swap meet.

"Am I ready to marry? Why are you asking me such a pointless question? I'm not even dating anyone."

"I know, but if you met someone and fell in love, would you want to marry him now, or would you wait?"

"Wait for what?"

"Oh, never mind," Sierra said, returning to her homework.

"When do you plan to pack, Sierra?"

"Tomorrow."

"Are all your clothes clean? Wait. That was a ridiculous question. Of course your clothes aren't clean. I want you to know that I'm not going to help you pull your stuff together at the last minute, and I don't want you to plan on borrowing any of my clothes once we get down there."

"Like I would," Sierra said. Even though she and Tawni were about the same size, their tastes were completely opposite. Sierra's style was carefree and casual. Tawni preferred color-coordinated, classic-style clothes.

A knock at their door was followed by their dad's clean-shaven face peeking in. "The boys and I are taking Granna Mae for a little ride down to Eaton's. You girls want to come? Shakes are on me."

"No."

"No thanks, Dad. I have too much homework," Sierra said.

"And she needs to wash her clothes for next week," Tawni added.

"Sure you can't take a break?" he asked, stepping into the room. Howard Jensen was a trim man with a receding hairline and a perpetual "open" look about him, which made him seem approachable any time, regarding any subject. He had a way of making Sierra feel as if she were his only child, not one of six. She suspected others felt the same way. "Free chocolate shakes," he said, trying to tempt them.

"I better keep at this," Sierra said, nodding toward the books surrounding her where she sat in bed, knees up, pillow against the headboard and notebook open in her elevated lap. "I'm glad you're taking Granna Mae. She'll be happy."

"I never need to be asked twice when it comes to having a malt at Eaton's. Should we bring something back for either of you?"

"Not for me," Sierra said.

"You know I'm on a diet, Dad," Tawni said.

"Right. I forgot." He ducked out, and a couple minutes later they heard him call into Granna Mae's room, "Your carriage awaits you, madam."

The sound of shuffling feet followed and then the echoing calls of their younger brothers, Gavin and Dillon, at the bottom of the stairs asking if they could take Brutus with them.

"As long as he's on a leash," Dad called back.

Sierra smiled. As if a leash made a difference with that walrus. She wanted to join them. It would be so much easier to forget all this homework and go have some fun. Plenty of light remained in the dusk sky this mild spring night. The endless Portland rains had let up for the past few days, and a warm, sweet scent filled the air. Sierra reminded herself that in a few days she would be having plenty of fun on a sunny beach in Southern California. For now, she had work to do.

"Do you think I should take both my bathing suits?" Tawni asked.

"Sure. Why not? They don't take up much room," Sierra said. "I'm taking all three of mine."

"I can't decide," Tawni said.

"Take both of them. Because once we get there, you're not borrowing any of my clothes!" Sierra playfully pointed her pencil at Tawni and shook it to emphasize her words.

"Like I would," Tawni muttered, placing both bathing suits inside her suitcase.

# four

THURSDAY AFTERNOON Sierra arrived at Mama Bear's a few minutes early and entered through the back door. She found her blue apron waiting, along with a pan of Mama Bear's famous cinnamon rolls on the lunch table. This is where they put the rolls jokingly referred to as the "burnt sacrifices" of the day. At least one pan a day was deemed unfit to sell by the owner, Mrs. Kraus, which left the employees free to eat to their hearts' content. Sierra pulled off a big piece. It was still warm—the only way to enjoy a Mama Bear's cinnamon roll.

"Hi, Sierra," Jody called to her from the front register. "I'm glad you're here. I have to leave early to run to the bank. Are you ready to take over?"

Sierra couldn't answer with the sticky wad in her mouth. She made her way to the front, tying her apron as she went and massaging the roll in her mouth. She faced Jody and nodded, still not able to swallow the bite.

"Good grief, girl," her fellow employee said. "A whole pan is back there. You don't have to down it all in one bite!"

Sierra quickly swallowed and joined Jody in a laugh.

"Okay. I'm all set now. You can go."

"You sure?"

Sierra nodded.

"I like you," Jody said. "Did I ever tell you that?"

Sierra thought, *Just every time I work the same days you do*. She smiled her mutual appreciation back to Jody and poured herself a cup of water.

"You add spunk to this place," Jody said, untying her apron. "I'm going to miss you next week."

"I'll bring you back some sand from the beach," Sierra said.

"No, don't. It'll only make me jealous. And don't you dare come back all tanned, with your hair bleached white."

"I promise my hair won't be bleached white, but I can't promise about the tan. That's one of the hazards, you know, of lounging on the beach all day for a week."

"Oh, hush. I don't want to hear about it. I'm leaving." Jody said, exiting with a friendly wave. She was in her early thirties and was the divorced mother of two. She worked two jobs and never seemed to have enough time to run errands. More than once Sierra had covered for her so she could drive her kids to the dentist or soccer practice. Sierra and Jody rarely worked the same hours.

The shop was quiet this afternoon, as usual for this time of day. Three women sat at a table by the window, bent forward in solemn conversation. Two men in business suits looked together at the screen of a laptop computer. Sierra noticed they both had coffee and went over with the fresh pot and offered them refills. She did the same for the women.

The door opened, and Randy stepped in, his crooked smile lighting up his face.

Sierra held up the coffeepot and, playing out the waitress role, said, "Coffee, sir?"

She tried to mask that she was irritated at him for being so mysterious. First, on Saturday he had said he would come see her. Then he pretty much avoided her all week at school. Now, here he was showing up on Thursday, as if this were what he meant all along. If he hadn't been so shy and inexperienced at dating, she would have been mad at him.

"Got milk?" Randy answered. "And the biggest cinnamon roll in the house. With extra frosting."

"Coming right up." Sierra said, returning to the area behind the counter. Randy followed her and leaned against the glass bakery case as she served his cinnamon roll and milk.

"Any chance you can take a break and sit down with me?" he asked.

"Not right now. I'm the only one here except Andy in the back. I need to stay behind the counter."

"Then I'll eat right here." He handed her some money and popped open the top of the milk carton, slugging it down all at once. "Better get me another milk," he said. "And a cup of water, if you don't mind, miss."

"Not a bit." Sierra felt a flock of flapping butterflies begin to dance in her stomach. Why should she feel nervous? She handed him the change and set another carton of milk and a cup of ice water on the counter for him. He was already two bites into the cinnamon roll.

"Good, aren't they?"

Now Randy was the one with the gooey ball of dough in

his mouth, and he could only nod his agreement.

*So, come on, Randy, what's the big mysterious thing you wanted to ask me? It took you long enough to finally come in. Are you going to ask me out or not?*

Finally he said, "What kind of flowers do you like?"

"Me?" It was the last question in the world Sierra expected him to ask.

He nodded and took another bite of his cinnamon roll. The white frosting dripped down the corner of his mouth.

Sierra motioned with her finger on the side of her mouth. Randy caught the hint and reached for a napkin. Another customer entered the store, setting off the cheery bell over the front door. At the sound, Randy stepped aside so the woman could order a box of cinnamon rolls to go. Then another customer came in who wanted a cappuccino. Sierra went through the familiar motions of preparing the specialty coffee drink and making change for the man's twenty-dollar bill. By the time she was ready to answer Randy's question, he had finished his snack and he was casually waiting for her with his arm across the top of the cash register.

"You wanted to know what kind of flowers I like?" she said. In the several minutes that had passed since he has asked, her mind had run through every possible reason Randy would pose such a question. All her hopes pointed to the obvious—and very flattering—conclusion.

"Right. What kind do you like?"

"That would depend. What would the flowers be for?"

"A corsage."

"And what would the corsage be for?"

"A spring benefit for the Portland Center for the

Performing Arts. Two weeks from tomorrow night at the downtown Hilton."

Sierra thought this had to be the most backward way a guy had ever asked a girl out in the history of the world. But Randy was creative—and a little shy. This seemed to fit his style. She remembered that his father had been in a band. Perhaps this was a yearly event Randy attended with his family. She immediately started to think about what she would wear to such a formal event.

"Roses are always nice. Or carnations. But carnations can be kind of bulky and heavy on a dress. Let's see. Orchids make me think of an old lady. I'd say rosebuds. A soft color like yellow or pink. Oh, I know—have you ever seen those peach-colored tea roses? Those would be really pretty in a corsage."

"Peach-colored tea roses. Okay."

Sierra smiled her anticipation at Randy. She had never been given flowers before, or asked to a formal anything. It would be fun to go to something like this with Randy since he was so easygoing and such a sincere friend. She wondered if she would have time to find a dress during the week after Easter vacation. Or maybe they could go shopping in California, as Christy suggested. It couldn't be too fancy, yet it would have to be nice enough so that the tea rose corsage wouldn't look out of place. Tawni would certainly volunteer to do her makeup. And her parents would want to take pictures.

Sierra's imagination continued to sprint through all the details as another customer stepped into the shop and ordered a single roll to go.

After she handed the customer the white bag and his change, Randy glanced at his watch.

"I have to run. Hey, do me a favor and don't say anything about this to Vicki, okay?"

"Sure." Sierra wasn't sure why he would say such a thing except maybe Vicki was beginning to be interested in Randy, and he didn't want her to be jealous of Sierra. "See you tomorrow at school."

"See you," he echoed, and he was out the door.

Sierra began her afternoon cleanup chores, starting with wiping down the counters. *Two weeks from tomorrow night,* she repeated to herself. *Maybe I can find a black dress and wear my ivory lace vest. Or something from the vintage shop in a sheer fabric with a full skirt. I should have told him white roses. White flowers would be easier to match than peach. Why did I ever tell him peach?*

A few more customers found their way into the shop during the next hour and a half. A few minutes before closing, the door opened, and Sierra looked up to see that her last customer of the day was her mom.

"Hi, honey." Mom wore jogging clothes, and her blond hair was pulled back in what Tawni called a nub of a ponytail. Tawni's hair was long and silky and hung past her shoulders, where it curled naturally on the ends. Tawni had little sympathy for Sierra's wild mane or Mom's thin, straight hair, which took a fair amount of effort to work into a presentable style. "I thought you might like some company on your walk home."

"Wait till you hear my news!" Sierra locked up the cash register and put her apron in the back. She said good night to Andy and left the shop, her arm linked in her mom's.

"Randy came in, and he asked me out to a formal dinner two weeks from tomorrow! It's a benefit for the music center downtown or something. He asked what kind of flowers I liked, and guess what I told him?"

"I can't imagine," her mom said as they marched up the street toward home.

"Peach-colored tea roses. Where in the world did I come up with that?"

"I don't know. And what are you going to wear?"

"I think I need something new."

"Do you mean new, new? Or new to you, from a thrift store?"

"Either. Whatever. Something nice. I know I shouldn't be so excited since it's just Randy," Sierra confessed, "but this is really fun! I can't believe he asked me."

"I can." She gave Sierra's arm a squeeze. "You just wait, Sierra Mae Jensen. Once the word is out, there will be standing room only as the eligible young men of Portland line up, waiting to ask you out."

"Yeah," Sierra said dryly, "don't I wish."

Sierra imagined what that line would look like. There would be half a dozen surfer-type guys from Christy's beach crowd, a few guys from school, including Randy at the front of the line, and way at the back would be a lone figure in a brown leather jacket, wearing an Indiana Jones-style hat, just like the one Paul had on when she met him.

It was only a dream, but an intriguing one, and one Sierra decided to carry around with her for a while.

# five

FRIDAY AT SCHOOL, all Sierra had were her dreams—her dreams and a headache. She had stayed up late packing for the trip, much to Tawni's disgust, and Randy said only five words to her the whole day: "'Bye. Have a nice vacation."

Everyone was a bit frenzied, though, turning in reports and homework before the week off. Sierra planned to tell Amy about Randy coming to Mama Bear's and asking her out, but there was never a convenient moment when they were far enough away from listening ears.

Mom and Tawni picked Sierra up from school the minute classes were dismissed. They drove to the airport in less than twenty minutes and Mom dropped them off. Everything went as smooth as could be, and Sierra and Tawni's flight left on time, which was a relief.

"Look how green everything is," Tawni said from her window seat. "I got tired of the rain this winter, but when you see the results from this view, it seems worth it."

Sierra didn't answer. She was lost in a memory of her flight home from England when she sat next to Paul and they had discussed life. She had been her usual blunt self, which hadn't scared Paul. Her relationship with Randy was different. She didn't feel as if she had to prove anything with him—but then again, it didn't matter as much if he liked her or not.

Christy's words from the other day returned to her, and Sierra thought about what it would be like if she met someone this week. Long walks on the beach. Shared jokes and goofing off with her friends. Good-byes and promises to write. Mom had always encouraged her to dream, and dream she did. Only, none of her dreams for this week included Tawni.

They exited the plane and made their way to baggage claim. Sierra began to scan the faces at the crowded airport as they waited for their luggage to appear on the designated carousel.

"Which of your friends has the red hair?" Tawni asked.

"Katie. Christy's hair is more like yours. Long, brown, and sort of straight."

"My hair isn't straight."

"Okay, long, brown, and sort of whatever."

"They're not here," Tawni said, looking around. "This is just great, Sierra. What are we going to do now?"

"Relax, will you? She said they would be here. Keep looking."

They stood together in the middle of the growing crowd, Sierra clutching her backpack and Tawni holding her vanity kit with both hands. The noise of the terminal began to close in on Sierra.

"I could call her," Sierra suggested.

"Do you have her cell phone number?"

"No."

"Sierra!"

"What?"

"How can you be so disorganized about everything?"

"I have her home phone number."

Just then, Sierra heard a loud, "Hey, Sierra! Over here."

They both looked and saw a tall, blond surfer dodging his way toward them. As he neared, Sierra noticed his screaming silver-blue eyes.

"Todd!" Sierra opened her arms to receive his breathless hug. The back of his T-shirt was wet with perspiration.

"How's it going? Hey, Tawni," he said, turning to Sierra's surprised yet obviously impressed sister. He gave her a quick, welcoming hug and said, "I'm Todd."

"Hello," Tawni said, all her best manners and posture coming to the fore. "It's nice to meet you."

"Let me carry that for you," he said, reaching for Tawni's makeup case. Sierra had teased Tawni about it, saying it looked like a little girl's play suitcase and should have the words "Going to Grandma's" printed across the side.

"That's okay," Tawni said, unwilling to surrender the case. "I've got it."

"I take it you have more luggage, though."

"Slightly," Sierra said with a laugh. "It hasn't come through on the carousel yet. Is Christy with you?"

"No, but she should be at Bob and Marti's by the time we get there. She was running too late with the Friday afternoon traffic, so she called and asked me to pick you up. Sorry to keep you waiting."

"Don't worry about it," Tawni said, stepping next to Todd. "We didn't wait long. We really appreciate your going out of the way like this. Thanks."

"No problem."

A loud buzzer sounded, and the luggage carousel clanged into motion.

"It's too crowded right here," Todd said. "Let's go around to the side. It'll be easier to grab your stuff."

He took off, leading the way. Sierra reached for Tawni, pulling her back by the elbow. "He's taken," Sierra whispered, making a face.

Tawni made a face back. A cloud of dread moved in and hung over Sierra's head. What if her sister went after Todd in a big way this week, and what if Todd fell for her charms? Tawni was, by far, more gorgeous than Christy, more refined, and much more aggressive. Was it possible that Sierra would be responsible for assisting the breakup of Todd and Christy by introducing her sister to him? The thought was too horrible to dwell on. She walked to the edge of the moving carousel and reached for her bag as it came around.

Behind her, she could hear Tawni's silky voice questioning Todd, "So, is this your senior year in college? Then what do you plan to do?"

"Not sure yet," Todd said.

"I have mine," Sierra said, breaking into their conversation and dropping her bag on the ground. "How many did you have, Tawni?"

"Only three," she answered with a veiled dark look at Sierra.

"I'll help you," Todd offered.

"Oh, would you? Thanks." Tawni's smile at Todd was

warmer than any Sierra had ever seen on her sister's face.

*Oh brother! So this is how my nightmare begins. Christy is never going to forgive me for bringing Tawni.*

They waited until the last piece of luggage had come through the opening and the carousel had stopped moving. They stood there for a few minutes more, expecting the conveyor belt to kick back on and pump out Tawni's three bags. It never did.

"This is awful," Tawni said. "Nothing like this has ever happened to me."

"Come on." Todd led them to a service representative at a nearby counter and explained the situation. After nearly an hour, Todd finally convinced Tawni that all they could do was fill out forms and leave Bob and Marti's address. The airport would deliver the missing luggage once it showed up.

"I can't believe this," Tawni said, clutching her makeup kit even tighter. "I'll have to go shopping right away."

"You can borrow some of my stuff," Sierra said sweetly, enjoying the irony of the situation. She couldn't imagine Tawni ever wearing her baggy jeans or gauze peasant skirts.

"Why don't we go to Bob and Marti's first?" Todd suggested. "You can make plans from there."

Tawni was silent as they walked to the parking lot. Todd led them to a Mercedes and unlocked it with a security pad on his key chain. The expression Tawni flashed at Sierra said, "Not only is he gorgeous, he's rich, too!" Tawni slid into the front passenger seat, and Sierra, without bothering to comment, climbed into the backseat.

"Nice car," Tawni said as they pulled out of the parking place.

"Yeah, it is," Todd said.

"Have you had it long?" Sierra asked.

"It's not mine. It's Bob's. He's had this one quite a few years. My mode of transportation is undergoing a transplant this week. We're all hoping the old guy makes it through."

As they pulled out of the airport into the heavy traffic, Tawni rolled down her window and stuck out her arm. "It's sure a lot warmer here than what we left this afternoon. So tell me, Todd, what are our plans for the week?"

"You'll have to ask Christy that. I'm just along for the ride."

"Oh, I am too," Tawni said. Sierra watched from the backseat as Tawni looked over at Todd and examined his profile. "I haven't been here since I was a kid. You'll have to show me all the hot spots."

Todd didn't respond. He looked straight ahead, speeding a little to make it through a yellow light. Sierra wondered if he would have acted any differently if Tawni weren't there. Certainly not. Certainly, Todd was as in love with Christy as she obviously was with him. At least he had seemed that way in England when Sierra first met him. But then, Tawni hadn't been there to mix things up.

# six

"WELCOME, WELCOME! Come on in." The dark-haired, middle-aged man in a white golf shirt and shorts showed them into his impressive beachfront home. "Which one of you is Sierra?"

"Me."

"And this must be your sister."

"Tawni. I'm pleased to meet you, Mr.—" Tawni held out her hand to shake his.

"Call me Bob. Please. Come on in. How was your flight?"

"They lost my luggage," Tawni said, stepping into the wide entryway. The house was decorated in a modern motif. "You have a beautiful home."

"Save all the praise for my wife," Bob said. "She eats it up. Marti? They're here!" he called into the living room. "I think she's out on the patio with the girls."

"Christy's here?" Todd asked.

Sierra thought his expression brightened. Before Bob could answer, Todd had deserted them, taking long strides through the living room.

"Shall we join him?" Bob asked. He led the way through the living room, with its picture windows looking out onto the inviting stretch of sand and endless blue ocean beyond. Early evening sunlight flooded the area, illuminating the white furniture and white baby grand piano in the corner.

Sierra peered through the sliding glass door that opened to the cement patio facing the beach, and saw Todd and Christy in a tight embrace. *Good,* she thought with a sense of relief. *Now Tawni will see that her efforts are wasted on this guy.*

They joined the small group on the patio, but before Bob could begin the introductions, Katie let out a squeal, hopped up from the chaise lounge, and gave Sierra a whopping hug. Christy hugged her next and then introduced her to Aunt Marti, which is where the hugging stopped cold.

The woman gave Sierra the shivers. It wasn't her appearance. She was very nice-looking—petite, trim, with dark hair and flawless makeup. She wore casual pants and a long, flowing top that looked like silk and was the color of persimmon. She wore a lot of jewelry, all gold. "Well maintained," her dad would have called her. It seemed to Sierra an invisible wall of ice surrounded this woman. She was not at all what Sierra had expected.

"Please," Marti said, taking command of the chatter. "Sierra, Tawni, help yourselves to the beverages over there on the tray. Then do come join us."

Sierra reminded herself that this woman, no matter how cold, was their hostess. "Thank you," Sierra said, forcing her warmest smile.

Beyond the small patio where they had gathered ran a wide sidewalk along the front of the house. The houses along the stretch of beach seemed to be built right next to each other, and almost all of them were two stories. Some homes down the way appeared older and considerably smaller in size. However, Bob and Marti's and the two next door were large, and their patios were well stocked with expensive patio furniture.

Marti showed the two sisters to the beverage cart a few feet away. Her glance rested only a moment on Sierra before landing soundly on Tawni. "Tell me, Tawni, how long have you been modeling for Nordstrom's?"

"Modeling? I don't model for them. I work at a fragrance counter at one of the stores in Portland."

"No!" Marti pressed her manicured hand to her chest. "You don't do any modeling?"

Tawni's laugh sounded innocent and sincere to Sierra. "No, I don't model."

Sierra dropped several melting ice cubes into a glass and reached for a bottle of kiwi-strawberry Snapple. Tawni stood right behind her and selected a bottle of mineral water. Her choice seemed to please Marti, who said, "What a terrible waste of such a face and figure. You really should consider modeling, Tawni."

"I never thought of it."

"Oh, come now, never?"

Tawni shook her head.

"It just so happens," Marti said, "that I know a few people in the industry, and well, that is, if you would be interested, I could make a few calls on your behalf."

"Interested in what?"

"In putting together a portfolio. Meeting with an agent. Starting your modeling career. That is, if you're interested."

Tawni looked as if her fairy godmother had just arrived and showered her with wish dust. "I…I don't know. I never thought of it before."

"Oh, come now. I have a hard time believing that. Surely you've looked in the mirror."

Out of the corner of her eye, Sierra caught Katie making a face to Christy. Christy only pursed her lips together and swallowed whatever her true reaction was.

"If you all will kindly excuse us," Marti said, aligning herself with Tawni, "we'll be in my office for a bit." With a grand, gracious gesture, she invited Tawni back inside.

Sierra sat at one of the chairs pulled out from around the patio table. Todd and Christy were seated a few feet away on the low, cement-block wall, holding hands and looking as if they should have their picture taken.

Katie had returned to her lounge chair, and Bob sat down next to Sierra at the table.

"What was that all about?" Sierra asked.

"Well, you did it, Sierra!" Katie said with a hearty laugh. "You made Marti's wish come true! You brought her the perfect Barbie doll. Something Christy could never be, and someone none of Christy's friends turned out to be."

Sierra turned to Bob, expecting him to be offended by Katie's outburst. His grin was subtle, but it was there, all right. A twinkle in his eyes tipped off Sierra that, although he would never admit it or join in the conversation, he agreed with Katie.

"I can't believe this," Sierra said, shaking her head. "What an introduction to Southern California!"

"It's only the beginning," Todd said. "We might not see

too much of your sister the rest of the week."

Sierra wanted to blurt out that that would be fine with her, but she held her tongue.

"Something tells me your sister can hold her own against my aunt," Christy said. "Marti means well. It's just that she..."

"She needs Jesus," Todd said, filling in the blank for Christy.

"Definitely," Katie echoed.

Sierra turned to Bob and said, "It must be hard being married to a non-Christian."

There was an awkward silence. Then Bob said slowly, "That would depend. Do you mean, is it hard for me being married to Marti or for Marti being married to me, since neither of us is what you would probably classify as a Christian?"

Sierra realized she had put her foot in her mouth big-time. "I didn't mean to say that," she stammered. Her cheeks turned red.

"Doesn't bother me," he said. "I firmly believe that everyone should believe in something. And right now I believe that I should start the barbeque." He rose and gave Sierra a wink. "Don't worry about it," he said. "I like it when a woman learns early on to speak her mind." Then, looking over Sierra's head at Katie, he said, "That's why I like Katie so much."

"The admiration is mutual," Katie replied. "Now if you would just get saved!"

"Oh, you never know," Bob said. "The prayer of a righteous person has a powerful effect. Wasn't that our verse last week, Todd? And I'd say you guys are about the most self-righteous young men and women I've ever met."

"Very funny," Katie countered.

"You want some help with the grill?" Todd asked.

"Naw. I got it. You can hold the spatula any day. What you're holding at the moment is much more important." Bob winked at Christy and then rounded the corner of the house, disappearing down the side patio, whistling to himself.

Sierra dropped her head in her hands. "This is the most bizarre first meeting I've every experienced! Are you guys always so intensely honest? And how come he knew that verse?"

"Bob has been going to a morning Bible study with me for the past few months," Todd said.

"You're kidding. He's not a believer, but he's willing to go with you?"

"Sure. Why not? The guys treat him like an equal. He's honestly seeking. There's no better place for him to be than with a bunch of other seekers and believers. My dad's been going, too, this past month."

"At least your dad is willing to look into Christianity," Katie said. "My parents won't even go to a Christmas service with me. They keep telling me I'll grow out of this delusion. Christy, however, had the storybook life."

"Your parents are Christians, too, aren't they, Sierra?" Christy asked.

"My whole family is. Parents, brothers, sister, grandparents. Everyone I know. I think I take it too much for granted."

"I know I do," Christy said.

Suddenly, from the side of the house came a loud whooshing sound like a gust of wind, immediately followed by frantic screams.

# seven

TODD BOLTED from the wall and ran around to side of the house with Katie sprinting after him. Christy and Sierra remained frozen for a second as ear-piercing screams filled the air. Marti came running out to the patio with Tawni right behind her. "What happened? What's going on?"

Sierra and Christy sprang from their seats at the same moment and rounded the corner to see Todd embracing Bob in a full body hug, then dropping to the ground and rolling on the cement. Smoke rose from the two men and the beach towel Todd stuffed between them. Reckless flames leapt three feet from the gas barbeque, lapping at the stucco wall of the garage.

Katie grabbed another beach towel, and edging her way to the grill, she reached to turn the knob.

"Katie, don't!" Christy screamed, causing Katie to momentarily withdraw her arm.

Marti arrived right behind them and began to shriek.

Katie yelled, "Call 911! Now!" Then, ducking from the flames, she turned the knob, and the fire began to decline.

Marti continued to shriek.

Sierra turned and ran into the house, frantically searching for a phone. She found one on the wall in the kitchen and dialed 911. Trying to think clearly and steady her breathing, she repeated to the person on the other end what had happened.

Christy dashed into the kitchen and took the phone from her, explaining the situation in greater detail and giving the address. She stayed on the line, and Sierra stood beside her, shaking, as they waited for the ambulance to arrive. The minute they heard the sirens, they ran to the front door and let in the team of paramedics and firefighters.

Everything was chaotic. Sierra couldn't watch as they loaded Bob and Todd onto stretchers. Marti had fainted, and they placed her on a stretcher as well. The firefighters checked the eaves and roof for flyaway sparks while a policeman questioned Christy and wrote down notes as she bravely tried to describe what happened.

Katie appeared to be the least shaken of any of them. She stood still while the paramedics examined her singed eyebrows and hair. The beach towel she had wrapped around her arm lay in a sooty mound next to the now silent barbeque.

"We'd like to take you in, all the same," the paramedic said to Katie. "Just to be safe."

"You guys want to come?" Katie asked. She made it sound more like a joyride than a trip to the hospital in an ambulance.

"I can follow you in the car," Christy said.

"Forget it," Katie said. "You need to be in there with Todd right this minute. I can drive these guys."

"We don't need to go, if it's a problem," Sierra offered.

"Tell you what," one of the paramedics said, interrupting their volley of car-pool ideas. "I'll make this decision for you. You're all coming, and you're going to ride where I tell you to ride."

Twenty minutes later, they were in the emergency room at the Hoag Memorial Hospital. Tawni and Sierra found empty seats in the waiting area while Katie and Christy went in with Marti and the men. Marti had come to in the ambulance and was crying hysterically. They could hear gut-wrenching moans from Bob as he and Todd were wheeled past them.

"This is so awful," Tawni said, the tears welling up. "I can't believe this happened!"

"I think they're going to be okay." Sierra said calmly. "It looked like Todd put a towel between them, and that probably put out most of the fire."

"But did you see Bob's arm?" Tawni whispered. "His ear..." Her voice trailed off.

Sierra hadn't looked on purpose. The ghastly smell of burnt flesh and hair overpowered her when she had gone back outside after the paramedics had arrived. She knew she couldn't look.

Five minutes passed before either of them spoke. "Do you think we should check on them?" Tawni asked.

"I think they'll come out and tell us," Sierra said. Over their heads, a television blared with a rerun of *Taxi.* Nothing was funny about any of it. The canned laughter made Sierra angry. Why did they have that stupid thing on, anyhow? Couldn't they let people sit and wait in peace?

A woman entered the emergency room with a crying baby in her arms. A nurse took her behind the double doors to the emergency area, and the infant's wail grew fainter.

"I could never work in a place like this," Sierra whispered to Tawni.

"Me either. Do you think they're okay in there?"

"I don't know. I think we should pray, Tawni."

"I have been."

"I know, I have been, too," Sierra said. "But I think we should pray together." She bowed her head, leaned closer to her sister, and started to pray before Tawni had a chance to agree or disagree. Sierra's prayer was long and sincere. When she finished, she looked up to see a guy sitting on the edge of the coffee table, head bowed, apparently praying with them. The minute she heard him begin his prayer with, "I agree, Father," she felt warm and comforted. It was Doug, her team leader from the missions trip in England.

When Doug finished, another guy, who Sierra didn't know, began to pray. When he said, "Amen," Sierra sprang from her chair and wrapped her arms around Doug's neck, hugging him and letting the pent-up tears come out. She pulled away, looked him in the face, and gave him her best attempt at a smile. "Hi," she said in a small voice.

Doug's face usually resembled that of a boy walking around secretly hiding a frog in his pocket. At this moment, he looked more serious than Sierra had ever seen him.

"We stopped by, and the neighbors told us," Doug said. "Have you heard anything?"

"Not yet. Bob and Todd were burned. Katie got singed, and Marti fainted."

"Sounds about right for Marti," Doug said. "Oh, this is Jeremy. Jeremy, this is Sierra."

"Hi," she said. "This is my sister, Tawni."

"Tawni," Jeremy repeated, nodding at her. The double doors to the emergency area swung open, and Katie stepped out. Her right arm was wrapped in gauze and resting in a sling. There appeared to be some sort of salve across her forehead and eyebrows.

"Hey, Doug! Jeremy! What are you guys doing here? Did we make the six o'clock news or something?"

"We were on our way to Tracy's and decided to stop at Bob and Marti's to see if you guys wanted to get together tonight. One of the neighbors was out front and told us what happened. Are you okay?" He rose and carefully gave her a side hug.

"I'm fine. I think the nurse who treated me was in training, and she receives extra credit for every bandage she applies. She wanted to wrap my eyebrows. Can you believe that?"

Doug looked at Katie closely. "What eyebrows?"

"I know," Katie said good-naturedly. "Freaky, huh?"

Sierra noticed that where the light reddish-brown brows had been, Katie now had fine, curly stubble.

"Feel my hair," she offered, lifting a section of the straight red hair that framed her face. Sierra could see that a large portion had "melted" from the bottom up and stuck out like the wacky, frayed ends of a rope. "And it smells awful."

"Do you know how Todd and Bob are doing?" Sierra asked.

"No. Christy is still in there. I heard one of the doctors talking about sedating Marti. She really flipped out, didn't she?"

"It was pretty gruesome," Sierra said, feeling for some reason she should defend Marti.

"I need to call my parents and ask them some information for the insurance," Katie said. "Do you want to come dial for me, Sierra?"

"Sure."

"I'll come with you," Doug said. "Tracy's probably wondering what happened to us. I'll give her a call, too."

As they walked away, Sierra could hear Jeremy saying to Tawni, "So, do you come here often?"

Tawni laughed.

Jeremy then said, "What an eventful way to start your vacation! Are you staying all week?"

When the three of them returned twenty minutes later from their phone calling, Jeremy and Tawni were still talking.

"Any news?" Doug asked.

Jeremy seemed to have a hard time pulling his attention away from Tawni to answer Doug. "No, not yet."

"I'm going back in," Katie said. "They'll let me in. And if they don't, I'll whine and say I want my eyebrows bandaged." She made her way through the double doors, being careful not to let her injured arm touch anything along the way.

Sierra slipped in between Jeremy and Tawni and returned to her original seat. It sounded as if the two of them were having a deep, spiritual conversation, something Sierra had rarely heard her sister participate in.

"I think there's room for both," Tawni was saying.

"I do too," Jeremy agreed. "But don't you find that most Christians today don't think that way?"

"They can always be taught," Tawni said. "I believe the responsibility falls on the people to seek these things out for themselves."

"You're right," Jeremy said.

Sierra wasn't sure what they were talking about, but she was impressed with her sister's approach to the dialogue. She had never seen Tawni talk like this before, especially with a guy.

A few minutes later, Tracy arrived. Sierra introduced her to Tawni as Doug's girlfriend, which extracted an instant smile from both Doug and Tracy but little more than a slight "Hi" from Tawni and Jeremy. They were on the subject of peace in the Middle East now, and it appeared as if the rest of the world barely existed.

"Did they just meet?" Tracy asked quietly. Her sweet, heart-shaped face reflected the same kind of surprise Sierra was feeling.

Sierra nodded and whispered back, "I've never seen my sister like this."

"I've never seen Jeremy like this either," Tracy said.

# eight

BY NOON the next day, the crisis seemed to have passed. Christy's mom, Margaret, had arrived that morning, which had a calming effect on Marti. Sierra found it hard to believe that Marti and Margaret were sisters because they were opposites in appearance and temperament. Sierra felt an alliance with Christy's mom. She also must know what it's like to spend her life in the shadow of a vibrant star for her sister. It made Sierra wonder if one of them was adopted, the way Tawni had been adopted in Sierra's family.

The house was full of people when Christy brought Todd home from the hospital. His right upper arm was bandaged, and his left arm rested on Christy's shoulder. He didn't need her support to walk, but neither of them seemed to mind the roles of "patient" and "nurse." Christy's mom and Marti followed them into the kitchen, where Sierra, Tawni, and Katie were sitting around the counter finishing their late breakfast.

"Give me five," Katie said as Todd entered the kitchen. She hopped off the stool and held up her free hand, which Todd swatted with his free hand.

"Does everyone know you're the hero, Katie? You told your mom, didn't you, Christy?" Todd asked.

"That's heroine, if you don't mind, and no," Katie said, her short, silky red hair swishing as she tossed her head. "They all know the truth. You're the hero who saved the day."

"If you hadn't turned off the grill, I think we might have all been blown to Jupiter." Todd sat down and pulled a big, fat dill pickle from the open jar on the counter. He took a bite that snapped the pickle and made Sierra inwardly pucker at the thought of that much dill and vinegar in her mouth.

"How much of your arm got it?" Katie asked.

Todd pointed to an invisible line about three inches down from his shoulder, about the place where his short-sleeved T-shirt ended, and marked again across his elbow. "That much. Not bad. Bob got it much worse. All the way across his left arm, up his neck to his earlobe and the back of his hair."

"It could have been much worse," Christy's mom said. "We're all thankful for the way each of you responded to the emergency."

"I don't know about you guys," Christy said, glancing at Katie and Sierra, "but I felt helpless. I don't know a thing about first aid. If I want to work with kids, I think I need to know a whole lot more about what to do in a crisis."

"That's right," Katie agreed. "The way preschool kids are today, you never know how many of them might blow up a barbeque during recess."

"You know what I mean," Christy said, giving Katie a

playful, exasperated look. "At least you thought to turn off the gas. I never would have thought of that."

"Did the doctor say when Bob might come home?" Marti asked.

"I didn't ask," Todd said. "Are you going over there?"

"Yes," Marti said. "Margaret and I will be there all afternoon. You young people make yourselves at home here, and Tawni, I haven't forgotten about making a call to the agent. I'll phone him on Monday."

"This is much more important," Tawni said. "Don't worry about it, please. You don't have to call him at all."

"No, no, I said I would, and I will. We'll all get through this weekend and then start fresh on Monday. By the way, did the airline ever call about your luggage?"

Sierra held her breath and waited to see how Tawni would respond in front of these strangers. That morning she had acted like a brat, saying she refused to wear the same clothes two days in row and slamming the bathroom door in Sierra's face when she held out a pair of shorts and a T-shirt to Tawni. In the end, Sierra's offering was snatched in silence and worn without comment.

"I was just thinking about calling them again," Tawni said calmly.

"Good idea," Marti said. "I don't suppose any of my clothes would fit you, since you're so much taller than I am, but please feel free to make use of anything you find in my closet. We'll be at the hospital if you need us. 'Bye, now." Marti made her grand exit with Christy's mom right behind.

Sierra couldn't help but wonder how many times in

their lives those two sisters had formed such a train. The image made her even more determined to never fall in line behind Tawni like some kind of shadow.

Christy and Todd began to make sandwiches for themselves while Tawni pulled a slip of paper from her pocket and reached for the phone.

"So, what should we do today?" Katie asked. "Did anyone hear from Doug?"

Tawni put her hand over the mouthpiece and said, "He and Jeremy are at Tracy's. They want us to call them when we decide what we're doing."

"What do you feel up to, Todd?" Christy asked.

"Anything."

"Except surfing, maybe," Katie suggested for him.

"I could wrap my arm up in a plastic bag," he said, picking up his sandwich with his left hand. The overly stressed slice of bread on the bottom gave way and dumped half of the roast beef and lettuce onto the counter.

"Right," Katie teased. "You can't even get a sandwich in your mouth. How are you going to keep your balance on a surfboard?"

Everyone laughed, and Todd said, "I'll take it one thing at a time. Sandwich first, then surfboard."

"Until those painkillers wear off," Katie warned. "Then all you want to do is take a nap."

"Is that what you guys want to do? Hang out on the beach?" Christy asked.

Sierra had been dying to sink her bare feet into the sand ever since her eyes met the yards and yards of inviting beach stretching to the sea yesterday afternoon. This morning she had almost slipped out for a walk while everyone else was still getting up and dressing, but she'd decided against it in case they wanted to be able to find her. Nothing sounded better to Sierra than spending the afternoon at the beach.

"Sounds great to me," Sierra said.

"Me, too," said Katie. "I want to see what kind of tan I can get where my eyebrows once were."

"I must go shopping," Tawni said, hanging up the phone with a slam. "Still no trace of my luggage. I don't even have a bathing suit!"

"You can borrow one of mine," Sierra said. She was enjoying this much more than she should and realized that if it had been her luggage that was lost, she wouldn't appreciate hearing Tawni offer her clothes every time she opened her mouth. Still, the irony of it was too good to pass up. "I brought several, you know. You can have first pick."

"Oh, let me see. Do I want the one with Tweety Bird on the front or the gym-class Speedo?" Tawni said.

"You have a Tweety Bird suit?" Katie asked. "Cool."

"No, I don't," Sierra said, deliberately not making eye contact with Tawni so that her icy glare would shatter in midair and all her invisible frozen daggers would fall noiselessly to the ground. "I did when I was ten or twelve. And I've never owned a Speedo."

"My aunt wouldn't mind if you borrowed one of hers. I'm sure she has several to choose from," Christy said.

"You think they would fit?" Tawni asked.

"One way to find out. Come on."

"I'll stay here," Todd said, managing to stuff another bite of his sandwich in his mouth without loosing any of it.

"Me, too." Sierra placed the lid on the mayonnaise jar

and acted as if she had been appointed as the kitchen cleanup crew.

"Not me," said Katie. "An open invitation to go through Marti's closet? Come on, Sierra! Don't you realize this doesn't happen every day?"

"I can live without the experience."

"Suit yourself," Katie said. "Oh, ha! Get it? Suit yourself?" Katie cackled away as the three girls walked out of the kitchen. "Sometimes I crack myself up."

"I guess we should call Doug," Todd said to Sierra. "They might already be on the beach." As he rose to head for the phone, he added, "I'm glad you came. Tawni, too. I'm glad you both came."

Sierra swung open the refrigerator door with more energy than the act required. *Well, I'm not glad she came. I wish I'd never suggested any of this to her. I wish she would find her own friends and leave mine alone. I wish she wasn't so picky and prissy about everything. I wish she wasn't so beautiful and so attractive to guys. I wish...* Sierra stopped herself right before she wished something she might regret later.

# nine

THE GREAT THING about the beach, Sierra decided, was that it treated everyone the same. Anyone, no matter who she was, could accept the invitation to cradle herself in the warm, rippled sand and feel the sun generously pouring out its gold with the same indifference (or was it benevolence?) on one and all.

Somehow, once she was stretched out on her towel, face toward the heavens, ears drinking in the laughing melody of the ocean's afternoon game of tag, all her envy of Tawni was evaporated. These people were still her friends. She was in Southern California, lying on the beach, with a whole week of vacation before her. Sierra refused to sabotage her own holiday.

One other factor calmed her, or at least redirected her focus of energy. When Todd called Doug, he found out a few more guys had arrived from the San Diego group. That tiny phrase, "a few more guys" rang like a bell inside Sierra. "Anger school is dismissed," it seemed to say. "The class in dreams and wishes is now in session." She remembered what

Christy had said on the phone the week before about the possibility that Sierra could meet someone here this week. One of Doug's friends, maybe. After all, Newport Beach was a wonderful place to meet someone special.

Sierra lay still in the sand, listening to the others talk around her, waiting for Doug and his bunch to show up. What if she opened her eyes and looked for the first time into the face of her future husband? What would he look like? What would his name be? Was she getting carried away with her hopes? Her mom had told her to dream, always dream. It wouldn't hurt to whip up a little for herself this afternoon, now would it?

Sierra hadn't allowed herself to do much of this daydreaming over guys before. Not that she wasn't interested in guys, but she lacked confidence in herself. Growing up in a small community as she had before her family moved to Portland in January, Sierra had been buddies with every guy in town—not only with the guys who were friends with her older brothers but also with guys her own age. She had known them all since she was in kindergarten and thought of them as little more than bullies and buddies.

Since meeting these new friends, and now spending time with them as couples, Sierra's thoughts had certainly turned around. It didn't seem as if she were one of the gang unless she was interested in somebody. So even though she knew that's what motivated her to dream up dating scenarios, she still let herself do it. After all, she was sixteen. It was time she took her feminine wiles more seriously. Tawni certainly had at that age.

"Jeremy, over here!" Sierra heard her sister call out.

Tawni had done well on her scavenger hunt in Marti's

closet, and she now wore a black bathing suit with straps that crisscrossed in the back. It was a bit too small on Tawni and rode up the sides, but it still looked ravishing on her, of course. She also had borrowed a cover-up trimmed in gold braid that looked like something a movie star would wear while lounging around her Beverly Hills pool. It was, Sierra decided, something she wouldn't be caught dead in.

Sierra could hear the voices of Doug and Tracy as they approached with their group. She hesitated before sitting up and opening her eyes. She had been pumping so much hope into this dream bubble that it seemed almost certain to burst if she even lifted one eyelash and traversed the gulf between dreams and reality.

And burst it did.

Sierra looked up and saw only Doug, Tracy, and Jeremy standing there. No "few more guys" were with them. Tawni went right to work smoothing out a spot for Jeremy's towel next to hers, which was already positioned behind and to the side of everyone else. A private sort of corner for the new people.

"How's the invalid doing?" Doug teased Todd.

"Rank. The afternoon set is starting to come in," Todd said, casting a longing glance toward the waves. "But Christy won't let me take my board out."

"Oh, right," Christy said. "As if I ever was able to stop you from doing anything."

Sierra thought Christy looked as if she belonged on the beach. She and Todd sat next to each other in matching beach chairs confiscated from Bob and Marti's garage. Christy didn't have a natural "show-off" body like Tawni's, just a round, nicely proportioned shape that looked good in her burgundy bathing suit. The color made her arms and legs look tan, much more tan than Sierra's. On Christy's right wrist was a delicate gold ID bracelet with the word "Forever" engraved on it. Sierra had heard the story of when Todd first gave her the bracelet and how it had been off and on Christy's wrist over the years. It certainly looked as if belonged there now.

The other thing Sierra noticed about Christy was that she carried herself well. She didn't "plop" when she sat, the way Katie did. Yet she wasn't petite and graceful like Tracy. She fit somewhere in the middle of those two, which made her approachable and the kind of person who was very watchable. Sierra wished she had a polished, mature look like Christy's rather than her own tomboy appearance.

"What happened to Larry and Antonio?" Todd asked after he seemed to realize that everyone was done giving him sympathy.

"Antonio needed to find a surfboard he could rent for the week," Tracy said, settling down next to Sierra. "Keep an eye out for them. So many people are out today that it'll be hard for them to find us."

"Too bad they wasted their money. They could have used my board," Todd said. Doug had brought a boogie board, which he placed on his towel. Todd's bright-orange surfboard was leaning against the back of his beach chair.

"I'll borrow your surfboard," Katie said, "if you don't mind."

"Sure," Todd said. "I know you'll take good care of Naranja. He's been all over the world with me." He adjusted his position in his chair and flipped on a pair of sunglasses.

Sierra knew naranja meant "orange" in Spanish. It made sense that Todd would call it that since it was such a distinctive shade of orange. But she wasn't sure what Todd meant by taking good care of it. It looked pretty beat-up to her.

"Katie," Christy said, trying to get her attention, "since when did you start surfing?"

"Ever since I found out Antonio was coming," Katie said with a sparkle in her green eyes. "If he's in the water on a surfboard, then that's where I want to be."

"Who's Antonio?" Sierra asked.

Katie was right next to her, and she turned her head from Christy on her other side to give Sierra the scoop. "Only the most gorgeous college student Italy has ever sent us."

Sierra laughed at Katie's "puppy love" expression.

Christy leaned over and said, "Katie has a thing for exchange students. Did she ever tell you about Michael?"

"He was the one from Ireland, right?"

"Northern Ireland," Katie corrected. "Can I help it if I'm a sucker for a guy with an accent?"

"I take it that it doesn't matter where they're from, as long as they have an accent," Sierra said.

"Yes," Katie answered, looking over Sierra's head and straining to see two guys walking toward them. "Is that them?"

Everyone looked, including Sierra. She was interested, of course, in how her little dream would turn out. If the "few other guys" consisted of Antonio and Larry, and Antonio was already spoken for, then she wanted to have a good look at Larry.

The two college-aged guys waved and made their way toward the growing group of friends. Sierra guessed Antonio to be the one on the right with the dark hair, and that would mean that Larry was...

# ten

HUGE! Larry was the largest guy Sierra had ever seen. He had to be a football player. As he approached, she thought he might be Polynesian. His surfboard looked almost like a skateboard under his arm.

Sierra had never thought of herself as a person who identified another individual by his size or skin color. But this guy was very noticeable because of both. In her daydreams, Sierra's potential new boyfriend never looked like Larry.

Everyone was introduced. Sierra smiled and greeted both guys while Katie announced to Antonio that she was going to take Todd's board and hit the waves with them.

"What are we waiting for?" Antonio said. "Let's punch it."

"Don't you mean, 'let's hit it'?" Katie asked, rising and brushing the sand off her backside.

"Larry is always saying 'punch it.' Is that not how you say it?" Antonio's accent would melt any romantic female's heart. He had broad shoulders, straight, white teeth, and engaging eyes. Sierra didn't blame Katie a bit for being attracted to him.

"That's right," Larry agreed in a deep, rumbling voice. "Punch it."

Katie held up her hands in surrender. "Okay by me. Let's punch it."

"You going out, Larry?" Doug asked.

"I sure am. Heather and Gisele are coming up this afternoon. I have a feeling when Gisele arrives, my week will be scheduled for me. I plan to enjoy my few hours as a free man while I can."

All of Sierra's fragile dreams of a potential romance with either guy fluttered away.

"Women tend to do that to a man's life, don't they?" Doug teased, leaning away from Tracy before she could hit him.

"Hear, hear," Todd said, lifting his bottle of seltzer water in agreement. It seemed to Sierra that Todd looked uncomfortable and a little pale. He wore a long-sleeved T-shirt with a sleeve covering the gauze bandage on his arm. He tossed a beach towel over his whole right side. The hot sun probably didn't feel too good pounding down its heat on his bandaged burn.

Antonio hoisted Todd's surfboard under his arm and trotted down to the water with Katie right beside him.

"Does she know how to ride that thing?" Larry asked.

"I've given her a few lessons," Todd said. "It's up to you guys to perfect her natural talent." Todd shifted in his chair and slowly stretched, trying to get comfortable.

"Hey, Sierra," Doug said, "you ever ride a boogie board? You can use mine if you want."

"I think I will," Sierra said, getting up.

Doug, Tracy, and Larry followed her to the water's edge, where the foaming waves came rolling up to their toes, cooling the hot sand. Larry jumped into the water and began paddling out to Katie and Antonio, who were already past where the waves broke. Doug gave a few brief instructions to Sierra on how to hold the board in front of her and lie across it with her feet straight behind her. Then she set out to sea, toward Katie and the guys.

A wave that seemed gigantic to Sierra rose and, like a big hand, closed on top of her, scooting her back to shore. She got up, soaked, still grasping the boogie board, and with a smile to Doug and Tracy, who were watching her, said, "That was my practice run."

"Let me get you past the waves. There are a few tricks to the trade." Doug dove into the oncoming wave and surfaced with his hair slicked back. "Go under," he called back to Sierra.

She followed his advice, and within two waves, she was bobbing with the others in the deeper water. Katie and the guys sat on their boards, floating on the calmer water. Clinging to the boogie board, Sierra realized she couldn't touch the bottom. She was a strong swimmer but hadn't spent much time in the ocean. It felt different from being in the deep part of a lake—maybe because she couldn't see anything in the murky water except clumps of floating kelp that felt slimy when they touched her legs. Sierra wasn't sure she liked this, but she wasn't going to let some globs of seaweed keep her from a new experience.

"I heard there was one down at San Onofre last week that came right up to the surfers," Larry said. "The water's really warm there because of the power plant. It probably attracts them."

"Attracts what?" Doug asked as he treaded water next to Antonio's surfboard. "Jellyfish?"

"No, sharks."

"No way," Sierra squawked.

Everyone looked at her with straight faces. "We get sharks around here every now and then," Doug said. "Not recently—but this *is* their home, you know."

"Why can't they live out there?" Sierra said, bringing her legs closer to the boogie board.

"They have to go where there's food," Doug said. "I saw one here three weeks ago."

"What did you do?" Katie asked.

"I got out of the water, of course."

"Wasn't there one up at Huntington Beach last month?" Larry asked.

"Yeah, did you see it in the paper?" Doug paddled over to Larry's board and held on to the side for support. "There was a bunch of them. Great white, I think. I heard about it from a surfer who said he knew another surfer who was out there. He saw them coming and thought they were dolphins, and then all of a sudden, they attacked him."

"Oh, stop it," Sierra said. "Not really."

Everyone, even Katie, remained serious, silently affirming Doug's story.

"Really," Doug said. "They showed a photo of his board hacked in half. The guy was in the hospital for a couple of weeks while they tried to reconstruct the lower part of his leg. He said the shark came up from underneath where he was dangling his legs in the water. One big chomp, and his leg was a hamburger."

The image forming in Sierra's mind was unpleasant. She tried to brush it away and change the subject. "So, are you going to give me your fine pointers on riding this thing, or do I have to figure it out myself?"

A gentle swell of salty water rose under them and pushed its way to shore.

"That would have been a good wave to catch," Antonio said. Then quickly glancing behind them, he said, "What was that?"

"What was what?" Katie said.

Now Larry snapped his head in the same direction. "I saw it, too. Was it a big fish?"

"Where?" Doug tried to boost himself up in the water to see what Larry and Antonio were looking at. "Are you guys putting us on?"

"It's right there!" Antonio said, shooting his arm in the direction of Larry's board. "Don't you see it?"

Sierra wished she were sitting on top of a board herself. She would feel safer and have a better view. She usually wasn't squeamish when it came to animals. Her younger brothers had brought home a variety over the years, including a slimy yellow banana slug they had put in her bowl of cereal one morning when she left the table for a couple of minutes. She had pretended not to notice and had eaten toast instead of her cereal, which blew all the wind out of Gavin and Dillon's sails.

This was different. The ocean seemed so huge and deep from where she bobbed in it. And she felt so vulnerable, especially because she couldn't see her own legs in the water.

"You guys are crazy," Doug said. He let go of Larry's board and paddled a few feet away from them, scanning the water. "Just seaweed, you guys. I don't see anything."

He began to swim back toward them when all of a sudden, he let out a blood-chilling scream. His arms went straight up in the air, and then he disappeared, straight down into the water.

"What happened?" Katie yelled.

Sierra was too stunned to speak.

"You guys," Katie hollered, "go get him!"

Antonio dove in with Larry right behind him. Sierra and Katie scanned the water for any sight of the three submerged men. But they didn't see or hear them.

"Where are they?" Katie said frantically.

Sierra stretched her neck and strained her eyes to see anything. Bubbles. Movement. Anything.

Suddenly, she felt something cold and slimy brush against her leg. "Katie!" she screamed.

Before she could form a complete thought, the cold, slimy things grabbed her right leg and jerked her into the water. The same instant she was going under, she saw Katie topple from her surfboard and fly into the water, shrieking all the way.

# eleven

AS SIERRA'S NOSTRILS filled with water, strong hands reached around her waist and boosted her back to the surface. She sucked in a panicked gulp of air and reached for the boogie board floating only a foot away. Doug popped his head out of the water directly in front of her and held on to the other side of the board. A mischievous grin hopscotched across his face.

"Gotcha," he said, laughing wildly. "That was totally awesome."

Sierra dished out her words slowly between gasping breaths. "That...was...the...worst...thing...you...could... have...ever...done!"

Katie had surfaced right behind Sierra. She wasn't wasting her time with words but went right to work, splashing Larry and Antonio and heaving handfuls of seaweed at them.

"Consider it your initiation to our little circle of friends," Doug said.

"You're a rat!" Sierra said.

"Don't tell Tracy that, will you?" Doug said. "She's crazy about me. I would hate to burst her bubble."

"I think I know now why she stayed on shore."

"You got it. She, Christy, and the others have all gone through their initiation in one form or another, usually involving seaweed, saltwater, and boogie boards. They're our standard operating equipment. Katie, however, keeps falling for it. We've initiated her half a dozen times already."

Sierra noticed Todd's orange surfboard floating out to sea. "Somebody had better grab that board."

The other two guys swam over and climbed back on top of their boards while Doug swam with sure, swift strokes to retrieve Todd's board, which he delivered to a breathless Katie.

"You just wait," Katie panted, glaring at Doug. "One of these days I'm going to get you back so good. You'll see."

"I'm still waiting," Doug teased. "I'm going to be an old married man before you get around to it."

"Oh?" Sierra said. "Is this an official announcement?"

Doug seemed to turn shy, embarrassed by his own words. "Come on. It's time for you to catch a wave."

Overhead, a small, low-flying airplane came into view. They all looked up as the plane motored overhead, towing a banner that read "Malibu Gold Sunscreen Products."

"What's that?" Sierra asked.

"Advertisement," Katie said. "Haven't you ever seen those before?"

Sierra shook her head.

"It got your attention, didn't it?" Katie said. "Easter

vacation, the beach is packed—it's a great way to advertise."

"Check it out," Antonio said. "The swells are really kicking it up."

"Don't you mean, 'picking up'?" Katie asked.

"Whatever they're doing, I'm taking the next one." Antonio lay on his stomach and paddled toward shore. They watched as he caught the crest of the wave with perfect timing and made a wobbly but successful attempt to stand up. He balanced himself on the board for a full minute and a half before toppling over the side.

"The guy's a natural," Larry said. "Time to show him up. Come on, Katie. Are you with me?"

"As long as you don't have any more shark attacks up your sleeve."

They paddled together quickly to catch the next wave. Larry caught the edge of it but couldn't get up. Katie missed it, too. Then, as Sierra watched, Katie quickly repositioned herself for the next wave, which she caught and rode to shore on her knees. Maybe she didn't want to push her luck by attempting to stand, so she had stayed low.

Tracy, who was standing ankle-deep in the foaming water, applauded Katie as she came to shore. Sierra liked being part of this group, practical jokes and all. She loved trying new things and determined that once she had mastered the boogie board, she was going to trade it in for a ride on that magical orange surfboard.

The boogie board turned out to be a breeze for her. Doug only had to run through the basics with her once, and she caught wave after wave, with Doug bodysurfing beside her, looking like a maniac otter. She loved the sensation, loved the pull and push of the mighty ocean giving her free rides. Sierra thought it would be great to live by the ocean and play like this all the time.

Quite a while later, she decided it was time to take a break. Doug said he'd had enough for a while, too, so they headed toward the shore. They passed Katie paddling out with Antonio as they took their last ride in.

"What are the chances of that relationship working out?" Sierra asked Doug as they wrung the water from their hair at the shoreline and walked back to the group on the sand.

"I stopped trying to figure out relationships a long time ago. Tracy says I'm clueless. She's probably right. The only couple I'd put any guarantees on would be Todd and Christy."

"And you and Tracy," Sierra added, spotting Tracy a few yards ahead, waving at them from her beach chair.

"Yeah, me and Tracy." His voice turned deep.

Sierra glanced over to see a tender look spread across his face. He looked even more mature at that moment than she had ever seen him, even with the drops of water clinging to his eyelashes and the goofy way his soaked hair stuck out on the left side. Sierra took note. *This is the look of a man in love.*

"She's the most awesome person in the world," he said, watching Tracy stand up and come toward him with a dry towel in her hand.

Sierra made another note. *And there's a woman in love. I can't believe it. I'm surrounded!*

"Hey," she said, breaking up the sweet moment between Doug and Tracy, "what happened to everyone else?"

"Todd was starting to feel the pain in his arm, although

he wouldn't admit it. Christy coaxed him into going back to the house with her. She said she wanted to call the hospital and check on Bob. I'm sure she was also going to convince Todd to take it easy, like the doctor told him to."

"What about my sister?"

"She persuaded Jeremy to take her shopping," Tracy said.

Doug wrapped the towel around his shoulders and reached into their small cooler for something to drink. "Jeremy went shopping?"

"I know," Tracy said. "Would you like something to drink, Sierra?"

"Sure. Anything."

Doug handed her a can of Squirt and said, "Man, Jeremy must have it bad! He went to the Ice Capades once when he had a crush on a girl last year, but shopping? This is pretty serious."

"And what's wrong with the Ice Capades?" Sierra challenged, stretching out on her stomach and letting her back "solar" dry.

"It's a chick thing," Doug said.

"Please," Tracy interjected, "don't get him started."

Before Doug could make another comment, an airplane engine roared over them, and Tracy asked, "What does that say?"

Sierra rolled over and sat up. Shielding her eyes from the lowering sun, she read the banner strung behind the advertising plane. "Good Planet-something," she said.

"Good Planet Restaurants," Doug said. "Sounds good to me. I'm starved."

"Do you want to go back to the house?" Tracy asked

Doug. "Christy might appreciate it if you could help her convince Todd he needs to take his medicine and rest."

"Sure. I'm ready. Are you ready, Sierra?"

Sierra decided to wait for Katie and the guys. Doug and Tracy left their ice chest full of drinks for the others and walked away, hand in hand.

*Let's see...* Sierra began reviewing for herself. *Doug and Tracy are in love, Todd and Christy are in love, Tawni and Jeremy are something. They're together, at any rate. Katie is interested in Antonio, and Larry said his girlfriend is coming up tonight. Am I the leftover pork chop here or what?*

She lay with her face to the sun, trying to decide if she should feel sorry for herself. She logically reminded herself that she was younger than anyone else in the gang. She also consoled herself with the reminder that Randy was taking her out next Friday. At least she was being asked out. It wasn't as if she had no attention from guys.

It was Tawni, really, who prompted all the jealous feelings. Todd and Christy belonged together. She had watched Doug and Tracy get together in England. And she couldn't wish for a better guy for Katie than Antonio. But why did Tawni deserve an instant boyfriend? What if Tawni hadn't come? Would Jeremy have been interested in Sierra instead? He was great-looking, intelligent, and slightly serious, and he seemed to be a strong Christian. Would she have been attracted to him? Would Jeremy have thought that Sierra was too young to take seriously, the way Paul had brushed her off on the way home from England once he found out how young she was?

Sierra loved the way the sun dried and warmed her all over. Even though she was lying still, it felt as if she were riding another wave. The sensation was similar to the way she felt after getting off a roller coaster. It was a sensation she liked, and it made her smile.

The late afternoon breeze began to pick up, bringing a sudden chill with it. Slipping into her beach cover-up, one of Dad's old white long-sleeved shirts, Sierra rolled up the sleeves and turned up the collar on her sunburned neck.

Katie and the guys were making their way through the sand with boards under their arms. Katie's face was shining as she carefully laid Todd's board on her towel. "Did you see that last one?"

"No, sorry. I missed it."

"I finally stood up all the way! This is a breakthrough for me, Sierra. And you missed it!"

"We saw it," Antonio said teasingly. "It wasn't anything to call home about."

"Antonio, we say, 'write home about,'" Katie corrected him.

"You can write if you want," he said. "I think calling is faster."

Sierra let out a giggle. Katie was the only one who didn't see that Antonio liked getting a reaction out of her. Sierra imagined his mind was working overtime trying to find ways to mix up expressions just to keep Katie attentive.

"Gisele wants to go to the Old Spaghetti Factory for dinner tonight. You guys want to join us?" Larry was looking at Antonio and Katie.

Katie cast an almost shy glance at Antonio. At least it looked as shy as Sierra had ever seen Katie appear to be.

"Sure, we would love to," he answered for both of them.

Katie smiled at Antonio. Antonio smiled back. Larry flipped the lid on the ice chest and asked, "Are these up for grabs?"

"Yes." Sierra swallowed the strong feelings that rose from her stomach to her throat. They hadn't asked her to go with them, had they? It sounded to her like a double date. If she went, she would be the oddball—again.

For the first time, she missed Amy, Randy, and her other friends in Portland. She thought of the wacky Saturday morning at the water fountain, and she realized she felt like Peanut, trying to keep up with Brutus. Maybe someone should stick her in a backpack and pull her out when the week was over.

"I'm going to head back to the house," Sierra said.

"Okay. We'll see you later," Larry said. "Nice meeting you, Sarah."

Sierra was about to correct him but then decided it wasn't worth it.

# twelve

BOB AND MARTI'S house was full of activity when Sierra entered through the sliding glass door off the patio. Tawni, Jeremy, and Aunt Marti were in the living room, and Tawni was pulling her new clothes from a shopping bag.

"Sierra," Tawni said, her face full of excitement, "you won't believe the selection of stores they have here! I found everything in record time."

"I bet you were glad for that," Sierra said to Jeremy, giving him a sympathetic look.

"We had a great time," Jeremy said.

For one instant, Sierra wondered if this guy was actually a well-constructed robot. Did she detect a hint of metallic resonance in his "We had a great time"? He looked human enough. As a matter of fact... Sierra looked at him more closely. Something was strangely familiar about Jeremy. She couldn't place it, but across his eyes around his mouth, he looked like someone she knew.

"How's Bob doing?" Sierra asked, forcing herself to look away from Jeremy and at Marti.

"Better, I think. They're still trying to make a decision about the skin graft. I wish they would decide. He's been sleeping all day, poor thing."

Marti seemed like a different woman from the one who had fainted only twenty-four hours ago—more calm and relaxed. Sierra still wasn't sure she liked her.

"What's everyone else doing?"

"I made Todd go home and rest," Marti said, her hand drawing up to her hip. "He's acting as if nothing happened to him when in reality he should still be in the hospital. At least he would take his medication and get some sleep."

"Did Doug and Tracy go home, too?"

"I think so. Christy's in the kitchen. She can give you a full report. I returned only a few minutes ago myself." Then, turning to Tawni, she said, "As I was saying, I wish you would have let me know you were going shopping. I have a personal shopper, you see. I could have given her a call, and she could have done all the legwork for you."

Sierra slid out of the living room and went to the kitchen, where she found Christy and her mom sitting at the round kitchen table. They seemed to be in a close conversation, so Sierra waved her hand and said, "I'm going upstairs to take a shower."

"Okay," Christy said. "I'll be up in a bit."

Sierra headed upstairs and pulled some clean clothes from her corner of the crowded guest room. The shower felt good, and it amazed her to see so much sand swirling around the drain. Even after she was out of the shower and dressed, she found more sand in her left ear.

It was quiet in the guest room. She stood by the window and looked out at the beach. The crowds from that afternoon had thinned. In the endless sky, the clouds topped the ever-churning, gray-green ocean like a gigantic dollop of whipping cream. "It's beautiful," Sierra whispered.

Just then the bedroom door opened, and in tumbled Katie and Tawni, laughing like old chums.

"Guess what?" Katie said to Sierra. "Tawni says she's going to glamorize me for our big date tonight. She thinks she can draw in new eyebrows!"

"I'm sure she can," Sierra said.

"What's that supposed to mean?" Tawni snapped.

"It means, if anyone can draw in new eyebrows for Katie, I'm sure you'll be the best person for the job," Sierra said, sounding innocent as she defended herself. Why was it that Tawni could read even the slightest pinch of sarcasm in Sierra's comments?

Tawni looked as if she were about to say something and then changed her mind. "I'll be only a minute in the shower," Tawni said to Katie.

Sierra wanted to say, "Since when?" but she held her tongue.

"I'll take my shower downstairs," Katie suggested, reaching into her disheveled bag for some clothes. "What are you going to wear tonight, Sierra?"

"This." She looked down at her jeans and T-shirt.

"I don't know what to wear. Did you see Tawni's new outfit?"

Sierra forced out a "Yes, it's great" just as Tawni slipped into the bedroom and closed the door.

"The Old Spaghetti Factory isn't a very fancy place. Have you ever been there?"

"No." Sierra's discomfort with the arrangements for the

evening grew. She wasn't sure she was actually invited to this dinner. The last thing she wanted to do was be the only one there without a date.

Fortunately, Christy walked in and said, "Are you talking about the Spaghetti Factory?"

"Yes. You and Todd are going, aren't you?" Katie asked. "What are you going to wear?"

"We're not going. Todd needs to take it easy, and I thought I'd keep my mom and aunt company tonight. We'll probably go back to the hospital. You guys go ahead. It's a fun place." Christy came over to Katie's bag and pulled out a shirt. "Wear this," she suggested. "I always liked this one on you."

"'Liked' is the key word here," Katie said. "Do you realize how long I've had this relic? I need to go shopping."

"That's a new one," Christy said. "You hate shopping."

"I hate looking like a slob more."

Sierra couldn't help but wonder what other bits of advice her sister had used on Katie to plant the word "slob" in her brain. It was definitely a "Tawni" word, and one she often used on Sierra.

"You can borrow anything of mine you want," Christy suggested.

"What I'd really like to wear is one of Sierra's skirts," Katie said.

The admission surprised and flattered Sierra.

"You're welcome to whatever you can find in there," Sierra said.

"Did you bring that one you wore in Belfast? The one with the silver thread woven through it?"

"It's in there," Sierra said. "Help yourself. There's also

a blouse with silver trim, if you want to borrow that, too."

"Cool, cool, cool," Katie said, pawing through Sierra's clothes. "You have the coolest clothes of anyone I've ever met. And I love your jewelry."

"Borrow whatever you like."

"Thanks, Sierra. What a pal!"

Sierra wouldn't admit it, but inwardly she couldn't wait to see Tawni's expression when Katie showed up, ready for her makeup, wearing one of Sierra's outfits.

"Are you going with them?" Christy asked.

"No. I..." She didn't know how to say it without sounding like she felt sorry for herself. "I'd rather stick around here tonight."

"You won't mind being here alone if we go to the hospital, will you?"

"Whatever works out is fine with me." Those were polite words, not words from her heart. What Sierra wanted was to be invited to be part of somebody's group, even if it was the group of women going to the hospital.

"You're welcome to come with us," Christy said, as if reading Sierra's thoughts. "I can't promise that it'll be very exciting."

"I don't need exciting," Sierra said. "Just an invitation, and I'll take yours."

Christy studied Sierra's face. "Are you okay?"

"Sure! Fine. Great, actually. It's really beautiful here. I loved being on the beach today. And the water was fantastic. I had a really good time." Even though Sierra felt certain she could trust Christy with her true feelings, she didn't want to pour out all her insecurities and put any more stress on Christy than she already felt.

"It looks like you got a little sunburned," Christy said, touching her finger to her own nose. "I wasn't out long enough to get pink. You should have seen me the first time I came here, though. It was in the summer, and I fried my first day out. Like a lobster! It doesn't feel that hot when you're lying out because of the breeze."

"I know," Sierra agreed. Before she could say anything else, someone rapped long fingernails on the closed door.

"Come in," Christy called. But the door opened before the words were out of her mouth.

Marti gave the room a quick surveillance and seemed surprised. By Sierra's standards of cleanliness, there was nothing wrong with the room. But Christy must have sensed something different, because she immediately said, "We'll clean it up."

"Oh, I'm not worried," Marti said, dramatically stepping over the wet bath towel Sierra had left wadded up by the futon bed on the floor. She realized how rude that must appear to Marti. "The maid is coming the day you all leave, so I'm not worried about a thing." She added, "I wanted to ask you, Christy darling, if you had a preference of where to go for dinner tonight."

"It doesn't matter to me," Christy said. "Sierra is staying home with us. Do you have a preference, Sierra?"

"What about the restaurant advertised on the airplane banner—the Good Planet?"

"Wonderful choice," Marti said, casting her fickle approval on Sierra for the first time. "Let's plan to leave here in, say, fifteen minutes."

"We'll be ready," Christy said.

"How about you, Sierra dear? Will you have enough

time to change or should we plan on twenty minutes instead of fifteen?"

"I'm ready to go now," Sierra said, not liking this woman one bit.

"Really?" Marti raised a finely shaped eyebrow.

Sierra didn't know how to answer without sounding rude. She was used to Tawni's occasional comments on her taste in fashion, but for this woman Sierra barely knew to show her obvious distaste was incredible. A half dozen stinger phrases raced through Sierra's mind. Her mother had told her once that it wasn't a sin when those thoughts came to her, but what she did with them determined whether or not they would be classified as sinful. Sierra decided not to take any chances, and she let each of the rude comments fly out the back side of her brain as quickly as they had flown in.

As the bad thoughts were on their way out, another one flew in. It was Todd's comment on the patio when he had said that Marti needed Jesus.

"I'll be glad to change," Sierra said, amazed to hear such words come from her own mouth. "Do you have any suggestions of what would be appropriate?"

Marti appeared to be so off guard that she only smiled and said, "Wear whatever you like, dear." With her dignity still intact, Marti turned. As she exited the room, she called over her shoulder, "Downstairs then, in fifteen minutes."

Christy looked surprised. "I wish I'd learned to do that years ago. I admire you, Sierra."

"You wouldn't if you knew what I was really thinking."

# thirteen

SIERRA LEARNED some hard lessons that night and the next day. She learned it's best to sit and listen when you're the guest, especially when Marti is the one treating you to dinner. It's also helpful to pretend to be asleep when your sister and friend come in from their night out. They will divulge plenty of information while brushing their teeth, which is easier to hear when they're not looking at your face, reading your expression, especially since they both had a wonderful time. All Sierra could do was wish she had been with them, with some terrific guy paying lots of attention to her.

Marti had made an appointment for Tawni with the modeling agent on Monday. When they returned late that afternoon, Sierra, Christy, and Todd had just come up from the beach and were sitting on the patio with Christy's mom. Christy reminded Todd for the second time to take his next pill.

Sierra had settled comfortably into a patio chair next to Todd when Marti and Tawni stepped onto the patio. Sierra felt sure she would soon have her own pill to swallow: the news that Tawni's career into fame and fortune was about to be launched.

"Before anyone says anything," Tawni said, "I'm not going to pursue this. There's too much required for a job in modeling. I'd have to move and completely commit myself to making it. I'm not interested in doing that."

"Really?" Sierra wasn't sure if she sounded as shocked as she felt. She never doubted that Tawni had what it took to be a great model and that she would probably be successful at it. But Tawni had never been much of a risk taker. Unless she was 100 percent sure of something, she rarely took a chance. She must have had serious doubts about succeeding at this, and her insecurities had taken over, drowning out the possibilities.

"He said she was a natural," Marti said, not trying to hide her disappointment. "I knew she was. Maybe you people can talk some sense into her."

None of them said a word. Marti threw up her hands and said, "I tried. No one can say I didn't try."

"And I told you I appreciated it," Tawni said. "It's just not for me."

Marti didn't respond.

"Bob called while you were out," Christy's mom said. "I told him we would go over to the hospital as soon as you came back. Whenever you're ready to go, I'm ready."

"I'm ready now," Marti said. "I probably should have been there all afternoon." The two women left, giving instructions that the group was on its own for dinner that night.

"Did Jeremy call?" Tawni asked.

"He said he would stop by after five," Todd said. "A bunch of us are going Rollerblading, in case you two want to come."

"Sounds fun. But you're not going, are you, Todd? Not with your arm still bandaged like that."

"I probably shouldn't," Todd said with a look of frustration. "Christy will get all over my case."

"Why do you say that?" Christy challenged him. She didn't look like she was teasing. "You talk as if I'm treating you like a baby."

Sierra saw a fight brewing. Tawni excused herself and went inside. Sierra wanted to, but the leg of her patio chair was wedged with Todd's, and she couldn't scoot her chair back from the table unless he moved his first. At the moment, he was busy.

"Aren't you?" Todd replied.

"No, I'm not treating you like a baby. I'm trying my best to do whatever I can to help you."

"I know."

If Todd had left it there, Sierra imagined the argument would have been diffused, and they could have gone back to their casual, friendly conversation. But he had to add, "Just like your aunt."

Christy's face turned deep red. "What is that supposed to mean?"

Todd's jaw seemed to stick out defiantly as he retorted, "I can take care of myself." Then, toning down his voice, he glanced at Sierra and pushed his chair back, saying, "Excuse me. I need to take my medicine." He strode into the house, slamming closed the patio's sliding door.

Sierra felt uncomfortable. She knew Christy must feel awkward, too. "You okay?" Sierra ventured.

Christy looked as if she were about to cry. "Can you believe it? We've never had a fight like this before. I've never seen him act this way." Tears glistened in the corners of her eyes.

"He's in a lot of pain with the burn, I'm sure," Sierra said. "The medication can do weird things to him, too. It did for my grandma after her surgery. She said a lot of strange things and snapped at my mom all the time the first week she was home from the hospital. I'm sure Todd didn't mean anything by it."

"No, he did. And he's probably right. I have been acting like my aunt, trying to take care of him. It's just that there's no one else to do it. His dad works all the time, and his mom is remarried and lives in Florida. He's been on his own for years."

"Well," Sierra ventured, "then maybe it's hard for him to get used to having someone else do stuff for him. He's probably not used to having you around all the time."

"But I'm not around. We only see each other on weekends. I thought we were so close," Christy said, wiping away a tear from her cheek. "I guess our relationship isn't as far along as I thought. Don't fall in love, Sierra. It complicates even the best friendships."

"I may be way off here," Sierra said, "but if you two only see each other on weekends, then this is probably really good for you. I mean, it's Monday, so you've seen each other for longer than usual, and the circumstances have been pretty stressful."

Christy nodded.

"I'm just saying that this is giving you both a chance to strengthen your relationship by working through this problem. That's not a bad thing, is it? I mean, all couples have arguments. Why don't you go talk to him? I'm sure you can work this out."

"I think you're right, Sierra," Christy said. "We've talked about this before. Ever since we came back from Europe, we've had this fairy-tale feeling about our relationship. We've been saying that we want God to test it and see if it's real and strong and lasting."

Sierra smiled and reached over to give Christy's arm a squeeze. "Didn't anyone ever tell you not to pray for stuff like that? The answer is always trials. Sounds like that's what's happening with you guys. You pray for God to strengthen your relationship, and look at what you get."

"You're right," Christy agreed. After a comfortable pause, she said, "I'm glad you're here. Thanks for coming down. You know, I really appreciate your encouragement. How did you become so wise?"

"Well, it wasn't from personal dating experience, that's for sure," Sierra joked.

"Your chance will come." Christy rose gracefully. "Don't wish it on yourself too soon, though, okay?"

"As if I had a choice," Sierra muttered as Christy left her alone on the patio. Fortunately, Katie showed up a few minutes later to ask Sierra if she wanted to go Rollerblading with them that evening.

Sierra agreed to go. Todd and Christy stayed behind, saying they were going to have dinner with his dad. From the expressions on their faces, it didn't appear that they had worked out their differences yet.

The gang rented Rollerblades at a little shop by the pier and buddied up as they raced along the miles of sidewalk separating the rows of beachfront houses from the sand. Sierra tried to be cheerful as she saw Jeremy reach for Tawni's hand and the two take off laughing. She watched Doug tie Tracy's skates for her and smiled to see how much shorter Gisele was than Larry. Katie persisted in telling Antonio they were skating on a "sidewalk" not the "boardwalk."

Sierra tried to find a buddy for herself. She felt as if she were back in grade school and the time had come to pick teams, but she was one of the last to be picked. Only, this had never happened to her. She was always the team leader and did the picking. For a few minutes, she considered writing notes to all those less athletic kids whom she had picked last all those years.

"Are you ready to go?" a friendly voice asked her. It was Heather, a thin, shy member of the gang whose wispy blond hair was whipping across her face in the evening breeze. Heather pulled a few strands out of her mouth. "Your name is Sierra, right?"

"Right. And you're Heather?"

She nodded. "I bet you're a pro at this. It's not my favorite activity, so if I make a complete fool of myself, you can go on without me. I'll understand."

"I'm sure you'll do fine," Sierra said. "Keep telling yourself to glide. Don't try to pick up your feet. There you go. Exactly. Come on, we can catch up with those Ricky Racers."

For the next two hours, Sierra had a blast laughing with Heather, playing tag with the other couples, and showing off her coordination skills by skating backward. She nearly collided with a man and his terrier but was able to inch past them by leaning way back. The wind felt cool against her sunburned cheeks. She didn't mind a bit that it was whipping her hair into knots.

As the sun set, Sierra decided this had been a memorable day. In the morning she had given surfing a try and had managed to stand all the way up for three seconds before crashing into the water. She would have tried some more, but her arms ached at the shoulders, and anyway, there was always tomorrow.

The gang returned the skates, and all decided to go over to Balboa Island for hot dogs at some place Doug liked. Sierra piled into the backseat of Larry's car along with Katie and Antonio. The hot dog place turned out to be a tiny stand that only sold hot dogs, frozen bananas, and "world-famous" Balboa Bars—creamy vanilla ice cream bars dipped in chocolate. Tracy teased Doug about being a real gourmet. Then everyone else teased him when he ordered six jumbo hot dogs and had no problem wolfing them down. He even went back for dessert.

Sierra managed to eat one of the jumbo dogs, but it didn't settle well, so she decided against dessert. When everyone was finished, they walked en masse down the shop-lined street, peering in the windows and laughing all the way.

Sierra hung out with Katie and Antonio, smiling when she saw Antonio slip his arm around Katie's shoulder. But his action also made her suddenly feel out of place all over again. They still included her in their conversation and acted as if they enjoyed having her with them. Still, they were becoming a couple, just like her sister and Jeremy, who were strolling with their arms around each other.

The next day, Todd and Christy joined the group on the beach late in the afternoon, but Sierra couldn't tell if they had settled things between them. The baseball cap she was wearing to shade her already peeling nose from the sun also shaded her view of the couple. She hoped they were getting along okay.

Just then, Doug and Antonio came up from the water with their boards under their arms. As Doug dropped his boogie board next to Tracy's towel, it knocked sand all over her. Immediately, she sprang up, wiping her eyes.

"Are you okay?" Sierra asked.

"I think I have some sand in my eye," Tracy said. "Can you see it?"

"Look," Doug said. "Here it comes." The sound of an airplane whirred in the distance.

Sierra leaned closer to Tracy, flipping the brim of her cap so she wouldn't bump Tracy's forehead. "Try opening your eye," she said.

Tracy's eyelid fluttered, and she said, "I can feel it. In my right eye."

"Trace," Doug said. "Look up. You have to see this."

"Just a second. I have something in my eye."

"Look to the left," Sierra said.

"Do you need some eyedrops?" Heather asked. "I have some."

"I see it," Sierra said. "Right along the lower lid. Don't blink."

The airplane engine roared closer. "Come on, Trace," Doug said. "You can't miss this!"

Now Todd was shouting at her too, "Tracy, look at the plane!"

"Just a minute!" she yelled, taking eyedrops from Heather. Two other girls huddled around her, asking if they could help.

"You're going to miss it!" Doug yelled. He stepped over, took her by the arm and pulled her up to his side. "Look!"

Tracy blinked, and in an irritated voice said, "What are you doing, Doug? I have something in my eye!"

"Just look at the plane for one second!" Todd yelled.

"Tracy, read the banner!" Larry called.

Sierra turned to see what the men were so worked up about. The plane was nearly past them, but the words on the banner were clear. It read, "Tracy, will you marry me?"

# fourteen

INSTANTLY, the whole group was crowding around Doug and Tracy. Tracy was crying, and Doug had his wet arm around her shoulders. He offered her his T-shirt to wipe her eyes, but she opted for the corner of the big T-shirt she was wearing over her bathing suit.

"Now you know what I was talking to your dad about last weekend," Doug said. "He's all for it. Of course your mom is, too. So are my parents."

"Tracy, I'm so happy for you!" Heather said, wiggling into the huddle, and hugging her.

"Just a minute, Heather," Doug said. "She hasn't told me yes yet."

Everyone grew quiet, moving back slightly to give the couple some room. Tracy looked at Doug with tears still streaming down her cheeks. "Well," she joked nervously, "at least it got the sand out of my eye."

Doug looked at her patiently, waiting for her answer.

Sierra wondered if the crowds of people on the beach staring at them because of all the commotion had any idea what was going on. The onlookers didn't bother Doug a bit. He stood like a rock, unwilling to move until Tracy gave him the answer he and everyone else in the group wanted to hear.

Tracy's expression grew soft. She looked into Doug's eyes, and tilting her heart-shaped face toward his, she whispered, "Yes, yes, a thousand times yes...you big lug!" Then with a playful thump on his chest, she said, "What if I hadn't looked at the plane?"

"I guess I would have had to pay the guy to come back tomorrow," Doug said. "Either that or find some other Tracy on the beach who *was* paying attention." He wrapped his arms around her, and they hugged.

"Isn't he going to kiss her?" Tawni said quietly to Sierra.

Jeremy was the one who answered. "No, not until their wedding day."

"You mean they've never kissed?"

"Doug's never kissed any girl," Sierra said.

"You're kidding!" Tawni said. "Isn't that taking purity a bit far?"

"Tracy doesn't think so," Sierra said quickly. "And neither do I."

"That's because you've never been kissed," Tawni said. "You wouldn't know."

Sierra blushed and felt like sinking into the sand. How could Tawni say that in front of Sierra's friends? Fury began to boil inside. It was one thing to decide you weren't going to kiss anyone, like Doug had, and a completely different thing to have your sister announce that no one had even tried to kiss you.

Sierra felt as if she didn't belong with this group. Here

they all were, going to college and becoming engaged, while she stuck out like a two-year-old. She wished she were home, planning her first big date with Randy and taking her time to grow up.

"Over here, honey," a male voice called out behind them. The man was wearing a blue baseball cap and holding a video camera. A blond-haired woman beside him came rushing up to give Tracy a hug. Apparently, they were her parents, and they were in on the scheme,

"Did you see the plane, Mom?" Tracy asked.

"Of course. Your dad captured the whole thing on tape. We were about ready to start yelling for you to look up, too!"

Another set of parents, quite obviously Doug's by the strong father-son resemblance, made their way through the sand and told the whole group to smile while Doug's mom snapped photos. Lots of hugs and pictures took place before Tracy and Doug left with their parents for what Tracy's mom called their "celebration dinner."

"I wonder when they'll get married," Katie said after the commotion had passed and everyone had settled back on the towels and beach chairs.

"Soon, if Doug gets his wish," Todd said with a smile. "He graduates in a few months."

"So do you." Katie challenged. With a twinkle in her eye, she looked at Christy and then back at Todd. "Any chance of a double wedding?"

Todd looked fondly at Christy. "I don't think so."

Sierra noticed that Christy didn't seem upset by his words, although Sierra couldn't help but wonder how their argument from the day before had ended up.

Todd reached over and covered Christy's hand with his. "I have some growing up to do," he admitted to the group. "Christy and I had a long talk about it yesterday. Do you mind if I tell them?" Todd asked her.

Christy shook her head. Sierra thought Christy's cheeks were turning red.

"You might as well," Katie said. "Otherwise we'll have to drag it out of Christy later tonight in our room under threat of a pillow war. She's not exceptionally cooperative about these things, so it might be in her best interest if you tell us now."

"I've pretty much been on my own since my parents divorced. This accident has been a good thing in that it has shown me I need to learn how to accept love from another person."

"That person being, perhaps, Christy?" Katie interjected in her spunky way.

Todd gave Christy another tender smile. "Of course Christy. There isn't anyone else. There never has been."

Sierra thought her heart was going to melt all over the sand, and she would have to scoop it up in her towel, take it to the house, and put it in the refrigerator before she could get it back inside her. She couldn't imagine a guy ever looking at her like that or saying those kinds of things to her.

"So, when I finish school, it looks as if I'm going to move down to Escondido, or at least near there, so Christy and I can get to know each other on a more consistent basis. Our relationship has always been in little pieces of time, separated by long stretches of being apart. We need to see how we do in average, day-to-day life."

"Isn't that what you find out once you're married?"

Larry said. "What's wrong, Todd? Are you afraid to take any chances?"

Sierra realized she wasn't the only one who assumed Todd and Christy would end up getting married. Everyone else seemed to think the same thing.

"You probably wouldn't ask that if your parents were divorced," Todd said. "It's like I said—I have a few things to learn about loving another person for the rest of my life and letting that person love me. I've been too much of a loner for too long."

No one said anything at first. They all knew he meant what he said. It made Sierra imagine how deep Todd's love for Christy must be. He wasn't willing to make any mistakes, even if it meant waiting to get married.

"I give him six months before he proposes," Larry said.

Christy glanced shyly at Todd.

"You're on." Katie reached over and slapped Larry a high five.

"Get me five," Antonio said, holding up his hand to Katie.

"You mean 'give me five,'" Katie corrected him. "Not 'get me.'"

"Oh, are you saying you're getting sodas from that ice chest over there?" Antonio teased. "Then I don't need five; I only need one. But perhaps my friends are thirsty as well. Larry? Gisele? What would you like? Katie's getting five."

# fifteen

SIERRA HAD A LOT of thinking time the next morning. Today and tomorrow were her last days at the beach, and so many things still seemed to be tied up in knots inside of her. She hadn't settled a thing with Tawni. Her jealousy seemed only to grow when Tawni and Jeremy had gone out alone last night for a long walk on the beach.

Her feelings of being a misfit kept her from sleeping well, so she was up at six. She quietly slipped into her clothes and went downstairs. After pouring herself a glass of orange juice, she settled into the plush white sofa in the living room, watching through the huge picture windows as the day began to wake up.

She prayed. She thought. She sipped her orange juice and prayed some more. Quiet footsteps padded down the stairs. Sierra watched the doorway and was surprised to see Christy.

"Hi," Christy whispered.

"Hi."

"Am I disturbing you?"

"No, not at all. I was just praying through some stuff."

"Do you mind if I ask you a question?" Christy said, sitting down beside Sierra. "Is Tawni one of the things you're praying about?"

"Yes. How did you know?"

"I don't have a sister, so I've never had to go through the kinds of things you and Tawni go through, but I think I know how you must feel sometimes."

"I'm jealous," Sierra said bluntly. "I know what the problem is, and I know it's wrong, but I don't know how to fix it. I try so hard to change my feelings and thoughts, but they keep coming back, even stronger."

"I know what that's like," Christy said.

"Somehow I find it hard to believe you've ever been jealous of anyone," Sierra said.

"You'd be surprised if you knew. As a matter of fact, I'm going to tell you. It was Tracy."

"Tracy?"

"I find it hard to believe now, too," Christy said. "When I first met Tracy, she and Todd were really close friends. I was so jealous of her. She and Todd gave me a Bible for my birthday, and I almost threw it back in her face. She even made me a fabric cover for it. Can you believe that?"

"No. When I met you two in England, you seemed like best friends who had never had a fight."

"Relationships take time, Sierra. That's what Todd and I are finding out. I think the main thing I'm learning is that it doesn't help to try harder. Remember what Todd said the other day about my being like Marti because I was trying so hard? The only thing that works is surrendering—giving up all your rights and expectations and asking God to do a God-thing in your relationship."

"Is that what happened with you and Tracy?"

"I guess so. Sort of. What helped me the most was when I got to know her. I realized that she and Todd were just good friends, and when I started to understand her, it was a lot easier to become her friend."

"You know what's really pathetic?" Sierra said. "I hardly know my sister. I mean, we live in the same house, but I don't understand her at all. Maybe I do need to pray about this differently. Instead of asking God to change her, maybe I should try surrendering our relationship to Him and ask Him to do a God-thing."

A smile dawned over Christy's face. "Exactly."

Sierra couldn't help but notice that Christy was a natural beauty. Here it was, early in the morning, and her eyes sparkled and her skin glowed. Though uncombed, her hair hung soft and natural from the crown of her head.

"Thanks," Sierra said. "I appreciate your advice."

"You know what's funny? Todd used to have this kind of spiritual discussion with me, and I'd never quite understand what he was saying. You're a lot more spiritually sensitive than I was at your age."

Christy's words acted as a bleak reminder that a gap of nearly three years existed between them. It brought up all those sinking feelings of not fitting in. Sierra's expression must have changed because Christy reached over and patted her arm, saying, "I meant it as a compliment."

Sierra gave her a forced smile and said, "I know. Thanks. It's just that I've felt pretty high-schoolish being around all you guys this week. It didn't feel that way in

England, but now I realize how much I'm behind the rest of you in experience and age."

"I don't think of it that way."

"I don't know, Christy. Have you ever felt as if you were caught between two lives? The one you're living, and the one you wish you were living?"

"I think everyone feels like that at one time or another. I know I did a couple of summers ago when I was a counselor at summer camp. I left home that week dreaming of adventure, romance, and great spiritual victories. I came home wanting all the familiar people and places in my life and wishing the old things would never change."

"Do you think we're ever happy?" Sierra said, glancing out at the brightness of the morning sun across the sand and sea.

"No," Christy said quickly. "But I want to learn how to be. The verse I've been trying to memorize and put into practice this month is 'Godliness with contentment is great gain.' It's 1 Timothy 6:6. Interesting, isn't it?" Christy took a handful of her hair and flipped it back. "We're both kind of learning the same thing: how to be happy where we are."

"What surprised me this week is how complicated life can be. Like with you and Todd. I thought my life would be so much easier if I had a boyfriend. But then I see how you two still have a lot of things to work out and how it takes a lot of time and energy. That means your life is still complicated, even though you have a boyfriend."

Christy laughed softly. "Uncle Bob once told me, 'If you think the grass is greener on the other side of the fence, try watering your own grass.'"

Sierra laughed. "That's what it's like, isn't it? Here I

am, watching everyone else carry on with his or her life and wishing I were on the other side of the fence. You're right, Christy. I am going to ask God to teach me how to live like that—godly with contentment and paying attention to my side of the fence."

"And don't forget to water your own grass!" Christy added.

"And watering my own grass," Sierra repeated.

They sat silently for a few moments in the large, quiet room. The rest of the household still wasn't stirring. Sierra knew she had found a rare treasure of a friend in Christy because they were able to sit together silently and it didn't feel awkward. The only other person she felt that level of comfort with was her Granna Mae.

"Do you feel like praying with me?" Sierra asked. "My mom and Granna Mae always pray with us, and well, this seems like a good praying time."

"Sure." Christy closed her eyes, and the two friends welcomed the new day with heartfelt prayers of praise and a few requests. Sierra surrendered her jealousy to the Lord and asked him to do one of His God-things between her and Tawni. Christy prayed for her aunt and uncle, and they prayed together for a swift healing for Todd and Uncle Bob.

Sierra was saying "Amen" when they heard someone come down the stairs. The both turned to see Marti in a purple silk robe.

"Whatever are you two doing up so early?"

Sierra was just about to say, "Just talking," but Christy answered first. "Praying."

"Oh really, Christina. Don't be so flippant."

"I'm not. We were praying for you and Uncle Bob," Christy said.

Marti seemed to brush off the comment and turned toward the kitchen. "I'm going to make some coffee. Do you drink coffee, Sierra?"

"No, but I'll have some tea if you happen to make any."

"Me, too," Christy said. "We'll come make it. As a matter of fact, we'll make the coffee too. Why don't you go back to bed? We'll bring the coffee to you."

"Well," Marti looked pleasantly surprised. "Now I know what they mean when they say 'Prayer works.'" She grinned at her own little joke. "I'll be upstairs. And you might want to bring a cup for your mother, Christy. She's going home this morning since Bob's coming out of the hospital today."

"We'll bring it right up." Christy said, leading Sierra into the kitchen. Christy pulled the coffee beans out of the pantry, but she didn't seem sure of what to do next.

"Do you know where the coffee grinder is?" Sierra asked.

"I'm not sure. My parents drink instant coffee. I don't know how to make this."

"Step aside," Sierra said. "I learned all about how to make the perfect cup of coffee from Granna Mae. Why don't you make the tea?"

They went to work searching for tea bags and the coffee grinder. Once the coffee began to brew, Sierra collected the cream and sugar and put them on the tray.

"Let's cut up some fruit," Christy suggested. "And bagels are probably in the freezer. Yep, here they are. Let's take breakfast in to everyone in bed!"

Fifteen minutes later, they were heading upstairs, carefully balancing their two full trays and trying not to giggle. Everything had seemed funny to them as they prepared their love offering in the kitchen. Christy had even snatched some flowers from a bouquet on the dining room table and put them in juice glasses, one vase for each tray.

"Room service," Christy said cheerfully as she opened the door to Marti's bedroom with her elbow.

Marti was back in bed with the covers folded all nice and neat as if she had been patiently waiting for them. She reminded Sierra of Granna Mae, except that Marti's comment was unlike anything Granna Mae would say. "What took you so long? You brought the nonfat creamer, I hope."

"Yes, it's all here," Christy said, patiently unloading the coffee cup and accoutrements onto Marti's nightstand. "Would you like some fruit or a bagel?"

"No. Your mother is in the shower, so you can leave her coffee over there. What's the rest of this for?"

"We thought we would serve breakfast in bed to all the women in the household," Christy said, still smiling. "Are you sure you don't want some fruit?"

"Well, maybe just a slice of that cantaloupe."

The other women were more appreciative. As Tawni took the coffee mug from Sierra, she said, "This smells wonderful. Thanks. Have the guys called yet?"

"Not that I know of," Sierra said. "It's still early."

"Jeremy wants to take me to some restaurant he likes in Laguna Beach. We'll probably make a day of it."

"That sounds fun," Katie said.

"He's such an incredible guy," Tawni said, sipping the

coffee and looking as if her mind were still in a dream. "I can't believe I met him."

Sierra was about to let her feelings start bubbling up when Christy said, "Tell us what you like about him."

"Well, you know him, Christy. He's strong-minded and yet tender about so many things. He's a deeply committed Christian, which makes all the difference in the world from the last few guys I've been interested in. He treats me like an equal, and at the same time he does little things to let me know he cares about me."

Sierra was about to interject one of her typically rude comments, but something stopped her. The Holy Spirit, maybe? She realized that if Katie were talking about Antonio or Christy about Todd, Sierra would be making all kinds of affirming comments to let her friends know how happy she was that they had found great guys. Why couldn't she be supportive of her sister?

"I'm really happy for you, Tawni," Sierra said, her voice and expression reflecting her sincerity.

"You are?"

"Yes, I am. I think he's a dream come true, and I'm really glad you met him."

"Thanks," Tawni said.

Sierra glanced at Christy out of the corner of her eye and caught a slight wink her heart-friend was sending her way—silent applause for this not-so-minor victory.

# sixteen

THE REST OF THE DAY filled up quickly. Christy's mom left, Marti went back to the hospital with Todd and Christy to bring Uncle Bob home, Tawni and Jeremy left at eleven for their big lunch date, and Sierra and Katie hung out at the beach with the rest of the bunch. Doug and Tracy didn't show up. Heather said they were spending the day making plans.

Sierra decided it was time to "water her own grass" and put her whole heart into teaching herself to surf. She bravely asked to borrow Todd's battered orange surfboard, and for more than two hours, she tried to ignore her aching arms as she paddled out again and again. Finally, she caught a wave and managed to stand up and keep her balance all the way to shore. No one saw her. No one was waiting to applaud. But she knew she had done something she had always wanted to do, and the feeling it gave her was, to use Doug's word, "awesome."

After a short nap in the sun, she challenged Antonio to a game of paddleball. They went down to the water and began to throw a ball to each other, catching it with Velcro-lined mitts. Katie had taken Todd's board back out and was hard at work trying to catch a good one. Sierra decided to be brave and ask Antonio if she could borrow his board. She took it out like a pro and bobbed about with Katie, waiting for the afternoon swell to pick up.

They talked, paddled, floated, and laughed. Sierra knew she would never forget this afternoon, not because anything spectacular was happening but simply because she felt so fully alive. Her heart felt fresh and clean, and she loved the sense of freedom the ocean gave her.

Katie began talking about Antonio. Sierra decided to bring up Randy and the date next Friday night.

"Good choice on the corsage suggestion," Katie said. "When I went to the prom, my date gave me this hilarious green carnation. It looked like a head of lettuce!"

"I don't know why I said peach. I should have said white roses. They would go with anything."

"Peach is a nice, neutral color. Green, on the other hand, doesn't match anything. What a disaster that night was! You know what, Sierra? If I knew in high school how much fun I was going to have in college, I wouldn't have been so paranoid about trying to get a boyfriend. Enjoy yourself, and don't make any bad memories with a guy just for the sake of having a date."

"I'll remember that," Sierra said.

"Whoa," Katie said, getting into position on her board. "Here comes the one we've been waiting for." She began to paddle furiously, and Sierra followed right behind. Katie was faster—she caught the wave, stood up, and rode to shore. It all seemed symbolic to Sierra as she watched and waited for the next decent wave. Katie was older, so of course she was ahead of Sierra and deserving to catch the wave. Somehow it didn't bother Sierra, being the one to watch and wait for romance.

She had more opportunities to watch and wait that night when everyone gathered around an open fire pit at the beach. Christy led them all to a certain fire pit she'd picked out of all the open ones on the beach. The group spread their blankets, and the guys started a fire. There was some teasing of Todd, telling him to stand back and have a beach towel ready in case the pit blew up. Sierra didn't think the jokes were funny, having been at the house and seen the accident. But the seriousness seemed to have passed now that Todd was doing better and Bob had come home from the hospital. He had gone right to bed, Christy told them. But he had invited everyone over for breakfast the next morning, so he must be feeling better.

The sun was making its grand exit as they gathered around the fire pit, and Sierra was glad she had worn her sweatshirt. She sat next to Christy, who offered her the other half of her blanket and said, "Anyone want to roast marshmallows?"

A chorus of cheers echoed from around the campfire.

"Then you get to untwist your own coat hanger," Christy said, pulling a handful from a bag and passing them around.

Todd, who was sitting on the other side of Christy, was right in the path of smoke. He sat there about two minutes before coming around and sitting on the other side of Sierra.

"Would you like me to move so you can sit next to Christy?" Sierra asked.

"No, this is fine. Pass me a couple of marshmallows, will you?" He took them from Sierra and slid them onto his coat hanger. "Okay," he challenged. "First one to brown a marshmallow nice and even without burning it is the winner."

Sierra promptly untwisted her coat hanger, grabbed two marshmallows and entered the competition.

"What's the prize?" Antonio asked.

"The knowledge that you're the victor," Todd said.

"You Americans are so contemplative," Antonio said.

"You mean 'competitive,'" Katie said.

"Oh, you've noticed it, too?" Antonio grinned at her.

For apparently the first time, it occurred to Katie that Antonio had superb command of the English language and had been teasing her all along. "You've been having a good time with me, haven't you?" she said.

"Of course. I thought you were having a good time, too."

"I mean with your words. You've been mixing things up just to—"

"Just to win your attention. And it's worked nicely, hasn't it?"

Before Katie could toss him a quick retort, Doug and Tracy, with their arms around each other, approached the group. Doug was carrying a guitar case, and Tracy had a plastic grocery bag.

"Marshmallow reinforcements!" Doug called out.

Todd reached across Sierra and grabbed some marshmallows from Christy's bag. "Excuse me," he said, and before Doug could see where they were coming from, Todd pelted him with flying marshmallows.

"Stand back, Trace," Doug said, holding his guitar case in front of them. "I'll protect you!"

"Oh, you guys, look!" Sierra said, pulling her twirling stick from the fire. "We almost have a winner here." Her marshmallows were nearly brown all the way around. Now came the tricky part of toasting the sagging underside before it oozed off the coat hanger and into the fire.

"We may have an early winner, folks," Todd said, sticking his marshmallow back into the fire. "But not without some competition."

Christy, who had been quietly roasting her marshmallows, now pulled her hanger from the fire and said, "Did you say competition?" As she said it, both her nearly perfect marshmallows began to droop beyond rescuing. She quickly grabbed them with her fingers. The sticky goo dripped down her hand as she tried to get it into her mouth. Christy's eyes grew wide, and she pointed to the fire. Sierra looked in time to see her own two perfect balls of sugar bursting into flames.

"I'm still in," Sierra said. "Second try. Somebody hand me a marshmallow."

For the next half hour, the gang roasted all the marshmallows in Christy's bag and Tracy's two bags. There were plenty of flaming marshmallow balls dropped into the fire, and in the end, Tawni was the winner with the most evenly roasted marshmallows. Sierra realized she shouldn't have been surprised. Tawni had the diligence to stick to it and wait patiently. Diligence and patience were two of her sister's good qualities that Sierra had never noticed much.

"You've kept us in suspense long enough," Christy finally said to Tracy and Doug. "When's the wedding? Did you set a date?"

"After spending the whole day with both mothers, you better believe we did," Doug said. "August 22, and you're all invited."

"This August?" Heather squawked.

"That was the only day all summer we could agree on. And if I go to graduate school," Doug explained, "we don't want to wait until next summer or try to squeeze in a wedding during Christmas break."

"Wow!" Todd said. "Wow!"

"I think it sounds perfect," Christy said. "I'm really happy and excited for both of you."

"Good," Tracy said, "because I have a favor to ask. Actually, Doug and I have a favor to ask you and Todd. Christy, will you be my maid of honor?"

"And Todd," Doug picked up, "you're the best man—okay, dude?"

"Wait a minute, wait a minute," Todd said. "This isn't like auditioning for parts for a school play. This is your wedding we're talking about. With all your family and all your friends, are you sure you want us?"

"Of course. We've already talked it through," Tracy said.

"With both mothers," Doug added. "So you know the arrangement has been sanctified."

"I'm honored," Todd said. "Of course I'll be your best man."

"And I'd love to be your maid of honor," Christy said.

"We haven't agreed on all the other attendants yet, but we're going to figure out a way to have all you guys in our wedding somehow. If nothing else, we really want all of you to be there."

"We wouldn't miss it for anything," Heather said.

"So, Doug," Todd said, poking the logs in the fire and watching them tumble, shooting off dozens of tiny red firecrackers, "exactly what does the best man do?"

"Isn't he the guy who kidnaps the groom the night before the wedding and has him dyed fuchsia all over?" Larry said.

"Wait a minute," Doug said. "I'm not planning on being kidnapped. Todd, as my best man, you're supposed to protect me from maniacs like Larry."

Sierra couldn't picture Todd's having much control over Larry, or anyone being able to stop him—except perhaps Gisele. She appeared to be his soft spot.

"That's the beauty of it," Larry said. "No groom ever plans to be kidnapped. Consider it a parting gift from us bachelors."

"I don't know," Doug said. "My idea to elope is starting to sound better and better."

"Can you believe you guys are getting married?" Katie asked. "I can't."

"Well, try to imagine it," Doug said. "Because we are." He put his arm around Tracy and squeezed her tightly. Tracy's face looked radiant in the glow of the campfire.

Sierra gazed into the warm embers and made a wish. Inside her heart, she wished that one day she would be as deeply in love as Tracy and Doug and that her love would be as pure as theirs.

# seventeen

WHEN THE GROUP gathered for breakfast the next morning, they found everything set up for them in the formal dining room. A caterer had been hired to serve the large group wedged around the table.

"Don't look so shocked," Katie said as she took a seat next to Sierra. "This is pretty typical of Marti. I'm sure it's her idea of a welcome-home party for Bob."

"It's pretty fancy, don't you think?" Sierra whispered back.

"Of course! The flashier the better in Marti's book. You should see the place during Christmas."

Bob sat at the head of the table, looking pale, but smiling. The gauze bandages came up his left arm and covered half of his neck and ear. Sierra knew he must be in pain. With Marti's help, he was bolstered up in the chair, making a rather regal appearance despite the handicap.

Once the orange juice had been poured into the crystal glasses, Bob tapped on the side of his with a spoon. Then he held up the glass, inviting a toast.

Everyone grew quiet, and Bob said, "Guess I missed most of the party this week. Sorry about that. I was probably looking forward to it more than you all were."

A ripple of laughter moved down the table.

"This makes up for it," Larry said from his position at the other end of the table. Sierra noticed his plate was heaped with eggs, sausages, and pancakes. Gisele sat on his right with only a few slices of fruit and a pineapple muffin on her plate. It reminded Sierra of a picture in her nephew's nursery rhyme book of Jack Sprat and his wife, only in reverse.

"I wanted you all to be together so I could make an announcement. I wish Margaret would have stayed," Bob said, looking at Christy. "You tell your mom and dad everything I say, okay?"

Christy looked solemn and nodded. Sierra wondered if this was going to be some big announcement about the family inheritance. She felt as if she had stepped into a remake of a Gothic mystery movie. All they needed was a change of wardrobe, a rainstorm with lightning, and a silver candelabra on the mantle.

But it wasn't that kind of atmosphere at all. The morning sun flooded through the front windows, piercing the crystals on the chandelier above them and sending dozens of ballerina rainbows across the table. The centerpiece bouquet was laden with large white gardenias. The fragrance floated through the air, intoxicating each of the guests with the sweetness.

Bob, sitting majestically before them, spoke with a lightheartedness that fit the joy permeating the room. Clearing his throat, he said, "What happened a few days ago caused me to take my life more seriously than I ever have before. I did a lot of what you would probably call soul-searching and have come to a decision. That is, I've realized...or, rather, it seemed the right time to..." His voice faltered. "What I mean is..."

"You got saved!" Katie blurted out.

All eyes were on Bob, waiting for his response. A wide smile broke across his face. "Thank you, Katie. That's what happened. I got saved."

Bedlam broke out. Christy, Todd, Katie, and Doug shot up from their seats like rockets, shouting and laughing and trying to hug Bob without disturbing the bandages. Marti was frantically trying to keep them from touching him. Larry was standing at the end of the table applauding and hooting like a football fan whose favorite team had just won the Super Bowl. Tracy and Heather got in line to hug Bob, while Gisele and the others joined Larry in clapping and cheering.

Sierra sprang to her feet and went over to hug Bob, too, even though she barely knew him. She realized how long Todd and Christy had been waiting for this day, and she shared in their excitement. She couldn't help but feel a part of it.

Tears were streaming down Bob's cheeks. It was rich to see a man cry over his welcome into the kingdom. When Sierra hugged him, she impulsively planted a little kiss on his cheek. Her lips tasted the salt of his tears. "Welcome to the family," she whispered.

"And now the toast," Larry said in his booming voice. He stood at the other end of the table with his juice glass lifted in the air.

Bob struggled to stand up, with Todd supporting his one arm and Sierra bracing the other. Bob lifted his glass. Making eye contact, one by one, with each of his guests, he said, "My brothers and sisters in Christ, here's to eternity."

Everyone cheered—except Marti.

She stood at the appropriate time, but Sierra noticed that she used the opportunity to step to the corner of the room and issue instructions to the woman serving the breakfast. A moment later, the server returned with a fresh basket of muffins and walked around trying to offer them to everyone.

No one accepted. Everyone was too busy cheering and talking.

Bob sat down and told how the men from the morning Bible study had come to visit him in the hospital, one at a time. "None of them said what I thought he would say. They each just came and sat with me, and most of them asked if they could pray with me. I kept thinking about things Todd had told me over the years, about needing to repent and yield my life to Christ, to ask Him to be my Savior. I never thought I needed a Savior before. But when your life is almost taken from you, I guess you stop believing in luck, and start hoping there really is a Savior."

"Oh, there is," Christy said, her eyes still brimming with tears. "And you found Him, Uncle Bob."

"Actually, I think He found me."

"Didn't take too much for Him to get your full attention, now did it?" Doug said with a laugh.

Bob tipped his juice glass in Doug's direction. "You know," he said, "I tried to explain it to Marti last night and

I couldn't find the words." He cast a loving glance at his wife.

Her expression was ice with a painted-on smile.

"I don't know what happened, but I am a different man inside."

The doorbell rang, and Doug, who was closest to the entryway, went to answer the door. A moment later, he stepped back into the dining room with three large suitcases. "The case of the lost luggage is solved, Tawni."

"Oh, that's perfect!" she said. "My plane leaves for home in two hours, and now they deliver my luggage."

Doug carried the suitcases back to the front door, and Sierra noticed Todd casting his silver-blue eyes first at Christy, then at Bob. He leaned toward Bob and said, "What once was lost, now is found."

Christy echoed Todd's ecstatic grin at her uncle.

Without a word, Bob lifted his glass and clinked it with Todd's and then with Christy's. "What once was lost, now is found," Bob repeated.

Sierra knew they weren't referring to Tawni's luggage.

# eighteen

ON EASTER SUNDAY, Sierra sat next to Granna Mae on the hard pew in Granna Mae's old church. Tall white Easter lilies lined the steps up to the altar, their heady fragrance filling Sierra with all the reminders of spring, new life, and the miracle of the resurrection.

Her heart was full this morning. It seemed so much had happened during the past week that pointed to this celebration of Christ conquering death. On the final hymn, Sierra helped Granna Mae stand, and with passion, Sierra sang alongside her grandmother: "Christ the Lord is risen today!"

The warm glow of the week and the holiness of the Easter morning service stayed with Sierra all day. She cheerfully helped her mother set the table after church for their big family dinner. Her oldest brother, Wesley, was up from Corvallis, and her brother Cody; his wife, Katrina; and their three-year-old son, Tyler, were there, too.

When they were all seated at the long table in the dining room, Sierra's dad stood to pray. When he sat down Sierra popped up and lifted her water glass, "I would like to propose a toast," she said.

"Since when did our family start giving toasts?" Wes said.

"Since your sister was influenced by a certain wealthy Uncle Bob in Newport Beach," Tawni told him.

"I would like to say thank you to God for my family, who are all believers. I don't ever want to take you for granted," Sierra said. "Here's to eternity."

The group didn't jump in as eagerly as the bunch at Bob and Marti's breakfast. But Granna Mae led the way, holding her glass up to Sierra, saying, "To eternity!"

Sierra still felt extra cheerful when she returned to school on Monday. Amy was the first person she saw in the parking lot that morning.

"No fair!" Amy said, holding her arm next to Sierra's. "You're so tan. Look at you!"

"Well, that can happen to a person when she lies on the beach in Southern California for days on end," Sierra said, enjoying the attention.

"I want to hear all about it," Amy said. "I can summarize my Easter vacation for you in two words: BOR–ING."

"Are you doing anything after school today?" Sierra asked. "I need to shop for a new dress." She knew Amy would be a good companion since they had similar taste in clothes. Sierra had never met anyone who dressed the way she did, until she met Amy.

"You, too?" Amy said, as she and Sierra walked together through the parking lot. "I spent three days shopping with Vicki last week in search of the perfect semi-formal outfit.

You know, don't you, that she asked Randy to go with her to some benefit dinner this Friday? I can't remember if I told you before you left."

Sierra stopped at the last row of cars, her heart pounding. "She asked Randy to go with her?"

Amy stopped alongside of Sierra and nodded. "The poor guy is such a nervous wreck. He made me go shopping with him last week, too. I finally talked him into renting a tux. You should see him in it. He looks so cute! Like a waiter. I didn't tell him that, though." Amy looked closely at Sierra. "How come your tan just left your face?

"I'm surprised. That's all."

"I thought Randy said he told you. Didn't he ask your advice on what kind of flowers to buy for the corsage?"

"Yes," Sierra said, finding her voice and feeling foolish, "he did. He came into work the day before I left and asked me."

A flash of understanding came across Amy's face. "Oh, Sierra, you didn't think he was asking you to go, did you?"

Sierra bit her lower lip and squinted her eyes to keep any stupid tears from exposing her. She didn't have a voice to answer Amy at the moment.

"Oh, dear," Amy said, leaning up against the nearest car.

The parking lot had filled up, and dozens of students were hurrying past them to class.

"That's right. He made a big deal at the park about going to Mama Bear's to talk to you, didn't he?"

Sierra found her wits again and grabbed Amy by the arm. She leaned close and said, "Amy, promise me you won't say anything to Randy or Vicki or anybody about this."

Amy looked startled at Sierra's sudden, dramatic request.

"Promise me," Sierra breathed. "It would kill me to have Randy find out. He deserves to have a great time, and I don't want to send any messages that might give him the wrong idea. Okay? It was just my own ridiculous misunderstanding. Promise me you won't say anything."

"I promise," Amy said solemnly. "You can trust me. I can keep secrets."

"Good," Sierra said, letting go of Amy's arm.

Just then the bell ran, and they took off running to their first class.

# nineteen

SIERRA MADE IT through the week without any awkward encounters with Randy. He seemed preoccupied with Vicki anyhow. Amy apparently kept Sierra's secret, which made Sierra feel loyal to Amy and appreciative of her friendship. Amy appeared equally interested in letting their friendship develop, because she invited Sierra to go to dinner at Amy's uncle's Italian restaurant downtown on Friday night.

"Just us girls," Amy said.

"You mean we leave the dogs at home?" Sierra said.

"You are referring to Brutus and Peanut, aren't you?"

"Of course? Who else?"

"Oh, nobody. But you're right. I don't think my uncle would like having a couple of canines there. He said dinner tonight would be his treat. Our reservations are at eight. I'll drive, okay?"

Sierra agreed and tried to explain to Amy how much she appreciated the invitation.

"Don't worry about it," Amy said. "I would have asked

you even if the Randy mix-up hadn't happened. Be ready by seven-thirty, okay?"

Sierra was ready early. The spring evening carried the fragrance of a mixed bouquet wafting from the trees surrounding Granna Mae's house. Sierra stepped outside onto the big porch that wrapped around the front. The white porch swing called to her: *Come, sit here and sway with me in the evening breeze.* Sierra obliged, nestling on the thickly padded seat her mom had made the week Sierra was gone. Freshly potted plants lined the porch railing. Mom had jokingly referred to the petunias, primroses, and pansies as her "three p's in a pot."

Swaying back and forth on the swing, Sierra drew in a deep breath of the spring sweetness around her. Two squirrels scampered across the telephone line, and a plump robin hopped across the yard, looking for dinner.

*Why do I feel so…what is this feeling? Happy? Settled? Happily settled into life in Portland. That's it,* Sierra thought. *No, a better word would be "content." What was Christy's verse last week? "Godliness with contentment is great gain." That's what it is. I'm content.*

Sierra certainly felt she had gained a lot. It had been great to see the gang last week, but now she knew this was where she needed to find new friends—friends her own age who were experiencing the same things she was, even if those things were crazy misunderstandings over corsages and dates. She wanted to take her time growing up, and she wanted to embrace all of it, good and bad.

She felt more certain than ever that God had His hand on her life and that He was working everything out the way He designed it to be. With a push of her feet against the wooden planks under the swing, Sierra rocked with an even, steady rhythm, the way a clock ticks off the passing seconds.

As she did, the thoughts ticked off in her settled mind. Trusting God in this big way made it hard to be jealous of Tawni or Vicki or anyone. Why would Sierra want what someone else had if that wasn't what God had decided was best for her? Didn't He know her best? Wouldn't He be faithful to work out His plan in her life? Sierra eagerly desired to slip into motion with that plan and not resist or hinder it in any way.

As she was letting those soothing thoughts lull her in the swing, a car pulled up in front of the house. She knew it wasn't Amy's. Sierra peered between the clay pots in the row of blooming flowers and saw a guy in a tuxedo coming up the front walkway with something in his hand.

*Randy?* "Hi," Sierra called as he stepped up to the porch.

Randy looked startled. "Oh, hi. I didn't see you." He ambled toward her.

"You look terrific," Sierra said, a grin spreading across her face.

"Thanks. I feel like a penguin."

Sierra laughed. "You don't look like one."

"Here. I wanted to drop this off for you." He held out a peach-colored tea rose tucked in a sprig of baby's breath and wrapped in green florist paper. "It's to say thanks for the advice on the corsage."

"You didn't have to do this," Sierra said, receiving the flower and drawing in its scent.

"I wanted to. You're a good friend, Sierra. I appreciate you."

"Thanks, Randy." She could feel her cheeks warm at his words.

"Well—" he let out a deep breath. "I guess I better go."

"Just a minute," Sierra said, getting up from the swing and going toward him. Randy looked even more nervous as she came closer. "Don't worry, Randy. I'm only going to fix your tie. Hold still." She tugged on the right side of the bow, wiggling it until both sides were even. "There. Now you're ready."

Sierra noticed two trickles of sweat coursing from his temple down his cheek. "Relax," Sierra said with a smile. "You look great, and I know you'll have a wonderful time."

The screen door opened, and Tawni appeared with the cordless phone in her hand. "I found her, Jeremy," Tawni said. "She was on the front porch with…Randy?"

He raised his hand with a stiff hello. "I was on my way out," he said.

"You look absolutely fantastic!" Tawni cooed. Then, turning her attention back to Jeremy on the other end of the phone, she said, "It's just one of Sierra's friends dressed up for prom or something."

Randy mouthed the words "See you later" and waved at Sierra as he galloped down the steps and dashed to his car.

"Thanks for the flower!" Sierra called after him.

Tawni was holding the phone out to her and said, "Here. You speak with him. I don't understand what Jeremy is talking about. He says he thought you knew."

"Knew what?"

Tawni pushed the phone into her hand, and Sierra put the receiver to her ear. "Hi Jeremy. What's up?"

"Flowers, huh?" Jeremy said. "Maybe my brother is up against stiffer competition than he thought."

Sierra gave Tawni a puzzled look. Tawni held up her

hands and said, "I told him I didn't know anything about it."

"Do you want to rewind a bit, Jeremy? What are you and Tawni talking about?"

"I'm planning on coming up there in a few weeks. Did Tawni tell you?"

"No, not yet. That's great. I'm sure you'll like meeting our family."

"Well, I was hoping you would like to meet someone in my family. But then, he tells me you already know him."

"Who?" Sierra said, switching the phone to her other hand. She put the rose on the swing and shrugged her shoulders at Tawni.

"Do you remember a certain letter Katie sent to you a while back?" Jeremy asked. "I gave the letter to her after my brother gave it to me. It was the only way he could think of to contact you after your encounter at the airport in London."

"Paul?!" Sierra felt an invisible hand push her against one of the porch pillars. "You're Paul's brother?"

"He was pretty shocked when he figured it out, too. I told him about Tawni and then mentioned she had a sister named Sierra."

"And what did he say?" Sierra asked.

"He figured it had to be you. He told me the whole story. The money you loaned him at the pay phone in London. Sitting by you on the flight home. Getting your luggage mixed up. And something about his calling you a daffodil queen and your getting upset and writing a flaming letter telling him he wasn't sincere."

Sierra closed her eyes and wished for the hundredth time that she hadn't so impulsively mailed that letter. If there were one thing she wished she could learn, it would be to keep her mouth shut. Or, in this case, to keep her words inside her head instead of committing them to paper.

"That was...it didn't really...I wasn't..." She fumbled to find a combination of words to explain. "It was kind of a mix-up. In the end, he brought my grandma flowers. I never got to thank him. Would you tell him thanks for me?"

"Sure. Is there anything else you would like me to tell him? I already told him that I saw you surf last week. That didn't seem to surprise him."

"Why should it?" Sierra challenged.

"That's right. Nothing about you or your sister should surprise me, should it?"

"What about your brother? Will he have any surprises for me?"

"What do you mean?"

"He's not dating Jalene anymore, is he?"

"No, they broke up months ago. The way I understood it, you had something to do with it. At least that's what I understand from Paul and my mom. You're becoming a little legend with our family."

Sierra suppressed a giggle. Here she thought Paul had long forgotten about her and their conversation on the plane, and he was still talking about her.

"Well, tell him hi for me."

"Okay. Anything else?"

"Tell him that godliness with contentment is great gain." Sierra caught the strange expression on her sister's face. "Never mind," she said. "Just tell him I hope he's doing well."

"Okay. I'll tell him. And hey, when I come up in a

couple of weeks, maybe the four of us can get together or something. Meanwhile, can you put Tawni back on the line?"

Sierra handed the phone to Tawni, who covered the mouthpiece and said, "I still don't understand."

"I'll explain the whole thing later," Sierra promised. She settled onto the cushion on the swing and drew in the rose's delicate fragrance.

As the porch swing gently rocked her, ticking away the moments, Sierra found an irrepressible smile had captured her lips. Her thoughts whirled with all the wild, romantic, wonderful possibilities that might be waiting for her down the road. Then, into the air she whispered to the One who already knew what she was thinking, "Oh, don't I wish!"

# SISTERCHICK® Adventures by ROBIN JONES GUNN

*SISTERCHICKS ON THE LOOSE!*

Zany antics abound when best friends Sharon and Penny take off on a midlife adventure to Finland, returning home with a new view of God and a new zest for life.

*SISTERCHICKS DO THE HULA!*

It'll take more than an unexpected stowaway to keep two middle-aged sisterchicks from reliving their college years with a little Waikiki wackiness—and learning to hula for the first time.

*SISTERCHICKS IN SOMBREROS!*

Two Canadian sisters embark on a journey to claim their inheritance—beachfront property in Mexico—not expecting so many bizarre, wacky problems! But there's nothing a little coconut cake can't cure...

**AVAILABLE NOW!**

www.sisterchicks.com

# More SISTERCHICK® Adventures by ROBIN JONES GUNN

### *SISTERCHICKS DOWN UNDER!*

Kathleen meets Jill at the Chocolate Fish café in New Zealand, and they instantly forge a friendship. Together they fall head over heels into a deeper sense of God's love.

### *SISTERCHICKS SAY OOH LA LA!*

Painting toenails and making promises under the canopy of a princess bed seals a friendship for life! Fifty years of ups and downs find Lisa and Amy still Best Friends Forever…and off on an unforgettable Paris rendezvous!

### *SISTERCHICKS IN GONDOLAS*

At a fifteenth-century palace in Venice, best friends/sisters-in-law Jenna and Sue welcome the gondola-paced Italian lifestyle! And over boiling pots of pasta, they dare each other to dream again.

**AVAILABLE NOW!**

www.sisterchicks.com

## About the Author

Robin Jones Gunn grew up in Orange County, California, where both her parents were teachers. She has one older sister and one younger brother. The three Jones kids graduated from Santa Ana High School and spent their summers on the beach with a bunch of "God-Lover" friends. Robin didn't meet her "Todd" until after she had gone to Biola University for two years and spent a summer traveling around Europe.

As her passion for ministering to teenagers grew, Robin assisted more with the youth group at her church. It was on a bike ride for middle schoolers that Robin met Ross. After they married, they spent the next two decades working together in youth ministry. God blessed them with a son and then a daughter.

When her children were young, Robin would rise at 3 a.m. when the house was quiet, make a pot of tea, and write pages and pages about Christy and Todd. She then read those pages to the girls in the youth group, and they gave her advice on what needed to be changed. The writing process took two years and ten rejections before her first novel, *Summer Promise*, was accepted for publication. Since its release in 1988, *Summer Promise* along with the rest of the Christy Miller and Sierra Jensen series have sold over 2.5 million copies and can be found in a dozen translations all over the world.

For the past twelve years, Robin has lived near Portland, Oregon, which has given her lots of insight into what Sierra's life might be like in the Great Northwest. Now that her children are grown and Robin's husband has a new career as a counselor, she continues to travel and tell stories about best friends and God-Lovers. Her popular Glenbrooke series tracks the love stories of some of Christy Miller's friends.

Robin's bestselling Sisterchick novels hatched a whole trend of lighthearted books about friendship and midlife adventures. Who knows what stories she'll write next?

You are warmly invited to visit Robin's websites at: www.robingunn.com, www.christymillerandfriends.com, and www.sisterchicks.com.

# Excerpt from *Secrets,* Book One in Robin Jones Gunn's Glenbrooke Series

JESSICA MORGAN GRIPPED her car's steering wheel and read the road sign aloud as she cruised past it. "Glenbrooke, three miles."

The summer breeze whipped through her open window and danced with the ends of her shoulder-length, honey-blond hair.

"This is it," Jessica murmured as the Oregon road brought her to the brink of her new life. For months she had planned this step into independence. Then yesterday, on the eve of her twenty-fifth birthday, she had hit the road with the back seat of her used station wagon full of boxes and her heart full of dreams.

She had driven ten hours yesterday before stopping at a hotel in Redding, California. After buying Chinese food, she ate it while sitting cross-legged on the bed watching the end of an old black-and-white movie. Jessica fell asleep dreaming of new beginnings and rose at 6:30, ready to drive another nine hours on her birthday.

*I'm almost there,* she thought. *I'm really doing this! Look at all these trees. This is beautiful. I'm going to love it here!*

The country road meandered through a grove of quivering willows. As she passed them, the trees appeared to wave at her, welcoming her to their corner of the world.

The late afternoon sun shot between the trees like a strobe light, striking the side of her car at rapid intervals and creating stripes. Light appeared, then shadow, light, then shadow.

As Jessica drove out of the grouping of trees, the road twisted to the right. She veered the car to round the curve. Suddenly the bright sunlight struck her eyes, momentarily blinding her. Swerving to the right to avoid a truck, she felt her front tire catch the gravel on the side of the road. Before she realized what was happening, she had lost control of the car. In one terrifying instant, Jessica felt the car skid through the gravel and tilt over on its side. Her seat belt held her fast as Jessica screamed and clutched the steering wheel. The car tumbled over an embankment, then came to a jolting halt in a ditch about twenty feet below the road. The world seemed to stop.

Jessica tried to cry out, but no sound came from her lips. Stunned, she lay motionless on her side. She quickly blinked as if to dismiss a bizarre daydream that she could snap out of. Her hair covered half her face. She felt a hot, moist trickle coursing down her chin and an acidic taste filling her mouth. *I'm bleeding!*

Peering through her disheveled hair, Jessica tried to focus her eyes. When her vision began to clear, she could make out the image of the windshield, now shattered, and the mangled steering wheel bent down and pinning her left leg in place.

Suddenly her breath came back, and with her breath came the pain. Every part of her body ached, and a ring of white dots began to spin wildly before her eyes, whether she opened or closed them. Jessica was afraid to move, afraid to try any part of her body and find it unwilling to cooperate.

*This didn't happen! It couldn't have. It was too fast. Wake up, Jess!*

Through all the cotton that seemed to fill her head, Jessica heard a remote crackle of a walkie talkie and a male voice in the distance saying, "I've located the car. I'm checking now for survivors. Over."

*I'm here! Down here! Help!* Jessica called out in her head. The only sound that escaped her lips was a raspy, "Ahhgg!" That's when she realized her tongue was bleeding and her upper lip was beginning to swell.

"Hello in there," a male voice said calmly. The man leaned in through the open driver's window, which was now above Jessica on her left side. "Can you hear me?"

"Yeath," Jessica managed to say, her tongue swelling and her jaw beginning to quiver. She felt cold and shivered uncontrollably.

"Don't try to move," the deep voice said. "I've called for help. We'll get you out of there. It's going to take a few minutes, now, so don't move, okay?"

Jessica couldn't see the man's face, but his voice soothed her. She heard scraping metal above her, and then a large, steady hand touched her neck and felt for her pulse.

"You had your seat belt on. Good girl," he said. The walkie talkie crackled again, this time right above her.

"Yeah, Mary," the man said. "We have one female, mid-twenties, I'd say. Condition is stable. I'll wait for the ambulance before I move her. Over."

Jessica felt his hand once more, this time across her cheek as he brushed back her hair. "How ya' doin'? I'm Kyle. What's your name?"

"Jethica," she said, her tongue now throbbing. From

the corner of her eye she caught a glimpse of dark hair and a tanned face.

"I saw your car just as it began to roll. Must have been pretty scary for you."

Jessica responded with a nod and realized she could move her neck painlessly. She slowly turned her head and looked up into her rescuer's face. Jessica smiled with surprise and pleasure when she saw his green eyes, straight nose, windblown dark hair, and the hint of a five o'clock shadow across his no-nonsense jaw. With her smile came a stabbing throb in her top lip and the sensation of blood trickling down her chin.

"So, you can move a little, huh?" Kyle said. "Let's try your left arm. Good! That's great. How do your legs feel?"

Jessica tried to answer that the right one felt okay, but the left one was immobile. Her words came out slurred. She wasn't sure exactly what she said. Her jaw was really quivering now, and she felt helpless.

"Just relax," Kyle said. "As soon as the guys arrive with the ambulance, we'll get you all patched up. I'm going to put some pressure on your lip now. Try breathing slowly and evenly like this." Kyle leaned toward her. His face was about six inches from hers. He began to breathe in slowly through his nose and exhale slowly through his mouth. The distinct smell of cinnamon chewing gum was on his breath, which she found strangely comforting.

Jessica heard the distant wail of an approaching siren. Within minutes she was in the middle of a flurry of activity. Some of the men began to stabilize the car while several others cut off the door to have more room to reach her. Soon a team of steady hands undid Jessica's seat belt, removed the steering wheel, and eased her body onto a long board. They taped her forehead to the board so she couldn't move her head, and one of the men wrapped her in a blanket. They lifted the stretcher and with sure-footed steps walked up the embankment and carried her to the ambulance.

Jessica felt as if her eyelids weighed a hundred pounds. They clamped shut as her throbbing head filled with questions.

*Why? Why me? Why now, right on the edge of my new beginning?*

With a jolt, the men released the wheeled legs on the stretcher and slid Jessica into the back of the ambulance. One of them reached for her arm from underneath the blanket, and running a rough thumb over the back of her left hand, he asked her to make a fist.

Another paramedic spoke calmly, a few inches from her head, "Can you open your eyes for me? That's good. Now can you tell me where it hurts the most?"

"My leg," Jessica said.

"It's her left one." Jessica recognized Kyle's strong voice. His hand reached over and pressed against her upper lip once more.

The siren started up, and the ambulance lurched out onto the road and sped toward the Glenbrooke hospital.

As the stretcher jostled in the ambulance, the paramedic holding Jessica's left hand said, "Keep your fist. This is going to pinch a little bit." And with that an IV needle poked through the bulging vein on the top of her hand.

"Ouch," she said weakly.

She felt a soft cloth on her chin and lips and opened her eyes all the way. Kyle smiled at her. With one hand he pressed against her lip, and with the other he wiped the drying blood from her cheek and chin.

"Can you open your mouth a little? I need to put this against your tongue," he said, placing a swab of cotton between her tongue and cheek. "The bleeding looks like it's about to stop in there. Now if we can only get your lip to cooperate, you'll be in good shape. We'll be at the hospital in a few minutes. You doing okay?"

Jessica tried to nod her head, but the tape across her forehead held her firmly in place. She forced a crooked, puffy-cheeked smile beneath the pressure of his hand on her lip.

Jessica felt ridiculous, trying to flirt in her condition. Here was the most handsome, gentle man she had ever laid eyes on, and she was a helpless mess.

*He's probably married and has six kids. These guys are trained to be nice to accident victims.*

The full impact of her situation hit Jessica. She *was* a victim. None of this was supposed to happen. She was supposed to enter Glenbrooke quietly and begin her new life uneventfully. Yes, even secretly. Now how would she answer the prying questions she was sure to receive at the hospital?

As tears began to form in her eyes, she remembered that today was her birthday. Never in her life had she felt so completely and painfully alone.